Once upon a time, John 'Jack' Mowgley was a Special Branch Detective Inspector based at Portsmouth's International ferry port.

Aided by the fiercely loyal and at other times just fierce Detective Sergeant Catherine McCarthy, Mowgley's ongoing brief was to investigate and bring to justice suspected drug and people traffickers, murderers and other miscreants passing through his domain. His approach to carrying out his duties was, his detractors claimed, along the lines of a particularly heavy-handed sheriff in the days of the Wild West. Though a firm believer in individual liberty if not licence, it was undeniably true that Mowgley would happily stretch, bend and even fracture the law to get his bad man or woman.

After one too many misadventures, he was given the choice of taking retirement or a possible stretch as a guest of HM Prisons. He chose the former, and moved across the Channel to work as a private investigator in Lower Normandy. *Kiss of De'Ath* is the sixth book in the series about a simple but complex man with an often-complicated life.

Leading Players

DS Catherine McCarthy. Former bag-carrier, mess clearer-upper and sole female confidante and friend of Jack Mowgley. An increasingly discontented member of the CID team at Portsmouth, McCarthy is the liaison officer with and lover of:

Colonel René Degas. In his mid-fifties and the most senior *Gendarmerie Nationale* officer in the Lower Normandy region, Degas is based at Cherbourg on the Cotentin peninsula. A widower who claims no family connections with the great Impressionist, he admires the non-conformity of Mowgley and is an enthusiastic Anglophile, at least partly because of his relationship with Catherine McCarthy.

Yann Cornec: Former colleague of René Degas, and the founder of the private detective agency, *Services d'Enquêtes Privés Cornec.* Thanks to his association and past amity with Degas, Cornec enjoys regular investigative assignments from the *Gendarmerie.* Some involve British nationals and expatriates, which is why he employs Jack Mowgley. Almost as wide as he is tall, Cornec is a very hard man in word and, especially, deed.

Christobel Hardy. 'Mimi' to the closest of friends, is beautiful, tall and elegant as only a French woman of a certain age can be. She effortlessly manages the agency office and cases and Mowgley, and is most likely a partner in bed as well as business with Yann Cornec. As well as kind and thoughtful, she is hard to shock, strong-willed and determined, as is evidenced by her continuing attempts to teach Mowgley how to eat, drink and speak French properly.

Kiss of De'Ath

A Jack Mowgley Mystery

George East

'Down these mean streets a man must go who is not himself mean, who is neither tarnished nor afraid. The detective must be a complete man and a common man and yet an unusual man. He must be, to use a rather weathered phrase, a man of honour.'

Raymond Chandler, creator of iconic private investigator Phillip Marlowe.

Kiss of De'Ath

Published by La Puce Publications

© George East 2023

This edition 2023

Paperback: 978-1-908747-86-0

Kindle edition: 978-1-908747-87-7

e-Pub: 978-1-908747-88-4

website: www.george-east.net

Typesetting and design Francesca Brooks

Other Mowgley Books

Death Duty

Deadly Tide

Dead Money

Death *á la* Carte

Dead and Buried

A small but significant player in Mowgley's life is **Madame Yvette**, doughty owner of the bar situated conveniently between the Gendarmerie and the agency office. She is particularly fond of her former lodger and now regular customer.

Author's Note

This sixth adventure for Jack Mowgley is as usual fictitious throughout and bears no intentional likeness to any situations or characters, living or otherwise. Or, that is, not any that I'd care to admit to. The references to famous fakers and art scams are true, however, and the plot is very loosely based on a true-ish story.

It is also true that Switzerland's Fine Art Expert Institute believes that fifty percent of all named art works are fakes. Some commentators believe that figure to be on the conservative side. For sure the worldwide trade in works of art is worth $65 billion a year, and some experts reckon that $6 billion of that figure comes from illegal, illicit and otherwise 'tainted' activity.

The naked man lay on his back, arms outstretched at shoulder level, legs spread-eagled. It occurred to Mowgley that the corpse was arranged in the familiar pose of Leonardo da Vinci's Vitruvian Man. The similarity was enhanced because the fingers and toes were touching a circle roughly chalked on the stone-flagged floor. Outside the circle were scrawled a number of what looked like cabbalistic symbols, and beside each stood the stump of a burned-out black candle.

Unlike the flowing locks of Leonardo's subject, the dead man was almost completely bald. A hairpiece lay like a small, dead animal alongside the head and lent an element of pathos to the grim scene. Sitting on the man's chest was a small framed painting of a red fish. Mowgley further observed that the dead man wore a small tattoo on the inside of his wrist, and could not help but notice that the corpse was far more generously endowed than the da Vinci illustration.

The strangest thing of all, Mowgley thought, was that the dead man was smiling an almost beatific smile.'

1

It definitely wasn't Jesus Christ, but at a push it could be Che Guevara; or maybe even Willie Nelson without the plaits and headband.

Former Special Branch Inspector John Jack Mowgley stretched, yawned and farted almost simultaneously, then resumed his study of the stain on the ceiling above his bed.

He'd read recently that a slice of toast miraculously branded with the face of Christ had fetched a hundred pounds in an online auction, while the asking price for a roof slate bearing the image of Jesus and Mary was ten thousand dollars.

He weighed the cost of removing the image and having the ceiling repaired against its likely value to iconic stain collectors, but decided to leave things as they were. Craftsmen did not come cheap, especially in rural France, and that's if they came at all.

On a positive note, he thought, studying the image might help him reflect on the nature and meaning of Life, humanity and the opposing arguments of kismet against pure happenstance. The stain was, after all, literal evidence that into every life a little rain must fall. For his part it seemed to have pissed down on him a lot of late, but things were hopefully on the up.

He looked around the room and felt a twinge of possessive pleasure. The tiny 18th-century cottage needed work, but it was more than habitable considering some of the places he'd lain his head across the years.

At least and at last he'd got shot of La Cour, the near-ruined Norman manor house that his wife had insisted he buy lest she leave him. Ironically she had left him anyway, and with the French property agent who had sold them the mouldering pile. Five years on and the sale of La Cour should have left him with the price of an apartment in Cherbourg and some rainy-day money, but the former Mrs. Mowgley had got wind of the sale and insisted on receiving half the profits. She had taken their house in Portsmouth and conceded him La Cour in the divorce settlement, but had obviously learned that French laws took no note of foreign agreements. What was left after her and the agent's and lawyers' share had bought the one-bed cottage in an unremarkable hamlet ten miles from Cherbourg. It was, however and on balance, good to know that the roof over his head was his own, even if it leaked.

~

A familiar squeal of brakes from below his bedroom widow interrupted Mowgley's reverie. Yawning, then swinging his legs out of bed he made his way carefully across the splinter-rich wooden floorboards.

'But soft, what light through yonder windows breaks?'

He leaned out of the window and down to where his

former colleague was standing by her car, looking up with eyes shaded against the early morning sun and one arm theatrically raised.

'It's not locked,' he replied, ' — go in and put the kettle on.'

'Do you think it'll suit me?'

Detective Sergeant Catherine McCarthy didn't wait for the groan or come-back, and pushed her way through the ancient and satisfyingly creaky front door.

The high-ceilinged room occupied most of the ground floor, which was modest in area. Overhead was a couple of roughly-hewn beams, and the stone flags beneath her feet almost glowed with the patina of centuries. These comfortable echoes of a time that probably never was contrasted sharply with the wallpaper, which bore a faded English hunting scene. The hanger had not bothered to match the strips, so a pack of sometimes grotesquely disjunctive hounds, horses and their riders pursued the front and back halves of foxes round the room.

One wall was thankfully free of wallpaper, which was because there was not room for a single strip. The huge fireplace with marble mantlepiece and majestic escutcheon above it took up the whole of the wall in which the chimney sat, and looked, she thought, almost as out of place as the wallpaper. Or, come to that, the new proprietor

'Did you know that "beam" is old English for "tree"?'

She turned to see her old boss framed in the doorless doorway to the kitchen. He had not reached the trouser stage, but his socks were in place. His top half was covered with an expensive-looking, diamond-paned sweater.

'I didn't,' she replied, 'but do now. That's a nice jersey.'

'Thanks,' he said, 'I got it at a boot sale at Carentan. It's a Walkers.'

'I think you mean Pringle.'

'That's it. I knew it was something to do with crisps.'

She looked to see if he could possibly be serious, then pointed at the fireplace. 'If you don't mind me saying, it looks as out of place as you at a temperance rally.'

'That's because it is out of place.' Mowgley walked the two steps from doorway to fireplace and laid a proprietary hand on the mantlepiece. 'According to the agent, it was looted from the château up the road after the Revolution. I like to think of the local serfs sitting round the fire and sharing a bottle of Château Lafite Rothschild '87 from the Count's cellar. That's the 1787, of course.'

'Get you,' said McCarthy. 'And do we know what happened to the former owner?'

Mowgley blew his cheeks out and raised an eyebrow. 'Nobody knows for sure but I hear he was away at his holiday château in the Loire valley at the time, and decided to stay there.'

'Very wise. And what about the Tardis in the kitchen? I don't suppose that came from the château?'

Mowgley looked to where she was pointing: 'Tardis?'

'Time and Relative Distances in Space. Dr Who and all that.'

He frowned. 'I think you'll find it's Time and Relative Dimensions in Space.'

'I know it is, just wanted to know if you knew. Anyway, what's it doing in the middle of your kitchen? Did it just materialise?'

Mowgley spread his arms. 'As you can see, nowhere much else to put it. It's a shower cubicle. Quite handy, really; you can keep an eye on the sausage and bacon while you're abluting.'

'A-whating?'

'Doing your privates.'

McCarthy shuddered. 'That's a picture I'll have a job deleting from the windmills of my mind. And what of the toilet — if there is one?'

Mowgley pointed to a door that looked like a pantry

cupboard. 'It's in there, but I haven't got round to using it, yet.'

'It's that grim, then?'

'No, just tricky to operate. The agent said it was salvaged from a boat in Cherbourg harbour. You have to pump it to force the doings through the pipe.'

McCarthy nodded. 'I know about boat loos. But where does the stuff go? A septic tank or cess pit? You don't seem to have much of a garden.'

'No. In the French way, the garden belongs to the lady next door. Mine is behind her house. The pipe from the toilet goes to a ditch alongside the road.'

'Ah. As you say, very French, in both cases.' She looked round, then said: 'Still it's a home of your own, and I can already see how much it suits you.'

He raised an eyebrow. 'What, you mean solid and dependable and full of character?'

She smiled almost fondly at him. 'More like old and a bit weird and dishevelled and full of contrasts and contradictions.' She looked at her watch: 'So are you going to get dressed or coming like that?'

'To where?'

'Like I said on the phone, we're going to meet René at a château up the road.' She nodded at the mantlepiece and escutcheon. 'It could even be the one where this came from,'

'And is the owner a count?'

She shrugged. 'Dunno, don't know anything about him, except that he's dead... and in somewhat unusual circumstances.'

~

They left the isolated hamlet and took one of the skeins of narrow lanes across the vast area of marshlands which bisected the Cherbourg peninsula. In summer the marais was a landscape of rich grass riven with tiny babbling springs. Cows grazed contentedly and rich flowers and rare salad plants bloomed. In a rainy winter it would become one vast lake, with only a handful of byways linking the marsh dwellers with civilisation.

Mowgley waved his hand in an almost proprietorial manner. 'Pretty eh?'

McCarthy grimaced. 'Yeah, but a bit spooky when the nights come early and the Undead start to walk. Or you lose the broadband and satellite signal.'

Mowgley puffed his cheeks. 'Think of all the books we never get round to reading. Would life be so hard without Netflix or a corner store down the road?'

'Probably.' She shrugged and steered round a pothole.

He patted his shirtfront, then experienced a moment of panic before he found the comforting bulge in his trouser pocket. 'Now remind me why your fiancé wants us at the scene of crime? I can see he'd want to impress you with his handling of the situation, but why me?'

'No idea,' said McCarthy, taking a hand from the wheel and tapping her lips with two fingers before blowing out a trail of imaginary smoke. 'Fag me. From what I gathered, the dead man is a Brit, and I think René thinks you could help out with enquiries amongst the local expat community in your new guise as a poor person's Phillip Marlowe. So there could be a nice few bob in it for you.'

'Ah.' Mowgley elevated his buttocks and pulled a lighter and battered packet of Gauloises Brunes from his trouser pocket. He extracted the last two cigarettes, lit them and passed one to McCarthy.

'Freedom forever', he said, raising the cigarette as if making a toast.

'Eh?' The car swerved as McCarthy took a long draw, then coughed and gagged and spluttered dramatically.

'It's the tagline for the Gauloises brand, or was.'

She took another tentative drag and coughed again, but with less disruption to her driving.

'Freedom to kill yourself, more like.'

'Quite. But I thought you were giving up to please René?'

'I am, but other people's don't count. And I know he's cheating on me with a sneaky Caporal when I'm not around.'

They left the hinterland and followed the road signposted for Valognes, Brix and Cherbourg, Mowgley winding his window up to capture fully the aroma and flavour of the cigarette smoke as he pointed out local points of interest. 'That's an old blacksmith's shop that specialises in *côte de boeuf* cooked on the forge with applewood. They say it makes the meat even sweeter. And that's...' he pointed with his cigarette, '... an old water mill that does a hundred fillings or more for crêpes and galettes. It's owned by a Breton couple. They do a blinding egg and bacon breakfast wrap.'

McCarthy looked away from the mill in time to pull up sharply as a tractor lurched from a field and on to the road. Even though it was no more than a track, she knew that traffic to the right had priority in some if not all towns, and this might be one of them. Either that was the case, or the brown-overalled driver didn't care. The old Massey-Ferguson was pulling a trailer with a cow in it, which regarded them with more interest than the driver had shown. Mowgley wondered if it was on its way to another field, or to market or abattoir. He smiled sympathetically at it, then observed: 'They say they know when they're nearing the slaughterhouse.'

'I hope not,' said his former colleague. 'There are some advantages to not knowing about mortality.'

'Yeh,' Mowgley agreed, 'and that you're going to end up on someone's plate alongside a heap of chips.'

'Almost enough to make you go vegetarian, isn't it?'

'Nope.'

The tractor crashed a set of lights at a crossroads, and they sat and watched the cow watching them as it travelled to its destiny.

'I suppose that's your local?' McCarthy nodded at a bar with a row of tables and chairs perilously close to the road. The plate glass window was garnished with heavily swagged curtains and lace netting, and an old-fashioned *carotte rouge* attached to the wall above the door proclaimed the premises to be a supplier of tobacco. A sandwich board beside the door notified passers-by that the dish of the day was rabbit in mustard with steamed potatoes, complete with pudding, cheese and a bottle of red wine thrown in for just fifteen Euros.

'Sort of,' said Mowgley. 'Pull over and I'll get some more fags. What do you fancy?'

'Don't care as long as it's not full-fat Gauloises.'

~

Catherine McCarthy tapped her fingers on the steering wheel and amused herself with a mild staring contest with a man seated at one of the tables outside the Bar Le Carrefour.

Rather than a bib and brace or overall, he was wearing what was obviously his working suit. The stained and shapeless jacket was tightly buttoned, and the trousers disappeared into an oversized pair of tractor-tread soled rubber boots. What was left of the man's copper-coloured hair was basin-cut, and the ears stuck out like jug handles. His eyes were small, close together and pointed in different directions, which made the contest harder for McCarthy. His age could be anywhere between forty and seventy. His nose was sharply pointed and bulbous at the same time. An ancient bicycle with an engine attached to the front wheel lay against the wall alongside the bar window. A fat rabbit sat regarding her unconcernedly from a wire cage strapped to the back pannier, while lashed to the crossbar was a piece of wood at least twice the length of the machine.

As the man broke eye contact to roll a cigarette, the

door opened and Mowgley emerged, wiping his mouth with the back of his hand. He was followed by a woman. She was tall by Norman standards, in her middle years and wearing a wrap-around apron over what looked to be a good quality and once-stylish blouse and skirt. She had what used to be called a statuesque figure, wore sensible low-heeled shoes, had clear white skin, a firm jaw and strong features. Her face was framed by the short, neat cut favoured by women who have reached the age when they know long hair is a no-go.

The woman and Mowgley stood talking for a moment, then she reached out, touched his arm and leaned forward. He looked quickly at the car, then pecked at her cheek, nodded to the man at the table and walked quickly to where DS McCarthy sat, smiling a knowing smile.

~

'Blimey, it doesn't take you long to get your feet under the table, does it?'

'What table?'

Catherine McCarthy repeated her lip-tapping cigarette request, then said: 'Madame's of course. Looks like she reckons you to be more than a regular customer.'

Mowgley tore the top off a pack of Gauloises Blondes and extracted two without spilling or crushing their neighbours. 'We are, as they say, just good friends. Madame Simon is a very nice, thoughtful and kind person — and she makes the best *Teurgoule* you've ever tasted.' He paused as he handed her a lit cigarette, then asked: 'What are you sniggering about?'

She drew gingerly on the cigarette, exhaled with evident pleasure and gave a slight shake of her head. 'It's you, and I'm so impressed. Teurgoule indeed. Once upon a time you'd have deliberately said rice pudding. I reckon you're going through the change.'

'What change?'

'Like the bloke in Metamorphosis. He changed into an insect, and you're changing into a frog. A typical Frenchman, I mean.'

'What, just because I smoke French fags and use a bit of the lingua franca out of respect for the language of my new home?'

'Nope. Because you've been telling me all about the best places to eat in the area, and raving about Madame's puddings. And you haven't asked if I brought over your full shipping order of chicken dansak, scotch eggs and pasties.

He raised an eyebrow as if suddenly reminded. 'Well, did you?'

'Of course; they're in the boot, if you're still interested.'

Mowgley nodded vigorously. 'Too right, squire. I haven't changed so much I'd turn a Scotch egg down.'

~

'So this is Brix,' said Catherine McCarthy as they entered a small village a mile or so from the RN13. 'Am I saying it right? Brie as in cheese?'

'Absolutely.' Mowgley nodded towards the two bars, convenience store, bakery and pharmacy taking up three sides of the square. The other was occupied by a church and graveyard. 'Actually,' he continued, 'in the local patois it was pronounced 'Broo' at the time of William the Conqueror.'

'How interesting,' said Catherine McCarthy, yawning pointedly then making a cigarette sign.

'Yes,' said Mowgley, reaching for the packet on the dashboard, 'Apparently, the local liege lord was a good mate and a big help to William in 1066, and was rewarded with coming up for half of Scotland.'

'Tell me more.'

'Well, spool on a couple of centuries, and a descendant

of the lord of Broo became—'

'Robert of Broo, king of the Scots,' interjected Catherine McCarthy triumphantly.

'That's right,' said Mowgley, his voice tinged with disappointment. 'How did you work that out?'

'Easy,' said McCarthy, sucking deeply on the cigarette Mowgley had placed between her lips. 'Being a detective, I used a combination of knowledge, deduction and observation...' she broke off to point through the windscreen with her Gauloises at a metal sign fixed to the side of the gate leading into the churchyard: 'and the valuable clue that we are driving through Robert The Bruce Square.'

~

As any visitor to France will have observed, châteaux take many forms.

The more overblown ones were built to impress other landlords and remind the peasants of the natural order of things. Châteaux-fortes were proper castles, built to keep unwelcome visitors at bay. Some were very grand palaces, created to upstage other courtiers if not the king. In agricultural France profonde, many were not much more than big houses with attitude. On a scale of one to ten in grandeur and pretension, the Château du Sourville would register no more than a pushy five.

Unlike the overblown confections lining the banks of the Loire, it was a sturdy, almost workmanlike building. The twiddly bits and vainglorious embellishments were limited to a couple of witches' hats and a square, crenelated tower complete with arrow slits. A curious addition, Mowgley noted, was a glass pyramid, sitting atop the main entranceway.

To one side of the arrow-straight drive were a stable block which echoed the design of the main house, a glasshouse more ornate than the château itself, and a pigeonnier considerably larger than Mowgley's new home. Half way along the drive, a working fountain splashed and gurgled in the midst of a sea of terraced gardens, topiarised bushes and manicured lawns.

Navigating around strips of yellow tape imprinted with the long-winded caution POLICE TECHNIQUE ET SCIENTIFIC — ZONE INTERDIT, Catherine McCarthy pulled up amidst the vehicles grouped around the main entrance.

Mowgley recognised René Degas' top-of-the-range blue Alpine 110, while next to it was a post-box red Porsche and a box-fresh Range Rover he assumed to be the property of the owner. Beyond that were two police cars and what Mowgley knew to be a scenes-of-crime van. By the open driver's door, a young woman in a flimsy-looking white coverall and hood was struggling with a pair of latex gloves. The roof lights on one of the police cars were slowly revolving, and a bored-looking gendarme was leaning against the bonnet, surreptitiously jabbing at his phone. He was either texting, Mowgley thought, or perhaps playing a French version of Candy Crush. An ambulance was backed up to the entrance, engine running and back doors open. For some reason it reminded Mowgley of an ice cream van.

As he opened the car door, Catherine McCarthy rummaged in her bag, found a tube of pastilles, then slipped one into her mouth. She saw him looking and gave him a mind-your-own-business glare, and he smiled placatingly. The aromatic pastille wouldn't fool her fiancé, but it was a small deception and done out of love as much as guilt.

The policeman leaning against the car put his phone away, straightened up and held up a hand as if stopping traffic as they approached. Catherine said something sharply and too quickly for Mowgley to follow, and the policeman thought about the least worst outcome of letting them through or refusing entry. Caution prevailed, and he dropped his hand, nodded at the entranceway and reached for his phone.

One of the massive, be-studded double doors was open, and beyond it lay an expanse of chessboard-tiled floor that would comfortably accommodate Mowgley's new home, back garden included. It was certainly too big and grand to call a hallway or even a vestibule. Natural light streamed in, and he saw that the ceiling had been replaced by the base of the glass pyramid which, he thought, was more than probably a nod at the bigger version outside the Louvre. The gallery theme was underlined by starkly whitewashed walls on which were hanging three paintings. Each was illuminated from above by a combination of strip and spot lighting, and were, he supposed, examples of modern art by favoured artists.

One of the paintings was a crude representation of a man with a penis for a head. Next to it was a stretched but unframed canvas dotted about with raised lumps of something brown. Probably not elephant shit, thought Mowgley as that had been done before. Perhaps it was literally all the artist's own work, he thought, in which case the cynics' judgement of modern art being mostly crap would be spot-on.

Its neighbour was a work which seemed wildly out of place. Even Mowgley knew it to be a copy of Vermeer's Girl with a Pearl Earring, and to his untrained eye it was indistinguishable from the original. Then he saw that the artist had added a moustache and the tip of a tongue, pierced by a pearl matching the earring. It changed dramatically the appearance of the model, and gave her a knowing and sensuous expression. He exchanged looks with DS McCarthy, and she shook her head, raised her eyebrows and made a don't-ask-me gesture with one hand.

As they crossed the room to the next set of doors Mowgley saw that, unless it was the ultimate statement of abstract art, one of the paintings was missing. The strip light was on, the hanging wire in place, and the focused spotlight trained on the blank wall.

~

The next set of double doors were at least ten foot high, of carved oak and, he thought, as substantial and enduring as the artworks on the wall were flimsy and ephemeral. It struck him how ironic it was that whoever perpetrated the dick head and pooh paintings would be hailed as artists, while whoever created the doors would be seen as just a craftsman.

It was curious, he thought as the right hand door reacted to no more than a gentle push, how good the French were at doors, windows and staircases, and how bad at electrics and plumbing. He supposed they thought more of eye-pleasing design and working with natural materials than putting a light switch in the right place and making sure it worked.

The doors led on to a huge room, which featured a lofty atrium-style glassed ceiling and a staircase leading up to a balcony serving the first-floor rooms. The current owner was clearly a fan of minimalism, and the room looked as if burglars had paid a visit and left only the stuff too big to carry. There was a glass-topped table surrounded by six chromium chairs with glass seats, and an almost painfully geometric black sofa with a long, low table in front of it. In contrast to the clean lines of the sofa, the table looked as if it were made of bits of a broken packing case held together by nails.

The sofa was being shared by two people of unusual appearance. One was a large, angry-looking woman with coarse features and green hair, dressed in a paint-stained bib-and-brace overalls. The short sleeves of her tee-shirt revealed muscular arms adorned with what looked like badly-drawn and probably home-made tattoos. She was also wearing what appeared to be aviator's goggles.

Next to and dwarfed by her, was a small, slight figure, huddled up and clutching a large wicker basket. Her long, dark hair was parted in the middle, bunched on either side of her face and tied with ribbons. She was wearing a white top with puffed sleeves over a blue gingham dress. The ruby-red sparkly shoes over pale blue ankle socks were the final clue to the character she was portraying. Toto the dog was missing from the basket, but could be, Mowgley thought, elsewhere.

Behind the sofa, a plain black metal staircase led up to the balcony giving access to six black doors. The staircase and balcony looked rather like a fire escape, and Mowgley wondered what sweeping oaken magnificence must have been ripped out to make way for it.

Outside one of the doors, a woman was leaning on the balcony rail, regarding the scene below her with a look of detached amusement. She was of middle age, tall and full-bodied, and reminded Mowgley of Vanessa Redgrave at her imperious best in Mrs. Dalloway. Unlike the lady in the movie, the woman was wearing a brightly-coloured headscarf, knotted at the front in the way housewives had once hidden their curlers while shopping. She was also wearing a sort of belted boiler suit, the legs of which were hugely puffed-out from hip to knee in the manner of a pair of Eric Morecambe joke jodhpurs. Her right hand was held imperiously above shoulder level, and from it dangled a long, thin cheroot. All in all, he thought, she was out to make an impression, and had got her way.

After a brief meeting of eyes which he found curiously disturbing, Mowgley looked away and saw that the white walls of the room were completely barren except for one work of art. It was a copy of the Mona Lisa on which a moustache and goatee beard had been daubed.

They crossed the room and went through the door to a

small ante-room. Again, the walls were white and the furniture minimal. A female police officer was standing behind a spindly chair, one hand laid comfortingly on the shoulder of someone who seemed to be doing their best to look like they needed comforting.

She was, Mowgley surmised, of Chinese or Thai heritage, and very young, very pretty and tiny and doll-like to a point of apparent fragility. Her glossy black hair cascaded onto her shoulders and looked, like the rest of her, extremely high-maintenance. Her skin was almost luminescent, and her eyes large and shining, but not, he thought, with tears.

The policewoman evidently recognised Catherine McCarthy, and nodded a sombre acknowledgement before pointing at a door in the wall beyond the staircase.

Mowgley followed McCarthy, passing the chair and trying for the sombre, sympathetic look favoured by funeral company employees when they arrive to pick up the body. Their eyes met, but the young woman did not acknowledge him or show any interest. This, as Mowgley had found when encountering young and beautiful females, was not at all unusual, regardless of circumstances.

2

The corpse and Colonel René Degas awaited them at the bottom of a flight of stone steps leading to what was clearly a very well-stocked wine cellar.

Unlike the minimalist/modernist styling above, this part of the Château du Sourville had escaped the vagaries of changing fashion. The brick walls of the first of a series of vaulted chambers were lined with rack after rack of bottles. Some carried a fine layer of dust, which Mowgley assumed meant they were older and more valuable than the shiny, newer ones. He assumed the three giant casks on another wall were filled with more wine, or perhaps even brandy. Either way, he would have been prepared to lay a lumpy bet that the dozens of racks contained not a single bottle of Prosecco.

~

The naked man lay on his back, arms outstretched at

shoulder level, legs spread-eagled. It occurred to Mowgley that the body had been arranged in the familiar pose of Leonardo da Vinci's Vitruvian Man. The similarity was enhanced because the fingers and toes were touching a circle roughly chalked on the stone-flagged floor. Outside the circle were scrawled a number of what looked like cabbalistic symbols, and beside each stood a black, lighted candle.

Unlike the flowing locks of Leonardo's subject, the dead man was almost completely bald. A hairpiece lay like a small, dead animal alongside the head and seemed to lend an element of pathos to the grim scene. Laying on the man's chest was a small framed painting of a red fish. Around his neck was a narrow belt, its end threaded loosely through the buckle. Mowgley further observed that the dead man wore a small tattoo on the inside of his wrist. He could also not help but notice that the corpse was far more generously endowed than the da Vinci illustration.

The strangest thing of all, Mowgley thought, was that the man was smiling an almost beatific smile.

~

Scene-of-crime tape had been strung around the chalk circle, and within it, two figures in full protective clothing moved slowly around the body. In a way and given the surroundings, he thought, they looked like celebrants playing their part in some arcane rite.

Scattered around the dead man were several small yellow numbered markers noting where items of possible interest had been found. One had been placed beside a small plastic bottle near the corpse's right hand. Another sat near to the painting on the dead man's chest. Outside the barrier of tape, an uncorked wine bottle was marked. It was dusty, Mowgley noted, but had no obvious finger marks disturbing the grey patina.

Inside the exclusion zone, also wearing a PPE protective suit, shoe covers and latex gloves and looking thoughtfully down at the corpse with one hand cupping his chin was a tall and what previous generations would have called distinguished-looking man. He appeared to be in his early fifties, was clean-shaven, wore his thick and obviously cared-for dark hair a little longer than the norm and had strong, regular features. Nowadays. Mowgley thought, he would more likely be described by admiring women as fit in both senses of the word. The man turned to look up at them as they came down the stairs, and it would, Mowgley thought, be no exaggeration to say his face lit up. He also deduced that it was not his arrival which had made Degas so clearly happy.

As a Colonel, René Degas was by far the senior officer in the Cherbourg department of the Gendarmerie Nationale. This made him a man with real clout. The Gendarmerie was the military half of France's two national police forces, and Degas could choose which crimes he would personally investigate. By logic and choice, they would always be the most serious of offences.

A man of sharp mind, the Colonel demonstrated a keen appreciation of irony and a quirky sense of humour not, in Mowgley's opinion, always found in the French.

Degas had met DS McCarthy while she was on a visit to see her old boss some two years before, just after Mowgley had moved across the Channel to begin his new life in self-imposed exile. Having failed to find a man to live up to her expectations, McCarthy had long ago settled on Mowgley as her sole male friend until she and Degas had met and the sparks of mutual attraction had sparked. Now they were lovers and the arrangement suited her and the widower well. Although neither would perhaps agree, it seemed to Mowgley that the distance between them across the Channel made their love deeper and their reunions so much sweeter. He knew that Degas would like to take their relationship further, but it would be a big step for Catherine McCarthy. From Mowgley's perspective, it was a win-win situation. The relationship gave him access to information and resources of the National law enforcement agency's data base, while his former colleague's increasingly frequent visits meant a regular supply of Scotch eggs, pastys and hard cheese. Despite his former colleague's observations about his metamorphosis into a Frog, he had learned the truism that you can take the man out of his country, but rarely the country out of the man when it came to long-established custom and taste and a love for Scotch eggs.

~

'Do you still miss it?' asked DS McCarthy while negotiating a narrow, hump-backed bridge.

'Miss what?' responded her former colleague as he waved absent-mindedly at a buzzard regarding them disinterestedly from a fence post.

'Well, everything, I suppose. The job, living in Portsmouth, being part of the team. The pub and the regulars and even Two-Shits and his mummified meat pies?'

Mowgley frowned and scratched a stubbly chin. 'Of course I miss some things… but not others.'

'Like?'

'Well, the paperwork for a start.'

DS McCarthy gave a fair impression of a horse snorting in derision. 'But you never did any.'

'True. But I certainly don't miss the way Dickie Quayle used to pick his nose, and especially not Madam bloody Hartley Hyphen Whatsername.'

Chief Superintendent Cressida Hartley-Whitley was an officer on the fastest of fast tracks, and the first female overseer of what had been Mowgley's patch. Apart from her personal distaste of the way he looked and spoke and breathed, she had made it quite clear from their first meeting that she was not in favour of 'old-style' policing methods, nor those officers who employed them. Especially, although she did not say it, of male officers with Mowgley's obvious attitude towards women.

It had been because of her that he had been presented with the choice of taking early retirement, or being suspended during an exhaustive trawl through his official and unofficial activities across the years. As Mowgley knew, no expense would be spared to uncover any minor or major misdemeanours, and there were a lot to uncover. He had chosen the stay-out-of-jail option, and taken up an offer to work as an associate with a new investigative agency in Cherbourg.

Services d'Enquêtes Privés Cornec was run by a former colleague of René Degas, and Mowgley had met and worked with Yann Cornec on a case involving deaths, disappearances and people and drug smuggling. The Breton was opening a branch in Cherbourg, and, with many thousands of Britons choosing to start a new life in Normandy and beyond, Cornec had assured him there would be plenty to keep him busy and earn a good commission.

~

As any seasoned Francophile will know and be sure to tell you, there is a trick to finding a good and cheap meal in rural France. It is simply to count the number of commercial vehicles outside any bar or restaurant offering a Relais Routiers lunchtime service.

At first sight, Mowgley thought, their destination looked like an over-subscribed lorry park. Sign written trades-men's vans, battered pick-up trucks, the odd car in the shadow of monstrous beasts with triple axles surrounded a shabby, brick-built building which looked under siege.

'I hope you booked,' said Mowgley.

McCarthy shook her head. 'You can't book here; it's first come, first served.'

'So, what if there's no room?'

'Don't worry, I think one of René's people had a word with the management. If not, we'll have to feast on your Scotch eggs and pastys.'

~

'Has everyone had enough?'

The Colonel's question having clearly been directed at him, and Mowgley looked at his empty plate and the severely diminished cheese board, nodded reluctantly and sighed. It was, he reflected, evident why The Relais du Cotentin was such a favoured stop.

The original building had obviously grown with the success of the business, and ninety-seven seats had been filled when they arrived at a few moments after noon. René Degas had overtaken them on route, and he and his guests had been shown to the mezzanine floor, overlooking row after row of trestle tables. In a cafeteria, the air would be filled with the buzz of conversation and the clash of cutlery on china. Here, it was more of a rumble of contentment and quiet appreciation, as if the clientele was worshipping at the altar of great regional cooking. There was no carte, as there was no choice but the patron's. Further evidence of his or her status was the lack of salt and pepper or any other condiments on the tables. It would have been regarded as a gross insult to augment the chef's idea of appropriate seasoning.

Everyone on the premises had feasted on duck pâté, then slices of perfectly roasted pork (sadly, in Mowgley's opinion, lacking crackling), potatoes boulangere and courgettes provencale. Mowgley pursued a shred of pork with a toothpick as he tried to imagine a similar set-up in

Britain, but could not.

The only disappointment had been the lack of an after-dinner cigarette. In the good old days, the air would have been dense with the aroma of tobacco as well as good food. He smiled ruefully and said: '*Formidable*. All I could do with now is an after-dinner fag.'

'I see that there is a cemetery across the road,' said Degas. 'It will be quiet and there will be seats and we could talk about the case while you have your cigarette.'

'Are you sure smoking isn't barred in cemeteries nowadays?'

'I don't think,' said Degas gravely, 'that it would be regarded as a health risk to the residents.'

~

A stick in one hand and a bunch of geraniums in the other, the old lady hobbled slowly and clearly painfully past the bench. She eyed them suspiciously and responded with no more than a curt nod to Degas' greeting.

On the first day of November — All Saints' Day — this and every other cemetery in France would be busy with families arriving to tend their departed loved ones' graves and dress them with giant pots of chrysanthemums. The traditional flower of death, they were also ironically a symbol of immortality as they survive the winter and need little attention. Still the sacred lunching hours and the road distant, the cemetery was proverbially as quiet as the grave.

Mowgley looked around and reflected on how, despite what people liked to say, death was not the great leveller. The status of the residents in life was reflected by the position and the munificence of their plot in death. In one eternally sunless corner, the markers were no more than plain wooden or metal framed crosses. The more elaborate and extravagant displays were sculptured creations of marble, with photographs of the residents looking out on the world they had left behind.

'Is my smoking bothering you?'

Mowgley held up his smouldering cigarette, which he had noticed both Catherine McCarthy and René Degas were regarding like a couple on a strict diet watching a food porn programme.

He took a long drag, smiled blandly, let the smoke drizzle seductively from his lips, then sat up straight and said; 'I'm sorry. I didn't offer you one, I thought you'd stopped.'

He held the packet out towards them and raised his eyebrows invitingly. They looked at each other, then Degas licked his lips and said: 'I suppose one would not hurt us…'

McCarthy gave a murderous glance at Mowgley, then smiled sweetly at Degas as if offering him absolution, and said: 'Why don't we share one?'

Licking his lips again, her lover nodded and they both watched as Mowgley took a cigarette from the packet, lit and held it out. René Degas nodded courteously to Catherine McCarthy, who reached over, took the cigarette and, apparently reluctantly, sucked daintily on it. She managed to look, thought Mowgley admiringly, like someone who had not been near a cigarette for weeks rather than a couple of hours.

'When I was at primary school,' Mowgley recalled, 'me and a couple of mates used to cycle to a quiet spot in Portsmouth Harbour to share a fag from a packet of five Woodbines we had stashed under a rock. We'd talk about what we'd do if someone tipped the police off and they arrived mob-handed to arrest us. Bobby Harrigan said he'd swim to the Isle of Wight.' He took another lungful of smoke.

'Mick Beacon said he'd give himself up.'

'And what was your plan?' Catherine McCarthy regretfully passed the stub of the Gauloises to her lover.

'I said I'd escape to France and claim asylum.'

'Which,' observed his former colleague, 'is more or less what you did a good few years later.'

'I suppose so,' he said reflectively, reaching for the packet and looking enquiringly at his companions.

~

'So, what about the dead bloke, René?' Mowgley asked. 'I assume he was the owner of the place and not someone who turned up in the cellar for a bit of self-abuse?'

'His name is — or it was — Piers De'Ath,' said Degas, dropping all pretence and reaching eagerly for a cigarette, '...and yes, he was the owner of the château.'

'And do you know who the strange lot in the sitting room are?'

'No, not really. I am told they are artists who had gathered for the weekend for an event staged by Mr. De'Ath.'

'What sort of event?' asked Catherine. 'Something arty...or something unsavoury in the cellar?'

Degas shrugged and lifted a hand. 'I do not know yet.'

'And the young woman of Asiatic heritage?'

'His wife. She is from Thailand and they had only been married a year. She was on an early morning shopping trip to Cherbourg market and came back to find him. It was she who called the police.'

Mowgley waited as the old lady walking slowly past them towards a water tap, then asked: 'Do you know what Mr. Death did before he lived up to his name?'

'It was not the time to question his young wife,' said Degas, 'and the cook and housekeeper were off duty. But the gardener was helpful. He said that Mr. De'Ath was very famous in the art world. Not as a painter, but a critic. They lived first in Bergerac and then moved here.'

'So, I know the body's still warm, but what do you

reckon to be the cause of death? Murder, accident or suicide?'

'It is, as you say, far too early to know, but interesting that you have presented the three choices.'

'Not really,' said Catherine McCarthy, 'there was what looked like an open pill bottle by his side, which could mean an accidental or deliberate overdose. Or the way the body was laid out, it could have been some weird statement by him — or someone arranged his body like that. And what about the painting of the dead fish and the other stuff? Part of some sort of weird sexual routine?'

'Or was he getting warmed up for the return of his wife and overdid it?' Mowgley added.

Degas gave a half-smile. 'Again, I know only what I have told you. But I think I understand the significance of the fish painting. It was, as we would say, *pour brouiller les pistes.*' Seeing Mowgley's blank expression, he continued: '…the fish was a *hareng* — a herring — coloured red. We think it may have belonged in the empty space in the gallery.

'Ah,' Mowgley mused, 'a bit of arty symbolism. But if it was, what did it mean? What was the red herring? The plastic bottle of pills or whatever was in it? The symbols round the circle?'

'Perhaps it didn't mean anything,' said Catherine McCarthy, thoughtfully. 'Perhaps it was just an arty-farty piece of distraction to get you trying to work out what it meant.'

'Yes,' agreed Mowgley. 'Or perhaps not.'

~

René Degas opened the gate and stepped back to usher Mowgley and McCarthy through. He waited while the old lady shuffled through as if herding them off the premises. She was carrying a small bunch of wilting geraniums, and nodded grudgingly at Degas as she made her way along the verge. Mowgley considered doing the old chestnut about it hardly being worth her going home, but thought the gag might not travel.

'Are you going to tell him our news?' Catherine McCarthy asked Degas as he re-joined them.

'What?' Mowgley looked his former colleague up and down theatrically. 'You're not pregnant are you?'

She did not deign to answer, but looked at Degas and nodded for him to make whatever the announcement might be.

'I have asked Catherine if she will marry me,' he said awkwardly, 'and she has said yes. Excuse me.'

Down the lane, the old lady had slipped on the verge and dropped her stick, and Degas moved swiftly to help her.

'So' Mowgley said to McCarthy as they watched him stride along the lane. 'It's a bit of a way to commute, isn't it? Unless René is moving to Portsmouth?'

'I'm leaving the job. I was getting nowhere and —'

'You missed me so much?'

'Not that much. I just got fed up with getting nowhere and having to clear up after my boss. At least you knew what a cock-up you could make of things. I've already put my papers in, and I'm moving over as soon as I can. We'll live at René's apartment until we find somewhere bigger. But,' she added almost as if in afterthought, 'I'm marrying him because I love him.'

'Of course.' Mowgley smiled a false smile. 'So, you'll be a busy housewife, knocking up light lunches and sophisticated dinners for René and your guests?'

'Erm, don't think so.' McCarthy looked almost embarrassed, then said: 'Yann has offered me a job.'

'Oh.' Mowgley stepped back in supposed shock. 'I'm going to get the bullet, then?'

'Not at all. Yann says there's more and more Brit expat work coming through, and René will be able to find some liaison work for me.'

Mowgley stopped and scratched his chin. 'Oh again. Then we'll be working together again?'

'Looks like it. Is that good or bad news?'

'Not sure, but I reckon we should mark the announcement.'

They waited for Degas to join them and walked to their cars. As Catherine McCarthy reached for her keys, Mowgley nodded towards the open door of the Relais du Cotentin.

'I bet they do a good bottle of sparkling wine in there. And we could sit outside and have a fag and toast the future you intend to share.'

'Sounds good to me,' said McCarthy, looking quizzically at Degas. 'But I reckon we could have a fag each this time.'

Famous Fakers: Han van Meegeren (1889-1947)

Taking place during World War Two and involving the deception of a top-ranking Nazi, the Case of the Fake Vermeers is said to be unique. It is considered by many to be the most dramatic art scam of the twentieth century.

In 1945, a relatively obscure Dutch artist called Han van Meegeren was accused of collaborating with the enemy, a charge which carried the death penalty. His alleged crime was to have been involved in the sale to Field-Marshall Hermann Goering of a Vermeer masterpiece. Meegeren's defence was that the Woman Taken in Adultery was in fact a forgery, and that he had painted it. In fact, he claimed, rather than a traitor, he should be regarded as a national hero for fooling the top Nazi. He also claimed that he was responsible for no less than five other Vermeer classics which had appeared on the art market from 1937.

In order to demonstrate his innocence, Meegeren offered to paint another 'Vermeer' while in captivity, using the same materials and techniques as in his previous forgeries.

As a result, the charges were changed from Collaboration to Forgery, and the artist was sentenced to a mere year's imprisonment.

The case caused a re-examination of the level of forgeries of Old Masters which might be in circulation at that time.

Claude-Emile Schuffenecker (1851-1934)

This contemporary of the great man is just one in a long line of fakers or alleged fakers of Vincent Van Gogh. Also a renowned collector, he was one of the first to acquire works by Gauguin, Cézanne and Van Gogh.

down to a sensible 50kph and concentrated on his driving as he reached the crest of the hill overlooking his adopted town. All things considered, he reckoned, he was doing okay, and increasingly had come to realise that he actually liked being a foreigner in a fairly welcoming land.

~

The Cherbourg headquarters of the *Gendarmerie Nationale* is an uninspiring concrete cube in a road close to the quayside and town centre. The new branch of the un-catchingly named Services d'Enquêtes Privés Cornec were to be found across the road and sandwiched between a Domino Pizza outlet and a car rental agency.

It would not take a trained detective to work out that it was no coincidence that the enquiry agency and the *Gendarmerie* were in such close locational accord. Another advantage to the agency was that the bar favoured by officers and employees of the *Gendarmerie* was but a step away, and made an ideal location for proprietor Yann Cornec and his so far sole enquiry agent to mix business and pleasure.

Using his unofficial official swipe card to raise the barrier, Mowgley drove into the *Gendarmerie* car park and left the Citroën in an inoffensive corner. Nodding affably to the closed-circuit camera and then the aged civilian washing a patrol car, he picked up a pair of still-warm croissants and a *pain au raisin* from the family bakery round the corner. The *8-a-huit* was nearer, but his colleague would be horrified at the idea of buying wine, chocolate and especially pastries from any chain store, no matter how convenient.

~

'You look…nice.'

Mowgley had no idea if shoulder pads and summery wrap-round wartime-looking dresses were in fashion, but he didn't suppose Mimi would give much of a hoot about what was *à la mode* – or even what he thought about how she looked.

For sure she had that knack – which even he had observed seemed more common on this side of the Channel – of making anything she wore look fashionable.

She eyed him up and down, gave a mock shudder, then said: 'Thank you. I wish I could return the compliment.'

Cristobel Hardy was tall and shapely, with finely-drawn, generous lips, sculpted features and what used to be called flame-haired hair. With it untied and down to her shoulders, she reminded Mowgley of Rula Lenska in her heyday, soon after her marriage to fellow thespian Dennis Waterman but before the toe-curling pussy-cat incident with George Galloway on *Big Brother*.

Cristobel or 'Mimi' to her friends was the office manager and more than probably lover of the proprietor of the agency, and Mowgley could see why in both cases. As he had quickly learned, she was as clever and witty and sharp as she was beautiful, and he had found that beneath today's summery dress rested a good heart. They had an easy understanding and, in spite of occupying different genders, did not need any degree of pretence or subterfuge in their dealings. It could never be the same, but was similar to his relationship—if that was the word—with Catherine McCarthy. Until now, he had found the comfortable, bantering and almost matey relationship rare as rocking-horse shit when it came to working with and getting on with women. He had certainly not had it with his wife, though had once thought he had, and then there were the two women who had almost caused his death. One deliberately so; the other perhaps not, though he would never really know for sure.

Arriving at his desk, he nodded to and sat beneath the 'down these mean streets' quotation by the creator of his favourite fictional detective. Catherine McCarthy had had the passage framed and presented to him on his retirement booze-up at the Ship Leopard. He knew he would never live up to the standards as laid down by Raymond Chandler, but it was good to have something to aim for.

'Tout va bien?'

Mimi arrived to place a stylish if tiny cup of espresso and a piece of paper on his desk. The cup had no hole in the handle, he noted, and the paper looked worryingly full of detail.

'Bah oui.' He replied and looked at her expectantly. Since his drinking companion, friend and occasional lover Lady Sarah had slipped anchor and sailed away from Cherbourg harbour, Mimi had taken on his tutelage in language and expected behaviour as a guest in a country where small things could be important.

'Bon,' said Mimi, *'tante mieux...'* then, seeing the edge of panic appear on his face, lapsed into English: 'You had a good time yesterday, obviously.'

Mowgley nodded and tried not to show his sense of relief. He could now pass the time of day, comment on the weather or swap an insult in passable French, but anything more complex was still beyond him. Old dogs and new tricks, as Catherine McCarthy had said. But Mimi was nothing if not resolute, and had presented him recently with a copy of Maupassant's *Bel Ami* and insisted on hearing him translate a paragraph a day. This was not a problem as he had bought an English copy, but he knew she knew he was cheating.

'I hear your friend is to be married soon,' said Mimi, perching her elegant bottom on the corner of his desk. '— and you are to be a witness?'

'We call it the best man.'

'Oh. But that is not very flattering to the groom?'

'No,' he said, 'I suppose not. But how did you know? About the wedding, I mean?'

She gave a careless and very French shrug, emphasised by the shoulder pads. 'Girl talk. And you will give the address in French of course?'

'Of course.'

'Don't worry, I shall make sure you can do it properly.'

She stood up, adjusted her dress and smiled down at him. 'Did you know it will be my birthday next week?'

'Ah, the big three-oh, eh?'

'No. I will be forty-two. Age is not an illness or to be ashamed of, you know.'

'Quite right. And what would you like for your birthday that I can afford?'

She seemed to give the question some thought, then said casually: 'There is that old necklace you brought back from Bulgaria.'

He grimaced. 'As I said to my wife when she asked for a divorce as a birthday present, I wasn't thinking of spending that much.'

She did the thing with her lips that French women do so well when registering disappointment or disagreement: 'But you told me it is only a copy.'

He shrugged: 'Still worth a lot more than I would spend on a present, even for you.'

The golden necklace had been a parting gift from a Bulgarian police officer in charge of a department trying to stem the tide of the illegal export of a billion dollars' worth of Thracian artefacts which left the country each year. Mowgley had been of life-saving service to Inspector Georgi Georgiev, who had managed to persuade Customs at Gatwick that the striking ornament was no more than a replica. But something about the Inspector and the result of their near-death experiences had made Mowgley think it might be the real thing. The delicate but substantial necklace sat in an old cigar box in his new home as a rainy-day standby, and even if a fake, it would be valuable. If the real thing, he figured it would buy a rather tasty château. Mowgley had resisted the temptation to have it valued, probably because he did not really want to know its true worth.

'So you have it safely in the bank?'

'No, safely hidden in my cottage. I'll tell you exactly where if you buy me lunch.'

She made another very French female facial expression, then said: 'It must be tomorrow. You have things to do.'

He looked at the piece of paper and frowned: 'Seems a lot of messages?'

'Perhaps that is because you have not answered your phone since yesterday morning.'

'True. Anything urgent?'

'There were calls from Colonel Degas and Yann. The Colonel wants to tell you about the dead man in the château.'

'And Yann?'

'He wants to talk to you about why you are not keeping proper records of your hours and expenses.'

'Okay, no problem.' said Mowgley defensively, opening a drawer in his desk and pulling out a fistful of crumpled receipts and scribbled notes. 'And?'

'And there is a man waiting to see you at the bar.'

'Does he want to see me about a dog or does he look like a jealous husband or a bailiff?'

She shook her head and frowned: 'I beg your pardon. What do you mean?'

'Never mind. Did he say what he wants?'

'He is English and it is about his son.'

'What about his son?'

'He was working here in the town, and has gone away without saying where. The father has got nothing from the police, but someone at the *Gendarmerie* told him about the English detective. I can see he is very worried and I think he is a nice man. I told him you were out and not answering your phone, but he said he would wait.'

~

Madame Yvette was as ever on duty behind the bar at the *Bon Parle* and insisted on coming from behind it to claim her four kisses. She had told him that the extra two were a Norman tradition reserved for the closest of friends, and that they should be on the lips rather than cheeks.

Mowgley was happy to oblige his former landlady, and looked around the bar as they kissed. He saw there were two uniformed and three plain-clothes officers gathered round the big table in the middle of the bar which was reserved for their exclusive use. Four were playing *barbu*, a card game which remained a mystery to Mowgley beyond that it involved elements of Bridge and was named for the bearded King of Hearts.

At another table and sipping delicately at their tiny pre-luncheon glasses of *suze* were two burly men in day-glow overalls who he recognised as dock workers.

More interestingly and occupying a marble-topped table in front of the plate glass window were a couple who were obviously approaching Defcon stage 3 in terms of a scene. The young woman's face was a crumpled mask of despair, and black streams of mascara trickled down her cheeks as her shoulders heaved. In front of her was an empty wine glass and the remains of what must have been several cardboard beer mats. Opposite sat a lean man in his thirties who had the misfortune to look not unlike Serge Gainsbourg at the time of his recording of *Je T'aime… Moi Non Plus*. His ears and teeth protruded far beyond the norm, and, together with his hooded eyes the overall effect was of a cornered rat. His ugliness was emphasised by the contrast with the temporarily distorted but obvious beauty of his companion. He was lounging back in his chair, looking out of the window, and Mowgley felt a mild urge to give him a slap. Whether because of the obvious distress of his companion or just the man's unfortunate looks, he could not honestly say.

'Mr. Begg?'

The small, worried-looking man in the corner had been toying with his coffee cup, and looked up sharply as if surprised to hear his name said in such a foreign location.

'Yes...?' he said with a tentative nod. Mowgley noted there was almost a question mark in his voice, as if he were expecting to hear something he did not want to hear.

'Jack Mowgley. From the agency. You called in this morning, I think...'

A wash of relief flitted across the man's features, then he stood and offered his hand. He was almost a head shorter than Mowgley, but large-handed, deep-chested, wide-shouldered and generally sturdy in appearance. *Costaud*, as the French would say.

'Pleased to meet you,' he said, and then as if Mowgley would not already know, 'Frank Begg. I came to see you this morning. Earlier.'

Mowgley waited a moment, but nothing more was forthcoming, so he looked at the empty coffee cup and said: 'Something to drink? Another coffee, or a beer or wine...?'

The man rubbed his chin in indecision as if Mowgley had asked him to name the last three kings of France, then reached for his pocket. 'Err, let me,' he said, waving an obviously unfamiliar twenty euro note vaguely in the air.

Mowgley held up both hands. 'No, I'll do it. I'm on exes. You can do the next one if you like. What's it going to be?

Before Begg could speak, there was a smash of glass,

the sound of a smack and a scream. Defcon had obviously reached stage 5. Mowgley looked to where the rat-faced man was standing by his upturned chair, smiling contemptuously down at the girl. She was holding a hand to her face and sobbing.

In some bars in the seamier dockside area, the incident would have caused little reaction beyond disapproving looks and perhaps comments of reproach if the assailant were not too big. But Rat Face had picked the wrong place to hit a woman. Or anyone.

Mowgley was quick, but the two uniformed officers were younger and fitter and quicker. They reached the man before Mowgley had taken more than a step, forcing him face down on the table and cuffing him with practised ease. Protesting loudly and profanely, Rat Face was hustled out of the door, managing to hit his head on the jamb as he was propelled through it.

Calm returned almost immediately. Madame Yvette bustled over to right the chair, sweep up the glass and shredded beer mats and comfort the girl with a large brandy. Cherbourg's Finest returned to their game and Mowgley noticed that one of the players took the opportunity to sneak a look at the abandoned hand of one of the arresting officers.

Dotty Swindle

In June 2017, Vincent Loptreto was charged in a Manhattan courtroom with selling $400,000 worth of fake Damien Hirst prints. The prosecution claimed that the alleged 'limited edition' prints had been advertised for sale alongside fake certificates of authenticity and purchase receipts. The alleged works by Hirst were mainly a series of coloured dots, and there was laughter in court when the judge asked how anyone could tell the difference between a genuine and fake blob of paint.

4

'I trust that's a purely decorative erection?'

'You're not the first woman to ask that.'

Mowgley stepped back to admire the bird-feeder now taking centre-stage in the patch of grass behind the cottage next door to his new home.

'Did you not know there are no small birds in Normandy now the bold hunters have slaughtered everything from a wren to a robin and above?'

'I bought it off an expat at a boot sale for a fiver,' said Mowgley defensively.

'And did you not wonder why he was selling it?'

'He said he was going home to Birmingham.'

'Well,' she shrugged, 'I suppose it'll give the locals something to shoot at if it attracts the last sparrow in all Normandy. And you'll certainly save on bird seed. Or perhaps,' she said, nodding towards the back of the neighbouring house behind which Mowgley's patch of garden stood, 'you're just staking out your territory?'

Mowgley gave the pole another tweak and waved vaguely towards where a small, stringy woman in a wrap-around apron stood at her kitchen window, regarding them with a mixture of curiosity and outrage.

Leading the way back to *Le Petit Bijou* and knowing Madame would still be watching, Mowgley ostentatiously avoided stepping on the patch of grass behind his house which, not unusually in France *profonde*, belonged to his neighbour.

'Silly question,' said McCarthy as they reached her car, 'but did you not ask the *notaire* if you couldn't just swap gardens with Madame?'

'I did, but he said she would rather die than give up her sacred plot.'

~

Despite McCarthy's reservations, they took Mowgley's car to their lunchtime rendezvous. Knowing of its condition and his road management levels, McCarthy at first demurred, but changed her mind when he pointed out they would be able to smoke on the way if they took his Citroën.

'Not that I'm ungrateful,' said Mowgley as they joined the RN13 and headed south, 'but is there a reason we always meet your fiancé in a bar or restaurant? Is he ashamed of seeing me in his office? It's all a bit...' he waved a hand as he searched for the right word, '...clandestine, isn't it?'

'Not really' said McCarthy, 'we get a nice meal and I get to come along too. But I also guess he doesn't want to advertise that he's giving his former colleague a regular earner in consultancy work.'

Mowgley nodded. 'Fair enough.' He paused a moment and then asked: 'Don't suppose you know how much he pays Yann for my services?'

'No, but Mimi would. Why do you want to know?'

'Just to know how much dosh he's making out of me.'

'What do you care?' she asked with female logic. 'As long as you're happy with your day rate, what does it matter how much he gets? And it would only upset you if you found out.'

'True.'

They travelled on in silence for a moment, then Mowgley fished out his packet of Gauloises. McCarthy took out two cigarettes, lit both, then leant over and put one between his lips. Mowgley nodded his thanks, took a deep draw then wound both front windows up.

'What are you doing?' McCarthy asked. 'You're not cold are you?'

'It's not that', said her former boss. 'It dilutes the atmosphere with the windows open.'

'Ahhh.' She sucked on her Caporal and sighed with contentment as the smoke drizzled from her nostrils. 'I'd forgotten that wheeze. See what I did there with "wheeze"?' She took another luxurious draw, then shook her head sadly. 'I know I've got to stop but it's so bloody good.'

She leaned back and aimed a jet of smoke at the smallest of the holes in the soft top of the DS21 'Here's a thing. Would you rather never having smoked and not known the pleasure, but saved on all the worry and cost?'

Mowgley thought for a second, then said: 'No contest. If you think about it, it's a bit like sex and marriage. You know how dangerous and expensive it's going to be, but can't stop yourself from doing it…'

~

With a swish marina at the head of a canal formed by the confluence of two rivers, Carentan-les-Marais is what guide books might call a picturesque and historic waterside market town.

In 1944, the then more plainly titled Carentan took on major significance at the start of the Allied Invasion. It was a vital beachhead and point of consolidation for the invaders, and airborne troops and ground forces took part in a fierce week-long battle with the German Wehrmacht. Because of the magic of movies, what most people remember about the battle would be the American trooper trapped when his parachute snagged on the church steeple, and John Wayne leading the way to victory in *The Longest Day.*

Nowadays, Carentan is a popular venue for tourists, sailors and D-Day enthusiasts, and is also distinguished by having a computer game named after it.

~

'We're going to have a job finding somewhere to park.'

McCarthy smiled smugly. 'It's okay; I've got a Gendarmerie-on-the-job card René gave me'.

Mowgley nodded in approval as he pulled up alongside a Park-and-be-Towed-Away warning sandwich board on the outskirts of the square and put the card on the dashboard. He generally disliked privilege of wealth or position, but admired how some things were approached in his adopted country. Across the Channel, police officers had to be ever more wary about taking advantage of their position; here the attitude seemed to be that there was no point in having access to civic privileges if you did not use them.

The national police were generally disliked and even feared, and, Mowgley suspected, were taught during training never to be amiable with or even smile at members of the public. Having had several encounters with *les flics*, he could not imagine any member of the *Gendarmerie Nationale* putting on make-up and donning high heels to show their support while monitoring an LGBT+ parade as now seemed common practice across the Channel.

They left the car in the shadow of the warning notice and walked toward the square. McCarthy inhaled deeply: 'Mmm, Camembert. Why can't we do it like this?'

Mowgley frowned. 'Do what like what? Make Camembert?'

'No, street markets. All we get is bric-a-crap boot sales or a load of people selling naff shoes and clothes, bin liners and toilet rolls and fake handbags. Or offering to unlock your nicked phone.'

Mowgley looked around, inhaled the heady aroma and nodded. 'You're not wrong, Sergeant.'

The square was crammed with stalls and vans, and all was colour, bustle and agreeable noise. The first pitch they passed was a big marble slab, covered in crushed ice and laden with mountains of glistening mussels and heaps of still-moving crabs. Next door was the pungently odiferous cheese wagon. On display were young and not-so-young varieties of Cantal from the Auvergne, blue-veined Roquefort and an almost liquid goat's milk cheese from the Loire Valley. Naturally, in pride of place were the twenty-seven varieties found in Normandy.

A little further on was a mobile butchery offering pots of family-made *rillettes* and a host of cuts of beef and lamb and whole chickens at eye-watering prices per kilo. At one end of the display, a whole wild boar hung suspended, turning slowly in the breeze and bearing an almost bemused look as if wondering how it came to be there. The recent time of its demise was demonstrated by the blood dripping from its snout into a bucket. That would be sold for making blood pudding, or even for direct consumption by traditionalists.

In a notable exception to the general rule, there were orderly queues at all the food stalls, with shoppers earnestly discussing the quality of the offerings as they shuffled forwards.

'What I don't get,' said Mowgley, 'is why so many women come here when they could get stuff at half the price in the local supermarket.'

Melons looked at him askance and sighed. 'You really don't understand women, do you?'

He lifted an eyebrow. 'Never claimed to. But what's that got to do with it?'

'In a supermarket you just load up your trolley and shove it to the check-out. Here you can catch up with your friends, talk about who's up to what and see what your neighbour is spending on the groceries.'

'You mean checking out if they're living beyond their means?'

'In a way. You must have noticed that It's a status symbol here to pay top dollar for what you put in your mouth, even if you could get it cheaper elsewhere. Just think of it as being the same sort of thing as women paying a fortune for a new bathroom across the Channel…or an eight-burner stove they'll hardly use.'

Mowgley sniffed dubiously. 'Yeah, I get that, but I wouldn't pay £20 for a chicken because it comes with a birth certificate.'

'Millions do. It's part of being French.'

Mowgley shook his head. 'I guess you're right. I don't understand women, wherever they come from.'

McCarthy smirked and patted his arm. 'Don't worry about it. They certainly don't understand you.'

Avoiding the invitation to stop and look at the wares of a very tall and black man selling silk scarves, kaftans, bongo drums and tribal masks, they arrived at the marina and a line of bars and *tabacs* and restaurants alongside the quayside. Mowgley led the way across cobbles, pausing to twiddle the ears of a dog guarding a classic *Mobylette* moped. The small black mongrel was sitting on the saddle, to which it was attached by a bungee cord. As they watched, a man came out of the nearby tabac, unwrapping a packet of *Disque Bleu*. Nodding to them, he thrust a cigarette in his mouth before pushing the dog back and taking its place on the saddle. Then he lit up, opened the throttle and whined off with total disregard to passers-by.

'An expensive habit,' observed Mowgley.

'What, smoking, you mean?'

'Yeah, but especially while riding a moped. The wind will have smoked that for him before he gets a hundred yards.'

~

Though the sign outside announced the premises as the Hotel Grande, their lunch venue was actually a very civilised combination of chrome-laden bar, unpretentious restaurant and betting shop with rooms above.

The large, high-ceilinged bar was ferociously busy with post-market customers sitting round plastic-topped tables, drinking and eating while they showed off their purchases.

As they stood and looked around for a spare table, a small elderly man with a long white apron, bow tie and painfully obvious wig appeared through the porthole swing door to the kitchen. He jinked his way through the tables with a laden tray held above his head, examined them sourly, then nodded towards a corner booth. It was laid for three and had a bottle of red wine on the table next to the *réservée* notice.

'Is there no end to your bloke's influence?' asked Mowgley as she thanked the waiter and slid along the banquette seating to the corner of the booth.

'If you ran a business like this and someone phoned from National Police HQ to tell you a high-ranking officer was coming for lunch, wouldn't you put yourself out a bit to make sure he got a good seat?'

'No, but I know what you mean.'

He squeezed in alongside and reached for the bread basket while taking in their surroundings.

'What's up,' asked McCarthy, moving the butter dish out of range, 'looking for a waitress?'

'No, just want to see if Mr. Syrup makes it back to the kitchen with his wig still in place.'

He turned his attention to a Van Gogh print hanging from a nearby wall. 'Is that great art or a great con, do you reckon?'

'What do you mean?' she asked, bartering a pat of butter for a slice of baguette and pointing at the wine bottle.

'I mean is the original worth hundreds of millions because it is the bestest-ever painting of a bunch of flowers?'

She looked to see if he was serious, then shrugged and spoke through a mouthful of bread: 'Simples. It's all about market forces, isn't it? Because it's Van Gogh and everyone loves Van Gogh, it's worth what someone will pay for it.'

'I get that. But what about its intrinsic worth?'

'What d'you mean, "intrinsic worth"? As I just said, it's worth what someone will pay for it, and that was many millions last time it changed hands. If it was by you or me, it wouldn't be worth a fiver.'

Mowgley screwed up his face and squinted at the bowl of flowers as if that would help him understand the painting and its possible merit.

'I get all that too, but I think what I meant was who *said* it's a great work of art?'

'The critics. Like the bloke in the cellar, I guess. They make a living by thinking up things to say about a painting, but only after it's been anointed as a Great Work of Art. Van Gogh is a good example. I think he only sold one painting in his lifetime, and that was for about five bob.'

'Unrecognised genius, then?'

'Dunno. I don't know enough about him, but I think he inspired other painters to try doing things differently.'

'Perhaps.' Mowgley poured the wine and looked reflectively at the bottle. 'Did I ever tell you I wanted to be a painter?'

'What, a house painter like Hitler, you mean?'

'Har de har. It was *The Rebel.*'

'The what?'

'The Tony Hancock film. He's got a really boring nine-to-five job and chucks it in to go to Paris and make a name as a painter. He's crap, but gets the credit for someone else's work and becomes rich and famous.'

'So that was your plan?'

'Sort of. Not much of a plan but I fancied spending my days in a garret in Montmartre painting great works, and my evenings in a loca*l zinc* bar, drinking absinthe and having heated debates about Art and Life'

'And what about sex?'

'Oh yeah, I figured there would be lots of that when I cracked it and became rich and famous. With a bit of luck I might get to do it with the Sex Kitten.'

'The who?'

'Brigitte Bardot. Don't tell me she was before your time.'

'I remember my dad telling me about her. And what really happened?'

'I hitched my way down to St Tropez and looked for Brigitte on the beach.'

'Did you find her?'

'No, but I met the guy who played Oddjob in Goldfinger.'

'Result. And then…?'

'I made it to Paris, spent a week sleeping in a park, then ran out of money and phoned home for help from my mum.'

McCarthy reached over and rested a hand on his arm.

'Never mind. It was probably all for the best. At least you realised your ambition about living in France.'

Mowgley looked around the crowded bar and waved to the wig-wearing waiter for another basket of bread.

'Yes,' he said, I suppose in a funny way I did, didn't I?'

Thomas Patrick Keating (1917-1984)

This was a faker with a mission. Londoner Keating was an art restorer who began forging paintings to protest against 'avant garde fashion, with critics and dealers often conniving to line their own pockets at the expense of both naïve collectors and impoverished artists.'

His specialty was the nineteenth-century landscape artist, Samuel Palmer.

He claimed to have created over 2000 fakes by more than a hundred artists. It is believed he made around $10 million at today's prices from his fakery. He is known for leaving 'time bombs' in his works in the form of clues that they were fakes.

His approach to creating authenticity was, however, meticulous. To create the right pigments for a fake Rembrandt, he would boil nuts for ten hours before straining them through silk.

In his book 'The Fake's Progress', he declared it to be a disgrace that so many now famous painters had died in poverty.

In an ironic twist, Keating fakes are now collectable items, fetching up to £11,000 apiece.

5

Both sun and market had reached their zenith, and Mowgley and McCarthy were on their third basket of bread. Degas had texted to suggest they start without him, but they'd settled for another bottle of the rich, fruity Merlot.

'René's been held up, then?' Mowgley said through a mouthful of crusty bread. 'Another job?'

McCarthy shook her head. 'He thinks I don't know, but he had an appointment in Cherbourg at a swish jewellery shop.'

'You mean…' Mowgley stopped chewing and made a dramatic gesture with the remains of the slice of bread.

'Yep. The engagement rings.'

'My God. He's not bringing it here to….'

'Relax. He's done the down-on-one-knee stuff. It won't get yucky.'

Mowgley let out a gust of air. 'That's a relief. I don't like to be moved to tears in front of an audience. So, when's the big day?'

'End of September. I need to work my time out, then it's on the next boat over.'

'With a removal lorry, I guess.'

'Hardly. I flogged the flat to a nice woman from Hackney who'd just canned her hubby and had plenty of cash from the settlement. She bought most of the furniture. The rest of the tatt went on e-Bay or to the tip.'

'So, I've got a couple of months to learn my speech.'

She smirked. 'Don't worry about it, none of the guests will understand what you're saying.'

'But I'm doing it in French.'

'That's what I mean.'

She poured another glass for Mowgley, took the bread basket off the table and put it on the seat out of his reach. 'And to think you used to like white sliced Wonderloaf. So, tell me about what's happening in your life. I've seen the cottage and your lady friend with the bar. What about work? Anything interesting?'

He made a half-hearted attempt at the bread basket, then said: 'I never knew there were so many Brits with a good reason for living on this side of the Channel and not letting people know where they are. Companies want to find people who owe them money or property or stuff. Husbands and wives want to know where their partners are, or what they're up to, particularly if they've cleaned out the bank account, or run off with the neighbour or the family dog. I even get the odd job from forces who're looking for someone on the run and want to go off the record.'

'Anything particularly spicy of late?'

'Apart from Mr. Death, you mean? Nothing in that league.'

She shook her head. 'You're going to call him that for the rest of the case, aren't you?'

'Yep.'

'What about this father with a missing son Mimi told me

about?'

'He's a nice bloke who's not had a particularly cushdy life. Left work early after playing with asbestos on the building sites and getting bad lungs. His wife died ten years ago, leaving him to bring up little Kai.'

'Kai?'

'Don't blame the parents. He was born Jack, and clearly didn't like it when he got old enough to care. He got into Class 'A' shenanigans with a little County Lines gang when he left school. To try and get him away from it and break the chain, his dad got him a job with a mate who's a builder in Cherbourg. Young Kai stuck it for all of a fortnight and then disappeared. He stopped returning his father's calls and left his lodgings down by the docks.'

McCarthy made a wry face. 'Any ideas? Cherchez la femme... or l'homme?'

He shrugged. 'Early days yet. Got to see the builder first.'

'I hope Mr. Begg's got deep pockets. He'll need them at Yann's prices.'

'Not at all. He's waiting for a pay-out on his asbestosis claim, but until then he's on supplementary benefits, or whatever they call it nowadays.'

'Ouch. How's he gonna manage to pay for your time and exes?'

'He won't. I'll tell Mimi to tell Yann he couldn't afford us, and I'll do it off the books in my spare time.'

'Does that mean you'll be working for free?'

'No,' said Mowgley defensively, 'I'll just charge my exes and keep a tally of hours spent. Then he can settle with me when he gets his compensation.'

McCarthy looked darkly at her wine glass. 'Bit risky, ain't it?'

'Not really. I reckon he's a straight bloke.'

'I meant about doing it on the side? What if Yann finds out you're doing a bit on the side?'

'I don't reckon Mimi to be a grass. I'll tell her the guy is skint and she'll understand. She's got a good heart.'

'True.' She looked at him and shook her head: 'Is this you living up to your Phillip Marlowe role model?'

Mowgley smiled and made another attempt on the bread basket. 'More like Don Quixote, maybe. Good intentions but crap execution.'

~

'I am so sorry. There was a hold-up.'

René Degas was carrying a bunch of what looked like very expensive flowers and a slim wallet file. He was as immaculate as ever, but slightly breathless. 'And I had a problem parking.'

Mowgley looked at McCarthy and asked innocently 'I would have thought you had one of those Copper on Duty signs for the car?'

Degas looked from him to her, nodded and smiled to say he got it, then slid into the booth alongside his fiancé. 'I have other cards. I was also delayed with calls to England about Mr. De'Ath.'

Catherine McCarthy smiled innocently and said: 'And don't forget your appointment with the shop in Cherbourg.'

'Of course.' Said Degas, 'and I had to pick these up.' He handed the flowers to Catherine McCarthy and the wallet file to Mowgley.

McCarthy accepted the lilies graciously, and Mowgley was relieved to see there appeared to be no small, ring-sized box lurking amongst the blooms.

Degas sat back, let out a sigh and visibly relaxed: 'Business before, over or after food? And drink now, of course.'

~

The man had one of the biggest moustaches Mowgley had seen in France, and certainly the biggest belly. He had rolled into the crowded bar, legs asplay, feet pointed outwards and leaning forward as if pushing an invisible wheelbarrow in which his enormous corporation sat. He had taken a table nearby, and though he had started half an hour later than them had got to the cheese and grapes stage before they had finished their entrée. Now he was looking glumly at his empty plate.

McCarthy saw Mowgley watching the man and smiled. 'I thought you were a big eater, but he makes you look anorexic.'

They'd eaten and drank exceedingly well at nineteen Euros a head for the four-course *plat du jour*, excluding wine and gratuity. As Degas had said, all French people loved good food, but it tasted even better when the patron was not trying to take your trousers down. They would also be leaving their cars at the hotel, and Degas had organised a lift home. Sirens off, he promised.

After extracting a grape pip from between his teeth, Mowgley leaned forward, twanged the band of elastic on the wallet file, 'I suppose I'd best not open it here?'

The Colonel looked round, lifted one shoulder and said: 'Perhaps not. Anyway, there is little of interest in there. It has the initial forensic reports...' he paused as he saw Mowgley's expression then continued: '...do not worry, they have been translated into English. Also, there is some other information like the cause of death options...'

'Options?'

'Yes. You will understand when you see the report. There are other contact details for relevant British people who knew Mr. De'Ath or who he had dealings with.'

'Dealings?'

Degas smiled again. 'As I said, you will understand when you read the contents.'

'Can't wait,' said Mowgley. 'How about some snippets upfront.'

'Yes please,' added McCarthy.

'Okay,' Degas patted his empty breast pocket, then

spoke with a poor attempt at guilelessness 'They will want to clear up here. Shall we not sit outside and look at the market while I give you a resumé of what we know about Mr. De'Ath?'

His fiancé regarded him with a 'don't kid a kidder' look. 'You mean you're dying for a fag. A cigarette.'

Degas put his head to one side and raised an eyebrow. 'Well, I hope I am *not* dying because I no longer smoke. But I read that each cigarette takes eleven minutes from your life. If that is so, I would be quite happy to pay that price for one of Jack's coffin nails.'

~

On the terrace with coffee and cigarettes, they watched in quiet contentment as the market came to a natural conclusion.

The food stalls and vans had long gone, but other traders were hanging on in the hope of a last-minute sale. Mowgley saw that the giant from Somalia was busy trying to sell a set of bongo drums to a little old lady who looked as if she had stopped by just to have a chat. The man with the invisible wheelbarrow waddled from the bar, and Mowgley felt the raised decking tremble as he passed. He must, Mowgley thought, have finally satisfied his appetite, or eaten the kitchen out of stock. The man reached an old *Mobylette* moped leaning against the kerb, and with difficulty got a leg over the saddle. For a moment it looked as if the whole machine might disappear up his fundament, but he hitched his belly forward on to the handlebars and cycled away till the engine caught and he disappeared in a cloud of smoke.

Mowgley aimed a squirt of smoke at a cheeky sparrow menacing the miniature macaroon in the saucer of his coffee cup, and said: 'So, Mr. D is a bit of a mover and shaker in international art circles? How did you find out so quickly and from who?' He glanced at Catherine McCarthy. 'Or do I mean whom? And what were your main sources?'

Degas frowned, then realised Mowgley's grammatical question had been rhetorical. 'The usual procedures and contacts within France and elsewhere, and we had some help from well-reputed experts and art crime investigators here and in England.'

Mowgley weighed the file in his hand. 'You mean you're still speaking to us — the UK forces? I thought Brexit was going to change that.'

Degas shook his head. 'Not really. The UK has officially lost access to the Schengen Information System and is no longer a member of Europol, but we still talk when it helps.'

'And were the Brits helpful with any shady stuff known about Mr. Death?'

'Not so much, as he has no record of misdeeds. But my friends at the Met gave me a name in the MPAAU —'

'The Metropolitan Police Art and Antiques Unit,' interjected McCarthy, looking at Mowgley.

'I knew that,' he said irritably, though he knew she would know he had not.

'Course you did,' she responded, scratching her chin to the bemusement of Degas. 'And you also knew they investigate art theft, illegal trafficking and fraud.'

'Naturally.'

'And that the UK has the second largest art market in the world?'

'Of course. Please proceed, René.'

Degas raised a hand. 'I was advised to speak to a private art fraud investigator. He used to work in the Unit and is highly respected and employed by the large art galleries, insurance companies and the art auction houses, Sotheby's and Christie's. If the media want to know the background to any major art crime stories, he is the man they will go to.'

'And what did this bloke…'

'Robert Bailey,' said Degas.

'…Robert Bailey tell you about our man in the morgue?'

'Mr. De'Ath is very well known in the international art world, and likes to move around. He owns — or owned before his death — homes in Spain, London and Paris as well as the château.'

'So if he was a critic, we could have a queue of suspects?'

Degas smiled to show he understood the joke and nodded: 'Yes, very much so. He had, as you might say, a very sharp tongue when it came to critical reviews. But his speciality was to discover young talent and promote them through his own and other respected critics' positive reviews and remarks. Mr. Bailey said he made a good profit by acquiring most of the artist's early work before he became famous and would then make a, what do you say, a killing by selling them when their value increased hugely.'

'Everyone a winner, then.' said McCarthy.

'Not all the time. Mr. Bailey said he could destroy an artist who would not fall in line and do exactly as he was told.'

'And was that often?'

'Yes, and so effective that there was a special name for what he did.'

'Which was?'

'The Kiss of De'Ath.'

'Blimey,' said McCarthy. 'And what about the circum-stances in which he was found? Why the magic circle and cabbalistic signs and black candles?'

'It's also in the dossier. Mr. De'Ath had some …unusual habits and friends.'

'Okay.' Mowgley broke the macaroon in pieces and threw them at the cheeky sparrow. The bird hopped over, sampled a few crumbs, then flew off. It was obviously, Mowgley thought, a French sparrow and had found the titbit below par.

A load of Pollocks

Over the course of twenty years, sixty fake art works supposedly by celebrated modern artists like Mark Rothko, Willem de Koning and Jackson Pollock were sold for more than $80 million through a New York Gallery. They were, in fact all originals by a lesser-known Chinese artist. The scam began with the appearance of a new and never-seen Rothko, being offered by an agent for a mysterious 'Mr. X'. He had apparently inherited a great number of famous original artworks, and wanted to dispose of them 'cheaply'.

6

Like an aged member of an old-money family fallen on hard times, the big house on the quayside was sorely distressed, but in a genteel sort of way.

The classic 18th-century merchant's home, he reflected, would have seen and survived much whilst looking out across the port and beyond to what Britons like to call the English Channel.

The house would have witnessed violent storms and sea battles, invasion attempts and local insurrections in its younger days. Then it would have looked on unimpressed as statesmen, musicians and movie stars steamed by on their way to and from America. Just as unmoved, it would also have looked on as the RMS *Titanic* made its final port of call before its rendezvous with fate and the giant iceberg.

Now, it was to be no more than a rarely-used holiday home for a British couple who lived in one of the 'better' (property-speak for even more unimaginably pricier) parts of London, who could not believe how little they had paid to add this gem to their property portfolio. Whatever the architectural sins committed on the quayside, Mowgley reckoned, at least this house would live on and to witness the frailties and fashions of humanity.

Guided by the sound of hammering and inventive cursing in English, he found their source on the first floor. A big man with a sledge hammer was making two rooms into one by removing the dividing wall, and Mowgley was pleased to see there were several upright scaffolding poles preventing the ceiling from joining the floor.

Between swings, he coughed politely to announce his presence. The man paused and looked over his shoulder, and Mowgley noticed he kept the sledge-hammer at a convenient level for sudden use.

'Morning. Mr. Nobes?'

'Could be' replied the dusty figure, 'depends on who's asking and why.'

Terry Nobes was of middle years and, apart from a drinker's belly, looked in good shape. This was more than probably because of his work rather than regular gym visits. He was bare-chested and his job had obviously earned him a tan a lot of people would need to spend a lot of money to rival. Following the builder's bum tradition, he wore a low-slung pair of denim jeans made into shorts by hacking off the legs at crotch level. On his feet, Mr. Nobes wore a pair of decidedly non-Health & Safety conforming flip-flops, and on his head a backward-facing ball cap. That, Mowgley reckoned, was more about keeping his luxuriantly thick black hair free of plaster dust and debris than a fashion statement.

Mowgley introduced himself, and noted the relaxation of the man's facial muscles and his grip on the sledge-hammer when he learned the reason for the visit.

'Okay, right,' said Nobes, leaning the hammer against the remains of the wall and fishing a packet of roll-up tobacco from his pocket. '…Frank said you'd be coming to see me.'

To give him time to roll and light his cigarette, Mowgley excused himself, stooped and made his way through the hole in the wall to the oriel window overlooking the quayside and what lay beyond.

It was lunchtime, and throngs of diners and drinkers were milling around or sitting outside the cafés and bars lining the quay. Also looking for lunch was a cloud of screeching gulls, following a couple of fishing boats, chugging towards the Turning Bridge, which was living up to its name.

He lit a Gauloises and turned back towards the dividing wall, where Nobes was framed in the hole. 'Putting in a door, eh?' Mowgley said, trying to sound as if he knew about such matters. 'Nope,' replied Terry Nobes as if talking to a person of restricted intelligence as he nodded at the old door propped against the pile of rubble. 'This was where it was. The wall's coming down to make one big room. '

'Got you,' said Mowgley, 'any other alterations?'

'Plenty. There's an en-suite for every bedroom as well as a spare one. A state-of-the-art kitchen that'll cost them more than the house, a woodburning stove that'll never be used, underfloor heating and, believe it or not, a gym, sauna and steam room.'

'Blimey.' Mowgley thought about how many rich people were really rich, and looked out to where a huge motor yacht sat bobbing in the approaches to the harbour. He could see tiny figures stretched out on the sun deck and one who was diving in. It was too far to see if the figures were male or female although none wore tops. He figured the person jumping off the boat must be male, as women on luxury cruisers did not generally like getting wet. He turned back to the builder. 'How the other five percent live, eh?'

'Yeah,' said Nobes, then: 'So I'm number one on your

call sheet, eh?'

'Number two,' replied Mowgley, 'I just went to the bar the lad had a room above. The owner said he'd not seen him for a couple of weeks, and he'd left most of his stuff in the room. He wasn't worried if anything had happened to him, as he was paid up to the day he left.'

'Nice to know people care,' said Nobes, coughing to clear his throat of the mixture of nicotine fumes and plaster dust.

Mowgley nodded. 'Yeah. I hear from his dad he did some work for you?'

'That was the idea. Frank's a mate from way back and we used the same boozer in Morden for years. I was there on a visit a month or so ago and he said his son had been getting into bad company and would I take him on. He even offered to pay me to give Kai a job. That was how worried he was.'

'And you accepted?'

Nobes looked sharply at Mowgley. 'Did I fuck. Like I said, Frank's a mate. I said yes, sorted out the transport and found Kai a place to stay. Where you went to earlier.' He looked thoughtfully at his cigarette before dropping it on the floor and stepping on it. 'Mind you, I should have taken Frank up on his offer of paying me to look after his son, 'cos I got fuck all work from Kai while he was here.'

'And how long was that?'

'No more than a month.'

'Did he not hand in his notice?'

Nobes gave a grunt of a laugh. 'Yeah, right. He just didn't turn up one morning. I gave it a couple of days for him to return to planet Earth and then phoned his dad.'

'Silly question, but do you have any idea where he went?'

'No, but I got a fair idea.'

'Umm?' said Mowgley encouragingly.

'He was coming in wasted every morning, still high on

whatever shit he was on or putting up his nose. That made him a waste of space, but I went with it for his dad's sake. I heard he'd got involved with a bad lot of foreign geezers who live on a boat in the marina. They used to come and pick him up some days in a flash motor.'

'Did you notice the make?'

'I did. It was a box-fresh Maserati Levante SUV. You don't get much change from a hundred grand for one of them.'

'So I believe,' said Mowgley as if he knew what Nobes was talking about. When you say foreigners, do you mean French?'

Nobes gave another short grunt of amusement. 'Nah. This is their country, after all. Someone in the pub said the geezers were Russian. Or maybe Bulgarian or Albanian. Eastern Europe anyway, for sure.'

'Don't suppose you know the name of the boat?'

The big man spat on his hands and reached for his sledgehammer to signal the meeting was over, then said: 'I do. It's a big lairy thing called *Zoete Dromen*. The boy told me that's Dutch for *Sweet Dreams*.'

~

Excepting the drone of a distant plane on its way to Spain, all was silent in and around the hamlet on the marshes. Though, to be fair, the silent rage of Mowgley's neighbour was almost tangible as she glared at him from her kitchen window. She was clearly not best pleased to see a large, pallid and flabby man in his underpants just a few metres from where she was working on an upside-down apple cake.

Mowgley made it worse by pretending to be unaware of her presence, put down his week-old copy of the *Daily Mail*, picked up his glass of Merlot and watched thoughtfully as, more than a mile away, a toy train moved lethargically across the otherwise lifeless marshland.

He was taking the sun in his new collapsible garden chair. He found most garden chairs collapsible when he sat on them, but this was stable enough and actually quite comfortable. It was one of a pair featured in a special summer offer at a LeClerc supermarket, and came with a glass-topped table and an umbrella to fit through the hole in the middle.

The garden furniture was phase two of the operation which had begun with the erection of the bird feeder. The plan was to generally make a nuisance of himself until Madame agreed to a swap so they would both own the patch of ground behind their homes. The intensity of the operation would depend on the level of the elderly lady's resistance and would range from merely sitting in his garden to putting on noisy barbecue parties or sunning himself *au naturel*. The barbecue was not really a feasible project as he hated them and anyway didn't know enough potentially noisy guests. The parading around in the buff would be easier to organise, but the sight of an ageing Englishman in nothing but his socks would be unlikely to shock the sensibilities of a seasoned observer of nature in the raw.'

Discussing the project with Catherine McCarthy, he had said that, when the exchange had taken place he would be able to dig a small fish pond, put up a garden shed and create his own vegetable patch. This, he further explained, was the reason for the code name Operation Market Garden.

Catherine McCarthy was not optimistic as to his chances of success. He may be becoming a Francophile by stages, she said, but he clearly did not understand the Gallic attitude to land. The logical fact that a swap would mean she would own the garden outside her back door and never have to see Mowgley in it clothed or otherwise would not come into it.

She also reminded Mowgley that he had chosen a

name with inbuilt failure possibility. It had been chosen for the ill-fated attack on Arnhem during the D-Day operations, and that had ended with disaster and humiliation for the Allied Command.

~

Looking at the cover of the out-of-date tabloid before fashioning it into a sun hat, he wondered again why he'd ever bothered to buy a daily paper and had felt a small sense of loss when he had missed an edition.

On the other side of the Channel the daily newspaper had been, like a bacon sandwich in Ginger's Caff, a daily habit. He still missed the bacon sandwich, but it was hard to see why a newspaper had ever become such a part of his daily ritual. Especially when you looked inside a typical issue. In this one and along with an in-depth analysis of the Wagatha Christie court battle and a rear view of a woman who had paid ten thousand pounds for grossly enlarged buttocks, the women's section gave tips on banishing the misery of flaky heel skin and announced that men lied more than women. The evidence came as a result of a survey, though it occurred to Mowgley that if the women lied more than the men about how much they lied, the truth could be the opposite of the findings.

The radio was tuned to a French music station, and Mowgley winced as a current favourite was introduced by a DJ apparently on the verge of vomiting with excitement. Strange, he thought, how a nation which could come up with Sartre, Marie Curé, Voltaire, Renoir, some really classy wine and several hundred varieties of mostly very edible cheeses could be so crap at writing and performing pop music.

After draining his glass, he laid back, closed his eyes and considered how a lack of news of any sort from the UK could be another reason he was beginning to feel so at home in this foreign land. Insulated by choice from

British radio, television and newspapers, he was free of the responsibility of keeping up with the latest happenings in the UK, which was mostly a relentless diet of gloom, doom and forecasts of a truly dystopian future.

He supposed things were not much better or different in France, but without the language skills or inclination to find out, he was able to live in a fairly comfortable bubble in his own little part of his adopted country.

~

Terry Nobes had been and gone, leaving Mowgley with an eye-watering estimate for the replacement of the roof that had been sitting on Le Petit Bijou for at least, the builder reckoned, a couple of centuries.

Over a cold beer, they had settled on a patching rather than replacement job, and Nobes had rattled off in his aged Renault pick-up as Catherine McCarthy phoned to take his order for British delicacies to be brought over with her goods and chattels.

'Only Cheddar cheese?' she asked. 'Are you sure?'

'I'm sure,' he said. 'Although a chicken pasanda with all the trims wouldn't go amiss.'

'I guess it'll put the sniffer dogs off if they give me a hard time at Caen,' she mused, then asked: 'How's the De'Ath case going?'

'It's not, really.'

'Have you not looked at the file?'

Yeah, but nothing much to go on, really. René reckons he needs me to do some digging and I'm seeing Yann later to talk about how he wants it handled.'

'You mean taking your time and building up the exes for his fellow French taxpayers?'

Mowgley nodded at his phone. 'I think that may be my boss's idea of the best way to proceed.' He reached for a cigarette, lit it and, for her benefit, groaned in near-ecstasy as he inhaled and blew out a giant cloud.

'God, that is so good.'

'Bollocks,' McCarthy said, 'I'm going to stay strong and René and I'll be able to help each other when I get over.'

'Yeah right,' Mowgley said, letting out another sigh of contentment 'By the way, none of my business, but I have to tell you that your intended has a date in a bar with a tall, curvy stunner this evening.'

'You mean you, don't you?'

'You guessed. And in a gay bar.'

'Don't worry, I reckon you'll be quite safe.'

Elmyr de Hory (1906-1976)

With more than a thousand fake works of art to his name, Hungarian-born Elmyr de Hory is reckoned to have been one of the world's most prolific of forgers. Claiming to be born into Austro-Hungarian nobility, he actually came from much more humble origins. He began his training in art at sixteen in Romania and completed his studies in Paris. During WWII he returned to Hungary and was imprisoned as a spy in Transylvania. He was released after a year, then arrested and put in a concentration camp by the Nazis as both a Jew and homosexual. He escaped back to Hungary, then returned to Paris after the War, intending to make his name as a painter. After selling a fake Picasso drawing to a British woman, he decided there was more money to be made by forging other more famous artists' works. He gained fame after appearing in an Orson Welles documentary 'F is for Fake' in 1973. While under investigation for forgery, he committed suicide in 1976 rather than face more jail time.

7

The two middle-aged British women and slack-faced man were sitting at a table near the door. The older and more determined-looking woman was adroitly spooling through an apparently endless collation of photographs on an Apple tablet as she gave a non-stop narration to her audience. She had developed the politician's trick of preventing interruption by taking short, quick breaths in mid-sentence. She was telling her victims about her and her husband's latest tour de France, while the couple sat like a rabbit frozen in headlights. They would clearly rather be elsewhere, but had not the courage or energy to make a stand.

In the old days, Mowgley reflected, being forced to watch the holiday snaps required attendance at the takers' home, and was usually at least compensated for by a meal. Nowadays, thanks to modern technology, there was no hiding place.

Relief came when a rowdy group of young booze-cruising Brit males arrived dressed as members of the Village People, and the lecturer spoke sharply to her husband as if it were his fault, turned off her machine and led the way from the *Café Moustache*.

~

Before attending a compulsory Metropolitan Police Race, Religion, Gender and Lifestyle Diversity and Inclusivity Workshop, Mowgley had not thought of himself as a particularly privileged white male racist homophobe.

In the discussion after his enlightenment, he'd been earmarked for further and more intensive sessions after saying some of his best mates were black or shirt-lifters, though he could not recall any that were both. He'd added that he was absolutely fine with whatever consenting adults wanted to do to each other — within the law, of course, and as long as they didn't try and shove it down his throat.

As Catherine McCarthy had observed when he had emerged from the hearing, he was either determined to make a quick exit from the Force, or just liked to shock people by appearing to carry prejudices he in fact did not hold,

Named to honour the near-legendary gay bar in Paris, the *Café Moustache* was busy. Ironically, the near-exclusively male clientele seemed low on the facial hair count, which Mowgley assumed was because gay moustaches were currently out of fashion.

In fact, apart from the ironic display by the Village People visitors, there was also a distinct lack of any under or overtone indicating the sexual proclivities of the majority of the customers. In Brighton at this time of year, he would have expected at least a sprinkling of short shorts teamed with Doc Marten boots, vests, short hair and bushy moustaches. The customers here were uniformly stylish but restrained in their costume and manner. Their attention to personal grooming was a constant, however, and most looked so honed and polished they resembled characters in a Hollywood musical, highly buffed and ready to spring into action when the music began.

Mowgley toyed with his beer and wondered how at ease Yann Cornec would have felt in the Moustache. From the expression on his face when Mowgley had told him where he was meeting René Degas, he suspected Cornec might benefit from a course with a diversity /inclusivity workshop.

They had met at Cornec's request in the office. Mimi had left them to talk privately, though Mowgley noticed she left the door to the store room open.

It was an awkward meeting, and although he thought he'd more than earned his keep with the agency, the relationship between the two men had become increasingly strained. As yet, Mowgley did not know if it was a natural clashing of antlers, or something more. Whatever the reason, it was obvious a clearing of the air would be needed before long. Perhaps Cornec liked the money Mowgley earned him, but resented another male in the company and just wanted to ensure Mowgley knew who was the boss.

After a review of other cases in hand and Yann's inevitable complaint that his sole investigator was not booking enough time or expenses to his clients, they had talked briefly about the De'Ath case and prospects. Cornec had not revealed the size of the budget from Degas, but made it clear he wanted his chief and only investigator to make the most of all opportunities to build up costs. His proposal was that Mowgley should push the focus of his enquiries beyond Cherbourg, and even France. It seemed that Cornec was making hay before René Degas retired and took up the offer to join the agency. And that Degas was going along with the over-charging of the French taxpayer.

Before leaving and as if in afterthought, Cornec had asked about the Englishman with the missing son. Having thought about the best approach, Mowgley said that the father had been open about having little money and been frightened off by the company day rate. It was, Mowgley had concluded, very unlikely that Mr. Begg would be using the services of Services d'Enquêtes Privés Cornec.

Cornec had done no more than grunt and shrug, but Mowgley wondered how much Mimi knew and would tell her boss and lover when they were alone in bar or bed.

~

'Hello Jack. You look…different.'

René Degas had left off his standard uniform of sombre suit and tie in favour of a more relaxed outfit. With aviator sunglasses on top of his head, he was wearing a slim-fit denim shirt with button-down collar and sleeves rolled up to the forearms. His fawn Chinos were held up by a narrow, faux-snakeskin belt and on his feet were soft leather loafers, mercifully, in Mowgley's opinion, without tassels. It first occurred to Mowgley that his style of dress was in accord with that of the customers of the Moustache. But then he realised it was typically French rather than gay, and made Mowgley conscious of his Hawaiian shirt, shorts and flip-flops.

The *Gendarmerie* Colonel put his shoulder bag on the bar and shook hands as Mowgley finished his beer, ordered two more and suggested they sit outside so he — or they — could smoke.

Threading between the tables, he realised they were under inspection by a couple sitting by the door. One was in his twenties, the other much older, and Mowgley wondered if they were wondering if he and Degas were a highly unlikely item. If that were so, they would be assuming that Mowgley was a rich eccentric who liked to show he did not need to worry about his appearance, or that Degas liked a bit of rough.

Outside, the weekly market in the *Place de Theatre* was winding up; traders were breaking down their stalls and loading vans and cars as municipal workers gathered up the detritus left after a busy day's trading.

Beyond the fountain and on the sunny side of the square, the terraces outside the bars were busy. The Moustache was on the shady side, and only one table was occupied. The four men sitting around it did not sound French or look as if they might be gay. If anything, to the former policeman's practised eye they looked distinctly dodgy. As he led the way past the group, a man with a badly-scarred shaven head and pug-like nose gave him a hard look, to which Mowgley responded with his simpleton smile. He had found the Forest Gump look either bemused or annoyed potentially aggressive males. He enjoyed seeing the outcome, if not always what it led to. The man looked more puzzled than angry, and Mowgley wondered whether he shaved his head to disguise a lack of hair, or to show off the crescent-shaped scar.

At the furthest-away table, he sat down and pushed a cast-iron chair out for Degas. As the waiter arrived with their drinks, Mowgley reached into his shirt pocket and pulled out a packet of Gauloises Brunes and a disposable lighter in the manner of a magician about to perform a trick. Putting them carefully on the table, he looked at Degas quizzically, then said: 'I'm not going to ask you if you want one, but....'

Degas looked at the packet and lighter, thought for all of two seconds, then nodded. 'Yes please.' He smiled wryly, and added: 'As long as you don't tell Catherine.'

Mowgley extracted two cigarettes from the packet, passed one to Degas and lit it. He thought about remarking that that was exactly what Catherine McCarthy had replied when he last offered her a cigarette, but instead said: 'Tomorrow's the big day, then?'

Degas drew long and deep on the Gauloises like a man who had been starved of oxygen, then nodded. 'Yes?' in an almost-absent-minded tone. He took another drag on his cigarette followed by a draught of beer, then looked over Mowgley's shoulder with a slight frown at the group of men.

'I meant Catherine coming over for good. I hope you're not getting cold feet,' said Mowgley in what he hoped was a jokey way, 'I've been working on my best man's speech.'

Degas gave a small smile to show he understood the idiomatic usage. 'No, my feet are quite warm, thank you.' He took another draught and draw, then said; 'You will understand how happy I am, but that it is going to be a little strange for me. I have lived alone since my wife left me. I mean of course when she... died, and I have become set in my ways. Sharing my home with someone will be a little unusual at first, I think.'

'Of course,' said Mowgley as if he knew what it would be like to have lost a beloved partner and then start again.

They sat and smoked in companionable silence, then Mowgley leaned over, caught the barman's eye through the open glass door and signalled for another round.

'So,' he said, 'before we get on to Mr. Death, can I ask why you suggested we meet here? Not that I have a problem with it being a gay bar, of course.'

Degas gave another small smile: 'I did not think you would. I suggested the Moustache because it was a favourite bar of Mr. De'Ath. I am known to the manager, and I thought it might be helpful to be seen together in case you wish to make any enquiries here.'

'Mr. D was gay, then?'

Degas raised an eyebrow and pursed his lips. 'Not exactly. I think the correct term would be bi-sexual. It seems he was equally at home having relations with male or female. And, it has been said though might not be true, with some animals.'

Mowgley winced. 'Ouch. You mean at the alleged devil-worshipping parties?'

'That is the rumour, but of course it may be just that. I don't know if they are Satanists, or merely like to exchange wives regularly.'

Mowgley looked thoughtful, then said: 'I went to a wife-swapping party once; I got a fridge.'

Getting little response beyond a polite if bemused smile, Mowgley waited until the barman had been and gone, then said: 'So, any news of the cause of death, yet? What does SOCO — sorry, I mean your pathology people — have to say? And what about time of death?'

A bright red sit-on machine with rotary brushes and a tank spraying water onto the square rumbled by, and Degas waited until the noise died down before replying. 'Time of death is the early hours of the day his body was found. We think we know the cause of death, but we have a choice as to the reason.'

'Reason?'

Looking thoughtfully at his cigarette as he stubbed it out in the goblet-shaped ashtray, Degas said: 'The latest report from the Forensic Pathologist concludes that Mr. De'Ath died as a result of taking amyl nitrite. You saw the small bottle alongside the body.'

'That's the stuff we call 'poppers?'

Degas nodded. 'So I believe. It is very popular with young people in France when they begin to experiment with drugs. It is also popular with gay people before sex. As well as mild euphoria and increased sexual arousal, it causes relaxation of the throat and anal passage.'

'Ouch again.' Mowgley reached for the cigarette packet and looked enquiringly at Degas, who nodded. 'So, it was probably an overdose that did for him?'

Degas took the offered cigarette, lit it, sucked in and exhaled smoke, then said: 'Yes, that is what the *pathologiste* thinks may have happened. Over-use can lead to long-term blood vessel and heart problems. On rare occasions, it can cause asphyxiation.'

'Then our man was getting ready for a sex session with someone… or just himself? Is that where the belt round his neck would have come in?'

'Exactly. I am told that coming close to asphyxiation by constricting the air flow is something some people do to heighten the pleasure while they are having sex on their own. The belt was an expensive one and identified as belonging to Mr. De'Ath.'

Mowgley nodded. 'What about fingerprints or DNA on the empty bottle?'

Degas made a wry face. 'Nothing. There were smudge marks but no fingerprints. There was no glass nearby and no wine of that type in Mr. De'Ath's body. It was,' he said almost absent-mindedly, 'a very good wine. Whoever opened it must have taken the cork with them.'

'So that means there must have been another person in the cellar at the time of death?'

'Maybe, but not necessarily. Mr. De'Ath could have brought it with him for some reason, or it could just be another red herring.'

'And what about anything in his clothing?'

'There was no clothing found at the scene, so he must have entered the cellar naked. Also no letter or anything which appears relevant in his office-bedroom.'

Mowgley frowned. 'Unless someone was down there with him before or after his death and then for some reason took the clothes with him. Or her.'

'That is true,' replied Degas. 'Just something else we must consider.'

'Quite.' Mowgley watched a disappointed seagull scavenging where the heap of market debris had been. 'And there was plenty of time for someone to have done the job on Death and leave the premises — or at least the cellar?'

Degas nodded. 'The forensic team were at the château within half an hour of when Madame De'Ath reported finding her husband's body, and the first police car arrived several minutes before them. Madame's call was registered at seven minutes before ten.'

'Okay. And no witnesses?'

'No. The gardener was working in the grounds, and saw nobody come or go except for Madame and the cook. He was out buying food for the evening meal.'

'Where?'

'At Cherbourg.'

'As was Mrs. De'Ath. Did they travel together?'

'No. Why do you ask?'

'No particular reason, just seems a bit…coincidental. And where was the housekeeper?'

'She too was away.'

Mowgley rubbed his chin. 'That's a bit convenient, isn't it?'

'You mean suspicious? Not really. Madame Leclerc was on a day off and visiting her mother, who is not well, in the Loire Valley. Neither she or the cook or the gardener had much to tell us. The cook said he saw Mr. De'Ath's car parked in front of the house when he left for market at around seven. Mrs. De'Ath's car was not there.'

'And the gardener? Could there be anything between him and the lady of the manor?'

Degas smiled. 'I think not. He is very old and not, I think the sort of person who Madame would choose for an affair.'

Mowgley scratched his chin absent-mindedly. 'And what about Butch Cassidy and the Friend of Dorothy and Biggles and co?'

'I beg your pardon?'

'The weird bunch hanging around in the sitting room when we arrived?'

'Ah.' Degas smiled. 'They were guests for the weekend

for some sort of event. It was their paintings that were displayed in the *hall d'entrée*. There was also a fourth guest.'

'Another artist?'

'Yes. He was the man who painted the picture of the red herring found with the body.'

'Ah.'

Mowgley waited as the cleaning machine passed by on its way out of the square, then continued: 'So where is he?'

'We do not know, yet. He has disappeared.'

~

The bars around the square were filling up. The two men were on their fourth beer and second cigarette each. The group of men at the end of the terrace were getting louder.

'So,' Mowgley asked, 'do you know any more about what happened on the night before the death of Death?'

'A little. The guests had dinner with their hosts at around nineteen hundred hours, which the stomach contents of the body confirm. Then the artists went with Mr. De'Ath for some sort of meeting. Madame De'Ath went to her room at around midnight, and the next she saw of her husband was in the cellar.'

'You say "her" room?'

Yes. There was a mutual bedroom, but Mr. De'Ath had a study with a bed in it if he was going to be late and did not want to disturb his wife. Or that is what she said.'

'So that left the artists as the last people to see Mr. Death alive?'

'Yes — apart from the murderer, if there was one. As I said, there was some sort of meeting and screening in the recording studio which had been built for Mr. De'Ath.

It obviously caused some upset, which we have yet to know fully about.'

'What about any phone calls to or from his phone?'

'Just one. To his daughter in Paris.'

'And not to his son in London?'

'No.'

'Do we know what the call was about?'

'Mademoiselle De'Ath says it was about an exhibition she was staging at her gallery, which features the work of one of the artists staying at the château.'

'Which one?'

'The tall English woman. Not the lady with red hair, but the other, more sophisticated one. Like Prince and Meatloaf and your Queen, she has only one professional name.'

'Which is?'

Degas raised both hands in a don't-ask-me-why gesture. 'Até.'

'Blimey. Do we know what it means?'

'I am told it derives from Swahili or Sanskrit and can mean "lion", "Lord Vishnu" or "saffron".

'That's a help, then.'

He took a ruminative draw on his cigarette. 'And what about the daughter of Death? Did you speak to her personally?'

'No. Why do you ask?'

'Just wondered how upset she was.'

'Not too much, according to my colleagues in Paris.'

'Okay.' Mowgley drained his glass and looked at his watch for no particular reason. 'And what's your gut feeling so far?'

Degas shrugged. 'So far, my guts tell me very little. As you know from the preliminary report, many people had reasons to dislike or even hate Mr. De'Ath. Whether to hate him enough to kill him is another question.'

'What about personal circumstances? Did he have serious money problems or any reasons he would want to kill himself?'

'Not that we know of. The sale of the château near

Bergerac would have given him more than enough to buy the one at Brix. We are looking into his bank accounts in France and elsewhere, and there appear to be no loans on his property in Paris. There is also an apartment in London.'

Mowgley fiddled with the ashtray. 'And if it were murder, it could be a jealous husband — or wife — or his own wife who. In French law she'd be entitled to a large share of the money and property, even allowing for what the first wife would be in line for.' He looked at the end of his cigarette, then said: Of course, that could put the ex-wife or her children in the frame. Or a pissed-off painter or even someone he had got the better of in a business deal in the art world?'

Degas raised a hand in acknowledgement: 'I am afraid you are right. After quite some work, all we know is that a man was found naked in the cellar of his home, dead either by suicide or accident —'

'— or murder,' Mowgley interjected. 'Don't forget murder.'

'*Oui*,' said Degas heavily, 'or murder.'

~

The old man was wearing a beanie hat, heavy overcoat and fingerless gloves despite the heat, and rummaging his way along the piles of discarded fruit and vegetables destined for the dustcart pulling into the square.

After filling a plastic shopping bag, the man made his unsteady way across the square and towards the bar. As he approached, Mowgley could see that he was not particularly old, just worn out by how he had treated life or it had treated him.

Arriving at the end of the terrace, he held out a hand and stood mutely looking at the group of hard-looking men. There was general laughter, then one half-rose, said something in a guttural tongue and threw a handful of coins at the mendicant. As he knelt to pick them up, the man with the shaven head who had given Mowgley a hard look took a banknote from his back pocket and held it up enticingly. Leaving the coins, the old beggar straightened up and made as if to step on to the terrace. Then the man picked up a lighter from the table and set fire to the note. It burned quickly as the beggar looked on with an expressionless face.

After a moment, he moved away and arrived at where Mowgley and Degas were sitting, where he adopted the same hand-out pose.

As the group at the end of the terrace looked on, Mowgley stood up, took a twenty Euro note from his pocket and handed it to the man.

There was no reaction or acknowledgement and he shuffled off, tucking the note away inside his overcoat. Feeling the eyes of the group on him, Mowgley took out another note and held it with a quizzical expression towards the shaven-headed man. The man's face flushed, then hardened and he made as if to stand, but the older man next to him held on to his arm and shook his head.

Mowgley sat down and reached for his glass and saw Degas looking at him with a half-smile.

'What?'

'Nothing' said Degas. 'But I see what Catherine meant.'

'What meant? I mean meant what?'

'She said that you were a mix of Irish and Scots and so cantankerous that you could start a fight in an empty room.'

Faking it

As part of a divorce settlement in 2018, a Californian woman was awarded a Picasso that had been jointly owned by the couple during their 31-year marriage.

It was later revealed that the woman had taken the painting from the wall of the family home several months before and replaced it with a copy she had painted herself. The original and genuine painting was later auctioned at Sotheby's, with a reserve price of $25 million.

8

The real problem was just how much he enjoyed a smoke, and how much it had become a part of his life. Triggers included every time he picked up a phone, sitting on the toilet if it was going to be a lengthy stay, after meals and before, during and after drinks.

He fleetingly admired the slim simplicity of the *briquet* lighter, then lit his third cigarette since taking to the terrace of the Café Moustache. That, he calculated, worked out at one every fourteen or so minutes, which would be at the lower end of his usual consumption rate when free to fully indulge himself.

Like all smokers he knew it was a costly, unhealthy and potentially deadly pastime, and now, like drink-driving, had become more than socially unacceptable. Like René Degas and Catherine McCarthy, he would have to try and quit, especially now that enjoying a cigarette seemed akin to farting in a lift. Or in the view of brain washed young people, not far below eating new-born babies. As Catherine and René had demonstrated, quitting was not just a question of stopping buying cigarettes. You also had to stop smoking other people's. And it didn't help that non-smokers were so intemperate. The same people who would wring their hands in pity over the plight of a heroin addict or alcoholic would be quite contemptuous of smokers without the willpower to quit.

He thought about whether it would be crueller to offer Degas the packet than not, then tossed it across the table. Degas picked it up, fought his inner battle, then took a cigarette like a man stealing from a charity box.

'Funny how we always smoke more when we're supposed to be giving it up, ain't it?' Mowgley observed.

Degas did not answer beyond a grunt, and they sat and smoked and watched passing life until Mowgley asked about the symbols chalked around the circle in which the body of Piers De'Ath was found.

'We have no idea…yet. I have an expert studying them. So far, he has said that they are not symbols, but runes.'

Mowgley raised an eyebrow. 'Runes? Never seen *Lord of the Rings*, so what's the difference?'

'I am told that each character represents a sound and meaning. They can tell a story or give a warning or make magic.'

He saw Mowgley's expression and added: 'I am only telling you what the man tells us. He is supposed to be the leading expert in Europe.'

'But if nobody else can read them, as well as him, he could just make it up as he went along.'

Degas pursed his lips and blew gently on the end of his cigarette. 'Yes, exactly. We will wait and see what he says they mean, if anything.'

Mowgley thought about it, then said: 'What about the official verdict? It's hardly an open-and-shut case?'

Degas nodded grimly. 'That is so. The *autopsie* or post-mortem can do not much more than tell us of the cause of death.'

'So, apart from the amyl nitrite, any or all of the stuff around the body and the way it was laid out could be red herrings, including the painting itself.'

'Yes, exactly. All we are sure of is that the guests were the authors of the paintings in the gallery and were there for a special occasion. Mr. De'Ath would regularly write about a new talent he had discovered and circulate a very favourable review to the influential art world media outlets. That would send the reputation of the artist and his work — and its value — soaring.'

'And were his reviews always positive?'

'Not at all. When it was a damning review, the opposite could happen.'

'That's where the 'Kiss of Death' comes from, then? Getting hung in the vestibule could be an entry point to fame and success…or certain death.'

Degas nodded. 'As I said, this was the first time these artists had been invited to the château, and to take part in some sort of special event.'

'And do you have any idea who was in line for the five-star puff or the turkey-of-the-month rating?'

'No. I spoke yesterday with the art fraud investigator in London, and I said you may wish to speak with him as part of your enquiries on our behalf.'

'Me?' Mowgley frowned. 'Why? I thought my brief was to find out about the local branch of the ex-pat devil-worshipping society?'

Degas shrugged. 'As you are British and a former police officer and homicide investigator, I think it would do no harm for you to become more involved. My lead officers will be talking with Mr. Bailey, but it could help for a former colleague in the Metropolitan police force to speak to him face to face about the painting and what he knows of Mr. De'Ath. It will give you a better picture, and — ' he smiled wryly, ' — I believe Yann will be happy for you to expand your areas of activity on our behalf.'

Mowgley nodded thoughtfully. 'I'm sure he will.'

~

Dusk was falling. Strings of coloured bulbs twinkled around the fountain, competing with the host of stars putting in an appearance in a cloudless sky. People ate, drank and talked animatedly and made extravagant gestures to make a point. Laughter was a common currency. The scene was not, Mowgley thought, as striking as Van Gogh's *Café Terrace*, but a pleasant and very French prospect.

Beyond and in the marina, more lights bobbed and weaved in tune with the wake of arrivals and departures and the changing tide. The door of the bar was in near-constant motion as customers arrived, looked inside, then entered or moved on. Like all young people on an evening out, Mowgley thought, they strode quickly as if anxious to be where they were going in case they missed something.

All the tables on the Moustache terrace were busy with mostly young and exclusively male customers. The group of foreigners had moved on, with the shaven-headed man giving Mowgley a long, hard stare before following his friends in the direction of the marina.

On the far side of the square, Mowgley saw the beggar. Curiously, he was walking with short, quick steps as if hurrying to be on time for an appointment. In one hand was the carrier bag; in the other he was holding two large bottles of wine close to his chest. He looked fleeting across at the terrace, but did not respond when Mowgley waved.

'There is a *foyer* in a road off the quay,' said Degas.

'Foyer?'

'A hostel for homeless or poor people passing through. They are usually *clothards* — tramps. He will not be allowed to take the wine in, but will probably share it with his friends outside while they eat what he has picked up from the market. Perhaps surprisingly, they like to share.'

Degas drained his glass, looked at his watch and reached for the plastic dish holding their tab. 'If you are ready, we can also go to eat. I know a place that does excellent seafood — or a steak if you prefer.'

'That would be good,' said Mowgley, picking up his cigarettes and lighter. 'By the way, I meant to ask if you had seen or heard anything about the missing boy I told you about.'

'I have asked for any reports, but nothing has come in yet. I am told you are taking on the case for the father at a special rate.'

Mowgley frowned. 'Who told you that?'

Degas smiled. 'I have my informants. I would just suggest you take care who else knows.'

'What do you mean?'

'I mean that Yann will not be happy if he finds you are cutting him out.'

'I'm not cutting him out. The father has no money and would never have employed the agency, I will do what I can for expenses only.'

Degas reached for his back pocket as the waiter appeared. 'I know that,' he said, 'but I still think you should keep your good deed from Yann.'

~

The meal had been good and Mowgley had insisted on paying. He might not have done had he known that the *Café Royal* was said to be the best and certainly the most expensive on the waterfront.

After shaking hands, Degas had taken a cab home, while Mowgley had turned down a lift and said he would walk his dinner off with a stroll alongside the water. There would be a bed for him at Madame Yvette's, or the sofa in the office if it came to it. That was something else he would not share with Yann Cornec.

Although close to midnight, the shutters were up and lights on in a small shop by the marina gates. It did well out of top-up groceries for owners, and also sold local and national newspapers. Mowgley bought a fresh packet of Caporal, a chocolate bar and a copy of *Ouest France*. He would not be able to read much of it, he thought, but it might come in handy.

~

There was a guard box and barrier beyond the marina gates, but the elderly man watching a portable TV showed no interest as Mowgley walked by with a confident smile and a wave of the rolled-up newspaper.

The metallic bronze Maserati sat smugly near to where the *Zoete Dromen* lay moored. Mowgley knew little about any boats, but guessed this one would come under the heading of luxury motor cruiser. It looked at least forty foot long, and had the rakish lines that suggested it would move very swiftly through the water if asked. It was very white and very shiny, and seemed to be on three levels. He guessed the top one held the wheel and controls.

All was quiet and there were no lights on the *Zoete Dromen* or any of the other boats lined up alongside the pontoon stretching from the quayside. Some were even bigger and grander than the one he had come to see, and some clearly more spacious than his new home. The owners of all the luxurious accommodations were either early to bed, he thought, or more likely at home in houses which would rival the in-your-face splendour of these rarely used ultra-rich man's toys.

He stood on the quayside looking at the line of boats, then turned as he heard the noise of disturbed shingle. A figure was walking quickly towards him and it was the shaven-haired man he had met at the *Café Moustache*.

The man's right hand was held unnaturally across his chest, and his left arm hung straight down. He was carrying a long and nasty-looking blade, commonly known as a butterfly knife.

'Good evening,' said Mowgley, smiling pleasantly, stepping closer to the edge of the quay, 'some lovely boats, eh?'

Confused by his amiable manner, the man paused, and Mowgley confused him further by stepping towards him, holding the rolled-up copy of *Ouest France* out at chest level.

'Have you seen this weeks' edition?' he asked, 'there's an interesting article about recent work on the nuclear power plant at Flamanville.'

Still silent, the man looked down at the newspaper fleetingly, and was raising his knife when Mowgley drove the solid tube up beneath his jaw.

The man made a retching, guttural sound, dropped the knife and instinctively reached up with both hands to his throat. This gave Mowgley ample time to take hold of the man's forearms and guide him towards and over the edge of the quayside.

He stood and watched as the figure surfaced, and, choking and spitting, began to swim towards the dinghy moored to a nearby motor cruiser. Satisfied he would make it safely, Mowgley leaned over and called softly: 'Sorry, mate, but I'm too old to fight fair. Not that I ever did.'

He turned and was about to walk back to towards the marina gates, when a shout came from the upper deck of the *Zoete Dromen*. Three men were hurrying down the gangway to the shore. They did not look disposed to be friendly to the visitor.

Suddenly and as Mowgley considered whether it was worth even trying to run, a blue light lit up the tableau, accompanied by a single, high-pitched wail.

The police car stopped between Mowgley and the men,

and a uniformed *Gendarme* got out from the passenger side.

One hand on the butt of his pistol, the officer walked slowly towards them. Through the windscreen, Mowgley could see the driver was calling-in the incident before joining his partner.

'Is everything alright, here?'

Mowgley recognised the man from Madame Yvette's bar, noted that he was speaking in English, and smiled ingratiatingly. 'Yes, fine thanks, officer.' He nodded towards where the shaven-headed man was hauling himself into the dinghy. 'I saw this man fall into the water and was about to dive in when I saw his friends were coming to help him.' He waved to where the three men were clustered around the top of the gangplank, keeping very still, then turned back to the policeman. 'I think he may have been drinking. Dangerous when you're around boats.'

The officer nodded. '*D'accord.*'

He gave the men a hard look, then gestured towards the car. 'We have been asked to take you home.'

'Most kind.'

With a mock-salute to the man in the dinghy, Mowgley followed the policeman to the car. There were, he concluded as they sped up the hill and out of Cherbourg, more than a few benefits to having a friend who was sleeping with the top cop in the region.

Fake or Fortune

As well as the thousands of forgeries uncovered and those still in the system, the authenticity of some works of art have long been hotly disputed. Depending on who you ask, a painting in profile of a young woman in the sixteenth century is either a priceless work by Leonardo da Vinci...or a fake worth thousands rather than millions. The authenticity of La Bella Principessa has been contested since 2008, when an art dealer claimed to have found it in the drawer of a friend's Parisian home. This proved to be untrue, and the debate on whether or not the painting is the work of the Renaissance genius continues. The current owner is unknown, and the painting—estimated to be worth $200 million if genuine, remains locked in a Swiss vault.

9

'So, what's this about you giving people midnight swimming lessons?'

'Now I wonder how you would know about that?' Mowgley squeezed the phone to his ear with a shoulder and held up his Diana and Charles mug while making a pretty-please face at Mimi.

'René said he had asked a patrol car to find you when you wandered off after the meal. He guessed you'd be getting up to no good and would need an escort home.'

'As it turned out, he was right. But I reckon I could have handled the situation.'

'Yeah, right.' Catherine McCarthy sighed loudly down the phone. 'I know you're getting worse as you get older, but why would you go and start trouble with a handful of iffy characters like that? You could've been found floating in the harbour with your willy in your mouth.'

'It's much too big for that, I reckon. Anyway, I didn't start any trouble,' said Mowgley in hurt tones. 'I was just having a look for the boat that my missper has been seen hanging around. One of the crew came at me. He must have thought I was a burglar or something.'

'Missper?'

Mowgley tut-tutted. 'Don't you watch any TV cop dramas?'

Another heavy sigh came down the line: 'The truth is you just like kicking wasps' nests to see what happens, don't you?'

'No. I know what's going to happen if I kick a wasps' nest. I was just pursuing my enquiries and it all sort of kicked off.'

'Quite. Don't you think you're getting on a bit to be wandering around at night being nosey?'

Mowgley did not respond, but reflected that she was right. It was probably not something he would have done if sober. On the plus side, the dodgy little crew that Kai Begg had got involved with would now know that Mowgley had friends in high places in local law-enforcement circles. On the downside, if they were really bad boys that might encourage them to get him off their backs permanently.

'So anyway,' he said brightly, 'how is it to be living in sin? Have you had your first row now you're on top of each other in more ways than one?'

'Bloody cheek.' She was silent for a moment, then said: 'It's a lovely apartment and great views, but a bit small for two of us.'

Mowgley made sympathetic sounds and gave his over-the-top village idiot smile of thanks as Mimi put the mug of Nescafe Gold on the desk as if ridding herself of something nasty. He took a sip and watched her sway back to her desk and thought what a lucky man his boss was.

'So,' he said, returning to the conversation, 'what have you done with all your gear? You know, the cuddly toys and cute toilet roll covers in the shape of crinoline dresses? It must be a bit of a tight squeeze as well as a culture clash of taste.' As he knew, Degas had down-sized from a house overlooking the town to a small apartment overlooking the sea after his wife had died three years before.

'As you very well know, I don't have any bloody toilet roll covers or cuddly toys. Well, only the monkey pyjama bag. It's just that I'm used to my own space, and there's not a lot of it here. Especially for my clothes and stuff.'

'Tch-tch.' Mowgley made concerned clucking and other over-the-top sympathetic sounds, which he knew would annoy her.

'Oh fuck off,' she said.

'Steady on. It was you who called me.'

'True. I was going to invite you to dinner this evening and we can mix business with pleasure.'

'Sounds good. If you think there'll be room?'

'Oh fuck off again.'

~

'That was very nice.'

'You say that to all the girls.'

'Oh, I thought René had done the cooking. You always told me you liked to eat out as you can't cook and didn't have to wash up.'

Catherine McCarthy looked like she was about to tell him to fuck off for the third time that day, but glanced at her fiancé before giving Mowgley a get-you-later look.

After the cooked and presented dinner which he knew had been a co-production, coffee was being taken on the balcony of Degas's small but enviably-located apartment.

It looked out to sea from the top floor of a tower block on the edge of the quay, and Mowgley reckoned that made it worth maybe twice as much as those on the blind side and with a view of rusting railway lines in a former goods yard. He had noted that, while the French didn't generally think much of rural property, they would pay almost English prices for a sea view.

He had arrived unfashionably on time, and there had been an awkward moment when he handed McCarthy a bouquet of chrysanthemums. It was not because they were the flower most associated with death in France, but that the act of giving his former colleague and sometimes fighting partner a bunch of flowers seemed somehow wrong to Mowgley, and, he suspected, to her.

The bottle of wine he had brought went down better, and he made a mental note to thank Mimi for the suggestion. Domaine Lafond was not a name with which he was familiar, but, he figured, it must be a good one at more than twenty Euros.

Over the goat's cheese and bacon salad, they had talked of their plans for the wedding and Mowgley's part in it. Over the perfectly, pinkily cooked duck with orange, wild rice, toasted almonds and green beans they had talked of their plans for a new home with more room and rooms. Somewhere, Catherine had said, just outside the town with a garden and view of the sea would be nice. When Mowgley looked at her fiancé for his comments, he did no more than shrug and smile in a whatever-she-wants way.

During the dessert, which to Mowgley was no more than a nice rice pudding, Degas explained with a straight face that the recipe and dish was unique to Normandy, and there was actually an official appreciation society for Teurgoule.

Finally, and with a selection of Norman cheeses and a fine Calvados, they had moved on to Mowgley's encounter in the marina.

As Degas explained, the luxury cruiser was on its second owner. Its former name had been *Beaux Rêves*, or — as Mowgley would know — *Sweet Dreams*. The French owner had also run a small fleet of fishing boats with home ports in Normandy and Brittany, with crews from each region. Though never proved, it was suspected that the fleet had been involved in a major people-smuggling operation.

With the pressure mounting on the more convenient points of departure like Calais and Dunkirk, the traffickers had come up with the idea of shipping their customers from sometimes tiny and obscure ports much further along the coast. Because they were constantly coming and going, fishing boats were a convenient cover. As Degas said, they would never know how many illegals had been ferried across the Channel, but fishing boats had lots of space below decks for their catch. After months of undercover investigation, a number of local boats were impounded and skippers jailed. One had killed himself — or that was the verdict — but the owner was never charged. This, Degas said, was either because he had not been involved in the scheme, or knew the right people. Ownership of the luxury yacht and fishing boats had changed hands a year ago, and the company was now registered in Amsterdam. Thus the change of name from *Beaux Rêves* to the Dutch *Zoete Dromen*.

Although there was no firm evidence, it was suspected that the trawlers were still going out to sea to do more than fish. And an extra line had been added to their endeavours.

The man who Mowgley had given swimming lessons to was an Albanian who was known very well to the authorities in his homeland. They had told Degas that they were happy that Terenc Malija was off their hands, and would be even happier not to have him returned to his native land when he fell foul of the law in France. Unsurprisingly, Degas added, Malija's record in his homeland showed a predisposition to violence. He was part of the crew of one of the Cherbourg-based fishing boats, and together with a number of fellow countrymen, also looked after and lived aboard the *Zoete Dromen* when the owner was elsewhere.

'Bit strange that the owner would want his fishy crew living on his luxury cruiser rather than one of the fishing boats?' Mowgley observed.

'Yes,' said Degas, 'that is what we thought. The owner has not been near it for over a year, but it goes out to sea about once a month.'

'So you have the crew under obo — I mean surveillance?'

'Yes. Of course.'

'And you think they're taking drugs and/or people across the Channel?'

'We do,' said Degas. 'But we have no evidence yet. They are obviously not taking drugs or people on board at the docks. The boat always goes out after dark, which makes observation from drone or another vessel almost impossible. The *Zoete Dromen* is also very fast. We think the Dutch company is made of straw and a front for part of a network of Albanian criminals. As you will know, a record number of young Albanian men are crossing to England in rubber dinghies. There are advertisements for the service on social media, and Albanian criminals run the cannabis trade in southern England, though much of the business is hard drugs. The gangs are involved in other sorts of criminal activity and sending hundreds of millions back to their home country.' He lifted his glass and looked through it at the sun as it headed for the horizon. He looked faintly embarrassed and even apologetic. 'I am afraid that the United Kingdom has become a very attractive target for Eastern European criminals since you left the Union.'

Mowgley grunted. 'And your people are of course helping them to make the crossing.'

'I would not say "helping",' Degas protested mildly. 'It is your government that picks them up and ferries them to your shores.'

'True.' Mowgley decided to steer the conversation in

another direction. He did not want the evening to end on a sour note, let alone upset the fiancé of his best friend as well as a very valued customer. 'So, I sort of blundered into your operation when I turned up at the marina?'

'Yes,' said Degas, 'but I do not think you will have done any harm. The crew were unlikely to think of you as some sort of undercover police officer, so perhaps assumed you were a man who had taken too much drink and had followed them back to the boat to cause trouble after your altercation at the gay bar.'

Catherine sniffed pointedly, and reached for the coffee pot. 'What, someone mistaking Mowgley for an elderly boozer looking for a fight? Heaven forfend.'

~

Later, and Mowgley watched the car ferry steaming through the breakwater on its way across the seventy-three miles of English Channel between his new and old homes.

The *Barfleur* was accompanied by a pilot boat and the usual horde of screeching seagulls. On the ancient ramparts, a line of cormorants sat, drying their wings and watching the action dispassionately. They knew that fishing was likely to be much more rewarding than following in hope of something remotely edible being jettisoned. The cormorants looked well-fed and glossy, and a French friend had told him there were so many more on this side of the Channel because the water was much cleaner.

He smothered a yawn, stretched and sighed contentedly, took out his cigarettes, lit one and put the packet on the table. 'So, moving on to the death of Death, you said over dinner that we've now got another suspect?'

The couple looked at the packet on the table and at

each other, then McCarthy reached for the packet and took two cigarettes out.

'When we have had our guilty pleasure,' said Degas after letting the smoke dribble from his nose and mouth, I have a film to show you.'

Mowgley frowned. 'Nothing too racy, I hope? My dinner's not gone down yet.'

Degas took a long draw on his cigarette and blew it in the general direction of the breakwater. 'No, not racy, but interesting, I hope you will agree.'

~

Unlike most of the few offerings Mowgley had seen on YouTube, Piers De'Ath's production was professional to the point of slickness. It had, Degas said, been posted in the early hours of the day he was found in the cellar.

There was something odd and even uncomfortable, Mowgley thought, about seeing someone so full of life who would be dead a few hours later. A sobering reminder that death was, as they liked to say at funerals, to be found in the midst of life.

His first reaction was surprise that a man of such status in the art world would bother with broadcasting on a channel usually occupied by amateurs, ego-maniacs and cranks.

After explaining the difference between vlogs and blogs, Degas had said how De'Ath had used the channel as a supplement to his regular columns in French, German, Italian and English-language newspapers and magazines. Besides, as a critic and commentator specialising in modern art, he knew how important it was to keep a high profile, and that any publicity was usually good publicity in his line of business. Besides, art programmes were thin on the ground in mainstream TV, and his monthly broadcasts drew a regular audience of more than a million.

Mowgley had expressed his surprise that there were so many modern art enthusiasts using You Tube, to which Degas replied he thought it might be the nature of the programme rather than the content which drew the high number of viewers. Piers De'Ath obviously knew how controversy and humiliation had a universal appeal, especially in the often very un-social world of social media.

The format, Degas had explained, was that the host would show four paintings by little-known artists, then dismiss three in savage terms. The fourth would be acknowledged as a true breakthrough and harbinger of the shape of things to come… and of future success for the artist. Transcripts of and articles about the programme would be distributed throughout the Art world, and dealers and collectors and gallery owners would often rush to buy up the winner's early works and so start the snowball of success on its roll. On the other hand, the mockery, humiliation and dismissal of the three rejects' talents would usually put a stop to their ambitions to make a positive name for themselves in the field of Contemporary Art.

It was, Degas concluded, an apparently more intellectual and certainly crueller version of the ubiquitous Saturday evening talent shows that no TV channel would neglect to offer.

~

Accompanied by a cacophonous squeal of modern jazz, the predictably titled *Art, Life & De'Ath* had opened with a kaleidoscopic, tumbling display of familiar works of modern art, dashing through, amongst others, *The Scream*, Lowry's matchstick men, Dali's melting watches, Picasso in his Blue mood, one of Lucien Freud's grossly fat ladies, Warhol's soup cans and a Hockney swimming pool, finishing with Damien Hirst's pickled shark.

The parade of, depending on your viewpoint, mediocrity, flim-flam or innovative genius eventually cross-faded to Piers De'Ath, sitting behind a desk in what Mowgley recognised as the vestibule/hanging gallery at the *Château du Sourville*. The host's hairpiece was resting comfortably if obviously in place and he was wearing a black, polo-necked sweater with a logo which Mowgley assumed would impress those who knew how outrageously overpriced the company's products were. Behind him, the four paintings to be judged were turned to the wall.

De'Ath began his presentation by announcing that the format of this edition would differ from the usual routine. The artists responsible — and he had emphasised the word 'responsible' — for the paintings had been his guests at the *château* for the weekend. They would be shown the programme and hear his thoughts on the innovative and impressive quality of their work — or their complete lack of talent. Their horrified expression and sometimes violent reactions would be tacked on to the end of the programme. The reason for the change of routine, De'Ath added, was because this would be the last edition of the series, and he had wanted to go out with a bang.

~

'Blimey,' said Mowgley as the programme ended. 'That was painful.'

Degas and Catherine showed their agreement. After hailing the painter of the Vermeer work as someone of insight and humour, of immense talent and obviously with an equally big future, De'Ath had gone on to savage the other three. The camera had cut away to the face of the artist responsible for the painting being rubbished. They had obviously not known they were being filmed, and their reactions ranged from shock to despair... and hatred for their tormentor. The last clip showed the woman in dungarees getting to her feet and rushing at the desk behind which De'Ath sat. As she strained to get at him, the picture froze and a caption came up, reading:

THE END…OR NOT?

'As you said earlier,' Degas commented, 'the list of suspects is becoming a queue.'

Mowgley grunted assent, then put his coffee cup on the table: 'I take it we are still agreed it could be a jealous husband or wife from the Black Magic Circle, or a jealous gay lover, but probably not a jealous goat or sheep. It could be his own wife for one reason or another, and certainly now, three of the four stars of the You Tube programme. And, of course, anyone he had previously destroyed through that programme or any other media source. I assume you will be checking out all past victims?' Degas nodded silently, and Mowgley continued: 'So, what do we know about the victims — and the winner?'

'The lady with green hair and a moustache who painted the man with the head of a penis is a self-acclaimed misandrist who lives and works in East London.' said Degas. 'Her professional name is Freda Cargo.'

'Misandrist?' asked Mowgley.

'A man-hating woman,' McCarthy explained.

'I thought you all did in one way or another,' observed Mowgley, then nodded to Degas to continue.

'The man dressed as Judy Garland is Dutch, who paints 'natural' works using his faeces and urine. As he says, his work is all about and of himself. He lives and works in Brittany. Gerard Dufour — the man who painted the red herring — is French and works in Paris. The Girl with the Pearl Earring and Pierced Tongue was the work of Até, the woman I told you of before. She moves around, likes to remain mysterious, but is thought to be British. I will have a dossier on each of them sent to your office.'

'And are they still helping you with your enquiries?'

'As you will know, we had no powers to hold them beyond forty-eight hours. Até is currently in Paris and the lady with green hair has gone back to London. Judy Garland has become Alice in Wonderland and returned to Brittany. Gerard Dufour has disappeared but there is a nationwide alert for him. Perversely, all the artists have become big celebrities since the murder and consequent publicity and are to be seen constantly on television.'

Mowgley made a wry face. 'So there really is no such thing as bad publicity?'

Degas looked momentarily puzzled. 'I suppose not.'

'And no sign of M. Dufour yet?'

'No.'

'Okay.' Mowgley reached for his wine glass. 'So it could be he who killed our man and left the red herring painting on the body—'

'—or it could have been any of the others, who left the painting *as* a red herring. 'interjected Catherine McCarthy.

'Quite,' acknowledged Mowgley. 'Or, of course, it could be anyone else on the list of suspects.'

'As you say,' said Degas.

'Or,' added McCarthy, it could have been a simple overdose while he was... pleasuring himself.'

'Sure,' said Mowgley, 'but what about it being the last programme — or not? Why the ambiguity at the end, unless he hadn't made up his mind about topping himself, if he ever meant to?'

'Perhaps,' said Degas, 'he wanted people to think he was... retiring, or going away. Even if he was not.'

'Ah. Approaching Menace? I can see that.' Mowgley reached for his glass. 'I suspect you have something more to tell me? Have you been saving the best till last?'

Degas smiled. 'Well, perhaps not the best, but certainly a new development.'

'And?'

The Colonel paused as if for effect, then said: 'While searching the cellar at the Château, a concealed room was found.'

Mowgley raised both eyebrows. 'What, like a chamber of secrets?'

'You could say that. It was hidden behind a wine rack.'

'Very James Bond.'

'Yes, I suppose so. The chamber was climate-controlled. By that I mean there was air conditioning, de-humidifiers and a constant ambient temperature maintained.'

'And what was all this for? Ritual sacrifices for the Black Magic Circle?'

'I don't think so. The walls were full of paintings, mostly Impressionists like Manet, Monet, Chagall, Rembrandt...and even what might be an unknown Vermeer.'

If Mowgley could whistle, he would have. 'So why keep them down there? Security? Secrecy?'

'Either or both. Or something else. Nearly all of the paintings, though signed by the artists, are unknown.'

'You sound as if you've got an idea of what was going on in there.'

Degas nodded and reached for the cigarette packet on the table top. 'There were restoration materials and tools, and a number of old paintings which the expert says are of no value and not by any known artist. They were unremarkable representations of animals or landscapes or people.'

'So why we would Death bother to keep them in the secret room?'

'They were all more than a hundred years old.'

'So?'

'Think about it,' said Catherine McCarthy. 'If you wanted to "discover" a previously unknown Impressionist painting, you're not going to use a nice new canvas to forge it on, are you?'

Mowgley did a Stan Laurel scratch to the top of his head. 'Duh. Of course. So Death was coming up with allegedly previously unknown works and knocking them out on the side, using materials of the time. That would explain where all the money and property and nice toys came from.'

'It would,' said Degas. 'And as an internationally known art critic and dealer, he could be involved in their "discovery" by an accomplice, then make a strong case that they were genuine.'

Catherine McCarthy took over. 'Here's the clever bit. The previously unknown paintings were all of subjects related to other works or known to have been mentioned by the artists as a possible future work.'

Mowgley made as if to speak and McCarthy held up a hand. 'Yep, you've got it. That gave the fakes a sort of unofficial provenance, especially when backed up by De'Ath's opinion. Now, here's the killer.' She took a lit cigarette from her fiancé's lips, took a long draw then said: 'There were several copies of two of the fakes.'

'So what?' said Mowgley. 'He could have been meaning to sell them to punters who wouldn't or couldn't want it known they owned them.

'Close but no cigar.' She took another draw then handed the cigarette back to Degas. 'The Vermeer had an estimated value of two hundred million dollars, and the other was a Monet.'

'So?'

'So, they were copies of paintings which were stolen and never returned or found.'

Mowgley held a finger up to show he got it. 'So when Death flogged them as the originals, the fact that they were missing would give them a sort-of provenance.' He paused. 'But a bit of a risky business, no? That works as long as the originals don't turn up. Or until one of the buyers finds out he was not alone in paying a fortune for the missing masterpiece. And he would have been dealing with some dodgy characters. And you know what that could mean.'

He looked out to where the Brittany Ferry boat was disappearing over the horizon and thought about the implications.

'Yep', said McCarthy. The list of suspects grows ever longer. Nightcap, anyone?'

Lost and Never Found

There's a long list of great or valuable paintings which have been stolen and ransomed or returned or never seen again except by whoever bought them. They include:

Poppy Flowers *(or Vase and Flowers) by Vincent Van Gogh was stolen from a Cairo Museum in 2010. Painted three years before his suicide, the painting was valued at $50 million when taken. It was in fact the second time the same painting had been stolen from the same museum.*

Le Pigeon aux Petits Pois *by Pablo Picasso was stolen along with four other masterpieces from the Museum of Modern art in Paris in 2010. The estimated value of the haul was $100 million. A man was convicted of the theft, but claimed he had thrown the Picasso into a rubbish skip.*

The Concert *was painted by Johannes Vermeer in 1664 and was part of a haul by two fake policemen who talked their way into a Boston Museum in 1990. Valued at $200 million, it is the most valuable stolen painting to remain untraced. Somewhat ironically, The Concert went missing for a hundred years when it was sold in Amsterdam in 1696.*

Portrait of a Young Man *is believed to have been a self-portrait by Raphael in 1513. Snatched by the Nazis in Poland as part of their orgy of art treasure looting and destined to become part of the Fuhrer's collection at Linz, it disappeared from a castle in Krakow and was never recovered.*

Other big-name masterpieces stolen and still missing are, The Just Judges by Jan van Eyck, Nativity with St Francis and St Lawrence by Caravaggio, The Storm on the Sea of Galilee by Rembrandt and Charing Cross Bridge by Claude Monet.

Monkey Business

In 1964, Swedish journalist Ake Axelsson put eminent art critics to the test by inviting them to study a series of paintings by an unknown but talented French avant-garde artist called Pierre Brassau. Four of the paintings were exhibited at Goteborg's Christinae Gallery, where they caused a buzz amongst the experts. After flattering comments about the artist's 'powerful and determined strokes' and how the painter had the 'delicacy of a ballet dancer', Axelsson revealed that all the works had been created by a four-year-old chimpanzee.

10

In his old job, Channel crossings had been routine. This time, taking the overnight boat from Cherbourg to Portsmouth had the makings of a treat. As the taxpayers of France were paying, Mowgley had booked a four-berth outside cabin which would have offered sea views had it not been dark.

After a dinner he would never pay for with his own money, he went to the bar, where a touring French rugby team were almost disappointing in their restrained behaviour, especially when taunted by a group of booze cruisers with an apparent death wish. On the plus side, there were no tribute acts, DJs or magicians on the stage, and it was too late for hordes of French schoolchildren pursuing each other at breakneck speed around the tables.

By two in the morning, he'd done substantial damage to the bottle of Johnny Walker from the duty-free shop. It had not been silly cheap, but worked out much better than buying it by the tot across the bar. In between drinks he'd been out on deck for reflective cigarettes while watching a full-ish moon dancing on the ship's wake. Back in the bar, he'd been making some progress with the History of Modern Art coffee-table book Catherine McCarthy had given him with her fiancé's compliments. It was a glossy and obviously expensive publication, and he wondered if it was Degas or the Kiss of De'Ath budget that had paid for it.

Preparing for another visit to the smoking deck he became aware of the middle-aged woman on the next table. She was generally elegant in appearance, looked like an undernourished stick insect, and was regarding him with a curled lip.

With typical French candour — or what some might regard as intrusive rudeness — she told Mowgley in heavily-accented English that he did not look like the sort of person who would be interested in art. When he said he was just a beginner, she replied that, if that were the case, he should know that the great French painters had invented Impressionism and were later imitated badly by foreigners.

After a moment's reflection, he smiled placatingly, yawned and bid her goodnight. This was partly because he was looking forward to his bed, and partly because he knew he would never persuade her that the French were not originators and world leaders in every art form in which they chose to partake. Making his excuses and leaving was also because he was getting old, had drunk far too much and anyway preferred women with, as the French themselves said, much more meat on their bones.

~

Not wanting to drive in central London or risk his aged Citroën being confiscated for breaking every clean-air regulation in the capital, Mowgley had crossed the Channel as a foot passenger.

Herded on to the shuttle bus for the short trip from quayside to Passport Control, he sat and looked out the window and thought how much his life had changed in just a couple of years. In his past life at this early hour he would have been found in his room above the Midnight Tindaloo, then later for a fry-up breakfast at Gingers Caff. Lunch time would usually have been taken at his local The Ship Leopard, or as the locals had it, The Shit Leopard. At some time he would even have been found in his office overlooking the quayside, probably wondering how long he was going to last under the command of newly-appointed Chief Superintendent Cressida Hartley-Whitley. He now knew that 'not long' would have been the answer.

~

At first sight, Mowgley liked the look of the proprietor of True Art Investigation Services. His reaction may have been influenced by the fact that the man he had come to see looked not unlike a taller, younger and better-looking version of himself.

Robert Bailey was an inch or two over six feet, with a wide, amiable face. It looked amiable in spite of the off-centre nose and small white scar on his upper lip. Unlike Mowgley, both his ear lobes were intact and he bore no visible tattoos.

His grip was as firm as Mowgley had guessed it would be, and his body looked more muscle than flab beneath the faded blue bomber jacket and baggy cavalry twill trousers. He was recently shaven and had a shock of dark hair that was naturally tousled and clearly not of the artfully deranged variety. As Mowgley had learned, Bailey had a reputation as the go-to man for discreet enquiries and speedy results while working in the murky waters of art fraud, and he obviously felt he did not need to dress to impress.

Something else Mowgley liked about Bob Bailey was his lack of the usual affectations and bullshit vocabulary associated with people making their livings from the Art World. He did not feel in the slightest patronised by Bailey's suggestion that they took a late breakfast at the greasy spoon close to his office, which happened to be a stroll from the Tate Modern. Mowgley was becoming acclimatised to breakfasting on croissants, butter and preserves, but he did miss the occasional fry-up. It just did not taste the same when he had tried to recreate an English breakfast at his new home. Black pudding was more than readily available, but proper, unsmoked back bacon was hard to come by. Anyway, that singularly British way of starting the day would always have a home in his heart. His host had said that The Tate had a café, but Fat Jack's did an all-day breakfast with beans, mushrooms and bubble and squeak as standard.

'So,' said Robert Bailey, through a mouthful of fried bread, 'you're being funded by Colonel Renoir and his boys to work on who or what did for Mr. De'Ath?'

'It's Degas, actually.'

Bailey smiled impishly: 'Of course; like a lot of people I get those two mixed up. Just a little arty-farty joke.'

As he prepared to worship at an overloaded plate, Mowgley paused to look in fascination over Bailey's shoulder at a man attacking a FJ's Gutbuster Special. His technique was almost professional, and he was using a spoon to scoop up the baked beans before hoovering them in as if it was his first meal of the week. Or perhaps month.

Against logic and like many over eating and drinking specialists, the man was almost cadaverously thin. In between mouthfuls, he was working on a self-made bacon, mushroom and egg sandwich, garnished with more of the beans. He ate with his mouth widely open, and yolk was running down his bristly chin and dripping on to the lapel of his greasy topcoat. Sensing he was being watched, he looked up for a moment, then turned his attention back to his plate when he saw Mowgley's expression was of admiration rather than condemnation. The detective almost sighed as he thought of the many ways ageing robs one of simple pleasures of over-indulgence. Once upon a time, he could eat and drink to almost those levels of excess. Now he accepted that those days were gone. Although he still over-indulged, he knew he would pay all day for too much food eaten too quickly. He had not understood the concept of a hangover up to a few years ago. Now it took him three days to get over a heavy session. Such were the small but significant and sad depredations of ageing.

'Yes,' Mowgley finally answered Bailey's question, '...sort of. The Colonel is paying my boss for me to make enquiries amongst the local expats.'

'Ah. Does that mean that he maybe upset some Brit badly enough to do him in?'

Mowgley made a 'who-can-say?' expression. 'Don't know yet, but there's talk of him liking to put it about a bit.'

'Sounds about right from what I've heard. And AC/DC to boot.'

As their heaped plates arrived and they set to, he told Bailey more about his job in Cherbourg, but not that his former colleague at Portsmouth was living with and soon would be marrying the top cop in the region.

Bailey was clearly already aware of the situation, and, after studying the half sausage impaled on his fork, he said: 'That's an interesting situation. I don't suppose you and she were ever...'

'No,' said Mowgley, more sharply than he had meant, 'we weren't.'

Bailey put a hand up in apology. 'Sorry, just being trunky.'

There was an awkward moment, then Bailey made an after-you gesture at the condiments, and said: 'Brown or red?'

Mowgley recovered his good humour and smiled as he pushed the oversized tomato to one side. 'Brown of course.'

'Spot on,' said Bailey. 'It's compulsory with bacon and sausages, or should be.'

~

'Do you miss being on the job?'

Mowgley looked up from dissecting a slice of fried bread and adding a soupcon of beans and egg yolk to each piece. 'A bit, but not as much as I thought I would.'

'That's good,' said Bailey. 'Unlike you I was lucky and didn't have to find work in the real world a bit sharpish. A good pension and plenty of punters looking for my help.'

He sat back and pushed his plate away as Mowgley wondered what his hourly and daily rates were, and if they reflected the levels even seemingly mediocre paintings reached. He had heard that Bailey had found or negotiated for the return of many millions' worth of missing art works.

Bailey seemed to know what he was thinking, and said: 'It's a funny old game, but not badly paid. So, do you want to talk about Mr. De'Ath now or in the pub?'

'Pub,' said Mowgley. 'But first, can you tell me what do you honestly think about modern art and what it's all about?'

Bailey smiled. 'Honesty is not a word I would expect to use in the same sentence as the modern art market.'

'So it really is all about hype and bullshit?'

'Yes and no. Or, if I'm honest, make that yes.' He looked around, then said: 'I love this.'

'What?'

'Sitting in a greasy spoon and talking about The Meaning of Art.' He looked across at an abandoned half-eaten breakfast on an otherwise empty table. A cup sat alongside a saucer filled with cold tea, and sauce dribbled from the encrusted neck of a bottle of brown sauce. 'To give you a snapshot of what I think about some forms of art nowadays and how the system works, you could probably make an installation work of that table if you had the front and name and right backing. If it did go large, some pratt would pay a lot of money for it. After all, they did it with a banana taped to a wall, so why not one of a Jack's fry-up?'

~

'Don't mind if I do. Just don't tell the missus.'

The two men were sitting outside the café, watching the traffic try to go by as Mowgley requested a cigarette break before going on to the pub.

As Bailey almost gingerly took a chunky Caporal, Mowgley reflected on how many people must be betraying their partners by sneaking a fag rather than a bit on the side.

'So,' said Bailey after exhaling and giving the familiar groan of a smoker trying to cut back or give up when falling off the wagon, 'where do you want me to start? With the history of art I mean? The cave paintings at Lascaux, a quick flit through the Renaissance?'

'What about starting with a definition of what art is?'

Bailey gave a grunt of amusement. 'Is that all?' He took another drag, followed by a mouthful of tea, then said: 'I'm still working on it, but then people much cleverer than me have been trying to make their minds up for a long, time. Tolstoy wrote a whole book about it, and ended up saying art was anything that communicates emotion.'

'And do you agree?'

'Again, yes and no. The problem with that is, if he was right, it would mean a punch-up or shouting match in *Eastenders* is art at some level.'

He picked up his mug and looked into it as if the answer may lay there.

'Another idea is that art is anything that is created for no practical purpose. Oscar Wilde said that Art is useless in the way that a flower is useless. He also sort-of went along with Tolstoy that art does nothing but create a mood. The problem with the useless line is it then means that any activity which results in something useful can't be art. Try telling that to an arty-farty chef or the owner of a classic Ming vase.'

'But there must be some stuff that's inarguably great art?'

Bailey wrinkled his nose. 'Of course there is. Da Vinci and Rembrandt and all that lot certainly made great art, simply because they did it so much better than anyone else. That's why they're called The Old Masters. And their job was to make the subjects of their paintings look …real. From an early age they worked countless hours learning about making and mixing colours, composition, perspective, shading, and textures… and most of all, light. All the tricks of the trade to get what we would call a photographic likeness. You have to remember they were the cameras of their day and the point of what they did was to make their subjects as real-looking as possible. Except for some obvious exceptions like Hieronymus Bosch, of course. When it comes to modern and then contemporary art, it gets a bit sticky... for all sorts of reasons.'

'And what's the difference between Impressionism and modern and contemporary art?'

Bailey sucked at his teeth, wiped his lips with the back of his hand and reached for his mug of tea. 'Okay, time for a quick whizz through the last couple of hundred years or so of fashion and foolishness, imagination and innovation mixed with affectation, bullshit and consistent greed. And remember this is very much a bullet-point *Reader's Digest*-type of presentation.'

He fiddled with his cigarette, balanced it on the edge of the metal table top. 'The official definition is that modern art applies to stuff from the hundred years or so between 1860 and the *1970s*. That would cover *The Scream* and Lowry's Matchstick Men as well as the Impressionists.'

'And that was a mostly French thing?'

Bailey screwed up his face. 'Yes, though a lot of Impressionists gave a nod to our JMW Turner as being a sort of forerunner. Anyway, like a lot of change, it began when the fairly young painters started questioning traditional approaches of making a photographic likeness. They said they were more interested in light and colour and creating an 'impression' with quick, short brush strokes which would make sense when you looked at it from a distance. Some people would give you a fight on it, but it's generally accepted that the first 'official' Impressionist painting was by Monet in 1874. It was an impression of dawn in the harbour at Le Havre. It didn't go down well to start with, but sort of opened the gates.'

He patted his chest with a bunched fist and belched softly. 'Excuse me. Of course, some cynics say the Impressionist Movement was just a club of rich people's sons who could get worked up over techniques and style while getting pissed and shagging anything that moved on the Left Bank.'

'As any couturier will tell you, fashions have to change to keep the interest up and the dosh coming in. So, unsurprisingly, after Impressionism, we had... Post-Impressionism, though it wasn't called that until the next century.'

'What was the difference?'

They both watched as a very pretty young girl in long boots and a short skirt hurried by as if late for a meeting with her lover.

Bailey sighed as if to remember other times, then said:

'Another good question. The movement started towards the back end of the 19th-century, and aimed at, as the official literature says, 'A subjective approach to representing emotion rather than realism.' He held up a hand to forestall Mowgley's next query. 'I know. Whatever the experts say, it was mostly all about slapping on more paint in more vivid colours. Or that's my opinion, anyway. This was where Van Gogh, Seurat, Cézanne, Gauguin and Rousseau and co came into their own.'

Another pause as another pretty woman passed by, then:

'So, a new century and a new movement. Surrealism started as a literary device, intending to, again, and I quote, 'release the unbridled imagination of the subconscious.' It became the latest thing in art, and take a bow René Magritte and company.'

'Magritte was the one who did the bloke with a bowler hat and an apple in front of his face?'

'Good boy,' said Bailey. 'You've got it. Other big names were Joan Miró, Max Ernst, and, of course, Salvador Dali. Picasso and Frida Kahlo are generally considered to be part of the group, though they never officially signed up.'

He paused and hefted his mug. 'More tea?'

Mowgley nodded and stood up, reaching for Bailey's mug. 'Hold that thought. Bit of bread pudding to go with it?'

'It would be a crime to say no. Jack's is known to be good brain food, especially for geezers planning a job.'

Mowgley went into the café, made and paid for his order, and came out to find Bailey had started on his second cigarette. He made an apologetic gesture and shoved the packet across the table. 'Get thee behind me.'

He took a long drag, put the cigarette on the edge of

the table, drank from his mug and took a bite of the thick, fruity bread pudding. 'Okay, where was I?'

'Dali and Picasso.'

'Oh yeah. Dali is a good example of a lot that was and is rotten in the art world.

He was a real showman and must have one of the most famous moustaches in history — not counting Charlie Chaplin and Hitler. To be fair, he broke with conventions and came up with all sorts of new ideas and memorable images like the lobster telephone and all those melting watches. He was a genuine one-off, but was seduced by the big money. They reckon he could put his signature on as many as 2000 blank sheets an hour. In 1974, French police made a routine stop of a lorry on its way to Andorra. It was carrying 40,000 blanks with the Dali signature. Forgery had become endemic in the art world.' He smiled grimly. 'I think that little example sums up what greed can do; it just seems worse in the world of artistic endeavour, where the performers were, they said, aiming for truth and not to become very, very rich.'

He shook his head, and looked at his watch. 'Must be nearly pub time, so I'll crack on. Let's pass over Dada-ism, Abstract Expressionism and enter the weird world of Pop Art, Op Art, Minimalism and Photorealism.'

Mowgley cleared his mouth of bread pudding. 'And this all comes under the heading of Modern Art?'

'Yes... and no,' said Bailey. 'Yet another good question. Don't ask me why, but the general consensus is that Modern Art ended somewhere in the mid-70s.'

Mowgley digested this, then pointed his mug in the rough direction of the Tate Modern. 'And what about Tracey Emin's unmade bed and the pickled shark and the pile of bricks up the road? What sort of art is that? If it is art?'

Bailey held up a cautionary finger. 'Ah, now we're talking about Conceptualism. Officially, the bricks in 1976 were an example of a movement to replace paintings and pictures with ideas. It dates back to the early Sixties, more or less.'

Mowgley reached for his cigarettes. 'Okay. But, whatever sort of art it is, who says it's any good — and what it's worth?'

Bailey screwed up his face. 'You are one for asking pertinent if awkward questions, ain't you? Officially, the king or queen makers have always been the galleries and dealers. It's also about something as simple as what someone will pay for a piece of work to start the ball rolling. Sometimes it can be a self-fulfilling prophecy. Someone pays a lot of money for a new artist's work, and off we go. He or she becomes the flavour of the month and everybody's happy — except all the other artists who don't make it. Sometimes it doesn't happen straight away. Andy Warhol and his soup cans attracted a lot of often hostile attention, then became 'collectable' and more and more valuable over the years.'

'Another thing is how time can lead to enchantment. We can admire a bit of Modern Art because it has become, like Van Gogh's *Starry Night*, familiar. As he found out, sometimes you have to wait till you're dead to get recognition. We all know about Van Gogh not selling a painting in his lifetime — which isn't true but makes a good story. He was on the verge of becoming a star when he shot himself — or allegedly shot himself. But that's another story. Anyway, that post-mortem success was happening way before his time. It took centuries for Vermeer to get recognition, though nowadays *The Girl with the Pearl Earring* is one of the most popular paintings in the world. That makes it virtually priceless.'

Bailey sat back and took a restorative swig of tea.

Mowgley sighed and scratched a cheek: 'Okay, I think I get that about the Old Masters. But is there a reason that some of the conceptual stuff is worth fortunes and others don't make it? Who decided an unmade bed was art, for instance?'

Bailey smiled and lifted an eyebrow. 'Well, you'll have to ask whoever shortlisted it for the Turner Prize. Or the gallery who showed it and gave it credence... or the German collector who thought enough of it to pay two and a half million for it at an auction.'

'But is it art — and was it worth it?' Mowgley persisted.

Bailey shrugged. 'The German — and those who worked the price up in the bidding — must have thought so.' He smiled sympathetically. 'With respect, I think your mistake is trying to make any sort of logic or sense of the wonderful world of art. I gave up yonks ago. I think the best thing is to remember the bit about art being useless, and being worth what someone will pay for it.'

'He broke off and nodded to a shiny and somehow menacing-looking black BMW trying to manoeuvre into a too-small parking pace. 'You know a top-of-the-range Beamer is going to cost you the best part of a hundred grand because of how and with what it's made and how good it is at what it does. In art, people say that a piece of French Impressionism is worth a million or two because of what it represents in the development of art after the camera had fucked up the old idea of artists trying to reproduce things exactly as people saw them. Nowadays, art is what people say it is, and, as I keep saying, worth what someone will pay for it.'

'Yeah, but who are those people?'

'What, those who say it's worth big bucks or those who pay the big bucks?'

He shrugged. 'That's easy. Collectors, critics and people like your Mr. De'Ath.'

Bailey looked at his watch, and Mowgley saw that it was a Rolex Perpetual Oyster. Business was obviously good... or perhaps it was a fake, and an ironic comment by the owner on the perceived and actual value of so many things.

'So, Leonardo to Tracy Emin in less than half an hour. Not bad eh? Pub?'

'Pub,' agreed Mowgley.

John Myatt (1945-)

This is the man credited as the author of the biggest art fraud of the 20th-century. The son of a farmer, Myatt attended art school; and discovered a talent for painting in the style of famous artists. Advertising his work in Private Eye *magazine, he offered 'genuine fakes' of celebrated 19th and 20th-century artists' work. Enter John Drewe, who revealed to Myatt that he had sold one of his copies of a French Cubist painter as an original for £25,000. The duo went into business, and police investigators estimate Myatt went on to paint more than two hundred imitations of artists like Marc Chagall, Ben Nicholson and Graham Sutherland. His accomplice sold them to auction houses such as Christie's and Sotheby's and dealers in New York, London and Paris. During their relationship, Myatt received only around £100,000 compared to the estimated £2 million made by Drewe.*

Myatt was arrested in 1996 after a raid on his studio by New Scotland Yard detectives, who also found materials used to fake certificates of authenticity. He was jailed in 1998, but only served four months.

Drewe was found guilty of conspiracy to defraud and given six years, of which he served two.

'The art world just didn't want to see they were fakes,' commented Myatt.

11

'Cheers.'

Mowgley tried to look enthusiastic as he took the pint of Theakston's Old Peculier recommended by Robert Bailey. He would have much preferred a nice, cold Foster's, but hadn't liked to risk upsetting his host by asking for a lager in such a temple of what people insisted on calling 'real ale.'

In his day, all ale had been real, and a lot of it had tasted like warm cat's piss. His grandfather had run a corner local, and Mowgley had often watched as the old man poured the slops from drip trays and part-filled glasses carefully back into the casks after closing time. It was common practice in those harder times for the booze trade. Then, like an alien visitation, something called lager beer had appeared on the bar counters of all British pubs. The gassy foreign import was cold and crystal clear, and took away the uncertainty. Unlike the punters in his granddad's pub, you knew exactly what you were getting, and what every pint would taste like, even if it was not much.

Apart from habit and familiarity, there was another reason Mowgley drank lager. For some reason, people always assumed he would be an ale drinker, and it gave him a perverse pleasure to prove them wrong. He also liked to upset and distance himself from the real ale aficionado poseurs who insisted on holding their pints up to the light and talking about SG, IBU's and, for Christ's sake, "hoppiness".

This was London, so even in mid-afternoon, the pub was rammed. Being an extra trendy part of the capital, he was by far the scruffiest and oldest customer. Some of the customers were too young to walk, and he watched as a grumpy-looking tot was carried around in a harness strapped to his minder's chest with designer-clad little legs and arms dangling free. It reminded Mowgley of an assisted parachute jump, or the scene in *Total Recall* where Kuato the mutant emerges from a resistance fighter's stomach.

Another peculiarity was the sameness of how many of the adult customers looked and moved. Bailey had said that the pub was favoured by "hipsters", and Mowgley had looked the term up on his phone while his new friend fetched the beer. Rather than the low-slung trousers of his day, it seemed that hipsters were part of a sub-culture of independent thinkers who 'eschewed trends and current fashions'. Given the commonality of Abraham Lincoln-style beards and man-buns, most of the adherents seemed keen to follow fashion in their own way. He also noted that, as well as looking much the same, most of the men were tall and thin and moved in a curious, swaying manner which put him in mind of a gathering of whatever the plural was for praying mantis.

'So, what do you think?'

Mowgley lifted his glass to head level and looked

through it in what he hoped was the appropriate manner and took a modest mouthful. He thought about rolling it around his mouth to show his connoisseurship, but refrained. 'Very nice,' he said.

'I think you don't really think so,' said Bailey, whose bullshit radar was clearly as efficient as Mowgley's skills of subterfuge were lacking. 'Sorry, mate, I took you for a real ale man. Would you rather have a pint of lager?'

Mowgley put the glass down and smiled with relief. 'Foster's if they've got it, please.'

~

Mowgley excavated for a particularly tough piece of pork scratching between his back teeth, then rinsed his mouth with a draught of Foster's. Admiring the expensive-looking business card Bailey had given him, he asked: 'So is there much work for you in this game?'

Bailey took a swig of his Bear Republic Hop Rod Rye Ale, and Mowgley was relieved that he did not smack his lips. 'Not so you'd notice, mate. Transactions in the worldwide art market came to over 60 billion dollars last year. Some experts reckon that half of all artwork in circulation is not authentic. There's certainly lots of dodgy stuff going on from outright criminal activity to "tainted" activity'

He saw the question on Mowgley's face, and continued. 'That's art world talk for what is defined as any level of immorality or outright criminality. It could be a minor bit of fakery, an auction house agreeing to sell a work they suspect could be iffy, a 'misattribution' or a drug overlord laundering his money through the transfer of pieces of modern art at hugely inflated prices.'

Mowgley reached for the pork scratchings bag and frowned when he found it empty. 'So how would that work?'

'Easy. Mr. Big spends out on a piece by a 'safe' artist

whose work fetches millions, then moves it into a high-security 'freeport' storage facility near a major airport. It sits there until it's sold to someone else with money to clean or burn. It may stay there, or move on to another tax-free security store. Either way, it's a universally accepted money token, and as long as all the participants buy into it, it'll only go up in value. The joke is that sometimes nobody will ever see or appreciate that work. It might as well be a pallet of gold bars locked away in a bank vault.'

He paused, then added: 'Of course, having a knocked-off Renoir or Vermeer can also be a handy get-out-of-jail-free card.'

'A whatter?'

Bailey smiled: 'It should really be a do-less-time-in-jail card but that don't scan so nicely.' He rubbed his cheek thoughtfully, then said. 'Basically, a much-loved masterpiece that is thought to have been lost to the world can be a great bargaining counter.'

'And how does that work?'

'Okay. Mr. Big has been caught bang to rights, and before the wheels of justice start to grind, he tells the appropriate representative of the law that he knows where to find a much-loved masterpiece thought to have been lost to the world. The deal is that he will spill the beans as to its location if he gets a lighter sentence.'

Mowgley nodded to show he was keeping up. 'And will he get time off what he would have got?'

Bailey held up his hands and shrugged. 'By definition we can't know, but it can't be a bad move.'

'And where if anywhere does Mr. Death come in?'

Bailey smiled knowingly. 'It's said he's acted as go-between for the people who nicked it and the potential punter. It's even said he's helped in steal-to-order cases, where the buyer wants a particular painting to act as a bargaining counter or an investment...or even just to gloat over it in the privacy of his own gaff.'

There was a moment's silence as Mowgely digested the information, then he blew out his cheeks and said: 'You know what that means?'

Bailey nodded. 'Yep. Not good news for you as it adds to your list of those who might want to see Mr De'Ath dead.'

~

A half hour had passed and another round of drinks bought and consumed. Talk had turned to current affairs and very briefly to football, a sport of which Mowgley was not fond.

Seeing the opportunity, he pointed at his companion's glass and said: 'So, back to business. I didn't ask exactly how you get involved in any of this immorality or criminality...and at what level?'

Bailey drained his glass, wiped his mouth with the back of his hand, then said: 'In all sorts of ways. A collector might come to me to check out a painting and how authentic the provenance is before he puts in an offer. It might be me tracing a missing or stolen piece of work, which can be fun. Or even a gallerythat's been done and wants me to find the malefactor. Or I might be called in by the insurance company as a sort of loss adjustor or negotiator when a painting has been nicked. Or by the gallery when it's being blackmailed. "Pay up or we'll burn it" sort of thing.'

'Does that happen often?'

Bailey smiled into his beer. 'You'd be surprised. Here's another little factette. Ninety-five percent of stolen art is never recovered. Or officially never recovered. It's a general rule that galleries and auction houses don't like to air their dirty washing, so enter your discreet but effective investigator.'

'That's you.'

Bailey nodded and smiled an almost smug smile.

'That's me, that is.'

'And there's only you in...' he looked down at Bailey's card, 'True Art Investigation Services?'

'Just me and a handful of freelancer specialists I can call on when I need to. Then there's my secretary—or PA as she insists on calling herself. I have to turn a lot of work down, but that's how I like it.' He paused, finished his pint and said: 'So, why all the questions? Are you after a job?'

Mowgley frowned and thought about his decaying relationship with Yann Cornec. 'I might be, but I know nothing about your world.'

'Doesn't matter. Being an ex-copper, observation and investigation is what you do... and I hear you're good at it. You can always call in help, or—' he nodded at the book on modern art in Mowgley's Lidl carrier bag, '— learn on the job and pick it up as you go along. But it's no different from investigating any crime. There's a guilty party and you have to find out who it is and how they done it. If it's a murder, we used to call in the SOCO crew. Nowadays I call on the experts, use my contacts and sometimes have a word with the shadowy figures of the art world.' He took a thoughtful swig and looked at Mowgley reflectively. 'Easy-peasy for someone with your experience and talents.'

Mowgley smiled and lifted his glass. 'I'll bear that in mind if it all goes a bit wrong.'

~

'*Mazele tov.* Here's to us.' Bailey reached out for his pint and chaser and took the top off both. They were on their fourth round and sixth packet of pork scratchings, and Mowgley was looking forward to the curry Bailey had proposed.

'So,' said the art investigator, 'I suppose we'd better get onto the purpose of your visit. What do you reckon to

Charlie Arnett? Was he done or was it an accidental overdose, or DIY?'

Mowgley settled into his seat, automatically reached into his shirt pocket for the packet of cigarettes he could not smoke, then asked: 'Charlie who?'

'Sorry, I thought you might already know. That's Piers De'Ath's real name. Or one of them.'

'You've done a bit of research on him, then?'

'Sort of. Someone he upset wanted the goods on him a few years ago, so I did a bit of digging. Mr. De'Ath first came to the public attention in the early Noughties, when he made an appearance on a late-night arts telly programme. You know the sort of thing, all murky lighting, a solo sax in the background and chromium stools for the guests. Anyway, he went down well, and became a fixture on *For Art's Sake*. From there he went from strength to strength, writing articles and pronouncing on new and existing artists, dabbling in buying and selling and being seen at all the right places.'

'But you found out where he came from?'

Bailey nodded into his glass. 'It wasn't hard. I did a bit of leg work and phoned around to old contacts and mates, and finally got a result. As Charles — he always insisted on 'Charles' — Arnett, he used to travel round, buying and flogging paintings at minor auctions and always on the lookout for the big hit. He also had a poncy art'n'antiques shop in the westcountry.'

'So he was on the hunt for the old Master in the attic? And did he find it?'

'Yes and no. In 1998 he suddenly came up with a Max Ernst he said a local woman had brought into his shop.'

Seeing Mowgley's blank look, he explained: 'Ernst was a German painter and sculptor, poet, graphic artist and all-round arty type, and a pioneer in Dada-ism and surrealism.' He paused again, then said 'Don't worry, we'll get into the Dada thing later.'

He looked at his expensive watch, squinting a little.

'Sorry about this bit of a history lesson and stop me if you've heard it before,'

Mowgley waved an inviting hand, and Bailey continued. 'Hitler hated modern art. When he became top dog he ordered all of the museums and galleries to get rid of anything that smacked of modernism and, in the Nazi view, decadence. This meant tens of thousands of paintings disappeared virtually overnight.'

'So a bit like the Nazi book-burning, then?'

'Not really. A lot must have been destroyed, but a lot more would have been squirrelled away by high-ranking officers. Nobody knows how many are still out there on private walls. That's where Mr. De'Ath-to-be comes in.'

Bailey broke off to pick up his apparently empty chaser glass, roll it energetically between his palms, then hold it over his ale. A couple of drops dripped from the glass and into the ale. He smiled and said 'It's a trick my dear old dad taught me. He was a Jock and said it was a sin to waste as much as a tear drop of good Scotch whisky. Anyway, back to the plot. De'Ath — or Charles Arnett as he was then — said the woman was the daughter of a Brigadier who had been a liaison officer for the Brits in the massive drive by the Allies to save and secure art works looted by the Nazis. You might have seen *The Monuments Men*. It was based on the true story about how European and American art experts became officers in an Allied task force which located and recovered millions of art treasures from Nazi repositories. Arnett said she had told him her father brought the painting back from Germany in 1946 as a souvenir. His missus didn't like it much, and it stayed in the attic till her granddaughter had a clear-out when the old lady died.'

'And did the experts buy into it?'

'They did — mostly because it sounded right and it suits everyone in the business when a previously unknown work by a very marketable artist turns up. Better still if he's dead so can't say if it was by him or not. Ernst had invented a technique called frottage in 1925, which was basically pencil rubbings. The one Charlie Arnett unveiled was a rubbing of — of all things — a bit of floor-boarding. It was true that a number of Max Ernst paintings had been removed from galleries as a result of Hitler's purge. Nowadays, a validated Ernst will fetch up to sixteen million dollars; Back then, the floorboard job was sold at auction for £20,000.'

'And what happened next?'

'Arnett took the money and ran. Literally, to re-emerge as art dealer and critic Piers De'Ath. In case you're wondering, I looked it up and Ath is a smallish French-speaking town in Belgium. I reckon Charlie thought the new name sounded memorable and just right for a big shot in the Art world.'

Mowgley went to work on his empty Scotch glass with no success, then asked: 'What about the Brigadier's daughter?'

'She disappeared too. Presumably with De'Ath-to-be.'

'And what happened next?'

Bailey shrugged. Piers went on to fame and fortune, but I could find no record of what happened to the lady. I guess that's where you come in. But the funny thing is that a whole heap of Max Ernst paintings came onto the market in the early 2000's.'

'Are you saying that the Brigadier brought back more than one painting?'

'Dunno. Could be that. Or it could be that the original painting was a fake, and De'Ath came up with a regular supply, giving a nod and a wink that they were the spoils of war. For sure, the story gave the painting a healthy provenance and made a sort of sense. The Brigadier could have acquired it genuinely or even nicked it and a lot more. Having sowed the seed, our man could then sell on more and more alleged Ernsts to all those people with a vested interest in believing them to be puckah.'

'Blimey.' Mowgley looked reflectively at his empty

glasses. 'So that's where Death got his money from?'

Bailey made an eyebrows-raised, palms upward 'don't know' signal. 'Sounds a bit likely, don't it? He might have made a nice few bob with that single painting, but I reckon he went on to be a player in quite a complicated scam. Or was until last week.'

'How do you mean?'

'Well, the original Ernst would have been a nice payday and got him out of messing around in the shop and touring round the auctions and boot sales. But there's his castle in Normandy, his apartment in Paris and his riverside place in London. He wouldn't have made really serious money from appearing on telly and writing articles, making and breaking artists and dealing in their works. I have more than a hunch that there was another stream of big income.'

'Yeah,' agreed Mowgley, thinking of the Chamber of Secrets. 'But you've got nothing more on him than the possible fake Ernsts?'

Bailey shook his head. 'Not really, but I haven't put that much time into sussing out the dodgy Mr. D. Unlike you, nobody's paying me to find out more. And anyway, the more I asked around the more I got a feeling it might not be too healthy for me to poke my nose in too much.'

'What do you mean?'

Bailey gave Mowgley a thoughtful look. 'Just things that happened when I was asking round and doing a bit of gentle digging.'

He drained his glass and looked at his watch again, and mimed eating. 'Ruby Murray time?'

Mowgley nodded. 'I'm your man. But, just to make that clear, are you saying you got warned off?'

'Not exactly. But, bearing in mind the sort of players involved and what may have happened to Mr. De'Ath, I'd say you should take care to take good care of yourself.

There's a lot of really big money involved in this game,

and big money always attracts more than just wealthy collectors. There's sharks aplenty swimming round in them murky waters, Jack boy.'

~

It was well into the witching hour, and the chief investigator of Services d'Enquêtes Privés Cornec was to be found in his hotel, sitting on the bed in his standard night-time attire of vest and pants. In the interests of self-respect, he had removed his socks.

Mowgley was finishing off a chicken tindaloo that he had started at the *Star of India*. Bailey had promised him the best curry in the capital, and it was Mowgley's judgment that he might be right. To be fair, it was, apart from the long-distance takeaways from across the Channel courtesy of Catherine McCarthy, the first proper sit-down curry on what had been home ground for more than a year. He had, as Bailey had observed, taken the opportunity to eat himself silly, but had been loath to leave the leftovers behind.

Reviewing the evening, it had been good to meet the art fraud investigator and share reminiscences of their time in the Met. To add to that, he'd learned a lot about the history of art and hoped to remember most of it. He'd also learned about the extent of fraud and corruption and hypocrisy in the art world, though he was not much wiser about the true value of what most people would call modern art. Bailey had been honest enough to admit that he might be missing something and be a philistine at heart, but after three decades he could not alter his opinion that, whatever those with a vested interest might like to think or say, much of the art world depended on the king's clothes syndrome and mountains of bullshit, created and propagated for obvious reasons.

Bailey had also come up with the goods on the life of

Charles Arnett before he became Piers De'Ath, and another possibility as to why he breathed his last in the cellar of his Normandy home.

His phone buzzed as he was flushing away the remains of his curry takeaway. It was Catherine McCarthy.

'Hello mate,' he said, 'couldn't you sleep, or were you feeling lonely?'

'If I was I wouldn't call you.'

'Nor would I.'

'Quite. So where are you and what are you doing—if it's within the bounds of normal behaviour? And I don't mean your normal behaviour.'

Mowgley affected a hurt expression and tone. 'I'm in a hotel. In London and just finished the leftovers from a blinding chicken tindaloo, as it happens.'

'I hope you've left the windows open out of respect for the chambermaid and future guests.'

'The windows don't open.' He waved the touch screen tablet connected to the wall as if she would be able to see it. 'I was trying to put the air conditioning on, but everything's controlled by this bloody computer thing,'

'Everything? I hope it doesn't operate the toilet.'

'No, but I can't even make the telly work.'

'So phone Reception.'

'I would if there was a phone. You're supposed to e-mail them.'

'Blimey, sounds trendy—and expensive.'

'Yeah. Just as well I'm not paying.'

'Quite. Oh, by the way, René sends his regards and to tell you the belt round the neck didn't offer up any prints, except for the owner's.'

'If it was someone else pulling it tight, they could have worn gloves.'

'Maybe. But René said it wasn't strangulation that killed him.'

'Might have kept him quiet so the killer could force feed him with the funny stuff, though.'

'True. Anyway, how was your evening and how did you get on with Mr. Bailey?' Mowgley nodded and rubbed his jaw. 'Okay. I met some hipsters and Bailey is a good bloke. And he knows his curry shops.'

'I hope there were some legs in the hipsters you met? Only kidding. What I actually meant was what Mr. B had to say about Piers De'Ath?'

'You mean Charlie Arnett. Okay. But you didn't call at this time in the morning to ask me that, did you?'

'True. Your detecting powers are obviously at full strength after a tindaloo and God knows how many pints of Foster's.'

'So,' he asked, 'what's to do?'

'You know the bloke who painted the Red Herrings picture?'

'Gerard Thingy? He's turned up, then?'

'He has.'

'So where is he and when can we talk to him.'

'That's never going to happen,' said Catherine McCarthy. 'M. Dufour turned up in the river Seine this afternoon.'

'Dead?'

'I hope so. He's lying on a slab in the morgue in the 12th Arondissement waiting to have his insides taken out as we speak.'

Mock Movement

In 1924, novelist Paul Jordan-Smith painted his first-ever picture, naming it Yes, We Have No Bananas, *later amended to* Exaltation. *He then presented it at an exhibition at the Waldorf-Astoria in New York under the name of Pavel Jerdanowitch, founder and creator of a new art movement called Disumbrationism. The movement was greeted with admiration and enthusiasm by influential critics, and Jordan-Smith created more paintings by the imaginary artist. He confessed to his hoax in 1927 after hearing that Disumbrationism was being taken so seriously and so praised that it was to be added to the curricula of a number of leading art colleges.*

12

A stiff onshore breeze clashed with an outgoing tide, making the choppy surface glitter in the morning sun like a host of broken mirror shards.

From the comfort of one of the loungers on the Degas balcony, Mowgley watched the usual line-up of cormorants on observation duty at the breakwater. According to some experts, they adopted their outstretched wing pose to dry their feathers between dives. Others observed they did it even in the rain, so drying could not be the primary purpose. Either way, the crucifix-like pose gave them an almost sinister appearance.

Mowgley wondered if they were the same birds he'd seen last time, and if, unlike the human race, all avian species looked the same. Give or take a few true doppelgängers, it seemed almost incredible how seven billion people on the planet had unique faces. Another puzzle was, if it were true about doppelgängers, how come they'd never found an Elvis imitator who looked remotely like the King of Rock 'n' Roll?

'More coffee, your Grace?'

Catherine McCarthy appeared through the sliding glass doors with a cafetière in one hand and a soup bowl-size cup in the other. 'Fag me, please. Don't panic,' she added, seeing his panicked look, 'this is for me. The Nescafé Gold jar is to hand in the kitchen. I have to hide it from René in case he sees it and thinks I drink the stuff.'

She sat next to him and put the cafetière and cup on the glass-topped table. He had interrupted her at work, and she was wearing an old, paint-spattered boiler suit, her hair protected by a scarf knotted in the front. He had to admit she made the outfit look stylish.

'I clocked the wooden louvre shutters when I came in,' he said. 'I suppose the leather furniture will be along soon. This must mean you're re-feathering the nest to put your mark on it... or there's a happy event imminent and you're changing the spare room to a nursery?'

'Oh fuck off,' she replied. 'For a start we don't have a spare room. It's called dressing for sale.'

'Ah, said Mowgley, nodding at a folder on the table, 'I did wonder about all those property details. Very nice,' he continued, handing her a lit cigarette, 'but I note some of them're priced at well over a million euros. I know that a lot of people like wasting estate agents' time by looking at houses way above their budget, but I didn't think you and René would be into that sort of thing.'

'Bloody cheek,' she said after taking in and slowly expelling an impressive volume of smoke, 'I know you paid next to nothing for your little place in the wasteland, but high-end property's shot up here in the past few years.'

'Perhaps so,' he observed, 'but a million euros? What are you after, a château like Mr. Death's place? Might be up for sale in a while, now I think of it.'

She sighed. 'You really do live in the past, don't you? A million euros would hardly buy the pigeon house and outbuildings at Brix. We're looking for a nice big place with a bit of character, no neighbours and a bit of land round it. And maybe a cottage in the grounds for guests.'

'Like me?'

'When you get too old to look after yourself. If you ever could? We'll see.'

She took a sip from the soup bowl and a mouthful of smoke. 'Anyway, René retires in a year or two and I might want to do a bit of B&B.'

'Ah,' he said, 'now I get it. It's that expat thing about buying a place that's got twice as many bedrooms and bathrooms you need with the excuse you'll be taking paying guests in, eh? You and a hundred other Brit ladies in this bit of France alone.' He scratched his chin. 'Still can't see why you need something of that size and price, though. I knew officers in the *Gendarmerie* were well paid, and you fancy yourself as Lady of the *Manoir*, but...'

She put her coffee cup down so firmly it threatened the integrity of the glass table-top. 'As I said before, fuck off. I did well out of my apartment in Portsmouth, and we got a pleasant surprise when we had this place valued. So we can afford to look at nice places.'

Mowgley looked at her eyes and thought it best to move on. 'Only teasing,' he said. 'So what about the Red Herring man?'

'René will be back soon,' she said frostily, 'and I told you all I knew over the phone.'

'Okay,' he said, 'sorry to pull your plonker, metaphorically speaking. Or do I mean allegorically speaking?' He shrugged, gave his little-boy-lost look and reached out with his empty mug. 'Any chance of that coffee? I'll swap it for another fag.'

~

It was a short but pleasant journey in the lift from the Degas apartment.

There was no tinny music, and no brittle female voice plied him with unnecessary information about where he had been or was going. The lift was also unvandalised and smelled of nothing more than a hint of perfume from a previous occupant. Very different to the blocks of flats he had visited in the line of duty on the other side of the Channel.

On the way down, he thought about the look in Catherine's eyes when he mentioned the price of the properties the couple were looking at. And how it was just as well he had not commented on the sporty new soft-top BMW in the apartment's parking space which she said had been an early wedding present from her husband-to-be.

~

From the outside, the fake British pub in the village square looked like a double-fronted shop with the windows painted over. More Old Curiosity Shop than *The Red Lion*.

Clues to what went on inside came with the sandwich board advertising coming attractions like a 70's Pop Quiz, Book Club meeting and the usual Friday night karaoke extravaganza. On the other side of the board, Mowgley saw that the Dish of the Day was cottage pie, with proper English chips.

Inside, he saw that the owners had made a fair job of recreating a British pub recalling a time and place that had never been. He had never seen the appeal of seeking out familiar surroundings from home when abroad, but could see how a transplanted pub and customers could be a comforting place to someone living in another land and missing their local.

He accompanied the sound of his footsteps across the

stone-flagged floor to where a hugely fat man sat at the bar, studying the screen of a lap-top computer. The man was so obese that his head, fingers and feet looked tiny in comparison with his body. He would give the wheelbarrow man in Carentan a run for his money, and the overall effect was that of a small man trapped in a mountain of lard, or a normal-sized actor wearing a fat suit. The heavy wooden bar stool on which he was sitting looked sturdy, which was just as well, Mowgley thought. Given the spread of his vast backside, it looked as if it could be lost between the cheeks of his arse if he made the wrong move.

The man looked up and nodded a neutral greeting before returning to the screen of his laptop. Bellying-up to the bar, Mowgley surveyed the row of fonts and pumps and ordered a pint of Carlsberg. The barmaid was as slim and petite and pretty as the man with the laptop was oversized and unappetising. Idly wondering if the two were partners in both senses of the word, he pushed the inevitable image from his mind and assumed that, if a pair, she would of necessity, be the one on top. Unless, that is, he had some sort of parachute-like harness attached to the ceiling. If they were indeed an item, he concluded, it was living proof that opposites do indeed attract.

'Might you be the landlady?' he asked, remembering to pay with his order in the British way as she put the glass on the counter.

'I might be,' she replied with what could be described as an arch smile, 'it depends on who you are and what you want.'

'My name's Jack.' He looked around the empty bar. 'I was supposed to be meeting a lady called Pat Futcher in here. She said she was a regular.'

'Ah.' The archness of the smile increased. 'She's bound to be late. Patsy's always letting things get on top of her and ending up all behind.'

'Not a problem,' he said. 'I'll just have a look at the paper till she arrives.'

Selecting a packet of roasted peanuts from the row of snack-bearing cards hanging on the back bar, he took a seat at a table in the corner. On the ancient stone wall above his head was a plastic fish of the sort which flapped its head and tail and sung a pop song at intervals. Mercifully, someone had forgotten to switch it on, or the batteries had run out.

He took the top off his beer, opened the packet of peanuts and thought how it had been a funny sort of day.

When Degas had arrived at his apartment, he had given details of how the Red Herring painter had been pulled out of the Seine the day before. So far, and in a faint echo of the circumstances in which Piers De'Ath had been found, there was no immediate evidence as to whether the death was accidental or deliberate.

Dufour's lungs had been filled with the soupy waters of the Seine, which meant he had been breathing when he fell or was pushed in. There were no obvious signs of injury to suggest he might have been unconscious when he entered the water. But high levels of alcohol and ketamine had been found in his blood. As Mowgley would know, ketamines were a class of drug used by the medical and veterinary professions as an anaesthetic. Known as 'Special K', 'kitkat', 'horse trank' or simply 'k', the substance was used by people seeking a detachment from reality. It could be swallowed, snorted, injected or smoked along with cannabis or tobacco. If swallowed it could take effect in less than thirty minutes and those effects last for an hour. As with LSD, the effect on the taker's co-ordination and senses could last much longer. Also like LSD, the effects range from slurred speech and blurred vision, a feeling of being detached from the body, visual and auditory hallucinations, and anxiety and panic. It was not known if Gerard Dufour was a regular user of ketamine or other mind-altering substances, excluding strong drink.

Nothing had been found on the body except a credit card, a small amount of money, a notepad and pencil. He had been seen in a number of bars along the Left Bank on the night before his body was spotted by the pilot of a *bateau mouche* pleasure boat on its way to pick up customers for a cruise along the river.

Dufour's studio and home — a suite of rooms in a large house in the heart of the so-called Latin Quarter — were being examined, and no suicide note or any other significant evidence of his state of mind at the time had been found. According to the regular bar users and local artistic community, Dufour had not enjoyed the intense attention generated by his appearance on the last edition of *Art, Life & De'Ath* and the subsequent discovery of the host's body with the *Hareng Rouge* painting on his chest. He had been questioned about his disappearance from the château, but had a solid alibi. He had filled his car at a rest stop on the A13 at about the same time as De'Ath had expired, and Paris had seen his image on a CCTV camera overlooking the petrol pumps. According to the pathologist's examination, Dufour had not eaten for at least twelve hours before his plunge into the Seine.

The death was, Degas conceded, in some ways similar to that of De'Ath, though there were no likely suspects if it had been murder. Dufour had few acquaintances and fewer friends, but no known enemies and seemed well-liked within the community of painters and writers and other creatives in which he moved. While continuing their investigations, the Paris police had pointed out that a drunk with an armful of drugs falling into the Seine was not a particularly unusual event.

After the meeting, Mowgley had walked the short distance to his office to learn that Frank Begg had been trying to get hold of him. When they spoke, the news was good.

A clearly relieved Begg senior reported that his son had

called the day before to say he was okay. He told his father he had not phoned for some weeks as he had had a lot on his mind. Now, he had a job working on a deep-sea fishing boat, and was enjoying being away from people and the distractions of drink and drugs. As his father had said, his son sounded relaxed and happy and positive. As Mowgley had thought but not said, those reactions were quite often the symptoms of someone who had recently taken a snort of cocaine or other Class 'A' drug with a similar effect.

Frank Begg had thanked Mowgley for his help and concern, and said he would gladly settle the bill for his time and trouble. Mowgley had told him how glad he was to hear the good news, and that there would be no charge except for a pint or two next time his erstwhile client was in Cherbourg. He had also asked Mimi not to mention the call to her boss.

~

A pint later and Mowgley was watching the monstrous landlord playing pool with an interesting technique.

Obviously unable to bend from the waist or get to within a yard of the table, he was using an extended snooker cue and rest to take his shots. Surprisingly, he managed the handicap very well, and was two games and drinks up when the old shop bell above the door announced a new arrival.

It was not Patsy Futcher or, he had a small bet with himself, any other British expat. Together with the unbroken shotgun, camouflage jacket and trousers tucked into heavy boots, the forage cap, and even the way the cigarette was hanging from the corner of his mouth, all the indicators were that the visitor could only be French.

For a nation which registered so many accidental deaths by shooting while hunting each year, it had always wryly amused Mowgley how many of the fraternity liked to wear clothing which helped them blend into rather than stand out from their surroundings.

The swagger as the man crossed to the bar was another indicator of nationality. Home was the hunter and with evidence of his proficiency. Rather than a dead rabbit, the man pulled a plastic bag of wild mushrooms from his rucksack and exchanged them for a glass of red wine. Then, and with a clearly disapproving look at Mowgley and his pint of lager and packet of prawn cocktail crisps, he sauntered over to the corner of the bar area devoted to British home comforts.

Lines of paperback novels and DVDs of popular television programmes and films sat on the top shelves. Elsewhere were a range of grocery items not to be found in the average French supermarket. Tins of British baked beans (with a thicker and sweeter sauce than the insipid French version) and loaves of cottony white sliced bread jostled for space alongside vacuum-packs of back and streaky bacon and Cheddar cheese.

Though he was clearly a regular, the French *chasseur* assumed an expression of irritated incredulity that anyone should have such an uneducated and even barbaric palate to want to buy and eat English cheese when they had a French variety for every day of the year. With a disbelieving shake of his head, he picked up a tin of Fray Bentos corned beef and examined it closely. After another shake of his head, he put the tin down in the manner of Mimi delivering Mowgley's instant coffee and turned back to the bar. As he passed, Mowgley smiled broadly in response to the incoming sneer, and reminded him to be sure to check that he'd removed all the shotgun pellets from the mushrooms.

The man looked at him as if thinking about taking umbrage, but decided against it and carried on. Feeling pleased with himself that the hunter had understood his quip, Mowgley rose to order another pint and to pay for and take a tin of corned beef.

~

Looking thoughtfully at the pile of what looked like mixed chicken and cow shit, Mowgley thought how it had indeed been a funny day, and had the makings of getting funnier.

He had enjoyed his brief and brisk exchange with the hunter, and liked Patsy Futcher, who had arrived preceded by an impressive and highly-strung frontage.

Her frilly white blouse with a deeply scooped neckline was struggling to contain its burden, and clearly losing the battle. In Portsmouth, the narrow strip of lemon-coloured cloth around her hips would have been dubbed as a pussy pelmet. An attempt to disguise the shortness of her legs and thickness of her ankles came in the shape of a towering pair of scarlet red high heels with bows on the back and thicker soles than a book by Marcel Proust. Parrots could have taken their ease comfortably on the hooped earrings and Ms. Futcher wore the first non-ironic beehive hairstyle that Mowgley had seen in decades.

But regardless of her dress code, Mowgley liked her. She was open and honest, clearly knew and approved of who she was, and probably unsinkable.

It had taken four vodka and oranges for Mowgley to determine that the goat or baby-sacrificing British expat devil-worshipping cult of popular local rumour did not exist. The clandestine society was no more than a group of women and men who liked to meet every week and exchange partners. It was a bit like, said Patsy Futcher, Saturday Swap Shop for grown-ups. After the fifth vodka, she told Mowgley that, though she had shagged him a couple times, she was not a fan of Piers De'Ath and did not know anyone in their swinging circle who was. But she could think of nobody who would dislike him enough to wish him dead. He would turn up now and then at their gatherings and enthusiastically join in, but never with his new wife, who he thought was unaware of the group.

In this he was wrong, Ms. Futcher had said. De'Ath's wife probably knew about the swingers' club, because she was having it off with one of the members.

It was, Mowgley concluded, a thin but feasible motive for a murder if Mrs. De'Ath was after freedom and a healthy share of De'Ath's assets. He would pass that information onto Degas at their next meeting.

They had parted after he had promised to attend one of the gatherings and at least consider buying one of the king-sized water beds she sold as a side-line. She had also offered for him to road-test one before buying, and gave him her number and website address. It was, unsurprisingly, www.pussypatsy.com.

When he had made his goodbyes and vague promises, Patsy had moved over to the pool table to show the landlord how it was possible to bend over a table despite massive encumbrances.

~

Dusk was falling as Mowgley looked at the odiferous heap. Almost certainly, the pile of manure had been left in the tiny garden behind his cottage by his neighbour. Madame was clearly responding to his use of the garden behind her cottage, which in the French way belonged to him. He thought about moving the muck, but it was her property and on her land. This being rural France, any such action would probably be grounds for calling in the hulking and unfriendly local policeman, who, Mowgley knew, was also her grandson.

It was as he decided to think about it in the morning and turned away that the figure came at him out of the dark.

The man was wearing a Covid mask, but his shaven

head with the white scar, size and manner of movement made him clearly recognisable from the occasion when they had previously met.

This time Mowgley had no rolled-up newspaper to hand, and there was another complication. In Terenc Malija's outstretched hand was a large knife with a serrated edge. It was of the type favoured by fishermen to gut their catch. Now it seemed Malija wanted to do the same to him.

With no other ideas, Mowgley feinted with his left forearm and swung with his right fist. It did not arrive on target, as a heavy blow to his head from behind caused him to lose his balance. Then came a searing sensation in his left arm. He shouted in pain and anger and staggered back, slipped in the heap of manure and fell on his back into it. With a grunt of triumph, Malija kicked him in the ribs, straddled his victim and steadied himself for the next blow.

As he changed his grip on the knife to better make a downward stabbing motion, there was a dull thud and Malija screamed as part of his right ear took flight.

A spurt of blood followed the ear as Mowgley rolled over and grabbed Malija's leg. He had no clear plan of action, but the problem was solved when another dull thud resulted in Malija ending up lying alongside him.

Cursing loudly, Mowgley smashed an elbow into the Albanian's face and had the satisfaction of hearing and feeling the pug nose give way. He took the knife, then looked up to thank his saviour. Somehow, he was not surprised to see his neighbour looking down and holding the small but clearly sharp-edged spade she had used to relieve Terenc Malija of his senses and a considerable part of his right ear. It was, he thought before suggesting she call her grandson, probably the same instrument she had used to shift the chicken and cow manure, and with luck it might give the Albanian a nasty case of sepsis.

Billy 'The Brush' Mumford (1949-)

Ex-faker and now celebrity Billy was rumbled in 2009 when a London auction house contacted the police to say they had been offered an unusually large number of paintings purported to be by Maqbool Fida Husain, the 'Indian Picasso.' Raiding Mumford's West Sussex home, police found hundreds of paintings, together with gallery stamps, ink pads and Victorian paper, used to provide false provenances. A gang of co-conspirators, the court heard, placed the works on e-bay and received a 20 percent cut. Some were sold on several times for prices of up to £30,000.

Billy was jailed for two years, and his wife Daphne — who admitted money laundering — received a suspended one-year sentence.

Now a reformed character, Billy the Brush gives talks on his life and crimes, makes guest appearances at galleries, sells paintings under his own name and has his own website.

13

'We must stop meeting like this.'

It was, in fact, a couple of years since Mowgley had first found himself in a Cherbourg hospital with Catherine McCarthy at his bedside.

'I have to say,' she continued, 'it comes to something when you need a 78-year-old widow with a garden spade to get you out of trouble.'

She took a grape from the bunch in the basket of fruit she and Colonel Degas had arrived with, popped it into her mouth, then continued: 'I guess you'll tread more carefully on her territory in future. And do you reckon the rumour's true that she only spanked your Albanian dance partner because she thought it was you on her patch after dark?'

Mowgley shrugged and shook his head, then winced as the movements caused the stitches to tug. Using his free hand, he explored the monk's tonsure on top of his head where Madame had mistakenly hit him when trying to deliver the first blow to his opponent. Or, as McCarthy had suggested, perhaps not so mistakenly. Whatever, he had to admit he was getting too old for that sort of rough and tumble, especially when his opponent was thirty years younger and clearly much fitter. It was lucky for him that an elderly French countrywoman with a sharp spade and strong sense of resentment at any violation of her property had witnessed the disturbance. He also thought about the indignity of lying spread-eagled in the muck as doors and windows around the hamlet opened and lights came on in response to the approach of Madame Ribet's grandson in a squad car. It was followed closely by an ambulance; both competing to drive most dangerously and make the most noise with their tyres and sirens.

'So what do the doctors say?' asked Degas as he fiddled with the foil around the neck of the bottle of Château Ramage la Batisse.

Mowgley looked down at the sling holding his left arm so high that the fingers grazed his neck when he shifted position. 'No problem. Nice clean cut to the forearm and not infected by any fish innards or chicken shit. Same with the cut to the head. They want to keep an eye on me tonight and then I'm out in the morning. And what about my mate Mr. Malija?'

'He is not so well.' Degas said. 'The missing part of his ear was stitched back on, but there is a risk of infection or rejection as it fell in and had to be removed from the… fertilizer. There was also an amount of damage to his head from the second blow.' He smiled. 'Madame obviously did better work on him than you.'

'Thanks for that' Mowgley grimaced, then asked: 'Is my mate Tel here? I'd like to go along with some grapes or at least send him a get-well card?'

Degas smiled again. 'I am sure you would. He is under guard and will be charged with attempted murder when he is awake and aware of his surroundings.'

'And what then?' asked McCarthy.

'He will be sentenced and then deported if Monsieur Darmanin has his way.'

'Who he?' asked Mowgley.

'Gérald Darmanin is the Interior Minister and has announced a zero-tolerance approach to what he called foreign delinquents.'

'And I guess Mr. Malija comes under that heading?'

Degas pulled the foil off the bottle and nodded. 'He is not a good person, to say the least. He is well known to the authorities in his home country and has served several prison sentences since the age of eighteen. Mostly for crimes involving violence.'

'But what if they don't want him back? In the UK there's loads of illegal immigrants from Albania that we can't send back.'

Degas put a hand to his mouth as if to hide a slight smile. 'I had heard that was the case. Since the United Kingdom left the European Union to, as they said, have more control over their borders, it does seem to have gone the opposite way. We will be able to send M. Malija back because he has been in the country illegally. I think it fair to say most French people only believe in Liberty, Fraternity and Equality should be applied to those who come to this country with good intentions.'

'And what of his mates?' asked Catherine McCarthy. 'What if they want to finish the job on Jack?'

Degas shook his head. 'I think that unlikely. The attack was personal, and our information is that the rest of the crew were getting tired of Malija. In fact, if he had been successful in his attack on Jack, he would probably have been disappeared. Whatever criminal activity the owner of the *Zoete Dromen* may be involved with, he will not want to attract our attention.' He saw the look on McCarthy's face and quickly said. 'But of course we have an officer here all night, and there will be…arrangements in the future.'

'Mowgley shifted himself to a more upright position and reached for one of the glasses on the bedside table. 'So I'm free to get on with the Death case?'

Degas nodded. 'Of course. When you are better.'

'I'll be better by the morning,' said Mowgley, 'and ain't it about time you opened that?'

McCarthy looked at the bottle and then the door. 'Do you think it's permitted to drink in the wards?'

Degas smiled as he reached for the corkscrew in his pocket. 'I should think it would be treated as medicine. Everyone knows that red wine is good for the health, and especially for replacing lost blood. If it were an inferior, foreign wine, that of course would be a different matter.'

~

The wine bottle was empty, his visitors departed and Mowgley was gasping for a cigarette with the frantic longing known only to a slave to nicotine confined to a strictly non-smoking environment. Just not being able to smoke made for desperation.

Before following her fiancé out of the room, Catherine McCarthy had presented Mowgley with a packet of Gauloises Brunes and a small transistor radio, to, as she said, keep him company through the night.

Given the choice of English language programmes on the radio and the ban on smoking, he doubted they would be much company. Earlier, he'd found BBC Radio Four and tried listening to a debate about the arrival of the latest new prime minister. One of the guests was a seemingly permanently angry young black woman, and when the presenter had pointed out it was the most diverse cabinet ever, with no white males in the most senior positions, she responded that it was the wrong sort of diversity. And anyway just a token display in a world ruled by pale and stale men. As he fitted into both categories, Mowgley had thought, it was another good reason for not living in today's disunited kingdom.

He had thought about and tried smoking under the bedclothes like Sid James in the *Carry On Doctor* film, but had nearly choked. Getting his breath back, he had slipped out of the room and ward in search of a hideaway where he could look at the stars and savour the heady mix of jasmine-scented night air and comforting nicotine.

~

Boarding the train and after the struggle to decide whether he would rather see where he was going or where he had been, Mowgley sat facing the future.

He spent the three hours and twenty-one-minute journey from Cherbourg to Paris St Lazare enjoying the rolling green landscape and trying his hand at deciphering a discarded copy of the regional newspaper, *Ouest France*. He also attempted the crossword, and was pleased to fill in most of the blank spaces. On the downside, he would never know if he had got the answers right, and had chosen the children-under-eight version.

A favoured place and painted several times by Claude Monet, the Gare St Lazare was now free of the all-enveloping clouds of steam and smoke, replaced by a swarm of humanity. Outside, the streets were even busier, and Paris was not at all how Mowgley remembered it from his first visit as a spotty teenager on a school exchange trip.

In those far-away days, the city seemed aflame with colour, while he thought of his home streets in a drab post-war monochrome. He had also been hypnotised by the freedom and lack of conformity and suppression of emotions which seemed the norm across the Channel. Most of all, it was the young people of Paris he envied and admired. In Britain, most working-class boys still wore short-back-and-sides haircuts and were uniformly clad in sensible shoes, flannels and tweedy jackets just like their fathers. Here, boys of no more than his age had Perry Como haircuts, stay-prest trousers and cool sweaters. They also smoked in public, and even more enviably, buzzed around on mopeds, with provocatively open-legged girls on the back.

The corrugated-iron-roofed delivery vans, the policemen with their kepi hats and mini-capes had long gone, but Paris was still very different from London, and he liked the difference. But like circuses, both were pleasant to visit, but he would not want to live in either.

~

In perhaps the same way Bob Bailey had chosen his business premises to be convenient to Tate Modern, Petra De'Ath had set up shop as close to the Louvre as was feasible when considering availability and cost.

Almost but not quite overlooking the river and just round the corner from the *Quai du Louvre*, the gallery made no bones about its lofty claims and intents.

Beaux-Arts du Monde was big on plate glass and chrome, with a very minimalist approach to window dressing. Apparently suspended in mid-air by no more than its own self-importance was a painting Mowgley had seen very recently. It was the Vermeer with the added-on tongue. Alongside it and also suspended by almost invisible wire was a pretentiously small and plain card announcing that other works of the renowned artist Até were on display inside for a limited season. Ms. De'Ath was obviously not too worried about cashing in on the financial benefits the publicity surrounding the death of her father had brought about.

Beyond the glass doors, the minimalist theme continued. Walls, ceilings and even floors were white.

Chrome spotlights picked out the paintings, all of which, without the embellishments, were familiar works of art across the ages.

Rembrandt's *Night Watch* included a Stormtrooper from *Star Wars* with his E-11 laser blaster pointing out of the picture. Van Gogh's *Starry Night* had a space shuttle crossing the firmament and leaving a glittering trail, and Leonardo's *Salvator Mundi* had a ribbon tied in a bow around the upraised fingers. A line of Andy Warhol soup cans had been joined by a tin of spaghetti hoops, with a heaving mass of worms emerging from the open top.

He then became aware of a tall figure standing behind a glass desk at the far end of the gallery, apparently trying to force her tongue down the throat of a petite, dark-haired woman in a black two-piece business suit.

Like father like daughter, he thought, clearing his throat politely like a butler happening upon a bit of hanky-panky in the withdrawing room.

The painter to be known as Até eventually released her hold and straightened up, regarding Mowgley with the mocking, humourless smile he recognised from the balcony at the Château du Sourville. Looking at her looking at him, it seemed that the tableau may have been arranged for his benefit.

'Have you come to the right place?' she asked.

'I hope so,' said Mowgley. 'Why?'

'You don't look like an art-lover. Or any sort of lover, come to that.' Her accent, Mowgley thought, was English, overlayed with shades and refinements from elsewhere.

'I've got hidden talents,' he said shortly, turning his attention to the other woman. 'Jack Mowgley. Sorry I'm late.'

Petra De'Ath straightened the collar of her white blouse and nodded. 'Yes. I'm sorry, I had completely forgotten you were coming.'

As she motioned towards the spindly chair in front of

the desk, Até narrowed her eyes theatrically: 'Now I remember you. Are you some sort of cop? I saw you at Piers' place. You were with a rather toothsome blonde with big tits. Are you fucking her?' She was obviously given to asking questions without waiting for them to be answered. Perhaps, he thought, that was because she was not interested in the answers, or already knew them.

Mowgley gave her his full-on Paddington Bear stare: 'The answer is 'no' on both counts, and you're the second person to ask me that this week.'

'What, if you're a *flic*?'

'No, the other one. I used to be a cop and the lady was a colleague. Nowadays I'm with an investigation agency in Cherbourg, and I've been asked to work with the police on...' he looked awkwardly at Petra De'Ath, then continued: 'the situation. I know you've talked to the Gendarmerie in Cherbourg about what happened, but I'd like a word with both of you while I'm here.' He gave what he hoped was an ingratiating smile: 'If you can spare me the time?'

The newly-famous painter ran her hand through her apparently carelessly cropped hair, took a cheroot from those lined up in the top pocket of her tweedy jacket, put it between her full lips, came from behind the desk and reached out for Mowgley to light it.

He did, and she kept her face close to his as she inhaled and then blew out the strongly aromatic smoke. 'I charge 500 Euros for an interview, Mr. private dick. As it's about poor Petra's papa, I'll settle for a bistro steak and as much beer and absinthe as I can manage. Deal or no deal?'

'Deal,' said Mowgley, as he wouldn't be spending his own money. 'When?'

'Tonight,' she said. 'Petra has my number. Though if I turn up, you may find it would have been cheaper to pay the standard interview fee.'

With that, she blew a kiss at Petra De'Ath, took a well-worn fedora hat and a Dr Who-length scarf from the spindly chrome hat stand lurking by the door, then exited in a haze of cheroot smoke.

Mowgley watched her through the glass door as she strode manfully down the wide pavement towards the river, and thought he might revise his impression of her. Not so much Mrs. Dalloway at her finest perhaps, but maybe Oscar Wilde at his worst.

~

'Hello mate, how's gay Paree?'

'Gayer in parts than I expected,' said Mowgley.

A sleek and crowded *bateau mouche* chugged by, its passengers drinking in the sights on deck or taking refreshment inside. Nearby, a chrome sculpture of tyrannosaurus kept an eye on the Eiffel Tower, and a pair of young lovers walked by his bench without seeing the beast, the tower or him.

His previous call had been to René Degas, and they had talked about his meeting with Petra De'Ath. She had, Mowgley reported, seemed generally unmoved by the death of her father and not said much more than that she would not be attending his funeral as it was important she kept the gallery open while the exhibition of Até's works was going so well. There was nobody she could trust to look after the exhibition, especially, she hinted, the artist herself.

She had not spoken to her father for three months or more (which Mowgley and Degas knew to be a lie), and said she had no idea of his general mood at the time of his death. She was sorry that his visit had been a waste of time. But, if Até turned up for their meeting, she was sure she would probably have a lot to say about her father and his mood and the events at the château that evening.

In return, Degas had told him that his officers had visited

and spoken to Piers De'Ath's son Charles in London, and he had been apparently as unmoved as his sister at their father's demise. Degas said dryly that they both would doubtless be more interested in the contents of the will and how much of De'Ath's assets would be destined to fall into the hands of his new wife.

'So what do you reckon to Ms. Até?' asked Bailey.

'Not sure yet, but I hope to find out more this evening.'

'How so?'

'We've got a date. She's going to show me the sights on the Left Bank and how to drink absinthe.'

'Blimey, good luck. From what little I know of her, I always thought she batted for the other side and wasn't too keen on blokes.'

Mowgley waved at another pleasure boat chugging by. 'I don't think she likes anyone except herself. What more do you know about her apart from being gay?'

'Nothing much, she's pretty new to the scene and the first I knew of her were snippets in the art world magazines and from word-of-mouth. From what I've seen of her work, she'd have done better as a forger than messing around with her add-ons. I reckon she got the idea from Duchamp's Mona Lisa with a beard, but better not mention that to her if she's as touchy as I hear.'

'I was going to ask about that. Not that I'd know, but her copying skills look very good for my money.'

'Yeah, they are. If it's all her own work she looks like she could be up there with Billy The Brush and Dave Henty.'

'Who?'

'Sorry. They're a couple of celebs in the world of painting fakery. They're the tops and reckoned to have knocked out at least a thousand 'copies' of famous or 'unknown' works in the style of some very pricey painters.'

'Do you mean forgeries?'

'Good point. The boys say they're just copies, or, as I say, "in the style of" tributes. If people want to buy them and claim they're originals, that's up to them.'

'So Até is that good?'

'I reckon. Before she came to sudden fame with the death of De'Ath, she might have done very well at the same game. Or perhaps she did. Now she can make a lot more by signing her copies as her own work.'

'So "original" copies of famous paintings are worth more than prints?'

Bailey grunted his amusement into the phone. 'A lot more. There's a village in China that knocks out tens of thousands of Van Goghs a year and sells them all over the world. They've a job keeping up with orders. The most popular are *Starry Night* and *Café Terrace*. The going rate on stretched canvas — that's without a proper frame — is around three hundred dollars.'

Mowgley licked his lips, tried to whistle and failed. 'So why would anyone pay that much for a copy?'

'Search me mate. I just find it a tad ironic that some poor peasant gets paid peanuts for making a spot-on replica of a masterpiece that the painter couldn't sell but is now worth hundreds of millions.'

'Quite. That is crazy, when you think about it.'

'Absolutely. Welcome to the wonderfully wacky world of Art.'

'I'm beginning to see that now.' Mowgley looked at his watch. 'Thanks for that, mate. I'll give you a call tomorrow morning.'

'Cheers. But if you're going to be quaffing the Green Fairy with Até, you'd better make that the afternoon.'

Making a Spectacle of Themselves

Visiting the San Francisco Museum of Modern Art, teenagers Kevin Nguyen and TJ Khayatan were so unimpressed with what was on show they decided to create their own piece of art. They left a pair of spectacles on the floor in an empty space, and the 'work' became a much-praised item until the couple revealed the hoax on Twitter.

14

'So you went to the Louvre and didn't bother to pay homage to the Mona Lisa? How refreshingly unorthodox of you.'

'There was a bit of a queue,' said Mowgley, 'so I just looked at the pictures outside.'

'And do you fancy her? Is she your type?'

'Not so much since someone told me that the reason she's smiling with her mouth shut is because she had no front teeth.'

'But you did drop in at the Musée d'Orsay?'

'I did.'

'See anything you liked?'

'I went to see an exhibition of Edvard Munch but it had closed.'

'Pity. I like his stuff and you might have learned something from it.'

Até emptied her glass and took a deep draw on her cheroot. 'So what did you think of the place?'

'Lots of people looking at lots of statues and pictures and trying to look as if they knew all about them. I hired one of those recorded guides but couldn't make it work, and the coffee was crap and really expensive.'

She gave a half-mocking smile of sympathy. 'Oh dear. And what about the permanent Impressionist exhibition? Not impressed?'

'To be honest, no.'

'Why not. Any particular reasons?'

He shrugged. 'I know what it's going to sound like, but I really couldn't see what the fuss was about. I liked the odd one because of the colours or...I don't know, just something appealed. But I reckon I could do as well as most of them if I put the time in. Not a lot of composition or perspective and just seemed they'd slapped the paint on and slapped each other's backs about their work.'

Another smile. 'Quite the little critic, aren't we? And all since you've been "investigating" the death of Mr. De'Ath.'

'Not really. I can see what all the fuss is about with Rembrandt or the bloke who did all the paintings in Venice. But to me it seems most of the Impressionists were just a load of blokes with rich parents and having fun drinking a lot and shagging around in Paris and pretending to be passionate and see things that weren't there in each other's work. If they were so clever, how come it's so easy to fake them?'

She raised an eyebrow. 'Well I suppose that's one way of looking at it. Even if it's the wrong way. I can't be bothered to educate you, although some of what you say is right. Anyway, ignorance can be bliss, and I like a man who knows what he likes. Sometimes.'

They were sitting in *Le Café Dôme*, the oldest and probably most famous bar in Montparnasse. As Até had told him, the celebrated arses which had occupied seat on the premises included painters of the stature of Picasso, Gauguin and Chagall. Writers who had taken and given offence here included Henry Miller, Ernest Hemmingway and Ezra Pound. The Dôme had also been a favourite haunt of patrons of the arts like Leo and Gertrude Stein, and even socialising revolutionaries like Lenin and Trotsky. Somehow, it pleased Mowgley that he was getting pissed in the company of such auspicious ghosts.

As they drank and smoked, he had also learned that the name of this area of Paris came from Mount Parnassus, the Ancient Greek home of the Muses, and was an arty nickname awarded by poetry students and other literary types who adopted the left bank in the 17th-century.

Unsurprisingly after what he had heard about and expected of her, Até had made her entrance no more than half an hour late. Knowing it could be a demanding evening, he had paced himself before her arrival, but they had quickly got through a dozen beers and had several encounters with the Green Fairy. Até had told him that a far stronger version of the original absinthe was the staple diet of a raft of enthusiasts from Oscar Wilde to Vincent Van Gough and Lord Byron.

So far, Mowgley had been pleasantly surprised to see that the drink made his companion bearable, and even amusing. Or, he reflected, that could equally be the effect of the Green Fairy on him.

Até was clearly a restless soul, and from the Dôme they moved on to other colourful and noisy bars, mostly well off the tourist trail. Their conversation had ranged from a potted history of the Left Bank to Até's scathing view of the art world. Like Bob Bailey, she was of the opinion that it was all one big scam, which she found disgusting and immoral. It was not the illegality, which would be found in any activity which involved big money, she accepted, but the hypocrisy and relegation of works of art to the numbers of dollars they were generally agreed to be worth.

If that was what she thought, he'd asked, why had she got involved… and learned to copy other people's works so well?

'Fair point,' she had laughed, snapping her fingers to be fed yet another Caporal now that her supply of cheroots had been exhausted. 'I went to art college because I liked the idea of a bohemian lifestyle rather than art for art's sake, if you know what I mean. I was also seriously pissed off that I'd missed out on the Sixties, when everything was happening. The Nineties were shit for originality and invention and any sense of adventure. So I did the tours of Marrakech and then on to India in the footsteps of John and Paul and co, took a load of dope and fucked myself silly. On the way I got married and unmarried a couple of times. Then I found out how easy it was to copy stuff.'

Mowgley lit a cigarette and passed it across the table. 'You mean famous and expensive stuff?'

She looked into her empty glass and smiled. 'Of course I did Picasso, Lowry, Dali—especially Dali 'cos he was so fucking easy. But I worked fucking hard on the Old Masters.'

Mowgley waved at a scurrying waiter, who nearly tripped over his long white apron as he came to an emergency stop. He ordered, then asked: 'So was it to prove you could get away with it? Or the money, or a bit of both?'

'That and something more. When it got serious, it was to take the piss out of all the stupid rich people who would pay hundreds of thousands of pounds to put one of my paintings on the wall.'

'And how did it work? Getting the pictures on the stupid people's walls?'

She looked through the smoke of her cigarette at him and gave a crooked smile.

'What's this, you get me pissed and I tell you everything and you grass me up and earn a lot of money? Not that I give a flying fart.'

He held a mildly protesting hand up. 'Nope. Just interested. Believe it or not, I'm not wearing a wire, and all you have to do is deny we ever had this conversation.'

She looked at him for a while, then said: 'Dunno why, but I believe you. Anyway, as you say, it's only your word against mine. And anyway,' she looked over his head and gave a secret smile, 'it's all over now and no witnesses are left.'

There was silence as he digested that remark, then said: 'So how did it start, and how serious did it get?'

'I met this… person who knew what I could do and suggested a deal. I'd knock out something that was either missing or in the style of someone collectable, then he'd have someone discover it at a boot sale or in an attic. Then he'd get a bent expert to say it certainly seemed to be kosher, and the art gallery would use weasel words in the catalogue to give it the best chance of making big money. They add a commission of up to a hundred percent on the reserve price and then charge the buyer a big whack. My "agent" would get a large slice as the seller, and he'd give me a percentage of his cut.'

'And when did it stop?'

'When it had to.'

'Someone sussed one of your paintings was a fake?'

'I made sure someone would. That was part of the fun.'

'What?'

'That was the clever part. Towards the end I'd take great care with the paint and canvas and the frame and soaking the nails in acid and water to make everything the right vintage. But I started making little mistakes like using a colour that wasn't in use at the time, or I'd put something in the painting which was only noticeable when it was pointed out.'

'Are you saying you wanted to get caught?'

'Not me, but the galleries and the bull-shitters and my agent. I liked the idea of them all being shown up as greedy bastards who didn't give a fuck about real art.'

Mowgley looked over her shoulder to catch the waiter's eye, then raised a hand. 'Did it work?'

She shrugged. 'Not really. There's always a bit of a fuss and then the circus carries on.'

'But I guess you must have upset a few people?'

Their drinks arrived, and Até added a sugar lump and a little water to hers and swirled the cloudy liquid round with a finger. As she said, she liked to keep up with some traditions. Then she emptied the glass and shuddered. 'Upset people?' She gave a harsh laugh. 'You could say that. I never admitted I was making the mistakes deliberately, and the only person who knew I was the painter was my "agent".'

Alongside the river, a Marcel Marceau lookalike was pretending to be trapped in a glass case. A statue of a knight sneezed and frightened a little boy, and a pavement artist was squatting beside his work and ignoring any comments or queries. Mowgley wondered what happened when it rained, and if the chalks were waterproof or would he cover them over and wait for it to stop. He certainly couldn't take his work home with him. A little further along the bank, a young woman with a shaven head was doing speedy caricatures of passers-by at twenty Euros a time. Her overheads could not be much lower and trade was brisk, but she would be earning not a lot more than the minimum wage. How weird a world, he thought, where a scribble by Picasso would be worth many times more than this woman would make in a lifetime of demonstrating her talent.

He looked back to where Até was taking a cigarette from the packet on the table. 'So', he asked, 'why the change from fakery to being a known artist? Necessity?'

'That—and I got bored, I thought of doing "honest fakes" with a little bit extra in them to show I wasn't trying to do forgeries. It started with me doing a commission for a rich and very vain arsehole who wanted himself to appear in a famous painting. I knocked out a copy of Manet's *Un Bar aux Folies Bergere* and added him to the mirror behind the barmaid. He loved it and then all his mates wanted one. It just took off from there and I got to like the idea of adding modern stuff to classic paintings.'

He nodded. 'It does seem it's all about the idea of something different rather than the quality of the work.'

'True. The melting watches and pickled sharks syndrome. But it's not as easy as that, and your idea's got to catch on. You need help, lots of luck, and lots of publicity.'

'Like the news of the sudden death in mysterious circumstance of your new patron?'

She looked at him thoughtfully for a moment, then shrugged and reached out for his glass of absinthe. 'I suppose so. Lucky for me, but not so lucky for him.'

~

Time had flown, but he was not sure how far it had flown and how far they had come or exactly where they were. The Green Fairy had waved her wand, and for the moment he was glad she had. He was at that stage when he believed his mind and brain were sharper and working much better than when he was sober. But he was enough of a veteran to know that it was a false if common belief.

The journey, he recalled, had been eventful in terms of absinthe-driven discussions on art, sex, Life and other aspects of the world and its ways, and now the odd couple had arrived in a basement which held some sort of club. The décor, customers and music made it very clear as they squeezed their way in that it was a jazz club.

Though close to hand, the stage was hard to see through the fume from cigarettes, cigars and more than the odd joint. Obviously, nobody had informed the management about the stringent non-smoking rules, and it was a pure pleasure to be sitting indoors and breathing in lungfuls worth of smoke even before you lit up.

Under a string of red lights, a five-piece band was making a fair hand of *Pent-up House*, with the Sonny Rollins role played by a big black man wearing an Abraham Lincoln beard and what looked like welding goggles.

It had been a long and hugely enjoyable pub crawl, and Mowgley and his companion had, if not drunk themselves sober, come close to it. Somewhere along the way they'd taken on board a plate of *couscous* in mind-numbingly ferocious harissa sauce. Next they had made a stab at eating the contents of a huge bowl of mussels, soaking up the liquid and hopefully the alcohol with lumps of the large loaf.

'Don't worry,' he said, 'I'm not going to ask you to dance.' He had seen that she was watching his shoulders moving a beat or more out of time with the music.

'Thank fuck for that, Mr. Mowgley,' she said. 'By the way, is it Mowgli as in *Jungle Book?*'

'No, it's Mowgley as in cutting the grass happily — but you can call me what you like if you keep the secrets coming.'

'Fire away, Jack The Lad,' she said, giving him a salute which she managed to make especially mocking. He noticed that she did it in the British way, palm outwards and hand almost vertical alongside the cheek.

'Okay,' he said, 'but first I have to caution you that anything you say will not be written down nor used in evidence in a court of law, as I haven't got a pen and won't remember it by the morning anyway.'

'Did you ever say that properly to people you were arresting when you were a real copper?'

'No,' he said in an affected manner, 'I had people to do that for me.'

'Ah,' she said, 'the lovely blonde with the big tits. Are you sure you weren't fucking her? I would.'

'We've been through this before,' he said, 'and the answer's still no. Best way to ruin a professional relationship, I found. So, are you ready?'

'What, for a sneaky shag?'

'Nope. It's Question Time again.' He drew deeply on his Caporal, then said: 'I get everything you said about how you came to be a forger —'

'Copier.'

'Okay, copier. But why the exotic stage name?'

'Seemed like a good idea after I packed up doing the fake stuff.'

'And what was it before then?'

'Sarah.' She said without hesitation, which, perversely, assured Mowgley it was a lie.

'Okay. Pretty name, if it's okay to say so. And your surname?'

'Fuck off.'

He tried for a look of mild surprise. 'Would that be hyphenated?'

'No, one word, followed by "Cunt" if I am not happy with the company'

Mowgley made an imaginary note in his imaginary notepad. 'Okay, so what about your arrangement with Petra?'

She gave a mockingly salacious leer. 'What, who does what to whom, you mean?'

'No. Happy to hear about that, but I meant did the deal with the exhibition of your work come before or after you met her dad?'

She blew out a plume of smoke and sat back in her chair, trying to make smoke rings. 'Before. Petra came to me and said that papa was going to bum me up on one of his shows, and she wanted to 'champion' my work in Paris.'

'And did the others on the show know they were going

to get a kicking?'

She shrugged. 'Dunno. Why, do you think one of them did the deed on Mr. De'Ath?'

'What do you think?'

'That's your job, not mine. What do *you* think?'

'Not a clue so far. What is it?'

He was looking at her clenched fist which she was holding out across the table.'

'Open your hand,' she instructed, and he did as he was told.

The transparent cellophane packet was about twice the size of a postage stamp, and he could see what he reckoned was around an eighth of an ounce of white powder.

'I'm going to powder my nose,' she said, 'and I thought you might like to join me.' She rose a little unsteadily, and rubbed her nose as if she had already ingested some of the cocaine. See you in five. Have fun.'

He tucked the bag into the back pocket of his trousers, looked at his watch and saw that it was just after three o'clock. Whether a.m. or p.m. he neither knew or cared.

'Perhaps I'll try it later. Do you live near here, by the way?'

She wagged a reproving finger at him. 'Again, none of your fucking business, Mr. private dick. Anyway, I was thinking more about your hotel. If of course you're up for it and up to it'

'Ah.' He looked at her and then said awkwardly: 'Thanks for the offer, but I thought that…'

'That I was of the sapphic persuasion? You blokes. Why has it got to be one or the other? Have you never heard of AC/DC?'

He nodded vigorously. 'And I really have got the t-shirt. High Voltage European Tour of '76.'

She smiled and gathered her things, wiped her nose on the back of her hand again and stood up.

'See you back here, Jack the Lad. If you've never done

a dyke, you don't know what you've been missing. And you know what they say about a change being as good as a rest.'

~

She was gone when he woke.

Mowgley stirred, sat up, thought better of it and laid back down, groaned and put a hand to his head, which made it worse. He then tried slapping the stitches to see if the distraction theory would work, but it did not. He didn't generally suffer from hangovers, but had earned this one, and felt truly terrible.

He practiced a little more groaning, and struggled to sit up again. This time he made it. As he reached for the pack of Caporal on the bedside table, it occurred to him that the way he felt might be a combination of the best part of a bottle of absinthe, the *couscous* and a possible bad mussel. Or it might be the unaccustomed gymnastics. Até had proved a demanding partner, and he had done his best to come up to expectations despite the vast quantity of alcohol in his system. She had obviously anticipated the likelihood of brewer's droop, and given him a blue pill before they left the jazz club. Unlike the cocaine wrap, he had taken it.

After tottering to the bathroom to relieve his swollen bladder, trying to vomit and then swallowing several glasses of tap water, he took a shower while he had another cigarette.

He flinched at the sudden sound of jangling chords and throbbing beat that introduced newscasts the world over, and realised the television must be on a timer.

Returning to the room and seeking the sock he had not worn in bed, he glanced at the screen and saw a young woman sitting at a desk. She was made up to almost *geisha* levels, and was wearing what he guessed was a designer jacket and crash helmet made of hair. She adjusted her expression to suit what was obviously going to be grim news, and began to speak.

She was talking much too fast for him to identify more than a few words, but then the picture cut from her deadpan face to a confused scene of rotating lights and flames and sirens. Several fire fighters were directing a jet of water at a building as two policemen stood by their car and looked on.

Although well alight and damaged, the corner building looked familiar.

He gave up the search for the sock and sat on the end of the bed and concentrated as the newscaster described a fire at a well-known left-bank gallery, not far from the Louvre. The blaze, he thought she said, had started in the early hours of the morning, and the cause was as yet unknown. Tragically, she concluded, a body had been found in a storeroom.

As footage of the château at Brix and a photo of Piers De'Ath flashed up, Mowgley became aware of an insistent and somehow authoritative knocking at the door of his room. Pulling on his underpants, he crossed the floor and opened it.

For some reason, he was unsurprised to find his callers were two large and unfriendly-looking policemen.

~

After all the turmoil of the capital, it was good to be back in rural Normandy.

It was still light when he parked on the verge and walked back up the lane to *Le Petit Bijou*, the name a previous and obviously romantically-minded occupant had chosen to impose upon the tiny cottage. Or, he thought, it could have been the invention of a cunning estate agent wishing to take advantage of the strange British predilection for giving sentimentalised, unsuitable and often indecipherable names to their homes. To be fair, he thought, the place certainly qualified for the 'little' appellation, but he was not sure about the jewel bit.

Before reaching for the giant key barely hidden under the Welcome mat presented to him as a housewarming gift by Catherine McCarthy, he decided to check out the back garden. It was unlikely there would be any Eastern European assassins lying in wait, but Madame next door might have dug the chicken and horse shit into the patch of ground that backed onto his house but belonged to her.

It was a surprise to find the mound of fertilizer gone, and more so that his garden furniture, umbrella and bird feeder had taken its place. Another item of interest was the lemonade bottle containing what could be urine from a sick horse or, more likely, home-made Calvados apple brandy. Attached to it was a sheet of note paper containing a message from Madame Ribet.

Inside and with the aid of the electronic translator he kept on the oversized mantlepiece and a call to Catherine McCarthy, he learned that the lady was, in principle, now in agreement with his suggestion that they should exchange their gardens. Naturally, as it was at his request, he would be expected to pay the fee of the local *notaire* which would make it an official, legal and very permanent and binding agreement.

Mowgley returned to his garden-in-waiting, reached for the bottle of *calva* and sat on one of the plastic chairs. As he thought about Madame's sudden change of mind, he unconsciously fingered the stubble forming over the stitches in his head. Perhaps the change of mind had come about because Madame Ribet had felt guilty for attacking him with her spade. Or even felt some form of camaraderie and consequent goodwill because they had been in battle together. The tussle in the manure and accompanying wounds had not been a pleasant experience, but, now he had won his garden back, it had been, on balance, worth it.

David Henty

Said by many to be the best 'copyist' in the world, Henty's imitations of Picasso, Lowry, Van Gogh, Rockwell, Caravaggio, Monet, Landseer. Magritte and a host of other huge names in the world of art have fooled scientists and art critics alike. His career as a master faker began appropriately enough, during a short spell in prison in the 90s for forgery. After selling thousands of fake masterpieces through internet auction sites, Dave was exposed in a Daily Telegraph investigation in 2014. The sites were closed down overnight and he found himself under investigation by the Criminal Tax Bureau.

Now creating masterful copies of great works in his own name, he is also the author of The Art World Underworld, *an expose of murky goings-on in that world, and his brilliant work can be seen at https://www.davidhentyart.co.uk/*

15

It was, he thought, a good day for a funeral.

Not that the departed would care, but for the mourners a cheery day could be taken as a spiteful reminder of how pleasant life could be. Today, the weather gods were in an obliging mood, providing a mournful drizzle, gusting winds and even the distant roll of thunder to accompany proceedings.

After a respectable delay and because of the possibly suspicious nature of the deceased passing, both the death certificate and burial permit had been issued by the Public Prosecutor at the local high court. This did not mean the case was closed for Colonel Degas and his colleagues, but that the dead man could at least be laid to rest.

As the owner of the nearby château, the hilltop churchyard at Brix was a proper setting for the inhumation of Piers De'Ath. Because of the short time he had been the unofficial Lord of the Manor, few local people had turned up to see him off, and media folk outnumbered mourners by a factor of two to one.

Although mostly unknown to the villagers, De'Ath was a big enough name to have drawn camera teams from as far afield as Paris and London. Regional and national newspapers had sent reporters and photographers, and there was even a solitary member of the *paparazzi* lurking by the cemetery gate. He was identifiable by his shifty manner, all-weather clothing and the size of his telephoto lens. He had hoped to secure some sellable close-ups of famous faces from the art world putting on a sad face at the graveside, but in that he had been disappointed. Now he stood dejectedly wiping rain from his lens, clearly regretting that he had made a bad call and wasted his time and train fare from the capital.

Apart from Mowgley, Degas and McCarthy, the only mourners with a current connection to the deceased were the gardener, cook and housekeeper. They looked appropriately downcast at their employer's departure, but that may have been mostly because of the prospect of losing their jobs.

Of De'Ath's three wives, only the second was present. The first Mrs. De'Ath — if that had been his name then — was awaiting her husband somewhere beyond the grave. His current spouse was, according to the housekeeper, too distraught to attend the ceremony. She had presumably also been too distraught to organise the French equivalent of a wake at the château. There would be, said Madame LeClerc with a hint of embarrassment, a limited supply of drinks and *amuse-bouche* at the bar across the square. She had had no hand in creating the snacks, she hastened to add, and they were the responsibility of the owner of the bar.

Pier's De'Ath's second wife was, however, in noticeable attendance, and Mowgley wondered if she was there out of duty, curiosity, or the satisfaction of seeing her former husband buried beneath the rich Norman soil. Or, he supposed, she might have made the journey to have a word with the notary dealing with the disposal of the château and other goods and chattels. As Mowgley had discovered to his cost, no matter what the divorce settlement, ex-wives still had a stake in the disposal of their ex-husband's property.

Mrs. De'Ath the Second was a tall, stringy woman, for whom the description of 'well-preserved' could have been coined. She had either an assumed or natural expression of disdain, and was dressed in an obviously expensive and, Mowgley assumed, stylish outfit in a deliberately, as he also assumed, shining white.

Mowgley had no idea whether the deceased had any beliefs apart from a devotion to making money and upsetting people, but the ceremony in the church was clearly Catholic, so ceremonial and lengthy. In Britain, seventy percent of people had their remains cremated. In France the ratio was the other way round, and the celebrants liked to give value for money. The fact that the current Mrs. De'Ath had opted for burial rather than burning, Mowgley thought, moved her way down the suspect list if her husband had been murdered. As even amateur murderers knew, it was better to get rid of any possible overlooked evidence by cremating the body and scattering the ashes.

After more than an hour of obedient standing and sitting for sermons and prayers and hymns, the handful of mourners were treated to a long poem about the corpse enriching the soil and the eternal nature of nature, read out and presumably composed by the gardener. Finally, and on their way out, the mourners shuffled past to sprinkle holy water on the coffin and its occupant. Although he found the idea of an open casket slightly uncomfortable, Mowgley noted that the occupant looked almost as content as when found on the floor of his wine cellar. Strangely, the inanimation of his waxen face made the carefully positioned wig look somehow more real.

~

Compared to the service, the committal ceremony was brief, almost as if the celebrant felt he had given more than full value inside the church and wanted to get out of the rain. The short, portly and glowingly red-faced minister irritably wiped the water from his spectacles and mopped his brow with one wide sleeve before making the final sign of the cross while the gravediggers lowered the coffin into the grave.

As the closest relative present, the second Mrs. De'Ath was first to be offered a palm-sized shovel with a small mound of earth on it. She hesitated, then took it with a pained expression and threw the earth with such vigour that it hit the top of the box with a loud, dull thud, amplified by the location of the box at the bottom of the natural sounding chamber.

Mowgley, Degas and McCarthy and a handful of other attendees dutifully followed suit. As they made their way across the road to the bar and as if on cue, the rain stopped, the clouds drew apart and the sun came out.

~

'What Ho, Jack, how's your Little Jewel?'

'It's not that small, mate. Oh, I see what you mean. Good, thanks.'

Mowgley turned away from the selection of filled brioche rolls to greet the man who had found him his new home.

Martin Benson was a tall, slim man in his fifties, with a young-old, long, enthusiastic face framed by a shock of dark curls, greying at the edges. He looked slightly ill-at-ease wearing a dark suit and tie, and Mowgley knew he would be much happier in a pair of work overalls as he clambered around the attics of decaying farmhouses with a torch and penknife. A lot of agents, Mowgley knew, saw the properties on their books as items to be disposed of to whoever could be persuaded to buy them; Martin Benson loved old houses, and tried to match those he was selling with the buyers he thought would be most happy with them. Mowgley did not know what it said about Martin's reading of him that he had matched him with an ancient and decaying if characterful cottage, but he was beginning to think the estate agent had got it right.

A shrill cry indicated that the owner of the bar had spotted them, and Madame Girolet left off harrying her daughter to throw a torrent of Norman patois at Martin, who replied in kind. As he explained after her departure, she was demanding to know why he had not found a buyer of the business at the price she had set. As he should appreciate, she added, for the sake of her physical and mental well-being, it was vital she be freed from the chains of running a bar for a crowd of mentally retarded customers in a village with no soul.

Martin Benson nodded sympathetically, took her hand and responded with a soothing flow of patois. He was, Mowgley reflected, one of the few expatriates he knew or had met who had managed the trick of becoming completely assimilated into the culture of his host country while remaining unmistakably a product of his own. He spoke as perfect Norman French as could be expected of any foreigner, and drove and ate and drank like a native. But he was quintessentially British, or rather, English in thought and manner and, where it applied, deed. As Mowgley had observed, many British expatriates lived a strangely disjointed life, pretending to be in their home country while constantly exasperated by French ways, laws and mores. A very few went native when they arrived, learned and spoke the local patois, and usually pretended to be French when they encountered a Brit at the supermarket. Martin Benson had managed the transition seamlessly, and as such was a mentor and even something of a role model for Mowgley. Except in the case of giving up Scotch eggs and Cheddar cheese.

As they sat and watched the landlady screaming at her slow-moving husband, Martin explained that he had dropped in to the funeral to pay his respects, and was on his way to see the grieving widow and discuss the best and quickest price she could get for the sale of the Château du Sourville.

'Why the rush?' asked Mowgley, reaching for another brioche roll and inspecting its contents.

Martin made a face. He did not find it easy to discuss the affairs of or be disrespectful of anyone, especially a customer, but knew it would go no further. 'Madame tells me she wishes to return to her native country as soon as possible. She says she hates the weather, people, food and everything else about France.'

'So why did she come here?'

'Apparently she and the recently departed met while he was on holiday in Phucket. Whatever his tastes and why ever he was over there, there followed — according to her — a whirlwind romance and he brought the blushing bride back to his then home near Bergerac. By the by, the lady's first name is Aom, which means in Thai, I learn from the superhighway of communication, to hug. Anyway, when she instructed me to put the marital home on the market with all haste, she said he had promised her he would retire, sell up all his stuff and then they could return to Thailand and live happily ever after.'

'Hmmm,' said Mowgley scratching the patch of stubble under his left ear that he always missed, 'can you see a sophisticated and publicity-hungry big-name art critic being happy to disappear to a country where nobody's heard of him?'

Martin Benson raised both hands and shrugged at the

same time: Absolutely not, but people do do strange things for lurve.'

'Hmmm again,' said Mowgley, thinking that the rush to cash in and return to her homeland certainly pushed Madame De'Ath up the list of those with a good reason to get rid of the decidedly queer Mr. Death.

~

'I think she has high hopes.'

Martin Benson had departed for his assignation with the widow, and Mowgley, McCarthy and Degas were sitting on the terrace, watching the sun fall towards the steeple of the church. The gravediggers had done their duty by filling in the hole, and had hung up their spades and were walking across the road to the bar, as a murder of homeward-bound crows darkened the sky directly above.

'Why do you say that?' asked Mowgley. 'Will she not be allowed to sell it?'

'Of course, as a widow she could put the castle up for sale, but I do not think she would be allowed to whisk the money away to Thailand before all the relatives have had their claims settled. And,' he paused significantly, 'there is another obstacle.'

'Which is?' Mowgley held his cigarette packet out and, after a glance at his future wife, Degas reached for it.

'Inheritance laws are complex, especially in unusual circumstances of death. I can tell you that, whatever Madame Aom told your friend the *immobilier*, the property is not in her name. Even if it were, past wives and children would have a claim and entitlement.' He took a cigarette from the packet, then Mowgley's lighter, lit the Caporal, sucked in and then blew a plume of smoke towards the string of fairly lights above the terrace. 'And there are two quite important other factors.'

'And they are?' asked Catherine, reaching for his cigarette.

'The lady was not married to Mr. De'Ath. In fact, there is talk that she is no lady.'

McCarthy frowned. 'Does her level of moral turpitude have any bearing on the case?'

Degas looked puzzled at the unfamiliar expression, then smiled almost apologetically and passed the Caporal over for her turn. 'I did not mean that she was not lady-like, although I suppose I did in one way. We have no proof so far, but there is an allegation that Madame De'Ath is not properly female. She is said to be what I believe is known in Thailand as a lady-boy.'

'Blimey.' said Mowgley.

'Ditto.' said McCarthy. 'Even in these gender-fluidity days, I can see that would complicate his/her entitlement to a share of De'Ath's assets.'

'Exactly,' said Degas. 'It was complicated enough that she is a foreign national and was not married to Mr. De'Ath. If she is indeed a he, it would as you would say, open a pretty can of worms.'

Mowgley looked impressed. 'And what would you say – for a situation that was a can of worms, I mean?'

'We would probably say "*Une affaire dans laquelle it vaut mieux ne pas trop fouiller.*" It means it is a business in which it is best not to examine too closely.'

'Ah,' said Mowgley, 'without being rude, I think ours works a tad better.'

'I would not say that,' protested Degas mildly. 'After all, who would keep a can full of worms — apart from a fisherman? And he would surely know what was in the can before he opened it.'

Catherine McCarthy held up a hand. 'Boys, boys, please. I don't think the issue here is whether Madame De'Ath is being misgendered, nor what it will mean to her chances of getting a lump of the dead man's leavings. For our — sorry, your purposes, surely what matters is the likelihood of her being in the frame for the killing?'

'*Au* contraire.' Mowgley wagged a thick finger. 'I think it could be a key factor. As we agreed earlier, it would be strange if the lady—if she is a lady—bumped off her meal ticket, unless she had good reason to think she would gain from it. If she—or he—had done his/her homework since arriving in France, he/she would know about the problems of getting his/her hands on any of the assets when it was discovered she/he was not married to Death. Or indeed that she was a he, if that is the case.'

McCarthy held up a conceding hand. 'Okay, fair do's'

Mowgley waved airily in acceptance, then turned to Degas. 'So who says the lady is a boy?'

'It came in the form of an e-mail which gave his name and said he used to work the bars in Phuket and was picked up by De'Ath in one of them. The passport giving her sex as female was, our informer said, forged. Easy enough to do in Thailand, he pointed out.'

'And I suppose the source of the email was a dead end?'

'Yes, but we are making enquiries about Madame De'Ath in Phuket now. That is not an easy job.'

'I can imagine. So until you know more, he/she stays as a contender?'

Degas nodded and McCarthy said, 'It's possible of course that, whether she did the deed or not, Madame Aom was planning to do a runner with any portable assets, and had put the château up for sale as a, if you'll excuse the expression, red herring? Who would suspect her of doing a midnight flit with such a valuable asset unsold?'

Degas nodded again, and McCarthy continued: 'So, you're no closer to finding the most likely culprit—if there is one?'

'That is so. Obviously, the death certificate was issued so that the remains could be buried, and I was hoping that Jack's investigations in Paris might have revealed something more about the daughter of De'Ath and the mysterious Até—' He paused, then said: 'Forgive me Jack, but I did not remember to ask you how you were treated by our colleagues in Paris.'

'Surprisingly well. But I think that may be something to do with your call.'

After his arrival at the Saint Chapelle Préfecture, Mowgley had been left in an interview room with a coffee and an ashtray for a little more than an hour. When the investigating officer reappeared, Mowgley had given him Degas's name and rank as a contact and referee. After a cynical response, the officer had left the room, and his manner was markedly changed on his return. Having made his statement, Mowgley was escorted back to his hotel in a patrol car, and had even been wished a friendly *bon voyage* by his driver.

'Yes,' said Degas. 'I talked to Captain Jann, and he was happy to leave you as it were, in my custody.'

Catherine held up one finger. 'Just a small point, but did you think to ask him how the police knew that Jack had been to the gallery – and the name of the hotel he was staying at?'

'I did. I too am a policeman and try to think like one, you know.' Degas gave her a half-smile and made a minimal Gallic shrug. 'It seems there was an anonymous call to the Prefecture at the Quai de Gesvres.'

'Male or female, any accent or probable age?' asked Mowgley.

Another barely perceptible movement of the shoulders. 'The officer who took the call said it was hard to tell. The voice was obviously disguised. He thought it sounded like Pauline the Hen.'

'Sorry pardon?'

'She is a character in Petit Poulet – Chicken Little as you say. The officer said his three-year-old daughter is very fond of the cartoon. The caller spoke in good French, but in an obviously assumed, high pitched voice.'

'Hmm,' said Mowgley, '…well that's something I suppose.

Cherchez le chicken.'

'La chicken', corrected Catherine instinctively. 'So, if Jack is in the clear and apart from Pauline the Hen, is there anyone else under suspicion for the poor woman's death? I'd been thinking that, attractive as Jack is, Até could have been using him as an alibi. She knew he was working with you, René and so his statement would carry more weight.'

'That is so,' Degas said. 'And the time of the explosion was in her favour, as it happened an hour after she met Jack. Of course, it is possible that she could have had an accomplice or set a timer to the device — though no evidence was found.'

'But,' said McCarthy, holding up a finger, 'surely the elephant in this room is if it was her, why would she want to kill the golden goose? Or the golden geese? De'Ath *pere* had put her on the trail to fame and fortune, and Petra was in the midst of a sell-out exhibition she had put on of her works.'

Mowgley pantomimed looking around as if to see if any elephant had in fact materialised, then said: 'At a stretch, you could conclude that she would've known that the explosion and death and massive subsequent publicity would have ratcheted up her fame and made her stuff worth even more.'

McCarthy shook her head. 'But it would've also destroyed all those valuable paintings.'

Mowgley shrugged. 'She could have done for Petra, left her in the storeroom and then swapped her paintings for some worthless ones. The news said all the paintings were completely destroyed, but there would have been traces for forensics to find and identify.'

'Everything you both say could be true,' Degas said, 'but you should also know there has been a claim of responsibility for the explosion.'

'What?'

Degas looked at his watch. 'I got the call in the church,

which is why I left before the service was finished. By now it will be on the news that a group calling itself Sword of Islam say they destroyed the shop.'

'The Sword of Islam? But why?' asked McCarthy.

'They say that a painting which was a reproduction of a work by Hieronymus Bosch had an added representation of The Prophet, waving a copy of the Quoran and giving the one-fingered salute used by the Isis terror group. The death of the owner of the gallery was not intended, said the spokesman, but she must bear the blame for displaying the painting.'

'Wow,' said McCarthy. 'If it is true, that means surely that Até is herself in danger?'

'Yes, which is why she is under protection by the police in Paris.'

'So where does that leave her as far as a suspect goes?' asked Catherine McCarthy.

'We must wait to see if the group exists and if it is likely they carried out the attack,' said Degas, reaching out for Mowgley's cigarette packet, 'and if so it would appear that Até is entirely innocent. What do you think, Jack?'

I think it's time for another drink,' replied Mowgley, pushing himself up from the table.

'The usual for me,' said Catherine. 'And before you go, do you know what your new lady friend's moniker means?'

'Nope, does it matter?'

'Could do. To the Ancient Greeks, the Goddess Até was the personified spirit of delusion, infatuation, rash action and blind folly who led men down the path of ruin'

'Sounds a bit like my ex-missus. How did you find that out?'

McCarthy smiled indulgently. 'Looked it up on the superhighway of information.'

Mowgley retained his blank expression, and she added: 'The world wide web. You know double-u, double-u, double-u dot and all that. You should try it someday when you want to know something.'

'Not when I have someone like you to do the clever stuff. Same again?'

Fake Fridas?

Claims that individual works of art are fakes are not unusual, but questioning the authenticity of an entire collection is probably unique. About 12,000 items connected with famed Mexican painter Frida Kahlo came to light in 2009, and many art historians, dealers and Kahlo experts have come out to denounce some or even all of the collection.

16

As a child, the annual week in a battered caravan uncomfortably close to the edge of a cliff in the westcountry had been a much-anticipated treat. In those days, North Cornwall had been the poorest part of one of the poorest counties in the land.

Now, the distressed caravan and a slice of the cliff had gone, and it was hard to move without bumping into former B&Bs re-invented as 'boutique hotels' and laughably overpriced restaurants masquerading as pubs.

But some of the treasures remained. Using his detecting skills, Mowgley had managed to find and return to what might be the last proper caff in Cornwall. It was full of memories and familiar smells, and even the wallpaper and plastic furniture was still in place.

Unless, of course it was an ironic and expensive 'retro' recreation.

In a window seat with his back to a wall and a fine view

of the car park (which was filled with lorries), Mowgley was mulling over the rivalling attractions of a full English breakfast (with chips or hash browns), a bacon 'n' egg roll, or the healthy alternative of the Vegetarian Breakfast (two fried eggs, fried bread, fried tomatoes, fried mushrooms and beans).

Regretfully, he remembered paying the dyspeptic price for Fat Jack's Full English and settled for another mug of tea and a bacon roll as he considered the recent events that had resulted in him sitting in Pat's Café.

On the down side, he was making the trip at his own expense, as Mimi had told him that the budget for work on the De'Ath case had run out. She'd also said that Yann Cornec wanted a meeting to discuss 'certain matters'. Mowgley had no idea what those matters were, but had an idea it might be to do with his no-fee work on searching for Kai Begg. He was not looking forward to the encounter, but had some questions of his own to ask Cornec. Mostly concerning the terms and conditions of his employment and their ongoing relationship.

The good news from Mimi was that there was a new job waiting his attention. A claims adjuster working for a major insurance company had called regarding a life cover claim from a woman in Bridlington. Her husband was a keen cyclist who had been in France following the route of the 2021 Tour de France. It was, he learned, something many *La Grande Boucle* enthusiasts and fans like to do, to take on the course and compare their achievements with the professionals. She had become concerned when about half way through the 3,414-kilometre circuit, Trevor had suddenly stopped What's Apping his daily reports (with photographs) of distance covered and problems overcome, best times and even vital signs readings from his top-range Fitbit.

Three days later, his mangled machine had been fished out of the Nantes to Brest canal near to the Breton town of Pontivy. There had been no word from or trace of the rider since. Though still officially investigating the case, the local police had issued what was known as a 'vain search' certificate after a year. The Presumption of Death time lapse in France for a missing person was ten years, but the wife had started the process of having her husband declared legally dead in an English court so she could claim the life cover of half a million pounds. Without any evidence that the missing man was dead, it would be a long and involved process. Then, as if on cue, the missing man's body had been discovered in woodland a dozen kilometres from where the bicycle had been found. It was, as Mimi said the insurance man had said, all very 'fishy' for various reasons. They had Mowgley's new friend Mr. Bailey to thank for recommending *Services d'Enquêtes Privés to* the claims adjuster. He had also been told that Mowgley was a former Special Branch officer who had investigated suspicious or unusual deaths in his role at the Portsmouth international ferry port. His own informal enquiries had revealed that, many years before, Mowgley had solved a case involving a woman who had made a large claim after her husband's death and then disappeared off an overnight boat to Cherbourg. The insurance company the claims adjuster represented said they would be pleased to pay Mowgley's employers for his assistance, and Cornec had ordered him to return to Cherbourg at the soonest opportunity.

Mowgley had promised Mimi he would be back after ensuring that his sick Great-Aunt Amelia was on the road to recovery or to the local crematorium.

He held up the bacon roll to study it in appreciation of times gone by. He would indeed go home at the soonest opportunity, but although he was no longer being paid to investigate it, finding out who — if anyone but the man himself — was responsible for Piers De'Ath's death was an itch he must scratch.

~

It was a big name for such a small place.

Chittilhampstead was the sort of born-again hamlet where farm labourers and their families used to shiver in leaky, rat-infested hovels. Now, the rural slums had metamorphosed into every well-off middle-class Londoner's wet dream as a green-wellie-woodburning-stove- let's- pretend- we- live- in- the- countryside- for- the-weekend retreat. Unsurprisingly, the properties had also become priced at London rates.

Some of these getaway villages were big enough to support a store, which would be patronised in both senses of the word as long as it sold the freshest of avocados and coffee that had passed through the intestines of a civet. Mowgley had long thought that fashion slaves would eat shit if it became trendy, and now it had actually happened. With just eleven homes, the scattering of picture-postcard cottages was too small to support any sort of convenience store, but surprisingly, it did have one commercial outlet.

Unfortunately for the sensitivities of part-time villagers, the premises of J. R. Harvey Esq. was not a trendy We-Saw-You-Coming high-end emporium but an in-your-face junk shop of the old school. The patina of dust and dirt of ages prevented any window shopping, but the accumulation of goods on display outside gave a fair idea of what might be on offer within.

An old zinc bath was propped against one side of the entranceway, and on the other rested a deckchair with its stripes faded to one indeterminate shade. Alongside a mangle with no rollers was a zinc watering can with a rusty spout, and a stack of plastic garden chairs which had once been white. On the seat of the top one was a stack of *Punch* magazines that had clearly not seen the inside of a dentist's waiting room for at least a decade.

Helping the sticky door open with a shoulder, Mowgley assumed there was a row going on within, but then saw it was a man sitting at a kitchen table and shouting at the radio by his elbow. It was a phone-in programme, but the man had obviously not bothered to call in. Becoming aware of Mowgley, he stopped in mid-curse, and from his expression Mowgley could see that a visitor was a rare event.

'Mr. Harvey? Bob Bailey sends his regards.'

Without answering, the man put down the oversized mug he'd been threatening the radio with, stood up and brushed past Mowgley. Opening the door, he hawked and spat out a gobbet of phlegm. He stood and looked at his handiwork with relish for a moment, then returned.

They stood eye-to-eye, and Mowgley saw that the man was so emaciated he looked as if his clothes would slip off his skeletal frame with any sudden movement. Or if he turned too quickly his threadbare tartan shirt might stay facing the same way. He was about the same height as Mowgley, and his lank, greasy, dark hair was thin on top, but hung down to his shoulders as if to compensate for the loss. It framed a face that put Mowgley in mind of a horse which had had a long and not always contented life.

'Nice car.' The man nodded his appreciation, then coughed and farted almost simultaneously.

'Thanks,' said Mowgley. 'It's a Citroën DS 21 Cabrio.'

'I know that. Wanna sell it?'

Mowgley smiled. 'Not really, how would I get home?'

'Buy another motor.'

'Thanks but no thanks. I like it.'

'So do I,' said the man, 'that's why I asked if you wanted to sell it.'

'I can see the logic of that.'

The man yawned toothlessly and absent-mindedly farted again. 'Bob Bailey, eh? You filth?'

'No. Used to be.'

'Thought so.' The proprietor looked at the car again. 'Cup of tea?'

'That would do nicely,' said Mowgley, 'How much do you want for it?'

~

The radio had been silenced and they were sitting at the old kitchen table.

The man Mowgley now knew to be Joe Harvey was sucking at what he called a tickler, and his visitor had been impressed to learn the roll-up was filled with strong pipe tobacco. The tea was also strong, and the colour and consistency of a muddy puddle.

Having turned down the offer of a tickler, Mowgley lit a Caporal, then asked Harvey if he had bought the shop from the art dealer who had found the valuable painting.

'No. I bought it from a shirt-lifter who only lasted a couple of years before going skint. Not a lot of call for old stuff dressed up as antiques in an empty village.'

Mowgley refrained from asking how much demand there was for a junk shop in a weekend retreat for London trendies, but instead asked if the owner had known Piers De'Ath, or Charles Arnett as he would have been known as back then.

'Of course. I lived here when he set up shop. I rented the thatched place along the road before the fucking landlord threw me out and did it up to sell to a pair of toffs from Primrose Hill. Mind you,' he said with a gummy smile, 'he had to put a new roof on after the thatch caught fire just when it was all tarted up.'

Mowgley assumed the thatch fire had been arson rather than accident, and wondered if J R Harvey Esq. had bought the shop and put all the junk outside as revenge against the part-time villagers.

'And you were in the village when the Brigadier's daughter brought the Max Ernst in for De'Ath to have a look at?'

Another gummy smile. 'The alleged Max Ernst.'

Mowgley frowned. 'So it was a fake…and the Brigadier and his bringing the painting back from the War was all bullshit?'

Harvey made a 'who knows?' expression. 'Pass. It looked good from what I saw of it, and the Brigadier and his daughter were certainly real.'

'So Arnett as he was then, put the story out, sold the shop and disappeared with the painting?'

'And the Brigadier's daughter. She was a bit loopy I reckon.'

'Do we know what happened to her?'

'From what I heard,' Harvey looked at the burning end of his Caporal and nodded in approval. 'She died.'

~

While the exterior of the shop had been as distressed as the goods on display, the inside was reasonably well-kempt. Beyond the table was a door leading to what could be the living quarters. Shelves on either side of the door were lined with books. Most appeared to be about art. A windowless wall was bare, except for one painting.

It was of a woman with what looked like ankle length white hair or some sort of overlong veil or headdress. She was holding a bunch of flowers and behind her was a goat playing a cello.

'It's Marc Chagall's first wife.' Harvey spoke in a surprisingly affectionate tone. 'He painted loads of her. It was love at first sight.'

'I've heard of him. Did he like to paint her, or was she just a free model?'

Harvey gave him a reproving look. 'He really loved her, but she died.'

He continued to look at the painting, then gave a small shake of his head, reached into a pocket of a coat hanging on the back of his chair and pulled out two very small bottles. They were of the sort found in hotel room minibars, containing measures of gin or Scotch or other spirits. He unscrewed the top of one and poured some into his tea. Without asking, he emptied the bottle into his visitor's mug, then dropped it into a plastic dustbin to one side of the table. There was a clinking noise, and Mowgley noticed the bin was half-filled with empties. He guessed his host must have a contact working in or supplying hotels with minibars, or perhaps an airline. Then, Harvey reached below the table and produced a large glass jar of the sort favoured by home brewers. It was filled with a murky urine-coloured liquid in which small pieces of unidentifiable matter lay suspended.

Putting the jar on the table, Harvey stood and loped over to a sideboard on which stood a variety of glasses. He picked up two of the largest, inspected them, then gave the rims a brisk rub with the end of a shirt sleeve. Returning to his seat, he pulled the rubber bung from the jar and glugged the cloudy liquid into the glasses. It had a strange sweet and sour aroma, Mowgley noted.

Looking up and seeing his expression, Harvey said: 'Don't go doing the one about that horse never working again. This is proper scrumpy and it's supposed to be opaque.'

Mowgley looked doubtful. 'More like impenetrable than opaque, I reckon.'

He picked up his glass, made an effort not to shut his eyes and took a swallow. 'Blimey,' he said after a moment. 'It's good.'

Harvey snorted. 'I should think so. I put more work into cider-making than knocking off a Picasso, and I've done some of my best work after a couple of pints of the golden nectar.'

They silently toasted each other, then Mowgley nodded at the painting: 'So that's one of yours?'

'No, it's one of Marc Chagall's. I just copied it.'

'Ah. So what's with the goat?'

'He painted a lot of goats.'

'He liked them, then?'

Harvey gave him an almost reproving look. 'Not for shagging, as far as I am aware. It was a comment on how badly Jews were treated across Europe.'

'And was he a Jew?'

'He was born Moishe Chagall. Can't blame him for changing his name in them days.'

'No. And what's so special about him?'

Harvey slurped his supercharged tea, then put the mug down and explored a spot on his chin. 'He's reckoned to be the last of the early modernists. And a pioneer in Cubism, Symbolism and Fauvism, if that means anything to you. When Matisse died, Picasso said Chagall was the only painter left who really understood colour. A bit strong, but I know what he meant.'

Mowgley tried to look as if he did too. 'So, is that why you like him?'

'Never thought much about it, but I suppose so. And he's easy to copy...and sell.'

'Is that what you do?'

'What, paint copies? Mostly.'

'And you sell 'em from here — the shop?'

Harvey grunted with amusement. 'No chance. On-line.'

'Do they cost a lot?'

Harvey shrugged. 'A couple of hundred quid a pop.'

Mowgley took a sip of his tea, and guessed the spirit was brandy. He reflected on how it would not be a bad life painting pictures in a quiet westcountry hamlet and knocking them out at £200 a go.

He looked at the painting and wondered how good a copy it was, then asked: 'So why all the crap out front?'

Another grunt. 'What do you think, Mowgley PI?' 'I think I get it. You like to get up the locals' noses...and put 'em off coming in at the same time.' He took another sip of enriched tea. 'Do your punters think the Chagall's are originals, or do they know they're fakes?'

A further grunt. 'If they think they can get an original

Chagall for two hundred quid, they must be fucking soft in the head. And they're not fakes, mater, they're copies. And some're in the style of the artist.'

'What's the difference?'

Harvey snorted, making his face look even more horse-like. 'A fake is pretending to be an original. A copy is just that, a copy. A painting in the style of the artist is what it says it is, and quite legal.'

'As long as the painter doesn't put the original artist's signature on the canvas?'

Harvey gave an irritated frown. 'Nothing wrong with that, as far as I know. It's only when he or she or whoever tries to sell it as an original that it becomes hookey.'

'And the difference between a copy and a fake can be tens of thousands of pounds?'

'The difference is about ten years in nick.' He pointed at the painting of Chagall's wife. 'That one fetched $28 million five years ago.'

'Did he do many? As well as his wife, I mean.'

'Thousands. A lot were burned in the purge of modern art when Hitler was in charge. But there's a lot about still, and God knows how many fakes. Probably even a lot more than the originals.'

'And people will pay two hundred quid for a copy when they could get a print for a lot less?'

Harvey shrugged and reached for his glass. 'It's how it is. It's up to them whether they hang 'em on the wall or keep 'em in the khazi to look at while they're having a dump.'

Mowgley smiled. 'Or try to pass them off as an original?'

Harvey shook his head and spoke slowly as if explaining something to a small child. 'They could try, but they'd have to be very stupid. The frame and the paint would be all wrong, just to start with.'

'Okay, got you. And why do you like doing Chagall so

much?'

Harvey thought about it, then said: 'It's the colours mostly, and he's so easy to copy.'

'But some forgers will paint stuff 'in the style of' a famous artist and pass it off as an unknown work?'

Harvey gave a sloppy smile. The cider was doing its job and his words were slightly slurred. He was clearly a seasoned drinker, but the hardest head could not hold off the effects of home brew cider and of varied spirits. 'Yep.'

'So how many 'copies' have you done, and have you ever sold one as an original?'

A pause, then another leery smile. 'Fucking hundreds to question one. And to question two, mind your own fucking business.'

~

Some hours later, and Mowgley left the premises more than a little unsteadily.

With him he took directions to the Brigadier's former home and a nearby pub which did B&B. He also carried a painting in the unmistakable style of Edgar Degas. He'd made the choice after being taken into the shop's back room, the walls of which were lined with a similar display to that in the chamber of secrets at the Château du Sourville.

In one corner was a brass bedstead and on it a mound of blankets. Nearby was a wooden easel, beneath a battery of lights. Beside the easel was a table, its top barely visible beneath heaps of tubes, jars of brushes and other painting paraphernalia. On the easel was a colourful work in progress which Harvey said was going to be a Jason Pollock. Or a painting that Jason Pollock might have painted.

Hanging from or stacked against the remaining walls was what amounted to a catalogue of the development of modern art, or as Harvey had said with no small trace of bitterness, proof of how simple it was for someone like him to paint pictures which were worth millions because some suited hooligans said they were.

Mowgley sensed that Harvey had invited him into the room not just to sell him a painting, but to show off and have his talent appreciated. He was, Mowgley concluded, one of the many forgers who set out on their illegal career path after their own work went unappreciated or even ridiculed. They wanted to show they could paint as well as the biggest of beasts of the modernist world, and at the same time fool the people who said what was real and what was not in the world of modern art.

After handing over half the asking price, Mowgley had arranged to meet Joe Harvey in the bar of the pub that evening to pay the balance, and promised to give him first refusal on his Citroën if and when he decided to sell it. As the forger had pointed out, if Mowgley chose to get someone to doctor the frame, add Degas' signature and pass it off as an original, he would be able to buy a brand-new mid-range DS9. Not as classy as the old Cabrio, perhaps, but more reliable. If it all went wrong he could expect to spend no more than a couple of years in nick and could claim to be a beginner at the game.

As Mowgley squeezed into the car and started the engine, Harvey appeared at the shop doorway, carrying with difficulty a stained and chipped toilet bowl still attached to an old-fashioned high-rise cistern. Mowgley assumed it was not the working model in the lean-to in the yard. He watched as Harvey dumped it amongst the collection of junk on the forecourt, then reached for the fly-buttons on his paint-stained trousers. Whether or not for Mowgley's benefit he did not know, and did not stay to find out.

Founder Figure

Hilaire-Germain-Edgar Degas is in the not inconsiderable queue for recognition as the 'founder' of the French Impressionism Movement. Perhaps best known for his soft pastel images of women ballet dancers, Degas is believed to have created more than 1500 paintings on that theme alone, and 'new' works — genuine or otherwise — surface from time to time. The sheer number of his works invite fakery, of course.

Degas rejected the 'Impressionist' label and preferred to be known as a 'realist.' He suffered from a retinal problem, which caused him to develop a technique using broader strokes and bolder colours. Reputed to be a cantankerous, misanthropic misogynist, Degas believed that 'the artist should live alone and his private life remain unknown.'

Manet famously remarked that Degas was not capable of loving a woman, and the life-long bachelor died in 1917, childless and alone.

17

Had the pub been owned by a company with a marketing department in tune with modern sensibilities, the sign and even the name would have been changed long ago.

Built around the turn of the 17th-century, *The Labour in Vain* had survived wars both civil and International, arson attempts and the decline of country pubs which did not become temples for the worship of fine foods. More recently, the threat had come in the form of a petition started by two self-righteous schoolgirls and which demanded that the proprietor come up with a name much less horrendously insensitive and racist.

After a tidal wave of publicity which had done his turnover no harm, a concession by the landlord-owner had been to replace the current illustrated swing sign with a board bearing no more than the name of the pub. In the way of these things, the original outcry had been caused not by the name, but the pictorial sign. It showed a woman in a mob cap trying to scrub the colour from a black toddler sitting in a wooden tub. The old board was, however, still on prominent show in the bar, which said something about the proprietor and his take on the situation and modern sensitivities.

Mowgley's room was at the top of a faltering staircase. The view from the unopenable window showed rolling meadowland, forests, farmers' fields and glimpses of what might be a sliver of sea. It was a view needing no more than a frame to put on the wall to celebrate what modern people liked to think rural England used to look like.

Warped by time and use, both the ancient staircase and floor of the room made the user as unsteady on his feet as a surfeit of house cider. The smell of old wood and plaster and the general unevenness of walls, ceilings and floor reminded him of Le Petit Bijou, and he found it pleasantly familiar. Since buying the cottage he had come to realise how much he preferred old buildings, despite their drawbacks and discomforts. They seemed to gain character just by being old. Perhaps it was some sort of genetic memory of past lives creating a feeling of nostalgia for a time he could not have known. Whatever, he was beginning to feel at home in the Little Jewel, with its quirky inconsistencies. He looked forward to his return, and even found himself thinking almost affectionately of the damp patch above his bed and the smell of the pump-up toilet.

Downstairs, the single bar was, like Le Petit Bijou, an agreeable mix of ancient and fairly modern. The stone-flagged floor had probably been in place Since the Civil War, while the red flock wallpaper was of 1970's vintage and more commonly seen in unreconstructed Indian restaurants.

The bar counter was a sensible mid-belly height, with a footrest heating pipe and hooks on which to hang handbags or perhaps belt buckles when legs began to sag. Other small but pleasing points and reminders of his old Portsmouth local were a jar of picked eggs and a hot pie display case on the counter. The difference was that this case contained clearly fresh pastys rather than veteran meat pies soon to have a life of their own. Another plus point was the lack of stools littering the space directly in front of the counter. A lot of the space in this area was, however, taken up with a very large, incongruous and tatty armchair.

'In case you're thinking of sitting there, sir, it's reserved for old Harry.'

The speaker was the landlord, a man who carried his extreme roundness easily and like a comfortable old coat. He had short hair, a long beard and a booming voice, and spoke and even moved in an actor-ish way. Mowgley noted a half-moon, velvet-lined shape had been cut out of the counter. Its purpose was revealed when the landlord shuffled in to it so as to let the barmaid pass.

'I inherited Harry with the pub,' explained the landlord. 'First thing I did was to tell someone to chuck the smelly old armchair out. Then I heard he came in every day and drank at least five pints of home-brew.'

The man picked up a glass and looked at it thoughtfully. 'He's over eighty and probably pickled. Someone helps him to the khazi when needed, and there's a free get-you-home service for anyone who drinks enough to earn a ticket.'

'Ah,' said Mowgley, who'd noticed the big red bus in the car park and that it had the old pub sign prominently displayed on both sides.

'Now sir, what do you fancy apart from the barmaid's tits?' asked the landlord, watching Mowgley watching the young woman in the low-cut top leaning over the pumps.

'Just thinking about the barmaid at my old local,' he said. 'She was called Twiggy by the regulars.'

He ordered a half of the house cider and a pasty, and

only protested mildly when a pint appeared on the counter. 'House policy, sir,' said his host, 'we don't sell half pints except to ladies. So, unless you are identifying as a woman...?'

Mowgley raised a hand in surrender, asked for the pint and pasty to be put on his tab, then took them to a seat at a table in the corner where his back would be to the wall. He took the top off his pint, noted the landlord watching him and so kept a neutral expression as the sweet and sour rawness hit the back of his throat. As he bit into the pasty, he studied the blackboard above the bar and saw that upcoming events included the annual nettle-eating contest, a mud snorkelling weekend and the Standing-on-your-Head-while-drinking-a-Yard-of-Ale Tournament. There was also a warning that itinerant Morris dancers would be shot on sight.

The cider was very cold and very good and Mowgley was glad he'd been given a pint. The pasty was all it should be and more.

As he sat and wished he could smoke, he took in the customer profile. It was, like his local at the Portsmouth ferry port, a diverse mix, but in a countryfied way. The single bar enforced diversity of occupation, class and attitude, and stroppy, leathered-up bikers and crusty domino-playing farm workers shared space with churchy flower-arranging ladies. At the bar with virtue-signalling pints of cask-conditioned ale displayed at chest level, dentists, accountants and solicitors in chukka boots and sweaters with leather elbow patches did their best to look like old-time country money. One, Mowgley observed, was even wearing a cravat.

As he savoured another pasty/scrumpy combination, he looked round the bar and thought about how he, his fellow customers and the landlord and his barmaid had ended up in this pub and part of the world at this time. The opposing conjectures of self-determination, kismet or just happenstance in life had been a long-time source of self-debate for Mowgley. However intended and planned and executed, the whole course of lives and, sometimes, deaths could be changed by a tiny and apparently inconsequential event, and have, by definition, immeasurable consequences. Thousands, perhaps millions of small events had occurred to determine the path that had led to Petra De'Ath working in her gallery when the firebomb came crashing through the window. And also, of course, the sequence of events which led to her father lying naked and dead on the floor of the cellar of his mini-castle.

As usual at this point, he gave up, looked darkly at his empty glass then got up to order another pint. Waiting at the bar, he went over his visit to the former home of the Brigadier, his wife and their daughter.

He'd called in at Branscombe Manor after leaving Joe Harvey's shop and, while there, had tried to imagine what it would be like to grow up and live in such a place. Now, the family had long gone and the new owners had added a superfluous 'Country Park Hotel' to its original name. Like so many fine old bastions of individual privilege, it had become the sort of place with a tv chef allegedly to be found at all times in the kitchen and a menu of what they liked to call high-end cosseting. Top of the list for price was the Wellbeing Weekend Experience, including Macrobiotic Yin and Yang Eating adventures, Colonic Irrigation and Korean Body Scrub.

As Mowgley had learned from the ancient gardener who had survived the change of ownership, the Manor had been sold by Honoria, the daughter of Brigadier Healey-Asquith after her mother's passing and before her divorce. She had, however, retained the gatehouse, and moved in to sit and look out of the windows at what used to be her birth right.

As the old gardener straightened his back, took off his beret and looked back into the past, he'd added that there had been something about a painting being found which was worth a lot of money, and the lady had sold the gatehouse and gone away, to that London, or so some said.

After ordering another pasty to help absorb the all-conquering cider, Mowgley had asked the landlord about the disappearing lady of the manor, who said it was well before his time. Pointing at the now-occupied armchair at the bar, he said Old Harry was sure to know about any murky goings-on in the parish. The usual fee for reminiscences was a pint of the house cider.

In fact it took half a gallon to keep Old Harry's whistle wetted as he told the tale. Then, not-so-old Harry Pollard had been a butcher, and served the Brigadier's daughter regularly. She was, he said, a strange, twitchy, nervy woman. She had married badly, and the husband had buggered off with his bow tie and lounge lizard patent leather shoes, but not before making her sell the manor and hand over a good slice of what it fetched. She was, said Old Harry looking meaningfully at his empty glass, a bit of a drinker as well.

'Do you know what happened to him?'

'Nah, he just slithered off looking for the next dopey woman, I reckon. But I did hear he died.'

'And their daughter?' Mowgley waved at the barmaid for a refill.

'Miss Caroline? Didn't really know her. Strange young woman, sort of arty-farty and a bit queer for my liking. She buggered off too.'

'There we go,' Mowgley had said, pushing the full glass along the bar, 'Just one thing more. Did the mother paint?'

A thoughtful fart, then a slurp and then: 'Only her face, and she were no good at that. Now I think of it, she looked a bit like that woman from Harry Potter. The one who was Mrs. Haversham on telly.'

'I know who you mean. And do you know what happened to her?'

'What, the woman in Harry Potter?'

'No, the lady from the big house. And her daughter.' Old Harry looked into his glass, sniffed and then said: 'No, but there was a rumour.'

'Rumour?'

'Yup. Someone said the mother died in a whatchermacallit.'

'A whatchermacallit?'

'Yup. A freak accident, they said. In a boat. I don't think the daughter was with her.'

~

Late afternoon, and Mowgley had delayed the drive back to Portsmouth and the ferry port until he judged enough alcohol had quit his bloodstream.

It had been a long evening at *The Labour in Vain*, with Joe Harvey arriving just in time for Last Orders, which lasted more than three hours from time of calling. Mowgley noticed that Harvey had paint on his hands as he passed a plastic bag over the bar. In it, he explained, was a Chagall copy in settlement for his monthly bar bill. He did not know if the landlord kept or sold them, but one *Over the Town* and two copies each of *The Fiddler* and *I and the Village* had changed hands since Christmas and had not appeared on the ancient but flock wallpaper-ridden walls.

~

The lights of Portsmouth and the Spinnaker Tower loomed, but Mowgley was so engrossed in a phone-in discussion on the local radio station that he came close to missing the turnoff from the M27.

The subject revolved around the grim statistic that two million Britons now found themselves unable to work because of mental rather than physical health issues.

Then there was the soaring rate of young people reporting depression and other mental health problems caused by the pressures of modern-day life.

The current caller had declared herself devastated and her life effectively ruined after being coercively controlled by her male boss and being forced to resign. She had admittedly received compensation, but had only taken the money to impress on employers the need to treat their staff properly.

It was, Mowgley reflected, an irony that the debate was taking place in a city where, just a couple of centuries before, life had been short and brutal for most Portmouthians. Theirs had been a life of squalor and unthinkable hardship, to say nothing of the likelihood of being transported to Australia for stealing a loaf of bread. And, more recently, had lived with the ever-present threat of death and destruction falling from the sky as the Luftwaffe aimed their deadly payloads at the Naval Dockyard. For centuries, the city's young men had sailed into the horrors of naval warfare and, relatively recently, for their rendezvous with Fate in the noise and carnage and horrors of the D-Day beaches.

Turning into the long-familiar ferry port gates, he wondered if it was people who had changed, or just their views on what made for mental distress.

It was almost bizarre to hear a string of distressed callers, devastated by being misgendered or obsessed with the size of their ears and teeth. Or breasts that were too big... or too small. Most had told the earnest counsellor in the studio that they had not realised how badly they were suffering until being advised to confront and open up about their concerns. As everyone knew, she frequently reminded the listeners, this was a terrible time to be young.

As he joined the queue to cross the linkspan, he thought about how it must have been to be on board a landing craft heading for Omaha Beach, bucketing towards lots of people who were waiting to kill you.

Switching off the radio and leaving the car while looking forward to a drink at the bar and a leisurely meal, he could not help but wonder if repeatedly telling people how awful their lives were was such a good idea.

In the days when life was truly hard and the lack of a television set was not a measure of poverty, the advice to those unhappy with their circumstance was routinely to put their shoulders back, pull themselves together and get on with it.

On the whole and with some noticeable caveats, the Jordan Peterson version of this approach seemed sound advice to Mowgley. Or, he conceded, perhaps it just demonstrated how out of touch with modern sensibilities and stresses he was... and what a dinosaur he had become.

Eric Hebborn (1934-1996)

In his creative lifetime, Jean-Baptiste-Camille Corot produced around 3000 art works. In the United States alone, more than 100,000 paintings are attributed to him. He is said to be the most forged artist of all time, and some of the most successful fakes in his name were painted by London-born art dealer Eric Hebborn. As with a number of art forgers, when critics did not show enthusiasm for his own work, Hebborn developed a talent for copying celebrated painters. He claims to have created over a thousand fakes, of which only a handful have been exposed. Documentaries and films and novels have been written about the master forger, and he wrote two books, entitled 'Drawn to Trouble' and 'The Master Forger's Handbook'. He challenged experts to differentiate between his fakes and the originals, and said: 'Forgeries should be enjoyed for what they are, rather than being questioned for what they are not.'

The Painter Who Never Was

Nat Tate was an abstract expressionist with a great future, but who destroyed 99 percent of his work, and sadly leapt to his death from a Staten Island Ferry. He was also a complete invention. With the help of writer and thinker Gore Vidal and popster David Bowie, author William Boyd created the character's name from the 'National' in the National Gallery of Art in Washington and the 'Tate' Gallery in London. He also created a detailed fake biography in 1998. Tate enjoyed a period of posthumous fame before the secret got out, and a painting by the author professing to be a Tate sold in 2011 for nearly $11000

18

'You look nice.'

'You say that always, whatever I am wearing.'

'Well,' said Mowgley weakly, 'you always wear such... nice... things.'

The reply was a puff of exasperation that only a French woman of a certain age and type could employ to such effect.

Mimi was not in a good mood, and the gift of Cornish clotted cream toffees and a picture postcard of Tintagel Castle had done little to improve it. He had also bought her a Cornish pasty from the *Labour in Vain*, but eaten it on the crossing.

On the plus side, it was clearly not he who was the root cause of Mimi's unhappiness. Yann Cornec was away on business, she had said with audible quote marks, and her expression confirmed she knew what sort of business he was conducting.

'So,' Mowgley said brightly, 'It's good news about the dead bike rider—I mean, good news that the insurance company wants us to investigate the situation?'

She emerged from the room beyond the office with his mug of instant coffee, raised an elegant eyebrow and sniffed. Then her face softened: 'Yes, but there is very bad news from Mr. Begg.'

He looked at her over the rim of his mug, knowing what she was going to say.

'It is his son,' Mimi said. 'He is dead. Drowned. In the sea.'

Mowgley put his mug down, shook his head and sighed. 'Do we know how?'

She gave a slight shrug. 'Mr. Begg says he was told that his son fell from the fishing boat and nobody knew till it was too late.'

'And the body?'

'There is no body. Yet. The men on the boat said they went back to search when he was missed, but could not find him.'

'But Frank Begg does not believe that.' He said it as a statement and not a question.

Mimi nodded and put her head to one side. 'That is right. He is very angry.'

'And what do the police say?'

'Nothing yet.'

'And he wants me to try and find out what happened?'

She raised a hand, palm upwards. 'I think he would like you to find out the truth and kill the men who he is sure killed his son.'

'What makes you so sure that he wants them killed?'

She raised her shoulders and came close to a full pout. 'Of course I do not know and he did not say that. It was just the way he spoke. If it were my son, I would want the same.' She took a sip from her cup, then reached over and tapped a piece of paper on his desk. 'I said you would call him.'

'Okay. But I hope you didn't tell him I would kill them.'

She shook her head. 'Don't be silly. And I will not tell Yann if you choose to help Mr. Begg. It could be, as you say, off the books.'

'Thank you,' he said. 'So is that it for the bad news?'

'No, though I do not know if you would regard a call from the famous artist lady as good or bad news?'

Mowgley thought about it, and was surprised to realise he felt it was pleasant news. 'What did she say?'

Another elegant and somehow disapproving shrug. 'Nothing, except she wanted you to call her. She said you did not give her your mobile telephone number. I think she likes you.'

'Hmmm.' He scratched his stubbly chin. 'I wonder. So what's the last bit of bad news?'

'I have heard from the *Direction Générale des Finances Publique*. They are the people who are responsible for ensuring taxes are paid, and they are not happy with you.'

'Why not? I've not even spoken to them.'

She gave a grim smile. 'That is why they are not happy with you.'

'But I thought my deal with Yann was that you — the company, I mean — did all that stuff and paid my taxes before paying me my dues?'

'I am afraid that it is not as simple as that.' She stood up, glanced at the wall clock and smoothed her dress over her hips. 'But it is nearly *midi*. I think I can explain better if you take me to eat. A nice meal and a glass of wine might help you understand better how we do things here.'

~

Mowgley ran a sticky finger between his neck and unaccustomed collar and tie as he surveyed his audience of two. He hadn't needed to bother with a tie as it was not a dress rehearsal, but had thought it might give him more confidence if he looked the part.

At a little over four minutes, his best man's speech was probably one of the shortest ever given in this country, but given his level of competence in French, that was, he figured, for the best.

Below the stage and in the middle of the vast function room, the soon-to-be happy couple had sat, smiling and nodding encouragingly like parents at the school nativity, though he'd noted that René Degas had winced at least twice. The only other witness had been a cleaner who had looked up from scrubbing an area floor, then stood and listened opened-mouthed with a look which seemed to blend confusion with horror.

'Well,' he asked, 'what do you think?'

'Very... good,' said René Degas, 'but I did not get the joke about the chips fly and the thin slice of pineapple.'

'It was a fruit fly and a banana,' said Mowgley. 'In English it's 'Time flies like an arrow, fruit flies like bananas.' He paused for a change of expression on his friend's face, then, seeing none, added: 'It's a play on words.'

'I see,' said Degas, who obviously didn't.

'It will help a lot,' said Catherine McCarthy, if you start by apologising in advance and saying how your French friends say you speak the language like a Spanish cow. They always like that.' She gave a beckoning gesture. 'Anyway, come and have some lunch; the gazpacho's getting cold.'

Mowgley fitted the microphone back onto its stand and joined the couple at the table in the centre of the large, lofty and totally over-the-top *salle de réception*.

The *Château Erzulie*, it had occurred to Mowgley, was a continental version of Branscombe Manor County Park Hotel, only even more so.

Like the Brigadier's former home, it specialised in high-end weddings, promising to make every bride's wedding day the happiest of her life. Also like Branscombe Manor, it was in English hands. The elegant but distressed property had been bought almost breathtakingly cheaply (to them) by a couple who had sold their home in Battersea at a price which had surprised even themselves. They had re-fashioned the sprawling property at a mind-numbing cost into what many British people might think a château did or should look like.

For once, what had seemed a great idea for a business in a trendy London wine bar over a few glasses of expensive wine had actually proved to be a winner, rather than ending in financial and emotional disaster.

The couple had instinctively understood how the more vulgar, over-the-top and expensive the setting, the more it would be valued by their sort of client. The Wedding Day Chateau Experience, they promised, was an event the bride and groom would remember and cherish for all eternity. The brochure also emphasised that same-sex partners were much more than welcome, and there were specially constructed celebrations completely avoiding the use of personal pronouns.

In summary and for a sum which was more than Mowgley had paid for his new home, the happy couple would be guaranteed a day and night in which they were the brightest and only stars in the firmament.

Before the guests arrived and after the attentions of an army of hair, make-up and other creative specialists, the couple would be endlessly photographed and filmed in front of the towering spires before the bride was led around the grounds on a snow-white horse in an homage to pop megastar Sting's wedding.

Following a wedding banquet of impeccable taste and variety, the speeches and toasts, their Day of True Magic would end with a spectacular firework display and then the launching of dozens of Love Lanterns, each bearing a declaration of the couple's commitment to eternal love and fidelity. For an extra consideration, a flight of white doves could be released from the *pigeonnier* to follow the Love Lanterns into the Heavens.

As Mowgley knew, Catherine and René were not availing themselves of any of the extras, and had chosen the Château Erzulie as it was the only venue on the peninsula able to accommodate nearly two hundred sit-down guests. Given his position and the profession of most of the guests, Degas had also negotiated a very favourable rate.

'Are you really sure you want me to do this speech?' he asked as Catherine poured the last of the contents of a cafetière into a tiny cup with a handle shaped like a bird's wing. Or perhaps, he thought, it was meant to represent half an angel's wing. Either way it was very hard to get a proper grip on. 'I'd be more than happy.' he added, 'if you'd like a better best man for the job.'

'Take that tie off and don't be daft,' said Catherine McCarthy in firm but affectionate tones. Looking from one to the other of the two men, she held up the cafetière and looked at Degas, who smiled, nodded, rose and made for the port-holed swing door to the kitchen.

'Don't worry,' she said as Mowgley watched Degas push his way through the two-way door, 'I'll leave you two to talk shop while I see the wedding arranger about some stuff. I just wanted to check you are okay with –' she waved an all-encompassing arm ' — all this. I don't want you getting too pissed to speak or pooing your pants when you get up on the stage. I can see you might find the surroundings not really… comfortable.'

Mowgley looked up at the lofty ceiling, from which was suspended a huge tent-like arrangement of lace and frilly trimmings. The ceiling itself was painted black, with hundreds of twinkling lights presumably representing stars. In all, it created the effect of being in a huge, translucent tent that was floating away from its moorings, or even an inside view of a giantess's nightgown.

'I know,' Catherine McCarthy said, taking in his expression.

'Don't blame me. I think René just wanted to do things big-time. He said he never expected to get married again after losing his wife...or to be happy again. Spending a bomb is his way of showing me how much he cares about me. And as he said, it's never going to happen again for him, and hopefully for me.'

Mowgley nodded. 'I can see that. Just promise you'll pass on climbing aboard for the trip on the white horse.'

She cautioned him with a look and changed the subject. 'So how was your trip to the westcountry? Anything turn up? Or was it a waste of time and René's money?'

He frowned. 'Didn't you know René has pulled the plug?'

'What do you mean?'

'Mimi told me that Yann said that the money for the investigation had run out and there was no more to come. I went to Death's old stamping ground at my own expense.'

She raised an eyebrow, 'No wonder you look so miserable...or is it that you're missing your lady friend in Paris?'

'Not really. Apart from my speech, I'm a bit worried because Mimi said the tax people want to talk to me.'

She stretched her lips out. 'That don't sound good. Have they caught you out at underpaying your dues?'

'Apparently I haven't paid them anything since joining the company.'

'Oh,' Her eyes widened. 'An oversight was it? You never were one for bookwork.'

'Nope. It was just that I was sure that the deal I had with Yann was that I would get day rate and expenses and they'd pay my taxes and other stuff and take it off my wages.'

'Oh, again. So what are you going to do?'

He scratched his cheek. 'Well, for a start I'll have a word with Yann and find out what the situation is.'

'I see. Just do me a favour and don't have the meeting till after the wedding.'

'What do you mean.'

She frowned and wagged a finger. 'I don't want you getting yourself beaten up by your boss as an excuse to get out of the best man's speech.'

~

'No, it is just not true that I have stopped the budget for your investigations into the De'Ath case. In fact, I signed off next month's tranche a week ago.'

Degas had returned through the porthole door with a pretty girl in an old-fashioned waitress's outfit, the cap and apron of which were almost as frilly as the giant tent above them. She was carrying a tray on which stood a coffee jug and a plate of mini-macaroons and other tit-bits the French liked to class as amusements for the mouth. There were also three glasses of Calvados apple brandy, and Mowgley bet himself it would be top quality and a matching price.

Degas' face had darkened when Catherine had explained that Mowgley had had to pay his own way for the trip to England, and that trouble loomed with the tax authorities.

He took a sip of brandy, then said: 'I have to tell you that things have not been well in our relations with Yann, for a number of reasons. He has been doing some bad things and lying to you about the allowance is just one of them.'

Mowgley made a mental note to suitably pad and then submit his expenses for the trip to Mimi the next day, and reached for a sliver of toast topped by a slice of olive in aspic. 'Can you tell me about the others?'

'For one thing, it is said he has been demanding money from the people he has tracked down on behalf of insurance companies and mortgage lenders. We believe he is asking for a payment not to tell the companies where they are.'

'Blackmail? Blimey. So he gets it from both ends?'

'That is right. He is being greedy. I told him yesterday that next month's payment for your work on the De'Ath case would be the last, and that we needed to talk about some of his activities if he wanted my business in future.'

Mowgley nodded and reached for a macaroon. 'So you're closing down the case on who killed Death, if anyone? I suppose my report didn't help much in terms of motive.' He had given the policeman a truthful but edited version of his visit to the westcountry, leaving out the details of his encounter with Joe Harvey and his purchase of a fake Degas.

Degas shrugged. 'It seems there is nowhere else we can go. Mr. De'Ath obviously made some enemies in his rise to success, but all the forensic and other evidence points to an accidental or deliberate overdose of the stimulant he was taking. Unless you have any ideas?'

'Not yet,' said Mowgley thoughtfully, but I'll let you know when I've been on another trip to Paris.'

~

In the absence of anything as down-market as a sheltered smoking area outside the château, Mowgley and Degas were having a sneaky cigarette in an arbour of intertwined hazel branches at the end of the Lover's Trail that led through a painfully twee copse on the outskirts of the grounds.

The selection of exotic trees and foliage seemed artificial, with not a fallen leaf, broken limb or animal turd in sight. Smoking was in fact strictly forbidden anywhere in or around the château, but Degas reckoned the cost of the day entitled them to break the rules. Elsewhere, Catherine McCarthy was locked in deep discussions on the fine details of the wedding with a severe-looking woman in a black suit and carrying a clipboard as if it were a shield.

'Do you know about Kai Begg?' Mowgley let out a geyser of smoke and watched a squirrel scurry along a branch overhead. It looked down at them for a moment, then carried on its journey.

Degas dropped the butt of his cigarette and screwed it into the damp earth. 'You mean that he is dead? Of course.'

'Why "Of course"?'

Degas reached for the packet of Caporal on the seat between them. He had, as he said, several hours of abstinence to make up for. 'He is a foreigner and not a resident, but he has been living and working in Cherbourg… and he is — or was — a person of interest. Working with people of interest.'

'And do you think his going over the side was an accident?'

Degas gave a grunt of dry amusement and lit his cigarette. 'I do not think so.'

'Fishermen do fall off boats.'

Degas smiled. 'Yes, but Mr. Begg was no fisherman.'

'No? So what was he doing in a fishing boat in the English Channel? The ship's cook… the cabin boy?'

Degas raised an eyebrow. 'None of those things, I think, but certainly he was not fishing. The boat was doing a delivery trip.'

Mowgley looked at the tip of his cigarette. 'What to where? I can guess the what bit.'

'As far as we know, the gang you had an altercation with at the marina had been delivering a consignment of heroin… and perhaps some illegal migrants as well. It was a clever arrangement. I am sure you know of the Isle of Wight?

Mowgley smiled. 'I went there on holiday once. That was enough.'

'Ah yes. The bucket and spade holiday I think you call it.'

Mowgley smiled at a distant memory. 'I was a bit older than that, but carry on.'

'The crew in the fishing boat belonging to the Dutch-based company had an arrangement with another group of fake fishermen. They and their boat set out regularly from the south of the Island, but few fish were caught. There is even talk that they bought hauls of fish from genuine trawlers to make it look as if they had been doing their work. The boat from Cherbourg would attach packages of heroin to the lines of lobster and crab pots put there by the fake fishermen. They would pick them up at a later date when the coast was, as again you say, clear.

Degas paused to light his new cigarette, and Mowgley asked: 'So what went wrong for them?'

'We had advanced warning, so were able to alert the authorities on the Island. They were waiting to witness the drop, but did not stop the French boat in case the men from the Island were watching from shore. The Island fishermen were arrested when they tried to pick up the delivery and are awaiting trial. They claim they were only fishing and did not know the packages were there, but I do not think they will be believed, as they were caught in the act.'

'And who gave you the tip-off? You had someone undercover?'

'Yes, you could say that.' Degas paused, then said: 'It was the son of your client, Kai Begg.'

Mowgley paused in the act of lighting his second cigarette of the session. 'Really? How did that happen?'

'He was... recruited ...by a senior officer, after a serious amount of heroin was found at his apartment. He was told that if he did not help with information, he would be charged as a dealer and would serve many years in prison.'

'But why did you not tell me this was happening when I was looking for the boy? Didn't you trust me?'

Degas held up one hand. 'I did not tell you because I did not know about this part of the investigation.'

'But you are the big cheese. How come —'

'I was not told because they knew I would not have allowed putting the young man in such a dangerous position.' Degas paused, then added: 'The officer in charge also said it was known that you and I were close, and he was worried about the boy being exposed and killed if I told you of the situation.'

'Which is what happened anyway?'

'Yes, I think so. The boat was stopped outside the breakwater here, and the crew arrested. It was known that Kai Begg would be on the trip, but the men said he had disappeared on their way to the fishing grounds.'

'Blimey.' Mowgley sat back and watched the squirrel amble along a branch of a nearby oak. Not for the first time, he thought about what it would be like to be thrown into a cold, dark and remorseless sea and left to die. He had heard it said that drowning was not an unpleasant death, but guessed the victims, if they could be asked, might not agree.

'So will the crew be charged with the murder?'

Degas shrugged. 'We hope so. If it is possible we will come to an arrangement with one of the crew. If he acts as a witness, he will receive a shorter sentence.'

And probably a death sentence when the rest of the gang find out, Mowgley thought. 'So what did your people tell Frank - the boy's father?'

Degas raised a hand and shook his head sadly. 'Only that Kai had disappeared overboard during a voyage of the *Zoete Dromen*. At that time the crew had not been charged and I thought it best he should know as soon as possible. I think he will suspect what happened when the details come out.'

'Yes,' said Mowgley, 'but I think perhaps he already does...'

Wolfgang Beltracchi (1951-)

Sometimes dubbed the 'forger of the century' and born in Germany 1951, Wolfgang Beltracchi is said to have produced around 1300 fakes during his career, though he says he has lost count. Many of his works are believed to still be in circulation, and it is estimated he made more than $100 million from his imitations of, amongst others, Max Ernst and Fernand Léger. Beltracchi did not imitate existing works, but created his own themes, claiming with his accomplices to have rediscovered lost masterpieces. He gave some of the forgeries provenance using old photographs which, he claimed, showed his wife's grandmother in the same room as the paintings. In fact, the photographs were of his wife, dressed in her grandmother's clothing. He was arrested after selling a painting for $2.88 million which contained a pigment not available in the time of the alleged artist, Heinrich Campendonk. Beltracchi was imprisoned in 2011, then released less than a decade later on the grounds of good behaviour. He has promised that his faking days are over...

19

At the busiest railway station in Europe, everyone except for him seemed to know where they were going, and moved as if they were in training for a walking race.

Choosing one of the various levels of the Gare du Nord at random he found himself face-to-face with a group of what looked like members of a school cadet force. They wore in-your-face baggy camouflage uniforms and the ridiculously tiny berets that French forces liked to perch on the side of their heads. How they were kept in place must be a trade secret, he thought. It certainly couldn't be hair grips, as the men were uniformly hairless from the collar up. Sharply contrasting with their youthful and otherwise generally amiable appearance, each carried an automatic rifle, held halfway to the shoulder and ready for action. They looked so much like children playing at soldiers that he wondered what the tally of dead and injured would be if they were let loose at a suspected terrorist on the packed platform.

Deciding it might not be a good idea to approach and ask for directions in bad French while wearing a bulky haversack, he then had to step back to make way for a line of burly men in SNCF Security uniforms. The leader was being towed by two attack dogs on uncomfortably long leads who were creating a parting in the crowds like the prow of a ship cutting through a choppy sea. Hoping they might be pursuing a fare-dodger towards the exit, he joined the end of the line and tried to look part of the team.

~

To someone used to the pace of life in rural Normandy, walking out of the Gare du Nord was like confronting a nightmarish chimera of Hieronymus Bosch's *Garden of Earthly Delights* and director George Miller's *Mad Max II*.

Inside, the station had been frantically busy but people seemed to know where they were going. There had been a sense of purpose about their determined shoulder-swinging bee-line movements. Outside, the viewpoint from the top of the steps put him in mind of an over-active ant hill.

Pedestrians elbowed from or voluntarily leaving the pavements generally ignored crossings or lights. They were in fact, in little danger from the traffic as it was mostly at a standstill. Cars and taxis sat sullenly resenting the brave (or apparently foolhardy) cyclists and scooterists who careered in between the tightest of spaces, some leaving a tangible reminder of their passing.

Like spectators at a gladiatorial encounter in Ancient Rome, people sat outside bars and enjoyed the spectacle. Some were watching a possible drama where an ambulance sat at the kerb, its blue light slowly revolving. A motor cycle lay on its side nearby with a leather-clad figure sprawled alongside it. Whether the ambulance was there to tend to the fallen rider or had caused him to fall was not clear. At the foot of the steps leading down from the main entrance, some sort of brass band was discordantly playing a rock anthem, and above all was the ceaseless honking and hooting and shouting from the sea of becalmed traffic.

Descending the steps, Mowgley avoided a garishly painted tuk-tuk mini-taxi, rewarded a banjo busker and paid off a persistent beggar, then passed a posse of gendarmes on pushbikes. They were corralling a skinny young man in pantaloons and a long robe. He was bearded, with shoulder-length hair, and had assumed a Christ-like position with arms outstretched and head down as he was being frisked.

Sidestepping a scooterist who had decided the pavement was fair game, Mowgley reflected on how Paris was accounted to be only the fifth most dangerous city in France. It would be interesting to learn which others were more dangerous, and in which ways.

~

She was sitting at a table outside the Dôme, a glass of Green Fairy to hand.

Rain drizzled half-heartedly on to and then dripped from the canopy, which seemed not to deter those who wanted to watch the world go by or have a smoke.

By the river, the pavement artist was shielding his work with a golf umbrella and looking optimistically at a patch of blue amongst the darkling clouds. Further along the bank, a statue of a Crusader came to life, looked up at the sky and the empty walkway, then stepped off his plinth and made his stiff way towards the bar. He was obviously going to take a break from standing still until the weather bucked up. As it was Paris and the Left Bank, nobody took much notice of a Knight Templar arriving for coffee and *croissant.*

'You look nice,' said Mowgley, resorting to his default opening pleasantry with women he was not entirely at ease with. That, he reflected as he said it, was nearly all of them.

'I know,' said the artist lately to be known as Até, opening her arms and striking a pose to show off her paint-stained Breton fisherman's top. 'I thought I'd make the effort to turn you on and see if it would improve your performance.'

He smiled and shook his head. 'I do like a girl who speaks her mind.'

She returned the smile and ran a hand through her short-cropped hair, which bore highlights of the same hue as those on her smock, then nodded at the chair opposite her. On the table in front of it was a flat-topped *demi* of beer and a large glass of the modern, scaled-down version of absinthe.

As he sat down, Até reached for her packet of cheroots, put one in her mouth and looked at him expectantly. He lit it and one of his Caporal*s*, then took a sip of the absinthe, washed down with the warm beer.

'Good journey,' she asked, leaving out the question in her voice as if to signal her lack of interest.

'Fine.' he said. 'The train was packed but a retro-punk gave me his seat. I didn't know whether to be pleased or pissed-off.' He bent over and looked under the table, then said: 'I see you're still at large.'

'They only use ankle tags on men who harm their women,' she said. 'not on suspected murderers.'

'And are you?'

'What, accused of harming my woman?'

'No, a suspected murderer of one of your women?'

She gave a wry smile, lifted her glass and rolled it along her cheek before emptying it. 'I don't think so. After our first meeting, the *flics* have not been to call. Yet.'

He raised an eyebrow. 'I thought you were under

protection after the threat by the jihadist gang?'

She smiled again and puffed out a cloud of smoke. 'Ah, the Sword of Islam? I think not. To the best of my recall I've never painted any image of Mohammed or any other Islamic figure, or anybody who could be mistaken for one. And it looks as if the so-called jihadi warriors don't exist. The police think it was either a hoax call or someone trying to shift the blame for the fire and Petra's death.'

Mowgley took another sip of warm beer, then pushed it away with a grimace. 'So they do think it was murder?'

She shrugged. 'If they do, they haven't told me. Most importantly, they obviously don't think it was me who done it. Investigations, as they like to say, are ongoing.'

'And who do you think could have done it?'

Another shrug. 'Not a clue. Someone with a grudge, or a really strong dislike of my work.'

'And you're completely out of the frame?'

'I hope so. I've got you as an alibi, remember. And why would I burn down a gallery which was showing my paintings and selling them like hot cakes? And why would I casually torch a quarter of a million Euros worth of my own work? Not for the insurance, that's for sure.'

Mowgley stroked his chin: 'Not unless you'd already removed your paintings and put a lot of tatt in their place for the forensic people to find. And I bet your stuff has doubled in price since the publicity from the fire.'

She looked coolly at him, then stubbed her cheroot out in a plastic ashtray bearing the Pernod logo. 'Do you really think I'd knock off a friend — and new lover — just to put the value of my paintings up?'

Mowgley stood, picked up his empty glasses and reached for hers. 'Of course not,' he said, 'unless you had another reason.'

'Like jealousy, you mean, if she was playing around elsewhere?'

'No. Perhaps because, let's just say you had a reason

to hate her or someone close to her. Same again?'

Até regarded him thoughtfully, then said: 'Where are you going? They have table service here, you know. You're not still in some English pub in the wilds of Dorset or wherever it was.'

'I need a pee,' he said, 'and this'll be quicker.'

'Okay,' she said. 'Just be sure to wash your hands like a good boy.'

He smiled and, as he turned away, nodded down at the table. 'I'm surprised that old Pernod ashtray hasn't been nicked by souvenir hunters.'

'It's not real,' she said. 'It's a copy. They even pre-stress them with burn marks and faded logo. They'll have dozens of them in the stock room.'

'Ah.' said Mowgley, 'I was forgetting about deception and fakery being all around us, all the time.'

~

'Pride and romance kill the one you love. Your mind makes you much older. Then you're gone.'

'Sorry? Did I miss something?'

Mowgley placed the glasses on their table and looked to where the Crusader was raising his coffee cup to Até and silently echoing her words.

'It's from *The Green Fairy* — by Kasabian,' she said. 'You know Kasabian, I hope?'

'Of course, we're old mates.'

Até lifted the glass to her nose and breathed in as if relishing the aroma. 'Oh Green Fairy, what you've done to me. There's a nothing in the sky, waiting to get high.'

'More Kasabian?' Mowgley asked.

She nodded, drained the glass and reached for the replacement. 'I wonder if he knows it's Friday the Thirteenth.'

'Who?'

'Him.' She nodded to where the Crusader sat under the

awning, keeping an eye on his plinth. He had taken off his mailed gloves to manage the tiny coffee cup and glass of Calvados, and his sword and shield were propped against the table. Against the grey of his costume and face, his hands looked very pink.

'Why would he care?' asked Mowgley.

'That's the day and date in October 1307 when the king of France ordered all Knights Templar to be rounded up and imprisoned. They were getting too rich and powerful for Philip's liking. They were charged with homosexuality, financial corruption and even spitting on the Cross.'

'So what happened to them?'

'Mostly they 'confessed' and were done to death, often quite horribly.'

'Ah.' Mowgley took a swallow of his cold, frothy beer and sighed. 'Funny what envy and greed leads people to do, isn't it?'

'I see you're becoming a philosopher,' she said. 'Is it living in France, exposure to the World of Art, or just approaching old age and looking into the abyss?'

'Bit of all that, I reckon.'

The Crusader felt them watching him, looked up and gave a salute with his coffee cup. Brushing croissant crumbs from his tabard, he put his gloves on, stood, picked up his sword and shield and made his way back to the plinth.

Até waved at a passing waiter, pointed at their glasses, lit a cheroot and directed a stream of smoke at the awning. 'So, how was your trip westward?'

'Interesting. I was going to ask how you knew about it?'

'Elementary, my dear Mowgley. I phoned your office and your colleague told me. Is she as fine-looking and fuckable as she sounds?'

'She's certainly fine looking, but I wouldn't know about her fuckability.'

'Not your cup of tea, perhaps?'

'She's my boss's cup of tea.'

Até frowned. 'So what?'

He smiled. 'You haven't seen my boss.'

'How disappointing. I always saw you as a man of action, in fear of nothing or no-one. Or not much.'

He smiled again. 'I'm getting a bit old for that.'

'So you're not the man you were?'

'Who is?'

'Oh dear, we're becoming philosophical. Perhaps it's all this exposure to the art world.'

'Perhaps.'

'And what do you think of it so far?'

'What do you mean?'

She looked irritated, then smiled. 'Exactly what I fucking said. Have you got over the Shock of the New and seen the light about modernity in Art, or do you think it's all bullshit and corruption and greed?'

He scratched his jaw. 'A bit of both, actually. I think people like Turner and Van Gogh and some of the Impressionists were genuinely looking for new ways to paint what they saw. Some of it works for me, especially when you know what the painter was trying to do. I think people like me like something instinctively — like a Beryl Cook fat lady or Hopper's *Nighthawks* — without analysing why. But bullshit baffles common sense as well as brains, I've found. When someone gets anointed, the suited hooligans and people who make a living by pretending they know what they're talking about get to work. As long as everyone agrees, a pile of bricks or can of soup is said to be a telling commentary on modern times — and worth a fortune. Call me a philistine, but it seems to me that not many people in the business stop to ask if something is a proper work of art, only how much it can be hyped and sold for. Fake or real. From what I've seen and learned, most of modern art is about money, greed, hype and bullshit.'

She smiled and brought her hands together in silent applause. 'There speaks a man who knows what he likes.

249

And are you including my stuff?'

'No…and yes. You can obviously paint, and you had a good idea with putting modern stuff in your copies of Old Masters. But why is your stuff worth ten times more now that you're famous…or infamous?'

She blew a cloud of smoke at him, then said: 'As you should know, it's called market forces. Or, as you say, hype and bullshit. With boxing or any sport, the winners —the best people at it—get the big money. With any form or art it has to be consensus of opinion. And that consensus has to start somewhere. That's where the arsehole Piers De'Ath came in.'

'Okay, I do get that. But…' Mowgley pointed at the pavement artist, who was holding his hand out and talking persuasively to an obvious tourist, '…how come his ability is worth whatever someone throws in his begging bowl, and a collection of coloured squares is agreed to be worth millions?'

She sighed and spoke as if explaining to a child: 'I don't get why you say you get it but obviously don't. After what you've been doing for all those years, do you still think the world is fair, or should be? It's all just a game. Winners and losers and all that. If you look at the most famous forgers, they started doing it because the critics said their work was shit, and they wanted to show them they could fool them with copies of paintings they said were modern masterpieces.'

'So Picasso and Dali and the rest were just good at playing the game, and the fakers are getting their revenge?'

'Of course. And why not?' Até reached over and put her empty glass on the table in front of him. 'And you have to remember, all those dealers and auction houses *want* there to be so many fakes. It's in their best interest.'

Mowgley showed her glass to a passing waiter, then turned back. 'Quite. So, aren't you going to ask me about my adventures in Devon and Cornwall?'

She yawned. 'No, but I sense you're going to tell me anyway. Was it business or pleasure?'

'A bit of both. I looked up some old mates and visited some new places.'

He flicked the ash off his cigarette and nodded to the waiter as he put two glasses of absinthe on the table. 'Do you know Devon?'

She picked her glass up and looked at him over the frosted rim as she took a drink. 'Not much. Where did you go – some tourist trap like Torquay?'

'No, a bit more off the beaten track than that. I had a bit of business to do with a man in a little place you won't have heard of.'

'Try me.'

'Chittlehampstead.'

She paused for a beat with the glass halfway to her lips, then shook her head. 'You're right, I've never heard of it. So what were you doing there?'

'I needed to talk to a man about a painting.'

'What man and what painting?'

'The painting was a Max Ernst. The man owns a junk shop in the village.'

'So what was he doing with an Ernst?'

'He wasn't. It was before his time. The painting had been taken into the same shop by the daughter of a senior army officer who brought it back from Germany after the War.'

Até looked as if she were about to yawn again, then said: 'And what happened to the painting?'

'It was sold for a lot of money and the shopkeeper went off with the Brigadier's daughter and her money.'

'So it was a happy ending?'

Mowgley scratched his chin, 'Not for both of them. The man went on to become rich and famous.'

'And the Brigadier's daughter?'

'Don't know, but I heard she died in an accident.'

She looked at her glass. 'Ah, so a sad ending.'

There was a moment's silence, then a tall black man arrived at their table. He was carrying an open briefcase filled with necklaces, brooches and sets of earrings. He showed a row of very white and big teeth and looked at Mowgley, who pointed at Até. She looked briefly at the array, then took a simple metal crescent of steel attached to what looked like a black bootlace. The man nodded as if she had made a good choice, then said something to Mowgley. He looked at Até for help, but she just lifted her shoulders and said: 'I don't speak Senegalese.'

Mowgley sighed, then reached for his back pocket. He held the wad of Euros in his left hand, then peeled off a twenty Euro note and handed it to the man. The man smiled even more broadly, shook his head and reached down and took another twenty, nodded and moved on to the next table. They watched as a succession of customers waved him away and the man snapped the case shut, then walked off into the night. As he passed, he raised a huge, pink-palmed hand to them and flashed another dazzling smile.

'He didn't try too hard with the rest of the punters,' Mowgley observed.

Até smiled. 'He knows when not to waste his time, and how to spot a soft touch. I saw him looking through the window and marking you as a near-certainty.'

'Ah. And what about you?'

'What about me?'

'Do you know how to spot a soft touch?'

She lifted her shoulders and gave a somehow sadly sweet smile: 'Perhaps I'm not as tough as you may think.'

'No,' he replied, 'I don't think you are…'

Paint it like Picasso

Though by definition it's unprovable, Pablo Picasso is believed to be the most faked painter of all time. This is partly because of his prolific output, said to be around 50,000 paintings, drawings, sketches, ceramics and sculptures. To further muddy the waters, Picasso was known to be 'difficult' about signing his work. Notorious forger Elmyr de Hory began his career with a copy of a Picasso drawing; nowadays, copies (and even forgeries) of his forgeries fetch a premium price.

20

'Thank you,' said Mimi, trying to sound enthusiastic or at least gracious, 'they are very…unusual.'

She was looking at a pair of earrings Mowgley had been persuaded to buy when the giant Senegalese jewellery vendor made a return visit to the Cafe Dome. They consisted of large metal hoops from each of which hung what looked like a representation of the bottom half of a zebra's leg.

As Até had said, the man obviously couldn't resist another raid on such a soft target.

'Not my sort of thing,' said Mowgley, 'but my friend picked them out and said she thought they would suit you.'

'*Ah bien*. Your friend would perhaps be the famous artist with the strange name.'

'That's right.'

'*D'accord.*' Mimi returned the earrings to the box and

put it on her desk. He guessed she would not be opening it again anytime soon.

She stood up, keeping her face turned slightly away from him. 'Would you like some coffee?'

'Thank you.'

It was not a full-blown black eye, but in spite of the camouflaging make-up, he could see the raised, blue-tinged weal on the right cheek bone. It looked so much worse, he reflected, as it was on the face of a woman. Although it shouldn't make a difference, it looked even worse on the face of a beautiful woman. A full punch from a man would have caused a lot more damage, and it was probably the result of a slap or back-hander. Whatever, he did not like men who hit women.

He watched her going into the back room and thought how it would not take a perceptively perceptive private detective to work out who had caused the damage.

She came back into the office, and he noticed her hand was trembling slightly as she put his mug down in front of him.

He thanked her, and they sat in silence for a moment before she took a deep breath, looked up and said: 'Do you have your cigarettes with you?'

'Of course. Why?'

Mimi put her cup down. 'I would like one, please.'

As she returned to the kitchenette, he crossed the space between their desks and took out his packet of Caporal. She came back into the office with a small, crystal ashtray, sat down, took a cigarette and leaned forward so he could light it. He stood looking down at her, then held the packet up and said 'Do you mind…?'

She blew smoke through pursed lips and smiled almost conspiratorially. 'Of course not.'

Mowgley lit up, then sat on the corner of her desk.

She took several drags, drawing the smoke in like someone who knew their way around a cigarette but had not smoked one for a long time.

After a while, she touched the undamaged side of her face with one finger, as if exploring it. 'So did your trip go well? Did you find out what you wanted?'

'Sort of.' He looked at the small stack of envelopes and post-it notes on his desk. 'Is there any good news for me?'

She smiled sympathetically. 'I do not think there is any. Mr. Begg has phoned every day to see if you will help him, and is coming to see you soon. Most importantly, you must phone the *Direction Générale des Finances Publique*.'

'Really? Does he want to invite me out to dinner?'

'I don't think so. It will be about why you have not declared any taxable income.' She frowned, touched his arm and said; 'You really must do this as they will not go away… and the longer you leave it the worse it will be.'

Mowgley raised his arms in mock-surrender. 'I'm not trying to avoid them. I just need to speak to Yann to find out what has been going on. I've called him a few times and he's never got back. Have you spoken to him about it?'

'Yes, but it is not good.'

She paused as if making a painful decision, then said. 'I have to tell you that he did not do what he said he would about your working arrangement. He did not ever intend to deduct your taxes and pay you the balance. He has been charging Colonel Degas three times what he pays you, and said to the tax authorities that he paid you much more than he did.' She paused, ground her Caporal out in the ashtray and held a hand out to show she would like another one. 'I know I should have told you, but I did not know exactly what was happening, and…'

She broke off and took the cigarette he offered. He lit it and then said: 'It's okay, let's talk about it later. Have you spoken to our employer about it today?'

She fiddled with her Caporal, then tapped it unnecessarily

on the ashtray. 'Yes.'

'And what did he say?'

'He said it was your problem.'

'And you have seen him?' he asked.

Mimi lifted a hand towards the bruise on her face, then realised what she was doing and brushed imaginary ash from her shoulder. 'Yes, I have seen him.'

'Can I ask when and where?'

In spite of herself, Mimi gave a faint smile at what she would see as his very English putting of the question. 'Yes, you can, and I will tell you. He was here this morning.'

'And do you know where he is now?'

Again the ghost of a smile. 'I think I do.'

'And will you tell me?'

She paused. 'He said he was going to the bar. But I think it would not be a good idea for you to speak to him now.'

'Why not?'

She made a fist of her right hand and twisted it in front of her nose. 'He has been drinking. He has big troubles, I think.'

'With the same department as me?'

'Taxes? No. Much bigger than that. He has a problem with the Colonel.'

'Oh? I thought they were friends?'

She shrugged. 'They were. But not now, I think.'

'Okay.' He stood up, leaving his cigarettes and lighter on her desk. 'I'll be back in a moment and then I think we should go to your favourite restaurant for lunch.'

'That would be good.' She gave a half smile and held up a hand as if to caution him. 'But Jack…'

He paused and looked back, surprised at the way she said his name.

'Yes?'

'Be careful.'

~

Yann Cornec was standing with his back to the bar, supporting himself on his elbows, two men who Mowgley knew to be police officers on either side of him. They were talking with their heads close together, as men do when speaking privately in a public place, or want to show they have something important and private to discuss.

From their posture and flushed faces, drink had clearly been taken, and with his shaven head and round face, Mowgley thought Cornec looked like a constipated baby. When he saw Mowgley, he looked more like an angry baby.

Pushing himself away from the bar, Cornec said something, and the two men looked at Mowgley with mild, unfocused interest.

With a nod to Madame Yvette and a couple of regulars, Mowgley walked to where the trio stood. Out of habit when unsure of a situation or the reception he was going to get, he stopped a clear two paces away from the trio.

He and Cornec regarded each other for a moment, while Cornec's cronies looked on with the heightened interest of men who sense a confrontation is imminent.

'So here you are, the great detective.'

Mowgley nodded at both men, then looked back at Cornec. 'If you say so. I can't be that good, though. I haven't been able to find you for weeks.'

Cornec frowned, then half-smiled and picked up his glass and waved it at Yvette. Mowgley noticed she was standing at the end of the counter, watching them. As the long-time owner of a dockside bar, she, like the policemen, had learned to sense potential trouble.

Cornec shrugged. 'I've been busy.'

'Yes,' said Mowgley evenly, 'I've just seen Mimi.'

Cornec's face went from red to white in a moment, and he pushed himself away from the bar to stand upright. He was swaying slightly, which gave Mowgley a rough idea of how drunk he was, how likely he was to take action, and how capable he would be if he did so.

The policemen had evidently gone through the same process, and one moved slightly away from Cornec, while the other laid a hand on the Breton's left forearm. Whether for restraint or encouragement, Mowgley could not know.

Around them and just before the eruption, the buzz of conversation died away. No voices had been raised, but the other customers had caught the mood.

~

For days afterwards, the talk in the bar was how bizarre it had been to see two ageing men fighting like rabid young dogs.

Most agreed that Madame Yvette was the star performer, in a drama which confirmed her soft spot for her former lodger. The story varied with the telling and the teller, but most agreed that the foreigner had moved surprisingly quickly for someone of his age and weight. Others said he was lucky that his opponent was so afflicted by drink.

Tables had been overturned, glasses smashed and some blood spilled during the brief fracas, with the policemen joining in. Later they would claim to be trying to stop the fight, but it looked to most onlookers as if they were helping the smaller man bring his opponent down. As one customer with a flair for theatrical metaphors said, it was like hunting dogs working together on an elderly but big and still game wild boar.

All agreed that most women café owners would have contributed by doing no more than scream and call the police. As they were already in attendance, that had not been necessary, and one of the officers had been laid low by a water jug wielded by the proprietor of the *Bon Parle*. Later she would claim she had been aiming to do no more than throw water over the participants, as one would do with rutting dogs to shock them apart. In the heat of the moment, she had merely forgotten to hold on to the vessel.

Eventually, the two officers had managed to restrain and handcuff the big Englishman, at the same time trying to stop Cornec's attack on him, and Madame's attack on them.

Regardless of the outcome, the spectators agreed it had been an entertaining diversion in a quiet day, with little damage to the fabric of the premises if not the leading players.

Shaun Greenhalgh (1961-)

This former forger kept the business in the family, who were known in police circles as 'the garden shed gang.' He produced a large number of forgeries over seventeen years from the family home near Bolton, with his parents dealing with clients and his brother handling money matters. Having left school at 16 with no qualifications, Greenhalgh was a self-taught artist who created his forgeries from photographs, catalogues and books on art. He was nothing if not diverse in his scope, and also created faked coins, sculptures and ancient busts. According to Scotland Yard, he and his family made up 'possibly the most diverse forgery team in the world, ever.' So celebrated was the master forger that London's Victoria and Albert Museum staged an exhibition of his works, and the Metropolitan Police's Art and Antiques Unit built a replica of the shed where the works were created.

21

Midnight had gone unannounced and largely unnoticed, and the party was coming to a natural and lingering conclusion. The DJ had reduced the volume and pace of his spiel and playlist, and no more than a handful of guests shuffled, swayed or stepped purposefully about the dance floor. Others sat and talked and drank and enjoyed the moment. As if in approval of the activity below, a gibbous moon sailed serenely on a sea of cotton wool cloud above the soaring spires of the Château Erzulie. It had watched benignly as the Anglo-Franco union had been well and truly notarised and celebrated.

As most guests would have agreed, the blessing ceremony had been satisfyingly emotional but not overly *émotif*, and the food acceptable when considering the inevitable problems of mass catering. The wine had been, like the food, as acceptable as one could expect in the circumstances. The firework display had been entertaining, and almost as spectacular as the speech by the English *garçon d'honneur.*

It was, the general consensus had it, a real achievement for anyone to speak French so badly. It had to be deliberate, like a skilled pianist hitting the wrong notes to win laughs. The spectacular black eye and sticking plaster across his nose had, if anything, enhanced the performance and may have been a sophisticated visual nod to what the groom could expect from his new wife if he did not toe the line.

His ordeal over, Mowgley sat alone at a table near to the stage, watching the gentle action on the dance floor and thinking about how fickle and unpredictable Dame Fortune could be. A few years ago, his wildest of dreams would not have portrayed him as an unemployed private detective, living in France and recovering from being the best man at his former colleague and closest friend's wedding to a very senior French policeman. Or that age would have taken such a toll on his physicality that he would need to be rescued in two fights in a row by women.

On the plus side, his speech had somehow gone down well unless the audience was clapping in sympathy and laughing in derision. The wedding and the guests being French, it had been a very orderly affair. There had been no dad dancing, fights between new relations or drunken or boorish behaviour. The only rowdy activity had come earlier with the convoy of guests' cars, hooting furiously and with broomsticks strapped to their roof racks for their procession from the Gendarmerie at Cherbourg to the wedding venue. There had been no hold-ups, as the convoy was escorted by two marked police cars which had joined in the fun with the occasional blast of siren and flash of lights. He had heard that the custom of displaying the old-fashioned besoms was a reminder of an ancient ceremony, but Madame Yvette had told him the modern view was that it was to let the groom know who was in charge and what would be his punishment for gross misbehaviour. The guests had ranged from the cradle to very close to the grave. Catherine's divorced mother and Degas's widowed father had got on well, and there had been some asides about them getting together in another Anglo-Franco alliance.

A loud belch with a follow-up rasping cough drew Mowgley's attention to a nearby table, where a fat, elderly man was solemnly regarding his empty brandy glass. With his pouchy, sad eyes, bibulous nose and veins suggesting the thread-like *craquelure* on an ancient oil painting, he was, Mowgley thought, almost a dead ringer for Rembrandt's self-portrait at the age of sixty-three. It was, he further considered, curious how, since the De'Ath case had begun, he had taken to comparing living people with long-dead artists.

Sensing he was being watched, the Rembrandt doppelgänger gave a smile as sad as his eyes, lifted his empty glass and waved it in Mowgley's direction. Whether in salute to a fellow reveller or request for a re-fill he could not tell.

On the dance floor, his best female friend and her husband of seven hours were locked together, dancing to Charles Trenet's *La Mer*. It was, Mowgley thought, the most French of French songs, rivalling Piaf and Maurice Chevalier at their most *emotif*. He did not know what it meant to the French, but to him the melody seemed to glow with warmth and comfort, innocent enthusiasm and hopes of what might be.

He reached for his breast pocket and patted his cigarettes ruefully and thought about going outside for a smoke. Accepting he had best be in attendance when the happy couple returned to the table, he reached for his glass of Champagne. He found it pleasant, if not as satisfying as a cold rough cider with bits of suspended apple adding to the flavour and zing. The fizzy nonsense could not possibly be worth the outrageous price the bridegroom would have paid for it, but his mild enjoyment perhaps marked another step on his journey to adapting to and even adopting French tastes. Perhaps, as with snails and frogs' legs, he would eventually acquire a liking for all sorts of Gallic fancies through osmosis or exposure. Having said that, he would draw a permanent line at consuming song birds, warm pig's blood and cows' intestines. It was true that he was beginning to feel almost at home in his adopted country, but that did not mean he had to do more than pretend to appreciate and admire some things about France. Despite or perhaps because of the British middle-class hectoring of and contempt for Little Englanders, he had no particular wish to become fully 'integrated'. He had always thought it peculiar how those who sneered at English expats for their preference for hard cheeses and roast dinners would not expect the same adaptation and integration from those from other countries who chose to make Britain their home. In fact, they seemed to encourage settlers to maintain their customs and traditions and dress and even otherness.

After topping up his new friend and pouring himself another glassful, he sat back to consider the largely unintentional irony of presenting his friends with wedding presents that were fakes. Or at least one fake.

The imitation Degas lay propped on a chair alongside him, and on the table top was the spectacle case in which he had placed the necklace which might once have adorned the neck of a Thracian princess. The Inspector had claimed the necklace to be no more than a clever copy when he presented it as a souvenir of their adventure. But Mowgley was unsure about the true history of the piece of jewellery or his friend's possible connections with the Mafia. Bulgaria, he had found, was a land of enigma and contradiction. He was sure Georgiev was a good man, but that did not preclude him being part of a system which had an unofficial as well as an official government. Either way, he had advised Catherine McCarthy to insure it for the value of its gold, keep it in a safe place and not wear it at any functions where an expert in ancient Thracian jewellery might be in attendance.

He reached again for his glass, toasted his fellow toper on the next table, then picked up his gift to the groom. The brown paper he had wrapped it in with the help of a few feet of sticky tape had been removed after some effort by Degas and the painting lay with its face against the chair back. As he picked it up, Mowgley noted that the framework looked as old and weathered as that of a genuine painting of that time; and that there was a faded label announcing that the work had been through the hands of a Paris dealer established in 1837.

Turning it over, he looked at the solemn face of the artist. It was, Joe Harvey had told him, an honest copy of one of the known forty self-portraits Degas painted at the start of his career. It showed the author as a pale-faced young man with a wispy moustache, and sulkily protruding lower lip. Mowgley wondered whether the look was one of frustration or impatience for the fame which he knew would one day enshrine his work. He knew that Joe Harvey had changed the high winged collar and the colour and hang of the coat so the painting could be taken as a genuine variation of the known version. As he had said, if Mowgley's mate had the bottle, he would just need to add a signature and have it 'discovered' in a convenient attic to increase its value from two hundred quid to a price almost beyond rubies.

Replacing the painting, Mowgley rubbed his jaw and thought about his experiences in the past month, and what he had learned about the Art world and those who inhabited it. Overall, the answer was not much.

Broadly, it seemed to him that most of the players in the game had honest intent and belief in the value and sanctity of their world. But in a world where billions regularly changed hands, it was inevitable that deliberate deception or the turning of a blind eye would be almost commonplace.

As to what made a painting great, he was clearly a philistine when it came to anything produced in the past century and a half. He recognised the obvious genius of the Old Masters, but could not see exactly what anointed a badly executed painting of a bunch of flowers or bowl of fruit a masterpiece. What he seemed to have learned in recent times was that, in Modern Art, it was obviously the idea and not the skill level that counted. But for him the mystery remained as to whose work was to be acclaimed, ignored or ridiculed.

~

'If I had a penny, I would give it to you for your thinking.'

'Thoughts.' Mowgley corrected her without thinking, then held a hand up in apology.

He looked up and almost flinched at how truly stunning Mimi looked. She was wearing what he guessed might be called a sheath dress. He briefly considered complimenting her on how it fitted her like a glove, but decided that she might not take it as a compliment.

The shiny red creation really was like a second skin, beginning at armpit level and revealing creamy white shoulders and arms and the smooth and seductive swell of her breasts. The lack of any jewellery except a pair of Vermeer-style pearl drop earrings added to the tantalising effect of near-nakedness.

It was, even to his limited understanding, a bold outfit to wear for someone of Mimi's age, and made only possible because of the taut firmness of her skin. No bingo wings or dinner lady arms on show here.

Her lustrous and glittering auburn hair was piled high, with ringlets cascading on to the flawless shoulders. Her make-up was restrained in comparison with the drama of hair and dress, except for the flaming crimson of her lips; looking closely, he could see that any bruising from her encounter with Mowgley's former boss had fully faded or been artfully concealed.

'Do you not like my appearance? You have not said anything all evening.' She smiled and gave a half-twirl.

'I'm sorry,' he said, 'but I was so terrified about my speech I forgot my manners. Now I see you as you are... the most beautiful woman here. Except for the bride of course. But I am sad that you are not wearing the zebra earrings I bought you from Paris.'

She smiled again. 'I do not think that Lower Normandy would be ready for the latest fashions of the capital.'

He stood up, grunted with the stab of pain in his back, moved the faux-Degas painting and invited her to sit with an overly courtly bow. She lowered herself onto the seat without a wrinkle appearing in her costume or exposed flesh, and he reached for an empty glass and a full bottle of Veuve Clicquot,

On the dance floor, a young couple were jitterbugging awkwardly to the Charles Tenet wartime hit, *Boum*. And he saw that she was watching them almost wistfully. 'I'd ask you to dance, but I can't,' he said.

'It is your back?'

'Nope. Just can't dance. My wife used to say I had two left feet.'

'Ah yes, I had forgotten you were married.'

He lifted his glass in salute. 'I'm trying to.'

'But how is your back. Does it hurt?'

'Only when I move.'

'I thought I would go outside with a cigarette,' she said, taking a sip from her glass and looking up at him over the rim.

He instinctively patted his breast pocket. 'Just thinking about it myself.'

'When you decide, please take me with you.'

He nodded, then they sat in companionable silence, watching the young couple bring their jive to a messy finale. Then Mimi asked: 'So what were you really thinking about?'

'Oh, this and that.' He looked to where the newlyweds were making an awkward attempt at the Twist to a Johnny Hallyday cover version of Elvis's *Burning Love*. 'And I was thinking how funny it is that the French don't do Rock 'n' Roll, just copy ours.'

'Perhaps because we taught the world to cook and paint and write — and love — we did not think pop music was serious enough to bother with.' She smiled to show she was not really serious. 'And I don't count Johnny as one of ours. Did you know he was a Belgian?'

'That accounts for it,' said Mowgley.

He turned the empty Clicquot bottle upside down, put it in the ice bucket and waved to a pretty young waitress standing in attendance with a circular metal tray held vertically against her stomach. She looked very bored and was probably thinking about how she was better than this and what she could do to change her life. As they waited for her arrival, he thought about what he had really been thinking about.

~

From the Dôme, she had led him away from the tourist haunts to a grimy bar in a winding, cobbled street a distance from the river.

Inside was a single, long room, with a serving hatch in one wall and a line of tables against another. Empty glasses and bottles had been left ungathered, and a handful of customers were seeing the night through. They were different but the same, he thought. One man was leaning forward with his head in his hands, muttering to himself. On the next table, a woman of indeterminate age sighed, shook her head and looked at her empty glass as if it might tell her something she needed to know. Nearby an elderly man was in earnest conversation with himself. All seemed to have accepted that Life had got the better of them. An old-fashioned billiards table occupied the centre of the room, its cloth torn and stained. The stain could have been beer, vomit or blood.

He felt her looking at him and saw she was waiting for a reaction. Then he realised what seemed familiar. It brought to mind the Van Gogh painting of a late-night billiard salon in Arles. Had it been nearer the river and a deliberate homage, the place would be packed and the prices tripled.

They took a seat near to the man with his head in his hands and ordered drinks. Disappointingly, the barman/waiter was not wearing the grubby white outfit in the painting, and was a sullen youth with dirty fingernails, spiky haircut and a tattoo of a snake emerging from his open collar. Até ordered absinthe, and included their despairing neighbour.

As the youth slouched away, she made an extravagant gesture, almost like an estate agent seeking approval from potential buyers. 'Do you like it? It's my favourite bar when I want to be with real people.'

'I think all people are real, just different,' he said in mild reproof, then added: '...but I know what you mean. And it's like I've stepped into the painting. Do you think it's deliberate or just a coincidence?'

She shrugged. 'Dunno, but it's funny that the clock is stuck at the same time as in the painting.'

He looked at the far wall and nodded. 'Spooky. Perhaps we're in a time warp, or the Green Fairy is doing its stuff. And it's got the same sort of colour scheme, hasn't it?'

'Well spotted. Van Gogh wrote to his brother that he was trying to express the terrible passions of humanity in red and green, with clashes and contrasts.'

Scrabbling around in the embroidered shoulder bag,

she fished out a tin of small cheroots, lit one and offered the tin. 'It's alright,' she said. 'The owner believes in the liberté bit of the national motto. The night shift cops come in for a fag and a beer on a dirty night.'

The drinks arrived and Até raised her glass as if toasting their surroundings: 'A café is where you can ruin yourself, go mad and commit crimes,' she said. 'Do you know who said that?'

'No, but I can guess.'

She smiled. 'Yep. Another corker from everyone's favourite mad genius. At the time, Vincent was getting excited about the arrival of Gauguin and the idea of starting an artist's colony. He said he'd sent Theo a *croquis* — a sketch — of what was to be *The Night Café*, gave a detailed account of how he'd spent Theo's money on the furniture he'd bought for the house, and how he was going to fill Gauguin's rooms with paintings of sunflowers.'

Mowgley rubbed his chin thoughtfully. 'I wonder if he ever thought his paintings would sell for millions after his death and he would become one of the most famous painters in history. It's sort of ironic that nobody wanted to know when he was alive but now, they say he was a genius. What would he have made of that?'

Até made a palms-up "who knows?" gesture. 'That's why his letters are so important. I don't give fuck-all credence to what the 'experts' tell us why he did what he did and what he was thinking, but when it's in his own words it works for me. He believed with God's help he would succeed in what he was trying to do, but he was absolutely sure he'd never amount to much as a painter. I don't think he ever gave a toss about fame and fortune, which may be why he never found it.'

They watched as the despairing man sat up, looked groggily at them and then reached for his glass of absinthe as if he were drowning and it was a life preserver.

Mowgley made a face, put his foul-tasting cheroot in

the ashtray and reached for a Caporal. 'What about you?'

'I've got my cigar.'

'No, I meant did you always want to be rich and famous?'

'Good question. Why do you ask?'

He shrugged. 'Just wondering about the death of Death and then the fire at the gallery...and how it all worked out for you.'

She blew a stream of smoke towards him, then smiled a hungry smile. 'You know, don't you? Or think you know?'

'I don't know if I know,' he had replied, 'but I know what I know. Why don't you tell me the rest?'

~

The newly-weds were still smooching on the dance floor, now joined by Mimi and a guest who could not believe his luck. It was the Rembrandt lookalike, who was at least a foot shorter than his statuesque partner and being held up by as much as dancing with her. His bulbous nose was at a level with and almost resting on her generous cleavage, and he looked blissfully happy.

Funny, Mowgley thought, how little it took to please most men, and how hope for sexual favour or conquest may diminish but never completely die with the passing of the years. Even when getting a hard-on is very much a thing of the past, most men still dare to fancy their chances.

He looked again at the fake Degas and thought of Até and her expressionless face as she had told him about the night of Piers De'Ath's death, what led up to it, and her part in it.

~

As he had concluded, Até was indeed Brigadier Healey-Asquith granddaughter and it had been her mother who took the Max Ernst to the man who would become Piers De'Ath.

The painting had proved to be genuine, and a gift from his French colleagues when he returned to the UK at the end of the War. It had been, they said, no more than a souvenir of their time and work together. Or at least, that was the family story.

Mowgley looked at her empty glass and waved at the young barman. 'So, is it true your mother left with Death when he took off for a larger stage?'

'Yes.'

'But you didn't go with them?'

'I was asked in a half-hearted sort of way, but I couldn't stand the thought of being anywhere near him. He'd tried it on the first time we met and seemed unlikely to take no for an answer. Mother gave me some money before they skipped — not a lot, but enough for me to hit the road to Marrakech.'

'And when did you last hear from her?'

Até looked away as if to try and avoid answering the question, then said: 'I didn't. I came back to the village three years later when I'd spent all my money, been to all the orgies and taken all the drugs I could ingest and stay alive. Then I learned that the police and the family solicitor had been trying to find me to tell me mother was dead and there was nothing for me to inherit. It turned out that Mr. Arsehole Arnett and Mama had set up home and shop in Brittany while he re-invented himself.'

She paused for a drink, then continued. 'According to the local police, Mother had gone out alone in her dinghy and only the boat came back. The coroner and local police were satisfied she'd been drinking and had died in a tragic accident. A bit like Rebecca.'

Mowgley frowned. 'Rebecca?'

'From the book.' She looked at his blank expression.

'By Daphne du Maurier.' A pause for reaction or recognition, then she said: 'Oh, never mind.'

Their drinks arrived, and he waited while they were served and the youth gone. 'And you thought it was more than an accident?'

She shrugged. 'I don't know what I thought. All I knew was that she was dead and I was broke and full of anger. At her for going off and at myself for not trying to stop her. But most of all at him for using her.'

'But perhaps he had loved her as well?'

She gave a puff of disdain. 'Perhaps.'

'So you planned to get your revenge?'

'Revenge?'

She glanced down at the table top as if looking into the past and considering her options, then said. 'Revenge? I never really thought of it like that, but I suppose you're right.' She looked at him with a weary smile. 'I guess it best I tell you exactly why and how Mr. De'Ath and I ended up in the cellar. Would that help?'

He gave a small smile. 'I think it might.'

~

Arriving home to find herself a penniless orphan, Caroline Healey-Asquith realised she would have to make her own way in the world. It came, she said, as a bit of a shock. And apart from lesbian prostitution, the only occupation she could think of that she had some talent for was painting.

This seemed a better option than becoming a shelf-stacker at Tesco, marrying a wealthy prick or sleeping with ugly women for a living. Ironically, her journey to making a name for herself in the art world would involve Piers De'Ath, both before and, most ironically, after his death.

To begin with, she could see no sense in trying to be an original painter. During her time at Chelsea art college and on the road to and beyond Morocco, she had learned how much easier it was to copy rather than create, and particularly so with most modern works. She had knocked out any number of Dalis and Picassos and Van Goghs and sold them in tourist trap bazaars for booze and dope money during her Eastern adventuring. She had found she was very good at it, but realised the market for honest copies was flooded and the going rate would hardly keep her in cheroots.

It was then she had the seedling of an idea for making big money while bringing down the man who had stolen and perhaps caused her mother to die. A big bonus was that her target now had plenty of money and influence.

Shortly after coming to national attention in the art world with his discovery of the Max Ernst, Charles Arnett had metamorphosed into Piers De'Ath. He'd also anointed himself as a leading critic and commentator on all aspects of pre — and post-Modern Art. In the process, he'd become extraordinarily lucky at unearthing lost or previously unknown works by not-too-famous painters of the era.

Based on his authentication of the Ernst, he had become the go-to intermediary and advisor for all those who thought they may have found a modern masterpiece in their attics. Mr. De'Ath was happy to help for a healthy commission.

His rate of progress meant that in three short years, he had buried his past as a small-time dealer in a seedy shop in the westcountry to live a privileged and indulgent life in a series of grand dwellings across France. With the collaboration and connivance of others who would benefit from his activities, pronouncements and 'discoveries', he had become a leading figure in a world which thrived on fakery, lies and deception. To build up such treasure and treasures in such a short time, the Brigadier's daughter's daughter knew he must be doing more than just talking and writing about art and making the occasional genuine discovery. He was obviously dealing in fakery, and in his new incarnation, in the perfect position to authenticate them. So, it would seem to be a good move to offer to service his need for lost treasures.

~

Unsurprisingly, De'Ath had been suspicious of but clearly intrigued by her request for a meeting. Thus, they had dined in a suitably anonymous bistro in Cherbourg while she laid out her proposals.

As he should know, she was broke, and as she saw it, he owed her. He had contacts and power and influence in the art world. She wanted to make a name for herself and had been working on an idea that, with his help, could make her the next big name in the Modernist Movement. Or a contender at least. Warhol had come up with his soup cans, Dali his melted watches and Pollock his stripes. Her almost Unique Selling Point would be to reproduce familiar works with a small but telling addition. Along the lines of graffiti, which would shock the purists and amuse the iconoclasts. As an example, she had brought a copy of *The Scream*, with the manic central character holding a phone to his ear so that his expression now suggested he was hearing not imagining the worst of bad news. Or had perhaps been put on hold in a telephonic queue that stretched to infinity.

With Duchamp's bearded Mona Lisa, she knew her idea was neither unique, particularly ground-breaking nor earth-shaking, but then neither had been the Emin's unmade bed or Damien's dots. By claiming her as his protégé and coming up with some inspirational bullshit, her mentor would make her a star—and share in the proceeds and reflected glory.

By the third bottle of wine, she had enhanced the offering with the proposal that, on the side, she would reproduce a stream of previously unknown works by dead modernists with a mid-range value. He could invent a source and validate and put them into circulation.

Finally, and as a clincher if one were needed, she said it was even possible that they could eventually become sexual partners as well as business partners. She knew about his unusual tastes, as he did about her Sapphic inclinations. Between them, they could come up with some interesting and possibly unique arrangements.

In fact, she had told Mowgley, the thought made her gag, but she would use the prospect of intimate closeness to De'Ath to find out more about and expose his illegal activities and try to discover the truth about her mother's death.

'So, what did he say?' Mowgley asked.

'He lapped it up. Within months he'd discovered me and got the campaign going with a series of articles and interviews about my iconoclastic approach to modern masterpieces and how my add-ons were a wry comment on the development of technology and its impact on our minds and lives. And lots more utter crap.'

'And it worked?'

She looked at her empty glass and then expectantly at him. 'It did, but, strangely, things only really took off for me after the… incident… at the château.'

'And…' he reminded her, '…the fire and death at the gallery.'

She looked briefly troubled. 'Yes, I fear so.'

He put his glass down, sat back and looked at her. 'So what really happened in the cellar — and the fire? And don't lie to me or I'll turn over what I know to Colonel Degas and recommend he pulls you in for suspected murder.'

'Okay, okay.' She held up a hand and waited till the waiter had come and gone, then said: 'The honest truth is that I found him in the cellar and had nothing to do with his death.'

'He pulled a face. 'I'm always worried when someone tells me they're telling me the honest truth. Anyway, what were you doing there? Why go down there in the early hours? To meet him for some funny business?'

'No. To be truly honest, I was very pissed... and a bit high. And I'd read an article in one of those poncy glossy 'lifestyle' magazines about his fabled wine collection.'

'So?'

'So I thought I'd go down and have some fun. Perhaps chug an 1811 Château d'Yquem and then piss in the bottle. That sort of thing. And perhaps visit the secret room — I'm sure you know about the secret room?'

He nodded and she continued. 'And then fuck up some of the paintings.'

'Your own paintings?'

'No, my predecessor.'

'Who was?'

She shrugged. 'Dunno. I realised after I started doing the fakes that my proposal was even more appealing because he'd lost his original fakester.'

'You mean they fell out?'

She grimaced. 'A bit more than that. He disappeared. Like my mother.'

Mowgley frowned. 'You think Death may have got rid of him? Why would he kill the golden goose?'

She shrugged. 'Pass. Maybe he got greedy or let the cat out of the bag. De'Ath was mixing with some not very nice business partners in America. The sort who look like characters from *The Sopranos*.'

'Was the States his best market for the fakes, then?'

She nodded. 'By far. I wondered at first why he got me to do mostly modern American stuff. I thought it was because they were the easiest to copy, but it was because there's such a huge market for it. Abstract Expressionists like Jackson Pollock and Mark Rothko are a piece of cake. They reckon there's ten times as many fakes than genuine works of those two on walls in the

USA than the rest of the world. The dodgy ones are easier to sell if they come from the place where they were allegedly created.'

'So you went down to the cellar just to mess up his fake pictures and posh wines?'

'That's right. No big plan, just impulse, fuelled as the briefs always say in mitigation, by alcohol and drugs.'

Mowgley nodded slowly, lit another cigarette to give himself time to think, then asked:

'And you found him there?'

'Yeah.'

'Dead?'

'No. When I got over the shock, I took a closer look. He was foaming at the mouth, but still breathing. I saw the pill bottle in his hand and knew what he'd been up to.'

'Did you not think about calling for help?'

She gave a dry laugh and looked at him as if he had said something really silly. 'Nope. Not for a fucking second.'

'But what about all the mumbo jumbo. The cabbalistic signs and the candles — and the Red Herring painting?'

'Guilty to the painting. I couldn't resist going back up for it and leaving it on his chest just to stir things up when he was found. But as to the other stuff, it was either how he liked it when he was having a session, or — .'

'Or what?'

'Someone else had been there before me. It would explain the symbols and his position. Perhaps it was someone from the local devil-worshipping club I heard about.'

'That doesn't actually exist.' He looked at her in a you-would-say-that way. 'Then what happened?'

'I picked a really nice bottle and drank it while I watched him die.'

Mowgley shook his head, then asked: 'How long did it take for him to stop breathing?'

'About an hour I guess.'

'And you didn't help him along a bit?'

'I did think about it, but there were no cushions to hand. And I was quite enjoying it and didn't want to bring it to an end. And I know about DNA and fingerprints and all that CSI stuff from watching the telly. I used a cloth from the secret chamber to hold the bottle and took the cork with me. I even glugged it without my lips touching the neck by pouring it Spanish *porron* style.'

'Okay.' He sat back and looked at her steadily for a moment, then said: 'And you really had nothing to do with the explosion and fire at the gallery?'

'Might not mean much to you, but I swear on my mother's life that I had nothing at all to do with that. You know the police know it, or they wouldn't have let me go. And you know what I've just told you about my visit to the cellar is the truth.'

She breathed out heavily as if relieved to have unburdened herself, reached for his cigarettes, emptied her glass and signalled to the waiter. The man at the next table was back in his default position, with his head ever closer to the floor. She gave their order and then looked at Mowgley with the question on her face. 'So, what are you going to do now?'

He raised a hand as if to look at the watch he was not wearing. 'I've got to be back in Normandy tomorrow to get ready for my friend's wedding next week. I'm the best man.'

She scowled. 'You know what I meant, you bastard. You do believe me, don't you?'

He looked at her steadily for a moment, then said: 'Yes, I think I actually do believe you. I think.'

'And what will you be telling your policeman friend?'

'At the wedding? I'll probably tell him a couple of crap jokes that don't work in France and give him some advice on how to handle my former colleague.'

She sighed. 'And what about what I've just told you?'

'To be quite honest — and I am being — I don't know. I'll

have to give it some thought.'

'And what about... us?'

He smiled wryly. 'I didn't know there was an 'us'. You're not trying to buy my silence with your body, are you?'

She smiled back. 'Nope. You already know I like having sex with some men as well as women.'

'What sort of men?'

She thought for a moment, then said: 'Umm, unpredictable and unusual ones. Ones who don't try to look better than they are — in both senses. And ones who don't always play by the rules and like to go their own way. But who stick to their own code of conduct. You know, oddballs.'

'Like me?'

'Like you. Fancy another drink before we go? And your place or mine?'

He looked at her through a haze of cigarette smoke. 'Both. I think I'll just walk you home...'

~

'How is your eye, Jack?

He suppressed a pantomime jerk as he was brought back to the present. 'Fine, thanks Mimi.'

'Good. Mine is too. And I see your head is almost mended.'

She slipped gracefully into the seat opposite him, then smiling sweetly, said: 'I hear it is the second time a woman has helped you in a fight.'

He smiled back. 'I believe in equal opportunities. Pity you won't be around to bail me out next time I get into a scrape.'

'Bail you out?'

'Yes. It means to remove water from a sinking ship, or posting bail to get someone out of prison. Or just to help someone out who's in trouble.'

'Ah, I see,' she said as if she did not.

Mowgley looked at her flawless features and make-up. Her elderly partner had retired to the bar, breathing heavily for, Mowgley suspected, more than one reason. Slightly flushed from her exertions on the dance floor, his former colleague looked achingly beautiful. She was, he thought not for the first time, the perfect embodiment of a stylish, beautiful and beautifully mature woman.

She shrugged an elegant shoulder. 'But why do you think I will not be around to... bail you out?'

'Well, you might be, but I may not. Not too much work about for a freelance private eye who has a punch-up with his boss and can't speak proper French.'

He put his glass on the table and absent-mindedly tapped the pocket where his Caporal had lain neglected for more than an hour.

'I could get used to this,' he said, looking round the room.

'You mean being the *garcon de honneur*, or drinking a lot of Champagne?' Mimi smiled, then added: 'Or do you mean getting married? I think René would agree to be your best boy.'

Mowgley made a sour face. 'Chance would be a fine thing. Anyway, the only woman I would want to spend the rest of my life with is spoken for.'

'Spoken for?'

'Taken... er, with another man.'

Mimi looked to see if he was joking. 'You mean Catherine? You should perhaps have asked her to marry you before it was too late.'

'Blimey, no. She's my best mate. You don't usually marry your best friend, and she would have said no, for sure. No, I meant you.'

'Me?' Mimi looked genuinely surprised. 'But if you are serious, why have you not made it clear?'

'A couple of reasons. One was because I knew what the answer would be if I asked you for a date, let alone to get married.'

'And the other?'

'The fact that you were in a relationship with my boss, and he would have given me more than a black eye had I made a pass at you.'

'Hmmm.' Mimi made a dismissive gesture with her free hand. 'Anyway, you need not worry about Mr. Cornec. He is no longer your boss or mine... and I am no longer in any sort of affair with him, business or of the heart.'

He gave a puzzled look. 'Oh, okay. But would you consider any type of proposal from an unemployed private detective.'

Mimi smiled. 'From what I hear, you may not be unemployed for much longer. In fact, you may be a company *directeur*, and a very good, catch, I think you say.'

'Eh? Sorrypardon?'

'Hello you two. Still upright?'

Another bottle of Champagne had arrived with the groom and bride, ready for what Mowgley estimated to be the fifteenth toast of the evening.

Mowgley looked from Mimi across to Degas and his new wife. 'Do you know something I don't?'

'She sure do,' said Catherine Degas-McCarthy 'We were going to proposition you tomorrow.' She looked at her watch and then continued, 'I mean later today.'

He shrugged. 'Feel free. I haven't been propositioned for years.'

~

Mowgley blew a plume of smoke towards the boughs of the majestic oak and looked at his old friend and former colleague. They had come to the place of the lover's tryst in the copse. It would not take a detective to work out that by some prior arrangement, her new husband and Mimi had stayed in the hall. They would join them for a cigarette later, they said, and when they had given due attention to the Champagne bottle.

She smiled contentedly. 'A bit like the old times, eh?'

'Not really,' said Mowgley. 'You're married and I'm unemployed and living in France on my own.'

'True… but don't whine. It's not like you. What I meant was just you and me, having a fag and a chat. I'm sure you'll meet the right person sometime soon, if you want to. She paused meaningfully, then asked: 'What did you think of my mother?'

'He gave her a sharp look, then said guardedly: 'A nice lady.'

They smoked in silence, then he looked at her and put his head on one side. 'You're not trying to fix me up with your mum, are you?'

She laughed a fake laugh. 'Are you kidding me? Do you really think I would wish you on to my mother? Or want you as a step father? And before you ask, I won't be trying to fix her up with René's dad. What is it with you blokes who think a woman can't live happily on her own?'

'She dropped her cigarette and ground it into the leaf mould beneath their feet, then made a signal for him to give her another one. She was obviously going to make the most of her nicotine ingesting time before her new husband appeared. 'So, what about your mum and dad? I know you lost them both when you were pretty young, but you never really talked about them. Were they happy together?'

Mowgley lit and passed her a fresh cigarette. 'Okay. And I wasn't that young, just past thirty.'

'And what were they like?'

'What do you mean, what were they like?'

'I mean what were they like?'

Mowgley looked into the past and then said. 'My dad was from Cork.'

'And what did he do?'

'Lots of things. Dug ditches, sold things from door-to-door, drove lorries and raced dogs.'

'Never settled to anything then?'

Mowgley shook his head. 'He was really easy-going and... wise and understood life and people, which was probably why he never amounted to much.'

She looked at his profile in the moonlight. 'And your mum?'

'She was very clever. Came from a 'good' family with a big house and even a maid and cook. She always said she could have done much better for herself, and when she let fly she would say that marrying him was the biggest mistake of her life, but I knew she didn't mean it.'

'So why did they marry? Opposite poles attract?'

'I suppose it was something like that. She said when they met, he had an old coat with a hole in the sleeve and a greyhound on a string and looked hopeless. She felt sorry for him.'

'Ah. And how did they...?'

'Mum got breast cancer. She was only in her fifties. Dad died less than a year later. I don't think he wanted to go on without her.'

'And how did he... die?'

'Lung cancer. The specialist said the tumour appeared and grew in weeks. He wouldn't say so, but I know he thought the same as me.'

They sat in silence again, then Catherine put a hand out and rested it on his knee. 'You haven't told me about your latest meeting with the Artist to be Known as Até.'

'Hasn't your husband told you about it?'

'She shook her head. Not a word. He's been a bit preoccupied for the past few days, to be fair. So, do you think she did it?'

'Tell you both about it later.'

'No advance briefing for your old bag carrier, then?'

'Nope.'

~

285

'So did Catherine proposition you?'

'No. We talked about the past a bit and she smoked four fags.'

Degas and Mimi had arrived with glasses, more Champagne and a bottle of Calvados.

'Fair exchange?' said Degas, waving the bottles and nodded at the packet of Caporal. 'We need to catch up. Along with the wedding vows, we promised each other we would stop smoking altogether tomorrow.

'You know that tomorrow never comes, don't you?'

'True,' said Degas, but we will do our best. And the office will be a smoke-free zone.'

'Office?'

'I will explain. But now, drink for cigarettes?'

'Done.'

'Okay.' Degas fiddled with the foil on the Champagne bottle and looked at his wife. 'Do you want to tell him, darling?'

'That's a Roger, René. Anyway, I'll start.' She sat on a gilded garden chair opposite their bench, took a thoughtful draw on her cigarette, then said. 'The thing is that you may be unemployed, but so is Yann Cornec.' She looked at Degas to continue.

He handed out the glasses then went and stood beside his wife. 'My former friend and your former employer is now in custody, awaiting trial.'

Mowgley raised an eyebrow. 'I wondered why he was not here today. Surely you're not doing him for giving me and Mimi a shiner.' He turned to Mimi. 'Black eye, as we say.'

'A little more than that,' said Degas. 'As you know, we had recently fallen out over his presumption on my indulgence as a past colleague. Then I heard some very bad things about him and that he was under investigation at the highest level. The accusations included malpractice, blackmail and extortion. They had not told me because they knew we had been close. As well as providing privileged information about rival companies to his clients, he was also blackmailing expatriate Britons who he had been asked to find because they had left big debts behind them. When he found them, he threatened to pass on the information unless they paid him a large amount. Less than they owed the companies, but still significant.'

'So, Mimi will be running Services d'Enquêtes Privés Cornec while the owner is away?'

'There will be no Services d'Enquêtes Privés Cornec,' said Mimi. 'There are big debts and the company would not be allowed to do their work while the investigations are taking place. I am glad to say I was never a *directeur* or partner in the business, just an employee. I resigned on the day that Yann...' she raised her hand to her cheek, '...gave me the present.'

'That makes two of us out of work then?'

'Not if you want to become part of a rival organisation,' said Catherine.

Mowgley looked at the three smiling faces. 'Tell me more.'

'As you know, I have reached the age at which I may retire and take my pension,' said René Degas. 'I had anticipated a long and peaceful retirement with my dear wife.' He reached out and took her hand, 'but she had other ideas.'

'He can't play golf and he doesn't like gardening and has no hobbies.' interjected Catherine. 'He'd just go mad sitting at home and getting under my feet. For thirty years he's lived and breathed investigating crime and bringing the bad guys to justice. And, although I love him to bits and want to be with him, believe it or not I'm already beginning to miss my old job.'

Mowgley held a hand up. 'And me as well, I hope?'

'A bit. Anyway, I am pleased to inform you that my husband—' she paused as if savouring the word, 'has put in motion the formation of a private investigation company, its headquarters to be in Cherbourg. As the premises are likely to be vacant in the near future, the offices opposite the gendarmerie would be a suitable location, and the owner of the premises has already expressed his enthusiasm.'

She exchanged glances with Degas, who toasted Mimi, then said: 'Madame Christobel Hardy has consented to join the company as director of operations, and Madame Catherine Degas... McCarthy will take the role of chief *investigateur* and director.'

'Blimey,' said Mowgley, 'and what about you.'

Degas smiled. 'I shall become the président, or chairman or as I think you now say, CEO. My role will be to generally oversee the business, find new customers and re-establish contact with old friends and colleagues. We will also be picking up business from past clients of Services d'Enquêtes Privés Cornec. This will mean we shall be busy from the beginning, and urgently need extra staff. A general secretary for office administration under Mimi, and also a trainee to assist my dear wife.'

'Ah. I think I can see where this is going. A role reversal? I'd be your bag carrier?'

'Not at all,' said Catherine. 'René means a young person to train as an *investigateur* while he or she gains the qualifications. But we will need a senior investigator with experience in the field. Someone with good contacts on both sides of the Channel. To ensure enthusiasm and commitment, he would become a director and partner and shareholder in the operation. Can you think of anyone who would suit the position?'

'It depends if there's an upper age limit,' said Mowgley. The person I would recommend is getting a little long in the tooth and set in his ways.'

'You don't have to tell us that,' said Degas. 'You can't teach an old dog new tricks I think you say, but a dog that knows all the tricks would be a valuable asset. And Mimi has said she would continue the French lessons so you would not need to be limited to English clients.'

With that, Colonel Degas smiled, walked across the space between them and reached out across the table with an open hand. 'Do you want some time to think about it, or can we seal the knot and bargain here? Salary and shareholdings and other things can be discussed at a later time.'

Mowgley rubbed his chin and looked as if he was giving the offer thoughtful consideration, then stood and took the proffered hand. Then, as if previously arranged, Catherine and Madame Mimi reached out and placed their hands on top.

'As someone said,' said Mowgley. 'One for all and all for one? Or would that be too cheesy?'

~

'I am sorry to talk more business, but —'

'Please do,' said Mowgley.

An hour later and they had decided to see the dawn in under the oak tree.

'As you know,' said Degas, 'and partly because of your conclusions and report on your investigations, I decided to cease any active investigation into the death of Mr. De'Ath as a case of murder. We can now leave the coroner to decide on a verdict of accidental death or suicide.'

'Okay,' said Mowgley. 'I think that's for the best.'

On his return from Paris, he had met with Degas and given him a final report on his conclusions as to Até's involvement in the events in the cellar. She had admitted to finding the body and leaving the red herring painting on the body, and had not reported it to the police for fear of what would happen when they found out who she was. They would then know she had motive as well as opportunity. She had been cleared of any involvement in the gallery fire and death of the owner, but if the local police knew she had been in the cellar it would be an obvious conclusion that she had killed the man who had stolen her mother and perhaps worse. It was a full and honest report, but Mowgley had chosen not to include how she had sat and relished watching Piers De'Ath take his last breaths.

Degas had listened intently, then said he agreed with Mowgley that she had no active part in the death. But she could and perhaps should have been charged with failing to report a death and wasting police time at the least.

But, after further deliberations in Mowgley's local bar, he had said it would perhaps be best for everyone concerned to close the investigation and leave the coroner to decide. It was not the official or even correct approach to take, but Até had been, he agreed, a victim, and he trusted his friend and future partner's instincts and assessment. In this case, he had said, it would be best to, as the English would say, let sleeping dogs lie.

~

Mowgley's phone rang as he arrived in his room at the Château Erzulie.

'I was just thinking of you,' she said. 'How did it go?'

'Okay. I think the punters thought I was putting on the mangled French.'

'I bet. But what about your talk with the groom? About me, I mean. What did he say? Did you convince him I didn't kill De'Ath?'

'Oh that. I didn't try to do any convincing, just told him what I thought. He saw it my way. The case is closed.'

A pause and then he heard her lighting a cheroot and sucking in a lungful of smoke. 'So I'm in the clear?'

'Looks like it. Unless you're going to tell me you did help Mr. Death on his way.'

'I did actually tell you the truth. You know that or you

wouldn't be on my side.'

'Yes, I think you did just what you said.'

'Only "think"?'

'What do we really know we can be sure of. It's just that's what my instincts told me.'

An audible sigh of what could be relief, then: 'I'm glad you followed them. So when do I get to see you again?'

'Oh,' he said, 'you mean you weren't being nice to me just to get me on side?'

'A bit of both,' she said with a small laugh. 'But then I found I liked your company. It's relaxing to spend time with someone of a lesser intellect.'

'Thanks.'

'Only joking. Will I see you again?'

'Could be. I do like the Left Bank.'

'And me?'

'And you. A bit.'

'How would tomorrow do? I could even change for the occasion.'

'You mean — ? Every man's dream. I didn't know I was that good.'

'Don't flatter yourself, I meant change my clobber and even wear a dress. Funny how after all my intellectual and rabidly sexual encounters. I end up fancying an old, washed-up private detective.'

'Yeah, he said, Life's funny sometimes, ain't it?'

Epilogue:

Abdyl Kurti's step was decidedly unsteady as he left the Theatre Square and took the short cut to the marina and the *Zoete Dromen*. The dark and narrow alleyway was lined with bins, crates and other detritus, and he cursed as he stumbled over a leaking plastic bag. It had been torn open by a fox or cat, and the debris from the kebab shop squelched under his feet.

So engrossed was he with maintaining his balance and navigating the obstacle course that he did not become aware of the figure blocking his way until they were almost within touching distance.

'*Lëvizni, pidhi*' he slurred, uncaring that the figure might not be fluent in Albanian profanities. He would get the message if Abdyl got hold of him.

The short, stocky figure did not move, except to pull a hand from the inside of his blouson jacket. As drunk as he was, the Albanian saw that it held a knife, and its blade shone dully in the weak light coming from the end of the alleyway.

Abdyl fumbled for his own knife as he backed away, but his reactions were dulled by the near-bottle of vodka he had got through on the terrace of the Moustache bar. Then, he slipped on the remains of a betyi kebab as the man took a single step towards him.

The Albanian small-time gangster felt little more than a sharp pain like a punch to his stomach, and was surprised to find his legs become suddenly weak. He fell and lay slumped against a wheely bin as his attacker knelt and leaned over in an almost solicitous manner. The man then reached out and gently took a hold on his left upper arm as if about to help him to his feet. Instead, he leaned closer, apparently to check that Abdyl was conscious.

'I have money,' said the Albanian in heavily-accented French. 'In my pocket —'

He fell silent as the figure held a gloved finger up to his lips, then lifted the blood-stained knife and held it horizontally against the fallen man's throat.

As the blade cut through the soft flesh and then one of the carotid arteries to let his life force gush free, Abdyl Kurti went into hypovolaemic shock. Soon, the blood flow to his brain would be compromised and he would lose consciousness, followed by death a few minutes later. As he headed into the dark tunnel of no return, he realised that the man had spoken in very bad Albanian before dealing the death blow.

'Goodbye Abdyl,' he had said, 'this is for Kai.'

The End

Dead and Buried

If you enjoyed this book, information about the rest of the series can be found on the author's website at george-east.net. In the meantime, here's a taste of the previous Jack Mowgley investigation:

Prologue

They adorned her naked and unresisting body with gold as the sun fell from the sky. Round her waist they fixed a golden belt and on her head a golden crown. Each of her remaining fingers was given an intricately worked golden ring, and around her body were strewn golden platters and cups as if to aid her journey to the next world. She woke from her opiate-induced slumber as the first clods of earth hit the lid of the casket. Still drunk from the effects of the drug she tried to understand why she lay on her back in the total darkness. Then she explored the confines of the box till gradually it came to her who and where she was. And why. She was the only one who could hear her attempts to scream, and soon they exhausted the air in her lungs and in the coffin. Then came a final shuddering gasp, and she was troubled no more as she became one with the earth and the buried treasures surrounding her.

~

'Does it hurt?'

'Only when I try to tap dance. I keep falling in the sink.'

'Har de har. Will you have a limp?'

'A limp what?' Detective Sergeant Catherine McCarthy tired of trying to get any sense out of her former boss, spat a grape seed into her hand and watched wistfully as Mowgley drew deeply on his odiferous cigarette. He made his usual pitiful attempt at blowing a smoke ring, and she thought fleetingly about taking the Gauloises and showing him how it should be done. It would have been some sort of an excuse to fill her lungs with deliciously toxic smoke, but she resisted and reached for another grape.

'So what happened to the roll-ups?' she asked.

Mowgley paused for a coughing fit, then replied. 'I am making a personal protest.'

'What against - the cost of English baccy?'

'No – this stupid idea to ban Gitanes and Gauloises.'

Former Special Branch Detective Inspector John 'Jack' Mowgley waved a copy of France Soir: 'It says here they're going to ban the classic brands for being too 'cool'.

His former colleague frowned. 'How do you know that's what it says?'

'The nice nurse told me.'

'Ah'. Melons raised an eyebrow: 'But "too cool"? How can a fag be cool?'

'I remember ones that were as cool as a mountain stream according to the adverts, but let that pass. You've obviously never seen a classic *film noir* or Jean-Paul Belmondo lighting up in bed after a bit of how's-your-father.'

'Jean-Paul who?'

'Never mind.' Mowgley maliciously directed a plume of smoke in her direction. 'How was Nice? And don't say 'nice'

'Well it was.'

'That's nice. So when are you going to make it official

with your Frog friend and come over here to live?'

'Why the concern? Do you miss me?'

'Yep.' Like a very unlikely snake charmer, Mowgley let smoke dribble seductively from his lip and, leaning forward, swung the bulky cigarette in a hypnotic arc under her nose.

Once upon a time, Catherine McCarthy had been Mowgley's aide, bag-carrier and constant bailer-out at Portsmouth's continental ferry port. Then he had been forced to jump before he was pushed and very possibly imprisoned, and had crossed the Channel to start a new life in Cherbourg. He'd found a job with a private detective agency, tasked with investigating the misdemeanours and excesses of British expatriates.

Sergeant McCarthy had taken on a new boss, but had continued to prop Mowgley up by using her contacts and official and unofficial resources at the ferry port. In the course of a recent cross-Channel investigation she had fallen for a tall, distinguished and widowed Colonel in the national *Gendarmerie,* and had just returned from a stolen and, she suspected, very expensive week in Nice. Such was her commitment to the new man in her life that she had stopped smoking and cut back considerably on her drinking. As her former boss had it, she was now in danger of becoming respectable.

She cast another wistful look at his cigarette, then asked: 'How are they treating you here now you're a regular?'

They were sitting in the sunlit courtyard of the Louis Pasteur hospital. Built at the behest of Napoleon in 1860, it had been Mowgley's place of residence for almost two weeks. He had arrived with a badly broken upper left thighbone after being involved in a hit-and-run incident which seemed very unlikely to have been an accident. It was the private investigator's third visit for treatment in the past twelve months, so the staff were becoming used to his funny little and often alien ways.

Mowgley dropped his cigarette butt into the saucer of

his coffee cup and tried to make himself more comfortable in the wheelchair. 'It's okay here, I suppose. But nobody speaks English… or they pretend not to, and the food's pretty crap -'

'By that you mean the food is French?'

'I suppose so.'

She shook her head in mock-disbelief. 'In a French hospital? How disgusting…'

Mowgley nodded absent-mindedly and scratched pointlessly at the plaster cast encasing his left leg.

Melons watched as he lit up another cigarette 'So when do they reckon it'll come off?'

'What, the leg?'

'Yawn, yawn.'

'Tomorrow, the nice nurse says. Did you know they call it plaster of Paris because the gypsum came from Montmartre?'

Melons watched Mowgley take a provocatively long and blissful drag on his Gauloises. 'You don't say?'

He nodded. 'I just did. But putting a cast round a broken bone goes back as far as the Ancient Egyptians.'

She licked her lips then bit into a ragged finger nail. 'I know you specialise in collecting mostly useless information, but where did you get that from? Nice Nurse again?'

Mowgley tried not to look smug. 'That's right. Suzi. She's teaching me French and I'm helping with her English. After I get out, we're going to have regular sessions.' He paused and gave her a concerned look: 'Are you okay? it looks as if you're sweating.'

'Bollocks.'

Melons reached out and grabbed his cigarette and inhaled a greedy lungful. She sat back and held on to the smoke for several seconds, then let it trickle decadently from her parted lips.

'Blimey,' said Mowgley, 'I thought you'd given up to keep your bloke happy.'

'I have,' she said, 'I give up after every bloody fag…'

The plane was full and as noisy, messy and unsightly as Mimi had predicted.

After comparing costs and contemplating the marathon car journey, Mowgley had opted for the round-about flight option. He was not mean, as he explained to Mimi, just unused to paying for any form of travel with his own money. When you'd spent a working life claiming expenses for every journey, it came hard having to settle the bills yourself.

But it had been some consolation that he had managed to trim the costs further. As he had hoped, Melons had found an excuse to deliver him to Luton airport in good time for the evening flight. On the way she confessed she was meeting her French lover in London later that evening to take in a show and spend the night at a boutique hotel in Bayswater. He, or rather the French government would be footing the bill as René Degas would be attending a special conference on co-operation between Euro-zone and British law enforcement agencies after Brexit.

This news only served to make Mowgley more resentful of paying his own way, but, he had to admit, the flight was almost embarrassingly cheap. There was of course an inevitable price to pay for the cheapness.

Some hours after saying goodbye to Melons he had found himself entombed in the narrow fuselage of a plane that seemed much too overloaded to take off. Every seat was filled to overflowing and the overhead lockers were crammed with bags, rucksacks, clothing and even sustenance to see the travellers through the journey.

Looking around, it was clear that some passengers should have paid for two seats and, as Mimi had predicted, they were the sort of people who would be taking a budget flight to a very budget country. The travellers were mostly British and either holidaymakers or those curious to know how a house in Bulgaria could cost less than a second-hand car in Britain.

There was also a number of mainly young Bulgarians intent on visiting their families and friends while reminding themselves of what they were not missing at home. They were easily identifiable by their lack of tattoos and their general preference to eating with their mouths closed.

Mowgley flinched as small feet hammered on the back of his seat, groaned inwardly and tried not to look across the aisle at a woman picking her nose while she demolished a jumbo-sized chocolate bar. He did not think of himself as a snob, but did not relish five hours in the company of people with whom he would rather not share a lift.

Another downside was his fear of flying.

To be fair, it was not the time in the air that worried him, but the take-off and landing stages. The official term was aviophobia, which curiously also referred to a dread of fresh air. He could see that a sudden influx of fresh air on a plane in flight could be disconcerting, but objected to the term 'phobia'. According to most dictionaries, a phobia was an irrational fear. As there could be only one result of an aeroplane dropping unintentionally from the sky, he could not see how there was anything at all irrational in coming close to shitting oneself at the most dangerous moments of the journey.

In the absence of Melons he had held his own hand and tried not to groan too loudly, and stopped panting and sweating only when the plane had struggled into the air. Now all he had to do was survive the company and the landing.

Knowing the even more breath-taking price of in-flight food and drinks, he had reluctantly paid the price for a fancily wrapped egg and bacon sandwich and small bottle of water from a W H Smith outlet in the holding area. His cabin luggage – a smart and very expensive mini-suitcase on wheels that Mimi had bought for him, also contained his toilet bag, a couple of clean shirts and a change of underwear and socks. He had no intention of staying In Bulgaria for more than a day or two, but Mimi had refused to let him leave without them. Distributed about the ancient tweed jacket were two Curly-Wurly chocolate bars, his notepad, phone, cigarettes and a paperback copy of *The Big Sleep*. He had been told it would be warm on the Black Sea, but the coat had many pockets and there was no weight limit or restriction on how many layers of clothing passengers chose to wear.

~

An hour into the flight, and Mowgley had learned more about Bulgaria than he had accumulated in the previous half century. He had picked up a guide book at the airport, and now reckoned he would be able to hold his own in any pub quiz about one of the most recent additions to the European Union.

Primarily he had learned that Bulgaria had a lot of history, and most of it not at all happy. Having recovered from five hundred years of Turkish occupation, Bulgaria had opted to join the wrong side in both World Wars. Worse, those in charge had welcomed Communism in 1948 and watched insouciantly as the economy disintegrated.

On the face of it, joining the EU in 2007 had been a no-brainer, but as with Communism it seemed nobody in charge had considered the law of unintended consequences. On the upside was the billions of Euros in subsidies and grants, but most of it went into the wrong pockets. The real disaster came with millions of young people leaving home to live a much better life elsewhere in the Union. As a result, Bulgaria had the most rapidly declining population in Europe. If things carried on as they were, it would have the most rapidly declining population in the world.

~

Two hours on and the plane was flying over a seemingly endless chain of white-capped mountains. Probably the Alps, Mowgley thought, but then all mountains had a certain similarity when viewed from above.

The aircraft seemed to be behaving itself, but Mowgley was becoming increasingly irritated with what was happening inside it. It wasn't just the lusty Bulgarian babe-in-arms who had been sick on his shoulder, nor the enormous woman on the other side who kept offering him sweets and crisps. Even the members of the hen party dressed as cowgirls were causing no trouble. They had drunk too much too soon and were now sleeping the journey away.

The focus of Mowgley's growing annoyance was a man sitting in line with him across the aisle. He was tall and bulky in a flabby way, with short hair and most of his exposed flesh taken up by badly-done tattoos. The man had small, mean eyes, a snout-like nose and prominent ears, the lobes of which bore star-shaped tattoos. He could have been anywhere between thirty and forty, and looked like trouble. He was with another, shorter man of around the same age but with less of a tattoo fetish. From long experience Mowgley knew that the taller man would be the instigator of any problems, and that he would almost certainly cause some.

The pair had obviously been drinking before getting on the plane, and the cabin crew had made the mistake of serving them more. Rather than placating them, it had made Snouty more determined to enjoy himself by spoiling the journey for everyone else. It had started with obscene soccer chants and propositions to the prettier women passengers and the two stewardesses, then threats to the obviously terrified steward. Most of the passengers pretended not to notice, but there was apprehension and even fear on the faces of those nearest to the pair. The flight was barely half way to its destination, and all the crew and passengers could do was hope the lout would, like the members of the hen party, fall asleep. For now, the lack of response was provoking increasingly aggressive behaviour. If the cabin crew had followed official procedure, Snouty would have already been given a pre-written printed warning from the captain. Known as a red card by on-board staff, it would say that unless the bad behaviour ceased the plane would be diverted to the nearest airport and the perpetrator/s dumped there. They would also be billed for the cost of the diversion, which could run into tens of thousands of pounds. The problem with red cards was that they were an attempt to reason with drunk and very unreasonable people, so could actually inflame the situation.

Twenty years before, Mowgley would have already done something about the situation. Now he had an injured leg and was too old to get involved for the fun of it.

Things started to get really nasty when Snouty called for more beer and got no response. After the third bellow, he left his seat and lurched to the front of the plane. The small and slight steward appeared from the galley and tried to reason with him, but was contemptuously pushed back through the curtain. The big man then started hammering on the door to the flight deck, when a woman screamed and babies and small children started to cry. Getting no answer from the flight crew, the big man pushed his way into the galley and reappeared holding up two bottles as if they were trophies. Stumbling back along the aisle, he threw one to his mate, then saw Mowgley looking at him. He smiled in anticipation, got a grip on the back of a seat and bent down so their faces were level.

'What's up, you old cunt?' he asked, 'do you fucking want some?'

Mowgley said nothing and looked rigidly ahead as the man considered his options. Eventually he grunted in contempt, looked round for other possible confrontation, said 'fucking wanker,' then straightened up, unzipped his jean fly and made his stumbling way towards the back of the plane.

Mowgley remained looking ahead but was aware of the reaction of the women on either side of him. The young mother held her baby tighter and looked at Mowgley with a mixture of sympathy and concern for herself and her child. The sweets lady seemed disappointed, as if she had expected some other reaction.

The former Special Branch officer stayed where he was for a long moment, then sighed, unbuckled his seat belt and stood up. Leaving his walking stick behind he got up and limped toward the rear of the plane. Looking over his shoulder, he saw the sweets lady watching and the white face of the male steward peering out from the galley. Everyone else was making a point of minding their own business. Pushing through the curtained-off partition, Mowgley rapped briskly on the toilet door.

There was no response so he knocked again. This time he was given an invitation to fuck himself. Saying nothing, he knocked again, and then again, more urgently. As planned, his persistence was rewarded. He stepped back a pace and braced himself against the partition as, following a fumbling sound, the door was yanked open. Before it opened enough to reveal the occupant, Mowgley placed the sole of his right shoe on the approximate centre of the door and pushed it as quickly and as hard as he could. He had learned at the start of his career that, despite what happened on TV and in films, it was virtually impossible to shoulder-charge or kick the most modest of doors down; in this case the objective was to use it as a weapon.

There was a satisfyingly meaty thud and a muffled shout as the door made solid contact then swung back towards him. This time Mowgley kicked it, and was rewarded with the sound of further contact. Stepping forward, he squeezed into the restricted space, one hand already balled into a fist.

He found Snouty straddled over the toilet, his back against the partition. He appeared semi-conscious, and a trickle of blood ran from his brow to the top of his nose.

Deciding further action would not be necessary, Mowgley put his hand round the man's throat and lowered him on to the toilet seat. There was no resistance.

Backing out of the cubicle, Mowgley paused to rub his right thigh and smiled a dark smile. Then he said pleasantly 'So who's the old cunt, now, mater?'

Arriving at the galley Mowgley smiled blandly at the fraught-looking stewardess and said, 'Just thought you should know someone has fallen asleep in the toilet at the back, miss.'

*****

Given their troubled history and after looking at a map of the Balkan peninsula, Mowgley could see that Bulgarians were entitled to feel a little defensive.

Like a wagon train under attack, the Republic was encircled by five other countries with the only relief a coastline on the Black Sea. Romania took up the whole of the northern border, Serbia and Macedonia shared the western boundary, while Greece and Turkey stopped the land of the Bulgars from falling into the Aegean Sea.

With time on his hands, Mowgley had also learned that if you were born and lived in Bulgaria you would probably die six years sooner and be fifty percent more likely to be murdered than if you lived in Britain.

Looking round the airport terminal, he was mildly surprised to see that the average Bulgarian looked no more or less unhappy than the average Briton. Some seemed positively eager to please. The pretty girl at the bar had given him a beaming smile, and he had returned it when he worked out how little his coffee and slice of cake had cost. Thanks also to his travel guide, Mowgley knew that the average wage in Bulgaria is a fifth of that in the UK.

He now also knew that Varna was the third biggest city in Bulgaria and began life as a Thracian seaside settlement at least five centuries before work on the Great Pyramid of Giza had begun.

'Hello John.'

Mowgley looked up from the guide book and felt an almost-forgotten disturbance in his stomach as he saw her standing there and thought of what might have been.

He got up, not knowing whether to hold his hand out or embrace his former colleague's former wife. He settled for keeping his hands by his side.

'There really was no need for you to come over, you know. But I'm glad you did. How was the flight?'

'A bit crowded and noisy but okay.' Mowgley didn't think it necessary to go into the toilet incident, or that the still-dazed Snouty had been helped back to his seat by two male passengers and then bound to it with gaffer tape by the cabin crew. Or that he had been escorted off the plane by a couple of armed and unfriendly-looking Bulgarian policemen. He also thought it unnecessary to mention that although no reference was made to his part in the proceedings, a constant flow of complimentary drinks had arrived at his seat for the remainder of the journey.

'Would you like a drink or something?'

'I'm fine' she said. 'I'd like to get back to the hotel. John will be happy killing zombies by the cart-load in his room, but I don't like to leave him alone too long.'

'John?'

'My son.'

'Oh. I didn't know you had a son.'

There was a pause as she looked briefly away, then said: 'Well, we've not been in touch much over the years, have we?'

'True.' Mowgley bent over and occupied himself with the handle on his case. 'Okay.'

She watched as he struggled then said: 'You need to push the button to pull it out.'

He looked up at her and nodded. 'Of course. I've always been rubbish with technical things.'

He mastered the art of pulling the case after a few capsizes as they walked towards the exit.

'How old is your son now?' he asked.

'Coming up for thirteen,' she replied as she slipped her hand through his arm. 'He was born after Den left.'

~

The Black Sea coast takes up Bulgaria's entire eastern boundary and stretches for 378 kilometres north to south. A third of the coastline boasts sandy beaches, and before the collapse of Communism was known as the Red Riviera. Nowadays it is a popular destination for Europeans in search of a cheap holiday. Like all places where people like to take their ease and spend money, it is also a popular destination with those of criminal intent. Corrupt governmental figures and members of the Bulgarian and Russian mafias are said to be amongst honest developers who own or build luxury apartments in the choicer spots. By Bulgarian standards, property can be breathtakingly expensive and the asking price for a penthouse overlooking the sea might approach that of a studio flat in a fashionable area of London. Varna is the most northerly and largest resort on the black Sea coastline, and it was here that Jenny Cullan and her son were staying.

'How's your *shopska salata*?'

Mowgley looked dubiously at his heaped plate. 'It's a salad.'

She smiled and wagged a reproving finger. 'Don't let the locals hear you disrespecting their national dish. They're very proud of it.'

Mowgley cautiously prodded a chunk of red bell pepper. 'So what sort of country has a salad with some *feta* cheese on top as a national dish? Are they all vegetarians?'

She shook her head. 'Anything but. The story goes that it was invented by the Communists in the 1960s to show off the best of their national produce and attract visitors.'

He raised an eyebrow. 'Didn't work though, did it? A bit like Communism, really.'

'Quite. And by the way, *feta* is what the Greeks call that sort of cheese. Here, it's *sirene*.'

Mowgley shrugged. 'Does it matter?'

She reached over and helped herself to some of the white crumbly cheese. 'It does to most Bulgarians. Remember they're still getting over five hundred years of Turkish occupation. They need to have things they can call their own. Now finish your *shopska* like a good boy or there could be an international incident.'

They were at dinner on the terrace of the hotel in which Jenny and John Cullan were staying. As she explained in a resigned tone, her son was having a burger in his room while busy saving the universe on his gaming console.

Their waiter arrived to clear away the first course, and looked puzzled when she spoke to him in what Mowgley assumed was his native language. He was a short but very wide young man with no visible neck, a shaven head and fingers like sausages. He looked, Mowgley thought, much more suited to minding the door of a dodgy nightclub than waiting on tables.

The man picked up the plates clumsily, said in badly fractured English that he would be back soon, then ambled off with the odd, swinging gait that muscle-bound men often adopt.

Mowgley watched him go, then looked questioningly at her. 'I thought you said you could speak Bulgarian?'

She shrugged. 'I do. Don't forget I'm a language teacher and I've been coming here twice a year for a decade. It's not me who doesn't understand Bulgarian, it's him. There's a big shortage of hospitality industry staff here because the locals have buggered off to where the pay is much better. The operators have had to recruit from non-EU countries, and the adverts actually say there's no need to be able to speak Bulgarian, but English or Russian is essential. I think our man is probably from the Ukraine.'

'Ah. Well I hope he knows we're not Russian.'

'Of course he does. Why?'

'Given their recent history, if I were Russian I wouldn't want a bloke from the Ukraine having access to my soup before leaving the kitchen.'

She smiled. 'I suppose not. Are you okay? You look a bit anxious?'

'Just dying for a fag. Is it okay to smoke here?'

She looked around and nodded. 'Don't see why not. I do. We're outside and everyone else seems happy to light up. Anyway, I don't think Bulgaria has got used to the EU non-smoking rules yet. All the bars have 'no smoking' stickers on the doors, but they don't seem to work. Mind you, they also put 'no guns allowed' stickers on all the bar doors and nobody seems to take any notice.'

He looked to see if she were joking, then asked: 'What about you; do you mind if I smoke?'

'Not if you give me one.'

Mowgley reached for his packet of *Gauloises,* thought about trying the tap-the-bottom-of-the-packet routine but settled for teasing another cigarette from the hole in the top of the squashy packet.

She watched him and smiled. 'You really are adapting to your new life, aren't you?'

He nodded then held the packet up. 'The trick is to tear just enough from the top. The flash blokes tap the bottom and shoot one or two out, but I haven't managed that yet.'

She giggled and laid a hand on his. 'I do hope you never grow up. I think you are one of the funniest people I've ever met.'

As she bent forward for him to light her cigarette, he looked at the soft swell of her breasts beneath her lightweight summer dress and remembered their past and wondered why she had chosen not to tell him about her son.

~

Mowgley reached across the table to top up her glass, then sat back, looked up at the night sky and said: 'This is nice.'

It was, he realised, not one of the great after-dinner lines but the best he could do at the moment. Although she always sent a card at Christmas It had been several years since they spoke on the phone and fifteen since they had briefly been lovers. He was not sure of why he was here, or exactly what Jenny Cullan wanted from him, and he was not even sure that she knew. But it was not a bad way to take a break before returning to work.

Andriy the muscle-bound waiter had delivered their second bottle of wine and left more than well-rewarded for his clumsy if well-intentioned service. This was not because Mowgley was feeling especially benevolent, but because he hadn't realised that the handful of coins he'd dumped on the table as a tip added up to more than the average daily wage in Bulgaria.

Over dinner, they'd talked about the time Mowgley had worked on attachment with Den Cullan in the Forgery Squad. Alike in some ways but not at all in others, the two detectives had got on well at work and play. Both had an appetite for getting results, but Cullan had an even more extreme approach to getting them. There were also dark rumours that he was too selective in which cases he pursued relentlessly and those on which he appeared to soft pedal. As Mowgley quickly learned, the Dirty Den sobriquet was not based on the then popular TV soap character or any shortcomings with regard to personal hygiene. In the best traditions of London-based policing in those days, Mowgley had turned a blind eye. It was also possible that part of the reason he took that approach was influenced by his growing attachment to his partner's wife. Unlike his own wife, he found Jenny Cullan gentle, understanding and tolerant. But however she might have found him, she was of course out of bounds.

The end of the partnership came suddenly when Den Cullan left the police force and his wife on the same day. It was possible that Mowgley had been the more surprised of the two. He did his best to support and comfort the abandoned wife, and it was almost inevitable that they had become lovers over one short but memorably hot summer. The only affair Mowgley had ever had ended by mutual if unspoken agreement. Jenny Cullan had got on with her life after Den, and Mowgley had tried to get on with his wife. One of the failed attempts at saving his teetering marriage was to agree to the purchase of an imposing but ruined manor-house in Normandy. His wife was not interested in the restoration of architecturally significant properties, but liked to casually mention their ten-bedroomed *château* during weekly attendances at the gym and Waitrose.

After a few months his wife had left him for the French estate agent who had sold them the property, and

Mowgley was still unsure who had had the best of the transaction. As a result of the settlement his wife had taken their home in Hampshire but graciously surrendered the wreck across the Channel.

Increasingly of late he had found himself wondering if the sequence of events ending in his becoming a tyro private detective in Normandy had been a whimsy of the Fates, pure chance or some form of subconscious self-determination.

'A *leva* for them…and may I have another drink?'

He looked up and saw she was holding a coin in one hand and her empty glass in the other.

'Oh sorry. Miles away.' He picked up the bottle, topped her glass up then looked at the indecipherable label. 'Blimey, I didn't know Russia made wine.'

She smiled. 'It's Bulgarian. The weird lettering is in the Cyrillic alphabet, invented by a monk and his brother more than a thousand years ago.'

'I won't ask why. Is it any good?'

'The Cyrillic alphabet or Bulgarian wine?'

'You know what I meant.'

She smiled again. 'I like it, and so do lots of people. Bulgaria is one of the biggest producers and exporters of wine in the world. And maybe the oldest. They will tell you the Romans learned about wine-making here.'

'Ah.' Mowgley filled his own glass, thought about making a toast to their reunion, then thought of why he was there. He reached for the *Gauloises* packet and said: 'So, do you want to tell me about it?'

'How long have you got? How far do you want me to go back? It's going to take at least another bottle of Bear's Blood…and probably another packet of *Gauloises*.'

He took the last two cigarettes from the pack, lit both and handed her one before crumpling the packet. 'That's the end of the French fags – we'll have to move on to a local brand. But there's no hurry if John's okay?'

'He's fine. I checked when I went to the loo. He told me

he's still standing in his game, whatever that means, and I got room service to send up another monster burger and a gallon of fizzy drink.' She rooted around in her bag and then pulled out a phone and laid it on the table. 'He said he'd text me if he runs out of food and drink or too many lives in the game.'

Mowgley shrugged then took a pull on his cigarette and sat back. 'Okay then. Let's go.'

'Where shall I start?'

'How about why and how Den went, and ending with how we ended up having dinner in Bulgaria?'

'Okay' She took a deep pull on her cigarette then laid it carefully in the ashtray.

'As you know, our marriage was heading for the rocks for a while before Den buggered off. I had my job, but I found it a real trial to try and keep things light on the rare occasions he deigned to come home. I know he worked long hours, but I saw enough blonde hairs and smelled enough expensive perfume on his shirts to know it was not all work.' She paused and looked directly at him.' For the last few months I felt depressed and lonely and, I suppose, neglected. I needed someone to show they thought something of me. And then there was you.'

Mowgley looked away and felt his cheeks colour. It was another unfamiliar experience. She saw his embarrassment, reached over and laid a hand on his and continued. 'Anyway, to cut to the chase I came home from work and found his wardrobe cleared. There was no note or even a text, but he phoned a week later to say he was working in Bulgaria. No apologies or reasons, just that he wanted to move on. But I have to say he tied up the loose ends and made sure I and John would be alright. He'd resigned from work and had the house and bank accounts put in my name, and I was the only one who didn't know what was going on. Unless you were in the dark as well?'

He shook his head. 'No, I didn't have a clue. My attachment to the forgery squad was coming to an end, and the last time I saw him was when we had a drink to, as he said, celebrate getting rid of me. Then you called.'

He picked up the bottle and waved it at Andriy, who was picking up the remains of a pile of plates he had been transporting from a table occupied by a noisy group of young women. Their waiter arrived sucking a cut thumb and put a fresh bottle on the table. He hung around a moment, but lumbered off when Mowgley showed no sign of putting another day's worth of wages on the table.

'But you kept in touch with Den?'

She raised a hand and shook it in a 'so-so' gesture. 'I thought it my duty to give John the chance to get to know his father as he got older. As far as I know Den hasn't been back in Britain since he buggered off to Bulgaria, so I've been coming over with John every year since he was four. It's a break for me and Den spoils John rotten while he's here. He takes him out on his flash boat and they go skiing together. John even has his own bank account here and there's a trust fund of some sort of shady set-up in his name with God knows how much money in it. Den says it's for the future, and that he can't send any money to the UK for obvious reasons.'

'And are they obvious?'

She nodded. 'Probably.'

'So what does Den do to earn so much money?'

She raised an eyebrow. 'I don't really know. It's something to do with trading in artefacts.'

'Arte-what?'

'It's a sort of portmanteau word covering anything made by human hands, but usually applied to ancient objects - particularly those of historical or cultural interest.'

'You mean like stone arrowheads and bone tools and stuff like that?'

She smiled. 'Well yes. But Den's customers are more interested in stuff made out of gold and silver.'

'Like buried treasure?'

'That's it. It never gets the credit, but this place bred one of the oldest civilisations in the world. Seven thousand years ago the Thracians were already renowned for their skills in making beautiful gold and silver ornaments and jewellery. More buried treasure has been found in Bulgaria than anywhere else on earth, and that's only the stuff that's known about.'

'So there's quite a bit of trading in loot the authorities don't know about?'

'You could say that. Not far from where we're sitting is the site of the oldest and one of the most valuable discoveries of precious artefacts. And just out there...' She waved her glass towards the sea, '...are hundreds of shipwrecks dating back thousands of years. The coastal waters are a graveyard for ancient shipping-and a lot of the ships would have been carrying very valuable cargoes.'

'Could that be why Den has a big yacht?'

She frowned as if she had not thought of the link. 'I don't know if it's because of all that buried treasure or that he just likes having a flash boat to match his flash apartment.'

Mowgley used his glass to indicate the rows of luxury apartment blocks lining the shore. 'Like one of these?'

She smiled. 'Just like one of those. He's got a penthouse he shares with Magda.'

'Magda?'

'His current partner. All I know about her is that she's Bulgarian and twenty years younger than Den and very attractive in a former pole-dancerish sort of way.' She paused and smiled. 'Meow. I couldn't help that. To be fair, she's been with him for a long time - it's funny to think they may have been together longer than we were. I've never met her as Den is thoughtful enough to make sure she's not around when I arrive with John.'

'So you stay with him when you're here?'

She looked troubled. 'Usually. The routine is always the same. I phone him a few days before we arrive, confirm with an e-mail and he gets the guest rooms ready and sends Magda off somewhere.'

'And what happened this time?'

'His car was in the car park when we arrived three days ago, and it's still there.

I let us in to the foyer with the code and I've got a key for the penthouse lift. When we got up there, I pressed the intercom button but there was no answer. I tried the landline and could hear it ringing inside till it went to answerphone. It was the same with his mobile.'

'But you couldn't just let yourself in?'

'No. I didn't have a key or the code. He was funny like that. I suppose he would have seen it as letting me too far into his life.'

Mowgley frowned. 'What did you do next? Do you have Magda's number?'

She showed a flash of irritation. 'Of course not. I kept trying his number, then booked into this hotel. You have to remember that I know virtually nothing about his life here or his business or his friends.'

He held up a hand in apology. 'I'm sorry. What happened then?'

'I kept phoning and visiting the apartment and checking his car was there. Then yesterday I went to the police and reported him missing.'

'What did they say?'

'Nothing much. I think they thought I was some mad, bitter ex-wife trying to stir up trouble. They said there was no law against him not being at home when I arrived, and he'd probably gone off somewhere with his girlfriend; or on business. He was probably trying to tell me something by not answering my calls. If he didn't turn up in a week or so, I should let them know.'

Mowgley rubbed his jaw and fiddled with the empty cigarette packet, 'So then you called me?'

'Yes.' She looked contrite. 'I'm really sorry to have dragged you into this, but when I got no help from the police, I thought of you. I thought you would be still be at the ferry port and could have used your contacts like'- she threw her hands in the air and then ran her fingers through her hair - 'I don't know, Interpol or something to find out or make the police do something…'

He reached across the table and patted her hand. It was an unfamiliar gesture and he did it awkwardly. 'It's okay. I understand. I'll see if I can have a word with the local police tomorrow and make a few phone calls. I know people who know people here. At least we'll be doing something.'

He took his hand away and tried to look confidently reassuring. 'I'm sure it'll all work out. In the meantime, do you fancy a stroll along the prom in search of somewhere that sells French fags?'

*****

Lights were coming on along the walkway. In the distant velvety darkness, rich men's toys were moored in the bay and lit like Christmas trees.

'Would you like a yacht?'

He saw her watching him looking out to sea and shook his head. 'Not me. I've enough trouble looking after a car. And I'm not a boaty person.'

'I don't think Den was, really, but he liked to show off.'

Mowgley nodded. 'And maybe his boat was useful for other things.'

She seemed not to pick up on his implication, and said: 'Yes, he liked to dive. He had all the gear and was quite good at it. He always took John out to dive on wrecks when we were over.' She lit a cigarette, then said: 'Apparently there are lots of sunken ships out there. Last month they found the oldest shipwreck ever discovered. It's a mile down somewhere off the coast out there.' She waved an encompassing arm towards the sea. 'For some reason they're not disclosing exactly where it is.'

'So there are treasure looters at sea as well as on land?'

'Of course.'

Mowgley picked up and looked at the empty bottle and its label. 'I like the idea of drinking bear's blood.' He stood up, smiled at the young couple on the next table, then looked at his watch. 'I'm off for a comfort break. 'Do you want me to order some food?'

'She shook her head. 'Not for me, or not yet. I'm enjoying this. We could do another monster kebab takeaway later and walk hand-in-hand like young lovers back to our room.'

He paused in mid-turn and looked down at her. 'Don't you mean rooms plural?'

She leaned back in her chair and aimed a plume of smoke in his direction. 'I know what I said and what I mean.'

~

After noting the shortage of paper towels in the dispenser, Mowgley ran his hands though his hair to dry them and was checking he'd zipped up when chaos erupted outside.

First came the scream of tyres, then a cacophony of shouting and screaming and crashing, interspersed with three sharp cracks. There was no mistaking what they were. He had heard people claim that a car backfiring could sound like a pistol shot but had never noticed any great similarity.

It seemed to take a long while to get to the outer door of the bar, and outside it was as if things were happening in slow motion. This was something he had found to be not uncommon in times of crisis. The first thing he noticed was a white van splayed across the cobbles, its back doors open.

Then he saw that the table at which they had been sitting was on its side, pieces of smashed bottle and glasses beside it. A man in a floral shirt and chinos lay on his side, blood spreading into a pool alongside his chest. Other customers were sitting as if frozen as they watched Jen Cullan being dragged towards the van. Much of the screaming was coming from her.

In a long couple of seconds, Mowgley realised that the man and woman dragging her were the couple who had been sitting at the next table. He suppressed the natural instinct to shout pointlessly at them, then lurched forward on his stiff leg, picking up the tubular black metal chair on which he had been sitting. By the time he had crossed the space between them, the couple had reached the open back doors. Someone inside was reaching out and had grabbed hold of Jen's hair, while the man and the woman were attempting to bundle her in.

Most civilians would have thrown or swung the chair at the couple; Mowgley held it out horizontally with one hand on the back rest and the other on a leg. Over many a close bar encounter he had found a chair or stool could be used much more effectively that way.

Now he went into shout mode, bellowing out a string of curses. This caused the man to look round at the source of the noise and just in time for the end of the chair leg to be driven into his right eye. Even amongst the screaming and yelling and his own shouting, Mowgley clearly heard the squelching sound and kept pushing. The man gave an agonised and strangely high-pitched scream, released his hold on Jen Cullan and fell to the floor.

Now Mowgley turned his attention towards the woman. Reaching out he grasped the front of her blouse and pulled her towards him. She was screaming and spitting, but was hampered by keeping her hold on Jen. As she pulled away from him and the front of her blouse ripped open, Mowgley threw himself forward and smashed the top of his head into her face. Her nose split open and blood spurted down and on to the cleavage revealed by her torn blouse. Her head snapped back and hit one of the van doors, but she clung doggedly on to her target.

Mowgley pulled his fist back and for a split second his eyes met those of Jen Cullan. Then, a hand appeared from the darkened interior of the van. It was holding a pistol, the muzzle pointing directly at him. He knew what was coming but had no time to react beyond instinctively shutting his eyes.

The flare of intense light burned through his closed eyelids as a great booming sound shut out all other noise, and his face was engulfed by a searing pain. Then he knew no more.

*****

It was the first time Mowgley had taken a ride in a helicopter, and within moments of clambering aboard he hoped it would be his last.

It was almost unbelievably noisy in spite of the padded headphones and the din rose to a screaming crescendo just before they took off. By the time he had opened his eyes they were high above the treetops.

He took a deep breath and tried to think about the nice things in his life, but gave up when he couldn't think of any.

'Cheer up.' Georgiev's voice crackled in his ear. 'You could be risking your life down there.'

Mowgley steeled himself and snatched a look at the road far below.

'Statistically,' continued the inspector, 'flying is a hundred times safer than driving. In Bulgaria it is much more so.'

'That's all very well,' said Mowgley after fiddling with the microphone attached to his headset, 'but if you have an accident up here it's likely to be your last one.' He looked round at the interior of the ageing Westland WAH-64. 'So where did you borrow this from - the Varna museum of aviation?'

'Don't let the pilot hear you say that - he will be very hurt. It was bought to patrol the borders some years ago when Bulgaria joined the EU.'

'That would explain the bullet holes in the bottom, then.'

'Not at all,' replied Georgiev. 'They come from an earlier time. This one has been grounded for the past year and it's the first time it has flown since then.'

'Oh,' said Mowgley, reluctant to ask the question in case the answer was not what he wanted to hear. 'Why's that?'

'There was a problem with the insurance,' said Geogiev.

~

As their flight got under way, Mowgley found the advantage of helicopter travel diminishing his fear level and was almost beginning to enjoy the experience. In a passenger plane the view was limited to what you could see through a small window and clouds seen from above look much the same. The comparatively panoramic view from the Westland made him see that it could be fun being above and beyond the restraints of gravity and almost as free as a bird.

The journey which would have taken three hours by car lasted less than one. As they approached the coast, Inspector Georgiev explained that they would be landing at an historic port.

'Nessebar has three thousand years of chequered history, and was known as the pearl of the Black Sea', he said. 'Nowadays it is a major seaside resort,'

'You sound disapproving,' said Mowgley.

'Not really. Times change. But I am a little sad that it is so full of history and yet most visitors lay on the beach or go to the bars.'

Mowgley looked down as the helicopter descended over red roofs, yellow beaches and lines of moored boats. Used to the limitations of fixed wing flying, it looked to him as though the pilot would overshoot the town. 'Am I missing something,' he said in a strained voice, 'or are there floats as well as wheels on this thing?'

'It's okay,' said Georgiev, reaching over and pointing past him. 'There's the landing pad.'

Mowgley looked to where the inspector was pointing and saw a circle enclosing a large 'H'. It did not comfort him that the circle was almost as wide as the narrow concrete jetty on which it had been painted. Moored nearby was a blue and white police launch, which began to bob and swing in the downdraft from the clattering blades as the helicopter descended. Then the Westland touched down with hardly a judder, and Mowgley resisted the urge to applaud the pilot.

Freeing themselves from harnesses and headsets, the passengers climbed down to the jetty and Inspector Georgiev led the way towards the launch.

'Aren't we supposed to be bending down and running?' asked Mowgley.

'I have always wondered why they do that in films,' said Georgiev, looking up as he patted his jacket pockets to locate his tobacco pouch. 'I think you would need to be a giraffe to be in peril from the rotor blades.'

~

The sharp-prowed police launch cut through the water, spray regularly cascading over the wheelhouse where Mowgley and Georgiev were taking shelter.

Ivo had refused a life jacket and was standing in his summer uniform of soaked tee-shirt and combat trousers at the stern. He had his legs braced and arms folded as he regarded the foam-topped wake from the launch's turbo-thruster. Two tough-looking men in blue ballcaps, blousons and trousers tucked in to Doc Marten-style knee-length boots were leaning against the starboard rail. Both wore heavy belts carrying pouches and holsters, and one was cradling what Mowgley now knew to be a Bulgarian police-issue submachine gun. Perhaps, he thought, their presence was why Ivo had chosen not to wear a life jacket and to stand so obviously exposing himself to the elements. He had noticed that many Bulgarian men liked to indulge in a bit of willy-waving.

He saw Georgiev looking thoughtfully at the two policemen, and asked: 'Are you expecting trouble?'

'Trouble? Ah, you mean our bodyguards? I did not ask for them, but someone senior obviously thought we would need taking care of.'

~

'What are they up to – diving for sunken treasure?

'I think that may be exactly what they are doing.'

Nessebar had dropped below the horizon and the launch was powering down as it approached a sturdy-looking craft sitting at anchor next to a large, yellow buoy.

Flying above the wheelhouse was a blue and white pennant which Mowgley knew to be the international warning that a diver was working below.

To Mowgley, the boat looked like a larger version of the one from which Den Cullan had fallen or been thrown. Unlike the *Treasure Seeker*, this one had a swim platform, sitting at the rear no more than few inches above the water.

A crackle of static filled the wheelhouse and the pilot spoke rapidly into a hand set hanging above his head. Another burst of noise, then a response came from the loudspeaker by the wheel.

Mowgley looked enquiringly at Georgiev, who nodded towards the dive boat. 'Our pilot is asking their business, and the man at the other end says they are on an official exploration.'

The inspector gave the man at the wheel a look of enquiry and words were exchanged. The patrol launch picked up speed, rose up out of the water and came on the plane, and Mowgley saw a figure on the dive boat wave. The officer with the submachine gun straightened up and returned the wave as the launch sped away. It was, Mowgley thought, a rather contrived gesture. The man with the gun did not look the sort of person who went in for waves.

Mowgley looked back as a wet-suited diver broke water and heaved a wire cage on to the dive platform. The man who had waved at them hurried to the stern, reached over and dragged the wire cage inboard. From that distance it seemed to be filled with nothing more exciting than a few rocks.

Mowgley watched and then turned to Georgiev. That was all a bit casual, wasn't it?'

The inspector frowned. 'What was casual, Jack?'

'Taking the bloke's word for it that they were on an official dive.'

The inspector shrugged. 'We have urgent business elsewhere, and I know the pilot knows the boat and its captain. They are archaeologists, not looters. I do not think even the mafia would go fishing for sunken treasure in the daylight so close to shore. Anyway, they don't like to do the dirty work; they prefer other people to find the treasure for them.'

'Like Den, perhaps?'

Georgiev nodded. 'Perhaps. Or perhaps not. I think Mr. Cullan got his loot from above the waves.'

Mowgley stepped from the wheel house and looked out across the water. 'Is there much down there, do you think?'

Georgiev joined him at the rail and smiled as he reached for his tobacco pouch.

'You could say that,' he said dryly. 'You must remember that for thousands of years this was one of the most important and busy trading junctions in the world. East met West here, and ships came from all over the world to buy and sell. But there was a cost. This has always been a place of dangerous waters, and the Greeks called it the 'Hostile Sea'.

Mowgley looked at the surface of the placid waters and thought about the secrets it held and how close yet far away its treasures were. 'So, lots of shipwrecks and their cargoes down there?'

Georgiev pointed with his pipe to the eastern horizon. 'Many here and probably more out there. There is what they call a 'dead zone', where the water is much deeper and richer. Below 150 metres it is so cold that the shipwrecks are in a very good condition. Nobody knows how many wrecks from across the ages lie down there, but there will be hundreds. Last month the oldest shipwreck in the world was discovered in these waters.'

'Yes,' said Mowgley thoughtfully, 'I heard about that.'

There was a shout from the stern and the two men looked to where Ivo was leaning over the rail and pointing at the bubbling wake. The two men stared at the water, then the inspector took the pipe from his mouth and said 'There!'

Mowgley moved along the rail and saw the torpedo-like shape pursuing the boat, twisting and turning in the wake.

'Is it a shark?' Mowgley asked.

Ivo looked to see if he were joking, then said: 'No, it is a dolphin. They like the extra oxygen from the wake. In Bulgaria the sharks are mostly to be found on land.'

~

'He must have been kept busy.'

For all its history, the island looked an unremarkable place to Mowgley. Once, Georgiev had said as they approached the small and mostly featureless piece of rock, it had been the site of a temple to the Greek god Apollo. As a son of Zeus, he was one of the most important deities and a god of music, poetry and healing as well as plague and sun and light and the truth.

More recently, the island had been home to a community of monks, and the ruins of their 5th-century monastery were the only thing breaking the skyline of the flat, treeless place. This enhanced its air of desolation and, Mowgley thought, added a hint of menace. Once-inhabited but now empty places often made him feel like that; especially if they were sitting alone in the sea and far from the mainland.

'Who?' asked Georgiev. He and Mowgley were leaning on the rail and looking at the island across a hundred or so metres of calm sea as Ivo and the pilot worked on lowering a sleek-looking craft from a pair of davits on the stern. Mowgley knew it was a R.I.B. or Rigid Inflatable Boat, which was in effect a permanently blown-up and solidly braced dinghy. This one had a large outboard motor on the wooden transom across the stern.

'Apollo. And wasn't he a messenger for the gods as well?'

'No. That was Mercury, He was a Roman god. In his spare time he looked after shopkeepers, travellers, thieves and tricksters.'

'Of course.'

A curt shout drew their attention to the activity at the

stern. The R.I.B. was dangling close to the surface, and Ivo had climbed on board. He was obviously calling for assistance, and after a moment one of the police guards left the rail and walked across to the davits. Mowgley noticed that, rather than move the harness to leave his hands free, he was still cradling the squat PM9 submachine gun.

~

The R.I.B. crossed the short distance to the shore in a couple of minutes, and Ivo did not bother to use more than a fraction of the power of the giant Mercury outboard engine. Georgiev and Mowgley were sitting on the bench seat directly behind the wheel position, and the two bodyguards were in the bows.

Georgiev turned and waved his pipe as the boat skidded up the beach, and Mowgley saw that the pilot was standing at the rail, watching them.

'Seems a nice bloke,' said Mowgley, 'is he a friend of yours?'

'Yes,' said the inspector, 'you could say that.'

~

They had left the somewhat oxy-moronically named boat aground on the narrow, sandy strip between the sea and the more elevated part of the island.

Beyond the beach was a mixture of rock and scrub, and only the ruins of what Mowgley took to be the old monastery broke the skyline. Ivo, Georgiev and Mowgley were walking abreast, followed closely by their bodyguards. Mowgley was in shirt-sleeves, but Georgiev had chosen to keep his tweedy jacket on. Although it was warmer than on the launch, Ivo was wearing his camouflaged, military-style body-warmer and forage cap.

'So where are we meeting the professor?' asked Mowgley, favouring his stiff leg as they mounted the rise.

Georgiev raised his hands in a small 'who knows?' gesture. 'He said he would be at the ruins.'

'I didn't see a boat?'

Georgiev repeated the gesture. 'Perhaps it is on the other side of the island or hidden somewhere. Remember he is a very frightened man.'

Mowgley looked at the grim, grey ruins and desolate surroundings.

'He must be to hide out here,' he said.

As they neared the remains of the monastery, Georgiev stopped and said something to his son, and Mowgley thought he seemed to speak more loudly than necessary. Ivo made an exasperated gesture, replied, turned and walked back towards the shore, pushing irritably between the guards.

'What did you say to upset him?' Mowgley asked.

'I asked if he had brought his sidearm, and he said he had forgotten it. He is going back to the launch to get it,'

'Aren't those two weaponised enough?' said Mowgley, nodding towards the two police officers. 'Are you expecting trouble?'

Inspector Georgiev had begun to answer when several events occurred in quick succession.

Mowgley had not previously heard a submachine gun being cocked, but knew instantly what it was as the man holding the MP9 swung round and away from them. Beyond the policeman, Ivo was standing with legs braced, holding a pistol in both hands. In his grip, it looked small. As Mowgley tried to take in what was happening, the barrel jerked and there were two sharp reports, followed by the yatter-yatter of the submachine gun. Mowgley watched in slack-jawed shock as the man who had pulled the trigger crumpled and fell slowly to the ground, the rounds he had let off drilling harmlessly into the scrub. Still numb and not yet grasping what was happening, Mowgley looked at Georgiev and saw that, pipe still clenched between his teeth, he had reached into an inside pocket of his jacket. He was struggling and grunting and whatever he was trying to pull out had obviously snagged on the lining.

Feeling as if he were watching something happening somewhere else, Mowgley looked back to where the shot man was laying on his side, curled up in a foetal position and cradling the submachine gun. A thin trickle of blood was running from beneath his chest. The other policeman was fumbling with his holster as Ivo moved his stance to point his pistol at him. Without thinking why, Mowgley took a step forward and threw himself at the back of the guard. The man grunted and pitched forward and Mowgley fell awkwardly on top of him as another shot sounded.

The policeman was younger and obviously fitter than Mowgley and threw him off with ease before getting to his knees and pulled a pistol from the now-opened holster. Mowgley was still spread-eagled on his back and for some reason recalled reading that turtles on their backs cannot right themselves.

He stared up with fascinated horror as the man pointed the pistol at his face. It was, Mowgley thought almost dispassionately, the second time it had happened in a few days. Two shots cracked out, and Mowgley winced and shut his eyes as he felt wetness spatter his face. Then he opened his eyes and saw that the blood was coming from the head of the man kneeling over him. His face assumed a bemused expression as he looked down at Mowgley and then towards where Ivo was standing. Then he gave a slight and almost deferential cough as he fell forward on top of the prostrate private detective.

It then became quiet and still, and Mowgley made no attempt to move until a figure loomed above him and hauled the body of the dead man aside.

'You prick,' said Ivo Georgiev, shaking his head as he offered Mowgley a helping hand. 'I wanted him alive.'

Other books by George East

The Mill of the Flea series (7)
Home & Dry in France
René & Me
French Letters
French Cricket
French Flea Bites
French Kisses
French Lessons

French Impressions series
Brittany
Loire Valley
The Dordogne River
Lower Normandy

A Year Behind Bars
A Balkan Summer
Just a Pompey Boy
Pompey Lad 1 and 2
How to write a Best Seller
Rough Diamond
Love Letters to France
The Naked Truth about Women
The Naked Truth about Dieting
France and the French

Un Pied-a-Terre en France
(*French translation of Home & Dry*)

Blesí mlýn v Normandii
Francouzské polibky
(*translations into Czechoslovakian*)

La Puce Publications
e-mail: **lapucepublications@hotmail.co.uk**
George East website: www.george east.net

Printed in Great Britain
by Amazon

40929764R00185